Di Morrissey is well known for her years as a presenter on Channel 10's 'Good Morning Australia'.

She trained as a journalist in Sydney and worked as Women's Editor for Northcliffe Newspapers in Fleet Street, London. Di then married American diplomat Peter Morrissey, and lived in the USA and elsewhere abroad. They have two children, Gabrielle and Nicolas, who attend university in California.

During her time as a foreign service wife, Di continued to work as a journalist, broadcaster and advertising copywriter.

Following her divorce she returned to Australia and worked in television and film before being commissioned to write *Heart of the Dreaming*.

Di lives in Byron Bay, NSW, where she continues to write novels.

HEART OF THE DREAMING

———— ❧ ————

Di Morrissey

PAN
AUSTRALIA

First published 1991 by Pan Macmillan Publishers Australia
a division of Pan Macmillan (Australia) Pty Limited
63-71 Balfour Street, Chippendale, Sydney
A.C.N. 001 184 014

Reprinted 1992 (twice) , 1993 , 1994

National Library of Australia
cataloguing-in-publication data:

Morrissey, Di.
Heart of the Dreaming.
ISBN 0 330 27283 7
1. Title.

A823.3

Typeset in 11/13pt Andover by Post Typesetters
Printed in Australia by McPherson's Printing Group

For the Revitt girls —

My lovely mother Grace (Kay),
grandmother Grace Louise,
Bette (Annette), Rosemary and Vivian.

And especially for Ken Cowley, the bush and
its people who inspired this book.

Acknowledgements

To my children, Gabrielle and Nicolas, for their constant love and encouragement; Jim Revitt who is more than Uncle. Ted and Dawn Herman for the peace in which to write; Selwa Anthony — super agent, friend and counsellor! Peter, Dorothy and Bill Morrissey, my American family I love dearly; Jim and Judy Hain of Warialda for their friendship. To all those who have been such loving and supportive friends.

In Aboriginal lore the place where you are born is where your spirit lives — a sacred Dreaming place.

It is a place of belonging, of being one with the land. A place where knowledge, peace and joy are found.

It is not a place recognised by white man's law, or marked on maps; but Dreaming sites blanket the face of Aboriginal Australia, exerting a pull on the spirit and soul always to return to the heart of one's Dreaming.

Prologue

The late afternoon sunlight slanted between the tall eucalypts, great runny slabs of hot primary colours sliding off an artist's pallet.

Against the reds and burnt golden tones, a flash of black movement darted between the trees. As swift as a shadow from some great black bird, it was accompanied by pounding earth and cracking twigs, as the beast thundered through the still landscape.

It was a horse as powerful and proud as any depicted in myth and legend. Despite its magnificent size and all-out flight, it moved lightly, gracefully responding to the touch of the small fingers which held its reins. For astride this animal sat an eleven-year-old girl, gently guiding the horse between the trees as they sped down the gully.

Slung across her back was a small rifle. The two dead rabbits hanging on the saddle attested to her skill with the weapon she had been taught to use with respect and care.

Ahead of them dashed their quarry — a small ginger rabbit; its white scut bobbing frantically as it scurried towards the safety of a hollow log or comforting warren.

Its salvation, however, came from another direction, diverting the attention of horse and rider.

Startled from its camouflaged stance in the trees, a huge grey kangaroo leapt forward with a push from its muscular legs and bounded ahead. Here was a new and stimulating challenge and, laughing aloud, the girl increased the pressure of her legs against the horse and the animal surged forward.

The ground became more open as it sloped steeply towards the creek running along the bottom of the gully. The hill rising on the other side had a thicker tangle of undergrowth, and this was where the roo headed.

'It's going to get away from us. Come on, Pegasus,' she shouted. The black horse headed down the slope at breakneck speed, never once faltering.

The horse was gaining, and as the kangaroo heard the snorting breath of the giant animal behind, it reached into its pouch and flung a tiny pink bundle to one side. Then, with a mighty bound, it crossed the creek, slipping on a rock before regaining its balance to land safely on the opposite bank, where it disappeared into the trees.

Horse and rider pulled up and watched the blue shadow bound away. Flinging one leg over the saddle the girl slid to the ground and went back over their tracks.

She was looking for the soft little bundle cast so desperately to one side by the mother roo. Finally she found it, smaller than her own hand, and gently laid it inside her soft shirt.

Pegasus lowered his nose into the muddy water and drank noisily. The burning ball of sun was reflected on the surface of the water before it slipped behind the trees. In seconds the shadows of the trees reached forward, swiftly enveloping the creek in deep purple twilight.

A cool breeze rustled through the gums, making the branches creak ominously as the young girl picked up the reins of the horse. Looking into the sky she saw a low line of inky blue clouds overtaking the setting rays of the sun. A chill ran through her; and the horse, sensing her nervousness, twitched its ears and snorted.

She smiled fondly at the horse and rubbed its nose. 'Time we were getting back, Gus. I didn't know it was so late. Maybe we'll get rain after all.'

She swung into the saddle, jumping up to grasp the pommel so she could pull herself up and wiggle a foot into the stirrup. Normally she would walk the horse to a convenient log to stand on, but she was anxious to retrace her steps.

She'd been gone from the homestead all day, and although she often spent hours away from home on horseback, today she had ridden through unfamiliar terrain and she wanted to find her direction home before nightfall.

Pulling her favourite knitted cardigan tighter around her shoulders, she settled herself in the saddle, patting the warm bulge nestling on her stomach, and moved the horse forward.

As they slowly retraced their steps, the girl glanced over her shoulder, as if she was being followed. But all was silent. A wall of trees seemed to close ranks behind them as if joined together to form an impenetrable barrier. In the gathering darkness the sky pressed down from above and dark thundery clouds rolled across the sky.

Far above there was an occasional spear of lightning, and the low rumble of thunder reached the girl a moment later.

Instinctively the young girl knew the longed-for rain was going to fall this time. The country was parched, and her father's worried expression had said all there was to say on the state of their dams and the condition of their cattle.

So often the dark rain clouds had gathered on the horizon, then teasingly dissipated, or dumped a heavy curtain of water on a wasteland far to the west. This time she knew the 'wet' would be right over their property and although for the moment she was fearful, she was also glad for her father.

As if sensing her trepidation, the heavens began to test her. It grew darker, the thunder began to rumble louder in the distance, and with each far-off flash of light, the black horse quivered.

The horse and girl came to a slight rise and she paused, judging the direction. Unsure, she stood up in the stirrups, peering forward before making her decision. She nudged the horse down towards the right, glancing up at the night sky, but lowering clouds obscured her guiding stars.

It was scarcely any time before the first heavy pellets of rain slammed into the parched ground, disappearing on impact. Drop followed drop, becoming an incessant drumming curtain. Persistent needles pierced the girl's clothing, drenching her.

Her hair streamed down her back, water ran around her neck and her skin was soon sodden. She pushed the horse into a gallop, but the confidence they felt when they had ridden out was gone. They were now rushing blindly, unsure of their direction. A feeling of desperation pushed them on in the faint hope of outrunning the gathering storm.

The trees, whipped to a frenzy by the screaming wind, were silhouetted against the blinding flashes which came one after the other. Each crack and flash was followed by a bellowing roar as the thunder rolled across the sky.

The horse was terrified and galloped unheeding, with the girl simply clinging on, offering no guidance.

It crossed her mind to pull up and find protection but she was afraid the lightning might strike any tree she sheltered near, and she knew there were no caves close at hand.

The wind was so strong she felt she could be blown from the saddle, and she crouched low, resting her head against the horse's neck as she clutched the shortened reins tightly.

Suddenly she felt a jolt run through Pegasus's body as the skies opened up, and it seemed the earth was cleaving in two. The horse reared in panic, taking faltering steps to one side.

In a burst of light she saw the ground suddenly splinter; great cracks widening as the earth gave way. At the same instant a low groan came from the depths beneath the stumbling horse.

It flashed through her mind that it was an earthquake, but instantly the thought was replaced by the knowledge that they didn't have earthquakes here. Or did they?

The horse stepped backwards, its eyes white with terror.

Looking up she saw the canopy of gum leaves from an ancient eucalypt shiver. In slow motion the tree began to fall, roots pulled from the earth as the wind whipped and lashed.

Screaming, she kicked the horse forward, its feet leaving the ground as the roots of the tree burst into the air. Ninety feet of solid wood thudded into the ground, making the surrounding trees tremble.

The trunk missed the horse and rider, but they were caught by the tangle of lower branches. The struggling horse was thrown off balance, rolling and twisting down the slope. Its small passenger was hurled into the undergrowth. The horse slammed into a boulder and lay motionless.

In seconds the girl was wrenching the branches apart to burst free, screaming the name of her horse above the wind and rain.

Slithering down the slope she looked for the horse in the next flash of lightning.

Sobbing, she reached the dark shape, and ran her hands over its body to find it was breathing in short painful gasps. The horse turned its deep brown eyes, filled with pain and pleading, to the girl.

She clung to the softness and strength of that proud head repeating over and over, 'Gus, I love you'.

Then, as the horse flinched with pain, and closed its eyes to cover its agony, the young girl rose.

With the rain still running in rivulets down her body, she reached for the rifle in its leather sheath now strapped to the saddle. With tears blinding her, she aimed the rifle just behind the horse's ear, squeezed her eyes closed, and fired.

It could have been just a small lightning crack which rang around the dark, wet bush, but the noise was that of a girl's heart breaking.

Oblivious to the now gentler, steady rain, she lay down beside the warm horse waiting for the pain to ease, but knowing in her heart it would never go away.

With the soft grey dawn the girl stirred from the gruesome dreamworld she had passed through during the stormy night. Her back was pressed against the cold, wet body of the horse, and she was curled on the ground, her arms folded protectively against her chest.

She opened her eyes and stared with great

concentration at the tightly furled, fern frond immediately in her line of vision. The clasped green fist would soon open into graceful trailing fingers, part of the beauty of a land which could also be so cruel.

Slowly the girl rubbed her hands over her stomach, probing gently. She breathed a sigh of relief and patted the warm bulge nestling against her skin. She ran her hands along her hips and legs, feeling for bruises.

Stiffly she got to her feet, picked up her rifle, and without looking backward, pulled herself back up the hill. She knew to look back would dissolve what little strength she had left.

She struggled on, still unsure of her direction, but as the sky cleared she looked at the sun and struck out for the north; a tiny determined figure in torn clothing, with mud-streaked face and tangled hair.

It was late morning when Snowy spotted the girl in the gully below him and called to her from the top of the ridge. 'Coo-ee... Coo-ee...' The tall, full blood Aborigine with the shock of prematurely white hair had been following her trail since dusk. He was an Aboriginal tracker and the head stockman from her father's property, Tingulla. He, too, had spent the night in the bush, sheltering in a cave before setting out again at dawn.

Although the storm had washed away the tracks made by the horse, he had put himself inside the horse's head and instinctively followed the direction they had taken.

The girl looked up and saw the black figure in a red shirt waving to her. The strength suddenly melted from her body, and she sank to her knees, unable to go on.

The understanding old man reached her, and picking her up he gently took the rifle from her hand. Holding her in his arms, he set off, feeling the warmth of her tears soaking through his shirt.

After about an hour he stopped, and balancing the girl in the crook of one arm, he cocked the rifle and fired into the air.

In seconds came an answering shot. He moved on, carrying the girl.

Soon came the sound of galloping hooves as her father, Patrick Hanlon, rode frantically towards them.

Lifting her head the girl asked quietly, 'Snowy, put me down please.'

Silently he lowered the small girl to the ground and she walked forward to meet the horse hastening to her.

Before the horse halted, the man swung down from the saddle and ran to her. Then, seeing her tragic face, he hesitated. 'You all right, Queenie?'

She nodded, calmly answering him. 'Gus is dead. I had to put him down.'

Reaching inside her clothing, from against her chest, she brought out the tiny joey flung aside by its mother, the grey kangaroo, in the hope of drawing attention to herself and away from the baby. 'I'm afraid this one has lost its mother.'

She stood there, her eyes closed in pain, the infant kangaroo cupped in her hands.

Gently her father took the joey and put it in his jacket pocket. 'I reckon we'll have to feed this fella with an eye dropper eh, Queenie?'

He took her hand and they began walking, while the Aborigine collected the reins of the horse, and leading it, followed behind Patrick Hanlon and his daughter Queenie.

I

1960s
Tingulla

Chapter One

Queenie sat on the splintery railing deep in thought, her wrinkled riding boots hooked over the wooden pole beneath, her favourite Akubra hat pulled into a comfortable shape low over her eyes, partly obscuring her face.

To the stockmen, drovers and casual workers around Tingulla homestead, Queenie had always been the boss's skinny daughter. They knew and admired her prowess on a horse and with a rifle, and she was regarded as a tough little tomboy who would one day grow up. They had grinned at the way she bossed around her younger brother, Colin, who was so different in temperament and ability.

But now the men were aware Queenie was more of a woman than a girl. Her beauty was startling. She had thick golden brown hair that, when loosened, fell in soft waves past her shoulders. Her face was wide and open with high cheekbones, and her lips curved upwards in repose or when she flashed her devastating wide smile. But it was her eyes, a deep emerald green, fringed with heavy dark lashes, which captured attention. She moved with a feline grace even when tackling rough jobs about the property. The men no longer joked around with her as they had done when she'd been 'just a kid'.

On this typical blue and gold Australian outback day, Queenie was surrounded by several dozen friends and neighbours who had gathered at the famed Tingulla Station to celebrate her twenty-first birthday. Sons and daughters of workers and wealthy landowners were spending two days at Tingulla for the festivities. There was no point in travelling miles 'just for a party'. Besides, Tingulla's hospitality, with Rose Hanlon's style and flair, was legendary, so they would stay as long as possible.

An informal rodeo was in progress and from beneath her battered hat Queenie studied the ring of friends perched around the stockyard. It was hard to tell the boys from the girls — all wore the same bush uniform of denim jeans with varying shades of blue or grey shirts, heads covered by worn hats, and dusty elastic-sided boots on their feet. Their shouts of derision and encouragement could be heard back at the homestead as each of them took a turn aboard an unbroken horse in the small yard.

Suddenly Queenie was aware she was being watched and she lifted her head like an animal sensing danger. She caught a flash of amused blue eyes studying her and a slow grin spreading across a tanned face.

TR Hamilton. He was a station hand at Bilbao, a nearby property. He was older than Queenie and she hadn't had much to do with him. She'd seen him with her father and the owner of Bilbao looking at horses several weeks back. Cheeky devil by the look of him. She turned her head, deliberately ignoring him.

Shouts rang out as another rider hit the dust and one of the station jackaroos yelled, 'Hey, Queenie, why don't you show these blokes how it's done? You're always saying there isn't a horse you can't ride. No one has been able to ride any of these to a standstill!'

The lad who was picking himself up from the dirt in the ring slapped his crumpled hat back on his head muttering, 'That's because they're flaming bloody brumbies only good for pet food!'

'Go on Queenie... let's see how good you are,' called one of the girls.

Queenie glared at her.

'Yes, I'd like to see the famous Miss Hanlon stop one of these fellows,' came a soft but challenging voice.

Queenie turned to see TR Hamilton smiling broadly at her.

She jumped down from the railing, smoothing her hands along the sides of her thighs, and jammed her hat firmly in place.

'Anyone want a side bet that she'll last the distance?' called another of the boys.

Charlie, the stockman who was helping in

the yard, grinned at Queenie as she moved along to where the next horse was penned in a small chute. A rope halter and light saddle were dropped onto the horse and buckled in place.

Queenie climbed to the top of the fence looking at the horse's frightened, angry eyes. She began to talk soothingly and didn't notice the two boys tighten the flank rope so that it would crush the horse's testicles once Queenie's weight was in the saddle.

'See if she can stay on this one,' hissed one boy, winking at the other.

Queenie lowered herself onto the saddle and twisted the reins around her fists. The horse flattened its ears and its nostrils flared as the whites of its eyes bulged in agony.

With a screaming whinny the horse rose upwards, pulling its feet together beneath the centre of its body, attempting to rid itself of the weight on its back.

The gate to the chute was flung open and the horse, seeing freedom and open space, exploded into the yard. But in seconds it realised it was trapped by the fence encircling the stockyard. With the bit pulling on its mouth, the horse lowered its head and began bucking violently, throwing out its legs and arching its back, as it leapt and thudded to the ground, slamming Queenie up and down in the saddle. She hung on grimly, her feet still locked in the stirrups, her braid of thick hair flying wildly about her head as her hat spun to the ground.

As the crowd cheered Queenie's bravura

performance with the wildest of the horses so far, TR Hamilton was studying the frenzied horse through the eyes of a horse-wise bushman.

Suddenly the horse stopped bucking and lunged at the far stockyard rails, determined to wipe this hindrance from its back by crushing it against the thick wooden poles and posts. In the same instant TR leapt down into the ring and ran at the horse, waving his arms. The horse turned sharply and reared, attempting to strike at TR with its front legs.

Queenie hit the ground hard. The watching guests gasped as TR ducked beneath the flashing hooves to grab the bridle. The horse tried to bolt but TR dug his heels in the dirt and pulled hard on its head. He was soon joined by Charlie and between them they managed to stop the wild horse, which now stood motionless, panting and glaring at the two men.

'You all right?' asked TR as he held out a hand to help Queenie to her feet.

She brushed his hand aside and stood up. 'Just what do you think you were doing, you fool? I was in complete control until you flew at him,' she snapped.

'Be careful who you call fool, my girl. That horse was going crazy. Your friends had tightened the flank rope.' TR turned away angrily. 'You were lucky he didn't try to wipe you off on the rails the minute he came out.'

The crowd had begun to drift away by the time Charlie had lifted the saddle and restraining ropes from the horse and let it loose in the stable yard.

'Well done, lass,' he said patting Queenie on the shoulder. 'That was a dirty trick they pulled. That flank rope would've made a dead horse buck.'

With that he turned back towards the house, leaving Queenie and TR standing alone in the stockyard. TR stooped to pick up Queenie's hat and, flicking off the dust, held it out to her. She didn't move.

'Hey, don't feel badly. You didn't lose face. Not many blokes could have stayed on that horse at all.'

Queenie still didn't move. 'I like to fight my own battles, thank you.'

'You could have been hurt. I was only trying to help you.' TR was still holding her hat in his outstretched hand.

'It was unlikely. Your intentions might have been good but you caused more trouble than if you'd left me alone.'

TR walked up to her and slammed the hat on her head. 'It wouldn't hurt you to say thanks, you know. But don't worry, from now on I'll leave you alone.'

He strode from the yard, wrenching open the gate as Queenie straightened her hat and glowered after him.

'She's not what you're thinking,' came a quiet voice beside TR. 'Queenie's no snob. She does ride better than most of the men on this station.' It was Charlie, talking as he coiled a rope.

'Is that a fact?' said TR tersely. 'I was thinking she seemed a bit of a spoiled brat.'

'Aw, Queenie gets her way most of the time

because she is generally right, although she can wind everyone around her little finger.'

'Well, she's not winding me around any finger, the ungrateful little wretch,' answered TR.

'She's as tough as an old gum tree despite being such a pretty little thing. Not many kids have to shoot their favourite horse when lost in a storm. No, mate, the spoiled one in the Hanlon family is her younger brother, Colin. You obviously don't know the Hanlons.'

TR fell into step beside the older man as they moved towards the homestead.

'No, I don't know them well. I met Mr Hanlon when he came over to Bilbao where I've been working. He asked me over to his daughter's party. By the way, I'm TR Hamilton. I've been breaking horses and doing a bit of mustering at Bilbao.'

The old stockman threw an amused glance at TR. 'A horse breaker, eh? You blokes all reckon you can outride the wind.'

TR shrugged. 'I do all right with horses.'

Charlie pointed in the direction of the homestead. 'The house is over that way. I've got to get the horses back. Nice meeting you.'

TR was tempted to help Charlie with the horses, preferring their company to the social round planned for Miss Hanlon's twenty-first. He hadn't come to this weekend party to meet the daughter of Tingulla but in the hope of talking her father, Patrick Hanlon, into giving him a job. His contract at Bilbao was due to run out.

*

Queenie walked around the rear of the large house past the cool side verandah where she could hear the girls chatting as they relaxed after the rodeo. The swinging seat creaked comfortably and ice cubes tinkled, but Queenie didn't feel like being sociable.

She stepped into the dimness of the house and edged past the kitchen where she could hear her mother Rose talking to Millie, the half-caste housekeeper who was part of the family. Millie had been with them for as long as Queenie could remember. Mission educated, she had come to the family as a shy young nanny to help Rose and Patrick with their new baby daughter. Millie now ran the entire household with steamtrain energy and efficiency.

Millie had grown up with the Hanlon family as Rose had blossomed from a hesitant young bride to the gracious and poised mistress of the great expanse of Tingulla. Millie had married Jim Nicholson, a white motor mechanic who now also worked at Tingulla looking after the vehicles and machinery. Jim and Millie had been together fifteen years and both were indispensable to the smooth running of the giant homestead and property.

Rose was hoping that since Millie had no children, she would pass on her skills to her assistant Ruthie. However, Patrick was not so sure Ruthie would become as efficient as Millie. Although she was mission educated since the age of ten, Ruthie, now seventeen, was a full-blood Aborigine and Patrick sensed there was still a tribal influence in her heart — even if she didn't know it yet.

Faintly, Queenie heard her mother and Millie issuing instructions to the nervous Ruthie and to Stan, the tough old shearers' cook.

Stan had been called in to slaughter a lamb which was now turning slowly on a roasting spit in the garden. Nearby a marquee had been erected and tables were set with Rose's inventive decorations and flower arrangements. Country hospitality was famous, but at Tingulla it was legendary.

Queenie tiptoed up the cedar staircase, past the collection of famous early Australian art her mother had acquired. She stopped to admire for the thousandth time a Turner landscape — one of several valuable English paintings Rose had inherited, and which hung as a reminder of her English homeland — a stark contrast to the Australian bush scenes.

In her room, feeling stiff and bruised by her fall, Queenie peeled off her grubby clothes and dropped them onto the shining cypress floor. The late sunset light streamed in through her window and the lacy curtains rose and fell in the breeze.

Queenie felt restless and was beginning to regret all the fuss being made over this birthday. She felt strangely alone, wishing she could share the tumbling thoughts and feelings inside her. She'd always been able to talk to her mother, but this was different — nothing specific, but somehow troubling.

As a small girl she had shared her secrets with Pegasus, the big black horse which had fallen during that terrible storm. Shooting Gus had been like crossing a chasm between childhood and the real world. Queenie now felt that another step lay before her, and she wondered what waited on the other side of her twenty-first birthday.

She had no desire to giggle and chatter with the girls gathered downstairs. Nor did she feel like galloping through the bush on Nareedah, her young white Arabian horse which had grown to replace Pegasus in her affections. She sighed and flung herself across the floral eiderdown on her bed where Snugglepot, her tortoiseshell cat, snoozed, escaping the demands of a new litter of kittens nestling in a box in the kitchen.

It was dark when her mother pushed open the door and switched on the light. The loud click caused Queenie to stir and Snugglepot to stretch.

'You lazy girls,' said Rose. 'Queenie, the party has started and everyone is wondering where you are. They think you're up here primping and preening and you haven't even started getting dressed.'

Rose sighed at the sight of her long-limbed daughter, her hair a tangle of loose waves, her bare body chilled from the cool night air. Queenie was such a tomboy that Rose knew getting her to dress up would be a battle.

'Come on, Queenie, get dressed quickly. And as for you,' Rose shooed the cat off the bed, 'down you go and feed those starving babies of yours.'

Rose, elegant in a soft grey chiffon dress with a strand of magnificent pearls swinging to her waist, left Queenie to dress and went downstairs. Patrick met her on the landing.

'When is she coming down? I've never known Queenie to take so long. I know she's not used to dressing up — she must really want to impress the boys.'

Rose smiled fondly at the tanned face she loved so dearly, with the crinkles round his eyes and the dimple in his strong chin. As he smiled at her she touched his cheek. 'She fell asleep, but she'll be here in a few minutes.'

Tingulla was ablaze with lights. The soft hum of the generator was drowned by music and laughter. Small lights were strung around the trees shading the homestead lawns. Flame torches on poles were set among the garden beds and along the driveway. Kerosene lanterns burned on tables set along the verandah. In the main entrance a crystal chandelier cast a glow around the beautiful vestibule with its antique furniture and grandfather clock.

In the music room a group sang around the Pianola, one of the boys pumping the pedals while another attempted to pluck a ukulele with hands more used to roping cattle than picking a tune.

The dusty boys of the afternoon were now scrubbed and slicked, their boots polished to a glass-like sheen. The girls bloomed in pastels, their hair curled in the latest fashion.

One of the girls leaning on the Pianola called across the room, 'Come and play, TR'.

TR smiled and reached inside his dinner

jacket. Everyone knew TR was never without his mouth organ. It had been his sole companion on many lonely nights out droving and he could play any song after hearing it twice. TR ran his lips along the little silver instrument then leaned against the Pianola and picked up the tune.

At twenty-six, TR Hamilton had the physique of a strong man and had already acquired more bush skills and horse knowledge than most men would ever learn. He was tall with sun-streaked hair, deep sky-blue eyes, and dark brows and lashes. He had a wide, engaging smile that tipped crookedly to one side, giving him a rather quizzical expression. He was softly spoken and had a gentle nature, yet there seemed to be a core of steel running through him. He appeared determined and not a man to be pushed around.

The mixture of young guests blended well. Outback life had made them tough and taught them to grow up quickly. Compared to their city peers they were responsible and competent adults. Most of them gathered for Queenie's party knew each other, though they met infrequently. There was an easy camaraderie amongst them. The practical bush girls didn't play coy games and understood the way of life in the harsh outback. The boys mainly came from prosperous stations or were hardworking station hands aiming to own a property of their own one day.

As TR breathed into the harmonica his eyes closed and he became totally lost in the music, remembering the times he'd heard his father sing *'Oh, Danny Boy'* — generally in his cups at the pub.

TR's father, Riann Hamilton, had been an Irish drifter and a dreamer. A handsome man with dark curling hair, his blue eyes and lilting brogue had beguiled the ladies. He was a moderately successful jockey who had come to Sydney to seek fame and riches. There he married Mary, the daughter of a well-to-do family, and fathered Terrance Ryan.

Once he'd spent Mary's dowry and what little he'd won, Riann had persuaded her to move to the bush with their baby son so he could ride the country circuit.

Riann was absent for weeks at a time leaving his wife and small son to the isolation of a tiny house in a country town where people minded their own business. Mary had only a nodding acquaintance with some of the local townsfolk and eked out what meagre funds she had to care for herself and TR.

When Riann did return he'd spend most of his time charming drinks from the locals in the pub, or sitting on the house's small front porch with TR on his knee, spinning tales of the horses and the racing world. He promised TR that one day he'd own a horse of his very own.

TR's father never got him that horse, and he never struck it lucky with the winners. The whisky finally claimed him in a dingy room in the Green Man Public House at Wattle Flat. His few possessions were forwarded to his wife — a fob watch, a tobacco tin of personal papers, and a pink and navy racing sash and cap.

TR's mother returned home to her parents and TR was sent to a fine school by his grandfather. The family were disappointed when, at fourteen, TR ran away to the bush. By the time he was eighteen TR had discovered he had a special way with horses. He could look at a horse and see not only its physical make-up, but also sense the animal's temperament, stamina and potential. He could tell which horse had the heart and guts to make it go on when others might falter. It was a treasured talent in the bush where men's lives and fortunes often depended on their horses.

During his years growing up in the city TR had hung around the Randwick Racecourse with the jockeys and trainers who'd known his father, and he'd listened, and watched, and learned.

But it was the tales of the bush and wild exploits of the country men that he remembered best. His father had instilled in him a passion for the wide open country and the land where a man was as good as his horse, his fists and his wits.

TR had risen from junior station hand to drover for one of the great pastoral families in the far north and he dreamed of one day making his own fortune. Deep down he wanted to fulfil his father's dream and vindicate him in his mother's eyes.

She had stuck by her man, too proud to ask family or friends for help, and her air of gentility had set her apart from the earthy country women who might have helped her. Instead, she struggled on alone, teaching her son about the finer things in life which she had once known. Although there was little food on the table, manners and etiquette were observed to the letter. She died when TR was sixteen, her son already won over by the bush.

The song ended and TR opened his eyes as the group about him clapped. Overwhelmed by memories TR excused himself and slipped quietly into the moonlit garden.

Upstairs Queenie tugged at the fastenings on the emerald green taffeta ballerina dress which Millie had painstakingly ironed. Gazing at her stiff and formal reflection, Queenie wrinkled her nose in distaste and squirmed uncomfortably in the boned and wired strapless ball dress with its flounced skirt. She lifted the heavy curtain of her burnished hair and coiled it in a looping bun, then decided against that and let her thick hair tumble over her shoulders. She reached for a tortoiseshell comb to pin it back behind one ear then stopped suddenly and smiled — she knew just the thing she needed to make her feel right.

In her bare feet, Queenie hitched up her dress and sat on the windowsill, throwing her legs onto the slanting roof. Gripping the corrugated iron with her toes and gingerly hanging on, she worked her way to the far corner where the branches of the peppercorn tree brushed against the roof. Entwined among the boughs spiralled a jasmine vine, thick with sweetly perfumed white clusters.

Queenie began pulling at the vine to bring the flowers within reach. As she leaned forward and tugged at the strong vine, her foot slipped and she slid with a clatter towards the edge of the roof. The strip of tin guttering broke her fall, and she flung her body flat onto the roof, one foot dangling over the edge, the other supported by the flimsy leaf-filled gutter. Her breath came in short startled gasps as she remained motionless.

A calm voice from below drifted up to her. 'Just what are you doing, exactly?'

It was TR standing in the shadows of the peppercorn tree peering up at the dangling leg and taffeta skirt. Despite the precarious position Queenie seemed to be in, he sounded faintly amused.

As TR watched, the leg disappeared and there was a scratching and a rustle as Queenie swivelled her body around so her legs were now angled up the roof and she could look over the edge.

'None of your business. What are you doing prowling around in the garden?' demanded Queenie.

'Oh, I was just taking a breath of fresh air. Are you planning on making some sort of entrance swinging through the trees like Tarzan?'

Queenie glared at him. 'Very funny. For your information I was just getting some flowers. I slipped.'

'You're obviously not as good on rooftops as you are on a horse,' said TR swinging into the tree and climbing till he was almost level with her nose. 'You were after these, I suppose.' He reached out to gather the heady sprays of delicate white flowers, and sniffed them appreciatively. 'Very lovely. Allow me.' He passed them to Queenie who silently took them from his hand.

'Now, how are you going to get back inside? Come down the tree with me.' TR held out his hand to her.

'No, thank you,' said Queenie stubbornly, feeling rather foolish. She gripped the stems of the flowers between her teeth and scrambled crablike back through her window.

She heard TR's soft laughter floating behind her as she slammed the window closed.

Rose swept into the kitchen where Millie and young Ruthie were putting the final touches to the bowls and platters of fresh salads, vegetables and fruit — luxuries flown in for Queenie's party.

Millie bustled about, wrapping her hands in a towel as she pulled open the door of the Aga cooker. The smell of fresh baked bread filled the room. With flour up to her elbows, Millie pulled out the tin pans and upended them on the bench, banging the bottoms to loosen the perfectly baked loaves.

Rose breathed in the delicious smell, tapping the base of the loaves which gave a hollow ring.

'Done to perfection as always, Millie. The nun who taught you to bake at the mission did a splendid job.'

Millie was too busy to be flattered. 'They taught us lots of things at the mission. Taught us to forget lots of things, too,' said Millie, beginning to whip a bowl of Tingulla cream with a wire whisk.

Rose was unperturbed at Millie's reference to the missionaries' attitude to the Aboriginal children in their care. Millie was a pretty, plump woman in her late thirties, light enough to pass as having Mediterranean blood. She had come to Tingulla as a shy young girl fresh from the mission, with a confused and blurred knowledge of her Aboriginal heritage. The nuns had preferred to ignore the fact that a white man had been tempted by black flesh and that the resulting offspring had as much claim to an Aboriginal upbringing as they did to a white one. Instead, the children, whether they were full blood or quarter-caste, were thoroughly schooled in Christian morals and manners.

Rose thanked Millie and walked through the ground floor rooms and along the verandah where groups of young people had gathered. Seeing Queenie's best friend, Sarah Quinn, crossing the lawn, she moved outside and stopped her.

'Sarah, where is Queenie? I can't find her anywhere,' said Rose.

'I haven't seen her since the rodeo this afternoon, Mrs Hanlon. She must still be getting dressed.'

'But it's been ages. And you know Queenie never spends any time getting fancified. I've already had to chase her up once.'

As Sarah moved away a voice made Rose spin around. 'Mrs Hanlon, your daughter was out on the roof a moment ago, I think she must still be upstairs.'

'On the roof! That little monkey. What was she doing?' asked Rose as she stared at the attractive young man before her.

TR shrugged. 'I just happened to be strolling past when I heard a bit of a clatter and saw her. She was by the peppercorn tree. I did offer to help her down but she seems a bit of a tomboy and insisted on climbing back up the roof to her room,' grinned TR.

Rose sighed. 'A bit of a tomboy! You obviously don't know Queenie well. I'd better go and see what she's up to . . . thank you.'

TR watched Rose disappear into the brightly lit house, and wondered how such an elegant and gracious woman could have such a gawky and haughty daughter. Shaking his head, he smiled at the thought of Queenie's face peering over the guttering at him, long hair falling past her shoulders, eyes wide and startled like a kangaroo trapped in a spotlight. There weren't too many girls TR could think of who would have been game enough to crawl around such a high and sloping roof.

Queenie intrigued him but he felt it best not to concern himself with the feisty daughter of the family. He was out to impress Patrick Hanlon, though TR suspected he might be able to charm Mrs Hanlon a little. Even so, he preferred to win a job on his own merits.

Rose snapped open Queenie's door to find her daughter, rumpled and flushed, looking at herself with dismay in the mirror. Her new dress was crushed and soiled with a rip at the front.

Rose caught her breath. Queenie looked upset enough, there was no point in berating her further. 'Oh, Queenie! Would you mind telling me just what you were doing on the roof?' asked Rose.

'So, he snitched on me, did he?' said Queenie angrily.

'Who?'

'TR Hamilton. He went running to tittle-tattle, did he?'

'No, Queenie, he didn't,' said Rose calmly. 'The point is, what are we going to do about that dress?'

Queenie slumped on her bed looking sad. 'I'm sorry, Mum. I know you went to a lot of trouble to have it made for me. But it just felt so... uncomfortable. I mean it was stiff and... unfriendly. I thought I'd pick some jasmine to soften it up a bit...'

Queenie looked forlornly at her dress and Rose moved to the bed and gave her a hug.

'Never mind, darling. Let's see what we can find in my cupboard. I know there are no party dresses in your wardrobe!'

With their arms around each other they moved down the hall to the main bedroom where Rose began rifling through the back reaches of her wardrobe.

'Queenie, try this on. It was my favourite party dress when I went out dancing with your father on trips to Sydney. I know it's old-fashioned but somehow I think you can carry it off... it will suit you, I'm sure.'

She handed the silvery satin dress to Queenie whose eyes lit up. 'I remember this dress!

When Sarah and I raided your clothes for dressing up, I always picked this one!'

Rose smiled to herself, remembering the times she'd found her clothes in disarray, knowing full well Sarah and Queenie had passed many a happy hour delving into her clothes, jewellery and powder, convinced she'd never known.

Queenie pulled off the ruined taffeta ball gown and slipped the shimmering dress over her head where it slithered around her, skimming the curves of her body, stunning in its classic simplicity.

'I used to call that my Jean Harlow dress,' smiled Rose. She took Queenie by the shoulders and slowly turned her around to face the full-length mirror on its stand.

The mirror was a legacy of an old woodcarver who had worked at Tingulla in her grandfather's day. Around the mirror he'd created a cedar frieze of Australian animals. Wombats, koalas and emus peered between flowers and leaves, framing Queenie's enchanting reflection.

Queenie stared at herself. Who was this tall, elegant creature in a dress that shone like moonlight on water, highlighting the soft curves, the creamy shoulders, the long graceful neck?

Rose rested her head on Queenie's shoulder speaking to her daughter's reflection. 'It's time you realised you're turning into a woman, Queenie. You can't stay a tomboy in trousers forever, my girl. You'd better start getting used to people looking at you as a grown woman.'

Queenie grinned and fell into a silly pose, spoofing the models in the fashion magazines her mother subscribed to. The graceful beauty in the mirror was replaced by a young woman giggling in amused embarrassment.

'I'd like to see me try and ride in an outfit like this!'

Rose laughed. Queenie was still her down-to-earth daughter. Smiling fondly at her, she smoothed Queenie's hair. 'Queenie, before you go...' Rose lifted a small blue velvet box from the top of her dresser and kissed Queenie as she placed it in her hands. 'Your father and I were going to give this to you later, but I think you should have it now. Happy birthday, darling.'

Queenie gasped as she saw the delicate opal necklace shining against the silk lining of the box. She lifted up her mass of shining hair and her mother clasped the necklace around her throat.

'These opals were from Great-grandfather Ned Hanlon and they have been passed on to all the Hanlon girls,' said Rose. 'Your father gave this to me the day we were married... now it's your turn.'

The milky opals set in dainty filigree gold seemed to come to life as they touched Queenie's skin, flashing and burning with a red-gold fire in their depths.

'I don't know what to say. You and Daddy are too good... I love you both so much. It's just lovely,' said Queenie, hugging her mother with tears in her eyes.

'You're a beautiful young woman and we

love you too,' said Rose softly, thinking how lovely Queenie was in her heart and mind and how unaware she was of her appearance. Rose patted her cheek. 'Off you go and put some of that jasmine in your hair as you planned.'

As Queenie skipped from the room in her bare feet Rose admonished, 'Queenie — wear those silver sandals I bought for you... *not* riding boots!'

A few moments later Queenie descended the broad staircase as music and laughter drifted from the rooms below. Patrick, crossing the vestibule, looked up as Queenie came down the stairs, smiling at him.

'Hello, Daddy... I'm ready at last. I had a few interruptions.'

Patrick was silent, simply staring at her.

'Well... what do you think?' Queenie twirled around on the bottom step.

Patrick shook his head and blinked. 'For a moment there, it was like seeing again the girl I fell in love with... You look so like your mother did then... How I remember that dress — how it felt when we danced... And I see she gave you our present. Happy birthday, precious girl.' He leaned forward under the twinkling chandelier and kissed her.

Queenie hugged him then touched the opal necklace. 'I don't know if I deserve this, but I'll treasure it all my life. I'm very proud to be a Hanlon. Thank you.'

Patrick grinned at her. 'I hope Great-grandad Ned can see you from up there. He'd be proud and happy too.' Patrick stood looking at the vision before him, the memories of falling in love with Rose flooding back to him. 'You certainly look lovely. I don't know where my Tingulla tomboy has gone. Overnight you've turned into a princess.'

'Not so, Dad, though I do feel like Cinderella. Tomorrow it's back to britches and bulldust for me!'

Patrick laughed. 'Enjoy your party, Queenie.' He watched her move away, a silvery sprite on the verge of womanhood yet still so much a simple girl.

Where indeed was the tomboy who worked so tirelessly beside him with such high spirits and the lithe strength of a young man? Queenie was better with horses than any of the men, and she was fearless and bright. She was still impetuous and convinced she could take on the world and win. She wanted to learn everything, do it all and do it better than anyone else. There was still so much she had to learn, but there was time enough to teach his daughter more about life, and men, and the land.

Seeing Queenie tonight, a lissome young woman, Patrick wondered what the future held for her. Queenie was so much stronger and more capable than her younger brother, Colin. There was such a small difference in age; such a huge difference in their attitude and approach to life.

As always when he compared the two, Patrick was troubled. Queenie would probably marry and move to another property, and Colin would run Tingulla. In his heart Patrick would have preferred his daughter to be boss, but in Australia it was the men who ran things. A woman at the head of a huge station was unheard of.

Patrick strolled into the garden, his attention caught by a burst of raucous laughter from several boys. Colin was in the group, obviously enjoying the smutty joke someone had told. Patrick sighed, knowing Colin would probably be drunk and unruly before the night was out.

By the barbecue Stan, the shearers' cook, was carving giant slabs of roast lamb from the carcass turning on the spit over the coals. As the heaped plates of meat, salads and baked vegetables began to diminish under the assault of healthy young appetites, Millie and Rose moved into the garden, carrying between them a silver platter laden with the classic Australian dessert — a pavlova. The meringue shell was surrounded by flickering candles and piled high with whipped cream topped with exotic fruit from the tropical north of Queensland.

Queenie smiled her way through the ritual of blowing out the candles, standing with her head bowed, looking shyly amused as the merry crowd roared the birthday song, which TR accompanied on his mouth organ, giving Queenie a cheeky wink as he played.

Then in groups they piled into trucks and moved down to the spruced up woolshed in the gully where a bush band was thumping out infectious country music. Light bulbs covered in coloured cellophane were strung along the beams and the woolshed floor had been swept and scrubbed. Clean sawdust was scattered in the shearing stands where the merinos, heavy with the wool which had made Tingulla wealthy, were shorn each season. Temporary tables and chairs were grouped along the galvanised iron walls.

The air was heavy with the sweet sticky smell of lanoline, the natural odour of wool. Outside, wooden kegs of beer were set on trestle tables and around them stockmen, ringers, drovers and workers from Tingulla, along with male friends and neighbours, too shy to join in the dancing, settled instead to serious drinking.

Queenie was in constant demand for dances. She was puzzled at first, then amused at the way the boys she had known as good mates for most of her life were treating her tonight. They were either deferential or restrained, holding this new ethereal Queenie at arm's length, unable to produce their usual teasing banter; or else they clasped her to their chest with clammy hands and breathed heavily into her hair. Queenie suffered the strained silences and moist breathing and hoped things would get back to normal tomorrow.

As she was twirled around the floor, she would occasionally catch a flash of blue eyes and lopsided grin observing her discomfort.

TR Hamilton. She'd learned a little about him, but as yet had hardly spoken to him, other than their exchange from the roof. Apparently he was some kind of wonderboy horse breaker, but that was all she knew about him.

As Queenie sat out a dance, Sarah, Queenie's best friend, flopped down beside her, fanning herself with a paper plate.

'Gosh, it's hot — you take your life in your hands out there. Most of the boys are taking their jackets off. Oops, here comes Mick O'Rourke. Be careful — he treads all over your feet in those great boots of his.'

Queenie looked away as the determined fellow threaded his way towards them.

A hand suddenly dropped lightly on Queenie's bare shoulder. 'My dance, I believe. Shall we?' TR was standing, smiling down at her, holding out his hand.

'Have you two met?' asked Sarah glancing from Queenie to TR who were staring at each other without moving or speaking.

Queenie was about to refuse him as he seemed to expect her to leap to her feet. O'Rourke was almost at their table when Queenie found her hand in TR's and she was pulled gently to her feet.

'Oh, yes, Miss Hanlon and I are old friends, Sarah. We've been climbing together,' said TR as he led Queenie away from the table.

Sarah stared after them murmuring, 'Climbing?' She shrugged and reluctantly rose to her feet to join the disappointed O'Rourke who was watching TR lead Queenie away.

'We haven't really met, you know,' said Queenie to TR who was still firmly holding her hand.

'Well, everyone knows the birthday girl. I'm TR Hamilton.' He touched his forehead, tugging at a mock forelock.

Queenie attempted to withdraw her hand but found that he only held it more tightly as they moved past the throng of dancers.

'What's the TR for? Terribly rude?' said Queenie pulling away from him.

TR was still smiling as he placed his hand firmly under her elbow and led her towards the woolshed door. 'Actually, it's for terrifically rhythmic. I'm a great dancer. Come on.' He propelled her out the door into the coolness of the night.

Queenie stopped, wrenching her arm from his grasp. 'Now just a minute, where are you going?'

'We're going dancing. Too crowded in there,' grinned TR sweeping her lightly into his arms and moving to the music which pounded from the band inside.

'Oh, really,' muttered Queenie as she found herself instinctively swaying in time to the music, easily following his sure lead.

They continued in silence for a few moments and she had to admit he was a good dancer. It was also very pleasant dancing in the freshness of the night. She could feel the rough fibres of his tweed jacket where her hand rested on his wide shoulder, and there was a faint musky smell about him which made her think of freshly cut hay. He didn't make small talk, although he didn't seem at a loss for words. He was obviously enjoying the pleasure of dancing.

Queenie's heel caught on a rough patch of ground and she stumbled against him. His grip tightened although he said nothing. Queenie pulled away from him and stopped dancing. Her cheeks were flushed and her eyes glittered.

'I think we should go back inside,' she said.

TR was about to protest but as he looked at her imperious and cool expression, he realised the haughty manner was disguising a shy and nervous girl. Gently, he led her by the arm back into the woolshed.

'I'm sure you have a long list of suitors waiting to dance with you. Thanks for the dance. I shan't forget it.'

He relinquished her arm just as O'Rourke came past holding two paper cups of Passiona.

'Queenie — I've been looking for you for a dance. Hang on till I give Sarah her drink and we'll hit the floor.'

Queenie turned but TR had disappeared into the crowd. She felt vaguely annoyed and didn't understand why. She had liked dancing with him but his presence unsettled her. Strange sensations had rippled through her as he'd held her. She felt he had known the effect he was having on her and was silently mocking her. Perhaps that was what had annoyed her, but she was also concerned at the way she had no control over her body — it just seemed to follow him and melt to his will. Queenie didn't like not being in control and the experience disturbed her.

Firmly she put him out of her mind and followed O'Rourke back to the table where Sarah was surreptitiously rubbing one of her feet.

Some time later, as Queenie sat with a group attempting to talk above the music, one of the boys pushed his way through the crowd, leant down and shouted in her ear. 'Colin is arguing with one of the ringers from Kandi, it looks like it could get nasty.'

Queenie rose to her feet. 'Don't let my father find out. Colin will only get into more strife. I'll see what I can do.'

'I'm coming with you,' said Sarah.

Outside a small group had gathered around one of the beer kegs and Colin's raised voice could be heard arguing with a thickset youth. Both were staggering and the watching boys egged them on.

'Let him have it. Go on, Hanlon.'

'Get in there, Richards.'

'Have a go!'

Queenie pushed through them to stand near Colin. 'Colin, what's going on... don't start a fight, it's not worth it. Please don't spoil my party,' she said quietly.

Swaying slightly, Colin snapped, 'I didn't start this. Push off, Queenie — it's none of your business.'

'Then act like a man and stop being so stupid, Colin. You're drunk and you'll get flattened,' replied Queenie. 'Walk away now before Dad finds out.'

The other fellow raised his fists. 'You going to let your sister boss you round, Hanlon? Or do you want her to finish your fight for you? I wouldn't mind going a coupla rounds with her!'

As the crowd laughed Colin turned to

Queenie. 'Get lost, Queenie, or I'll give you something to cry about, too.'

A voice from the sidelines cut in. 'It takes a really tough man to threaten a girl, unless he knows she can beat him.'

TR stepped forward, smiling at Colin, but his eyes were hard. 'Easy does it, boys. Come on now, let's not spoil the girl's birthday party.'

Queenie stared at TR who was standing casually, his arms loose by his sides, his eyes fixed on Colin.

'TR, this isn't your fight,' she said softly.

'Who's fighting?' he replied, not taking his eyes from Colin. 'It wouldn't take much to put these two on their backs.'

As the crowd tittered, Colin lunged at TR, his fists flailing. TR didn't raise an arm but swiftly sidestepped and ducked past Colin's wild swing, sticking out his foot to trip him up. Colin fell forward, landing heavily on the hard ground.

Colin's opponent burst out laughing. 'You win, mate. Never hit a man when he's down. He's too grogged up to worry about, anyway. Let's get a drink.' With that he moved away with the rest of the boys and Sarah leaned down to help Colin to his feet.

Roughly he pushed her away, glaring at TR. 'I won't forget this. You made a fool of me. Keep out of other people's fights or you'll get yours, mate.'

'Oh, Colin, stop making stupid threats. Just be glad it's over and you won't have a black eye at breakfast,' said Queenie.

'What makes you think I'd be the one with

the black eye, eh? Always telling me I'm no good. One day I'll show you I'm better than the whole bloody lot of you.' Angrily Colin turned on his heel as Sarah, ever the peace-maker, pattered after him.

Queenie called after him, 'Colin, that's not true. I don't think that at all...'

TR put a restraining hand on her arm and shook his head. 'Let him go and lick his wounds, he's in no mood to be rational.'

Queenie looked at TR. 'I guess I should thank you for breaking it up, even if Colin did lose face a bit. Dad would have had a fit and taken his allowance away for the next month, or something awful... so thanks for coming to his rescue.'

She smiled at him. TR smiled back as they exchanged their first frank and friendly look, their guards down and no pretence between them.

'If you ever need assistance, Queenie Hanlon, I'll be first there.'

Unaware of the fracas involving Colin, Patrick was enjoying himself in the thick of the dancing in the woolshed.

Rose was sitting out the energetic dances, smiling as she watched Patrick spin from partner to partner, lifting the girls off their feet so they squealed with delight. Surreptitiously Rose stifled a yawn and glanced at the small diamond watch Patrick had given her when Queenie was born and wool prices were booming. The tiny hands pointed to two am.

Rose excused herself from the group at the

table and moved to the edge of the dance floor where she finally caught Patrick's eye. She pointed to her watch and put a hand to her mouth miming a yawn and nodding in the direction of the homestead. Patrick hesitated, signalling 'Do you want me to come too?' as the dancers swirled past him.

Rose shook her head, blowing him a kiss. He waved and returned her kiss, turning back to sweep the next partner around in the circle of perspiring dancers.

Rose slipped quietly outside to the cool air where a group was still gathered around the beer keg. Seeing Millie busily picking up discarded paper plates and glasses Rose stopped beside her. 'Millie, you don't have to do that now. Go and enjoy yourself, Jim is inside dancing with all the girls.'

'I'm not much for dancing and crowds, Mrs Rose. Though I might go watch for a bit. I've finished at the house. Me and Stan put away all the food and tidied up. You off now?'

'Yes, I'm tired, but it's been lovely. I hope Queenie has enjoyed it,' said Rose, looking at the gaily festooned woolshed where light and laughter spilled into the night.

'She's having a good time all right, and my goodness, she looks a picture. Our Queenie is growing up, I reckon.'

Rose sighed. 'That she is, but I don't think she realises she is a beautiful young woman. I worry about her, Millie.'

'The way the boys have been around her she'll wake up soon enough,' said Millie matter-of-factly. 'Trouble with Queenie is, she wants to be better than the boys at everything and she don't take kindly to advice.'

Rose smiled. 'You're right as always, Millie. There's Colin at university who doesn't seem to be learning anything very useful, and Queenie learning to run Tingulla better than the lot of them.'

'Learn by doing is better than books, I reckon,' sniffed Millie. 'Well good night, Mrs Rose . . . it's been a real special day.'

As Millie headed into the woolshed Rose moved to one of the Tingulla vehicles parked nearby with its key ring dangling from the ignition. Carefully tucking her long chiffon skirt about her legs Rose put the truck into first gear and pushed in the clutch with a dainty kid shoe. The truck gurgled to life and Rose switched on the lights and headed over the bumpy grass towards the homestead on the hill.

The silhouette of the big house loomed against the moonlit sky. Tingulla homestead was no mere country home but one of the great Australian 'bush palaces' of the outback. The property had been carved out by hand from virgin scrub by Patrick's grandfather, Ned Hanlon, who'd found a fortune in gold in the late 1890s. Over the years the homestead had grown from a slab hut of split logs to a gracious double-storey mansion. Known throughout Australia, it was a grand house, not stately, but spacious and charming in the classical Australian style.

Stone blocks had been quarried and dragged by bullock teams to build the ground floor structure. Ancient cedar trees had been felled on the coast and hauled inland to build the upper storey and interior features.

A turner-carpenter from England with a dubious background but talented hands had worked for years on the property, turning and crafting the magnificent cedar staircase, interior fittings and fretwork, as well as some special pieces of furniture.

He had lived in a shack at the rear of the main house down by the river and seemed reluctant to leave as he kept offering to do more jobs in return for bed, food and 'baccy' money. He devoted weeks to creating the floor of the entrance vestibule with an inlaid bouquet of wild flowers made from different coloured woods. The old man took pride in his work and simply explained, 'I ain't in any hurry to move along'.

When he overheard the shearers' cook comment, 'That pommy bastard has settled in for the duration, he'll be making cedar dunnies next', the old carpenter took delight in presenting the cook with a polished cedar lavatory seat. It became the cook's pride and joy and he carried it from job to job on his packhorse along with his camp oven and cooking utensils.

The homestead appeared to ramble as room followed room through a formal entrance and forecourt and into an inner rear courtyard. But its overall design created a poetic harmony that contrasted against the harsh climate and its setting.

The verandah which ran around the upper storey had polished cypress floors shaded by a curved bull nose iron roof. Visible from every window, balcony and French door, was a breathtaking panorama of grazing land sweeping away to the river with its ghost gums and planted willows. Rising from the water was a hilly ridge studded with eucalypt trees which shimmered a hazy violet. It was said the vaporising oil from the gum leaves caused the blue effect and the ridge was known as 'Blue Hills'. The further reaches of the two hundred and fifty thousand acres of the Hanlon spread edged into harsher, drier country where it became acres to the sheep rather than sheep to the acre.

At the spectacular front entrance, a broad flight of stone steps led up to the ground floor verandah. Beside it stood a magnificent fountain which had been made by Duncan, a bohemian artist friend of Patrick's, during the Great Depression of the thirties.

Down on his luck, Duncan had arrived unannounced at Tingulla and offered his artistic services in return for food and board. Good as his word, he had painted a formal portrait of Rose seated in the garden in the shade of a jacaranda tree. The graceful and romantic portrait hung above the landing on the staircase in pride of place in Rose's fine art collection.

Duncan then declared he would sculpt an imposing statue for the entrance, which made Patrick and Rose nervous as they recalled the lascivious nude sculptures Duncan had created in the city. However, he had surprised and delighted everyone with the great swooping lines of a bird above the water of the lily pond.

The grey stone brolga stood elegantly poised for flight, as if ready to rise in the air.

Rose walked softly up the stairs to the upper hallway, her hand trailing along the deeply polished cedar bannister and her footsteps muffled on the richly patterned Persian carpet.

In the master bedroom she hung her chiffon gown over a chair and placed her pearls back in their special box. She uncoiled her hair and wrapped a peignoir around herself before stepping through the French doors onto the upstairs verandah. Wicker furniture and ferns stood beneath the curve of the tin roof and canvas blinds could be unfurled to keep the heat of the sun at bay.

How many evenings had she stood there, she wondered, breathing in the perfume from the night blooms and lemon-scented gum trees? All those nights when Patrick was away fighting the war in New Guinea when Queenie was just a baby. How she had stood there alone in the quiet darkness, gazing at the stars and praying for the safe return of her man.

Rose always drew strength and serenity from her nightly sojourn with the stars over Tingulla, but tonight, despite the distant sounds of revelry, she felt vaguely perturbed and disquieted. She stared into the sky trying to see through the curtain of night, sensing something was out there, threatening the safety and security of Tingulla.

She shuddered and turned inside, wishing Patrick had come back with her after all. As she drew the bedroom door shut Rose paused, her body stiffening. A sound downstairs drifted up to her, indistinct but unfamiliar. Whatever she had feared was in her home. Calmly, Rose took Patrick's rifle from behind the door and, barefoot, walked softly back down the carpeted hallway.

At the woolshed the beer keg was empty but another was rolled out in its place 'for breakfast'. Stan had promised those still standing at dawn, 'a feed of sausages, steak and eggs'.

Queenie stretched, feeling restless. She glanced past the slow dancing couples, their arms around each other's shoulders, to where TR was deep in conversation with her father. Queenie looked at the slim muscular man with the broad shoulders who stood taller than her father. He was good-looking in an even-featured, but rugged fashion, his gold-flecked hair flopping over his forehead. He was using his hands to describe something and she could see from across the room the long brown fingers which looked quite delicate in contrast to his strongly developed arms.

She turned away and shivered. The memory of his arms holding her was suddenly overwhelming.

Sarah was dancing with a sleepy-eyed O'Rourke; Colin was stretched out along a bench, sleeping off too many beers. Queenie quietly walked unnoticed from the woolshed.

She wanted to walk in the cool night air. The noise of the music, laughter and voices, the crowd, and, more disturbingly, her exchange with TR, had unsettled her. She wanted to be alone, and the tranquil bush, day or night, was always calming.

The moon seemed very high and far away as Queenie trudged up the rise from the gully. Despite the rough terrain she walked barefoot, swinging her silver sandals by their straps, hitching up her mother's dress with her free hand.

Fifteen minutes later she reached the crest of the hill, having identified most of the night noises of animals. She chuckled, remembering the startled wombat waddling back into his hole near the peak of the hill.

Suddenly in the stillness two shots rang out, and Queenie paused, listening.

All was quiet. Probably one of the boys horsing around. Most of them carried small rifles strapped to the outside of the trucks ready to shoot a snake or an errant kangaroo.

An engine started up and roared away from the homestead, but didn't head towards the woolshed. Puzzled, Queenie came to the clearing where she could see the house. Instantly she knew something was wrong.

A vehicle without lights was speeding away and the homestead was dark and silent. The generator was quiet and there were no lights on, save for the flame torches which still flickered in the grounds. Two of the dogs began howling.

Queenie broke into a desperate run, dropping her shoes as she held up her skirt and flew across the grounds towards the dark house.

As she approached the verandah steps

Queenie slowed down and, gasping for breath, her chest heaving with exhaustion, she called out, 'Anyone home?'

There was no response. Grabbing one of the burning torches from the lawn she rushed into the house.

In the same second a picture suddenly flashed into Queenie's mind — her mother blowing her father a kiss and slipping outside to go home.

Frantically she raced up the stairs, the kerosene-soaked wick flaring and trailing black smoke.

'Mum... Mum are you here? Are you all right? Mum!'

Queenie raced down the hall, a hard knot of fear in the pit of her belly. She hesitated at the door of her parents' bedroom before stepping inside and holding the torch high. In the flickering orange light she saw Rose's dress on the chair. Spinning around she wrenched back the door to find her father's rifle missing.

Running back down the stairs Queenie stopped in the darkened vestibule, straining for any slight sound. The ticking of the grandfather clock sounded hollow and ominous.

She ran through the downstairs rooms before finally heading towards the kitchen. As if knowing what she would find, Queenie slowed to a walk, appearing for all the world like some nymph bearing a golden beacon. The flame illuminated the corners of the room.

Queenie's breath came in sharp gasps as if squeezed from her chest with an iron fist when she saw the pale shape of her mother lying on the floor by the pantry.

She knelt by her mother, leaning the torch against the table. Gently she lifted her head, smoothing the hair from her forehead. Softly she spoke to the still and limp figure.

'It's all right, Mum. I'm here. Everything will be all right now.'

Carefully she laid her mother's head back down where it had been lying in a pool of blood which had seeped into a spilt bag of flour, turning the white powder deep red.

Almost unable to breathe and making no sound, Queenie walked outside and stood by the back steps. Stabbing the flame torch into the earth and with shaking hands, she inserted two fingers in her mouth and let out a shrill whistle.

She waited, then whistled again, an urgent sound which pierced the stillness of the night.

Breaking into a run Queenie clambered over a fence as the sound of galloping hooves echoed in the large paddock where Nareedah, her white Arabian, came obediently to her call. Leaning down from where she sat on the railing, Queenie gripped the horse's mane and, holding her dress above her knees, flung herself onto the bare back before stabbing her heels into its flanks.

With a lunge the horse charged down the paddock taking the fence in a powerful leap.

Through the moonlight the silver horse galloped with the girl in a dress the colour of starlight clinging to its back. The girl's face seemed carved from white marble, no tears fell from her eyes and no breath seemed to stir in her body as they raced towards the sounds of merriment echoing from the woolshed.

Chapter Two

‎🙚

Rose, born in a land of soft skies and misty mornings, was buried under a blistering blue canopy in parched red earth. It was not yet mid-morning but the unyielding sun burned down on the assembled mourners at the graveside, causing sweat to soak through unaccustomed jackets, while the leaves on the trees curled and hung forlornly.

Queenie and Colin stood on either side of their father as the Reverend Peters read the final words of the service. Queenie had pulled from her wardrobe a simple dress of pale green, sprigged with tiny sprays of flowers. Her hair hung straight down her back with a wide-brimmed straw hat with a black band upon her head.

As she had marched defiantly from her room, Patrick had hesitatingly asked if the dress was appropriate.

'Mum liked it,' replied Queenie, and looking at her grim face, Patrick didn't argue.

At least she was wearing a dress and not pants as he had feared. Patrick found he was focusing on such small matters, afraid to take in everything that was happening around him. He simply couldn't comprehend that he had lost his gentle Rose. Through his sedated sleep the nightmare had haunted him and he worried that she had been frightened or in pain when he had not been there to help her.

Colin spoke little and kept his grief to himself. Patrick had tried to comfort him but at the catch in his voice Colin had turned away and Patrick let him go. Queenie and Colin tended to keep their emotions to themselves. Patrick had learned to share sympathy and comfort with his partner in life and he wished his children had their mother's understanding and forgiving nature.

Millie, red-eyed, held Jim's hand as Patrick stepped forward to sprinkle a handful of powdery ochre dust on top of the coffin. She watched as Queenie had taken charge of the family group at the church, quietly speaking to friends and workers from the station who had muttered their condolences. Millie watched her face as Reverend Peters read the last words of the poem Rose had loved. Still not a flicker crossed Queenie's stony face.

Reverend Peters' voice continued.

' . . . and wherever I may die,
I know to what far country
my homing thoughts will fly.'

'She has got to give in to the heartache inside her,' thought Millie, 'or that girl is going to crack into a million tiny pieces.'

The memorial service had been held in the tiny Tingulla church at the foot of Blue Hills. It had been Rose, as a young bride exploring her new home, who had spotted the derelict building.

Once a district church for the travelling minister, it had been neglected. The foundations of stone had begun to collapse and the weatherboard building was cracked and peeling. The window panes had been shattered except for a stained-glass window set high beneath the peak of the rusting corrugated iron roof.

The solid wooden door was broken from its hinges and inside the six cedar pews had been stained by birds. Small animals had made their home amidst the rubbish, twigs and leaves. Cobwebs draped in every corner and as Rose had inched slowly forward towards the altar, Patrick had warned her to look out for snakes, causing her to squeal and hurry back to him as he laughingly hugged her.

Rose had insisted the church be restored, and then it was used for family occasions — Queenie and Colin had been christened there — and Rose had hoped they would be married there as well. A track wound behind the church through tall gum trees to the tiny graveyard in the shadow of the ridge of the hills. Surrounded by a rusty iron picket fence, headstones dated back to Great-grandfather Ned Hanlon.

Patrick drew a sharp breath as the memories returned to him and Queenie gently touched his hand as the sound of singing brought him back to the present.

When the service ended the group turned away and began walking to their cars and horses at the front of the church.

Patrick remained standing at the graveside, head bowed, and eyes squeezed shut as he reached for the hands of his children on either side of him. It was Queenie who turned away, gently guiding her father to follow.

Standing by his horse, holding his hat in his hands, TR nodded to Queenie with a sympathetic smile. She appeared not to see him and slid across the car seat as her father got in beside her.

Back at the homestead, Millie and Queenie, dressed once more in comfortable pants, served the tea, handing out cakes and sandwiches on the verandah as the mourners chatted quietly before returning home.

The old police sergeant stopped to speak to Patrick, and placed his gnarled hand on his shoulder. 'No news yet, my friend. I'll keep you posted.' He shook Patrick's hand and left.

It was believed Rose's killers were two escaped prisoners, but as yet her murder remained a disturbing mystery.

There were farewell condolences and offers of help; and finally they were alone. Patrick leaned back in his chair and closed his eyes. Colin sat on the step in his shirt sleeves, his jacket lying beside him as he distractedly pulled at the leaves of a shrub. Queenie followed Millie into the kitchen with the dirty plates.

Millie glanced at the tall young woman beside her. 'You all right, girl?'

Queenie nodded but didn't speak.

'You're going to have to cry some time, Queenie, love... you can't keep it all inside you.'

Queenie fumbled with the dishes she was carrying, dropping them onto the sideboard with a clatter, then turned and ran from the house.

'I'm here if you need me,' called Millie, but she'd gone.

Bolting like a colt from the confines of a corral Queenie ran and ran, her hair flying as she headed for the paddock. She ran without direction or plan. It wasn't until she reached the small stockyard where the wild chestnut stallion was penned that she stopped.

A scene she had witnessed in the early evening of her birthday party clicked into focus in her mind. As she had drifted amongst her guests, she had paused on the verandah where, screened by shrubbery, Patrick had been speaking to TR Hamilton. As if a tape recorder had been turned on, she heard once more her father saying:

'That stallion is a mad thing. Wild and cunning. No one has been able to break the bastard yet. If he wasn't such a good sire I'd get rid of him, but I've been wanting to start breeding a few good horses of our own.'

'I'd like to have a go at breaking him,' said TR.

'You'd like to have a go at maybe breaking a leg, you mean! Listen, TR, if you can tame that unruly buccaneer you've got a job. But take no risks and the responsibility rests on your head, son.'

'I don't take risks unless I'm sure of the outcome. You've got a deal, Mr Hanlon,' and they had shaken hands as Queenie had turned indoors.

Recalling that incident Queenie's distress and grief turned to blind fury. Just who did TR Hamilton think he was? *She* was the horse breaker at Tingulla. *She* would prove it to that arrogant fellow pushing his way into her father's pocket.

If only her mother could see her now.

'Queenie, my fearless pride and joy,' her mother had always said.

'Oh Mum! Watch me... watch me!' called Queenie aloud.

Then with icy calm she fetched a saddle, reins and a rope from the tin shed by the yards.

Drained of all emotion, she moved in close to the suspicious stallion. Making soothing noises in her throat, she moved slowly but deliberately towards the horse until she was standing by his head. He stood still but tense, his muscles twitching, ready to run.

With a touch so light and movement so smooth Queenie slipped the rope noose about the horse and tied it to the railing as the stallion whinnied aggressively. While she fetched the rest of the gear, the horse eyed her warily, ready to lash out if startled.

She let him smell the horse blanket before slipping it lightly onto his back. As the stallion got used to her, Queenie finished saddling him, then lowered the rail blocking the gate.

She had swiftly untied the horse and mounted before he was aware what had happened. As the realisation and sensation of the weight and movement on his back hit him, the stallion bolted.

To Queenie's surprise he didn't even attempt to pig-root and shake her off, or to kick or buck. Instead, the stallion streaked for freedom, plunging towards the rocky, log-strewn gully. Queenie's arms felt as if they were being pulled from her body. There was no way she could hold back this angry beast. She knew it would simply be a matter of trying to stay on as the horse veered through the dangerous terrain.

She could hear the sound of hooves in the distance but she was concentrating intently on the stallion as he skittered and slipped down the slope at full speed. Like a shadow flashing on the edge of her vision, she was aware of another horse gaining on them and a figure leaning forward to grip the halter of the panicked animal.

The stallion slowed and tossed its head, trying to break free of the man holding its reins and the horse nudging its flanks. As the two horses clashed, Queenie turned to see TR shouting at the stallion to ease up.

Both horses came to a stop, panting heavily. Queenie turned and screamed, 'What are you doing! Leave me alone!'

TR hadn't loosened his grip on the stallion and without looking at her he snapped, 'Get on behind me, he's going to start bucking the minute I let go and we'll both roll down this hill.'

'Why are you always interfering?' shouted

Queenie. 'I can control him if you'd just let *go!*'

She yanked the reins, nearly pulling TR from his saddle as the stallion started to buck. Queenie could see they were on a dangerous slope where a bad fall was inevitable if the horse started fighting her.

Before she could make any decision, TR leaned over, and in a swift movement, grabbed her around the waist and pulled her onto his horse in front of him. Queenie was still holding onto the stallion's reins.

'Keep leading him, so he'll follow us,' ordered TR.

Carefully TR turned his horse back up the slope. Queenie held her reins in an outstretched arm, and the stallion followed.

'Don't trust him, he'll make another try at bolting,' warned TR.

Queenie turned her attention from the wild horse to TR's blue eyes. 'I'm only doing this because I don't want the horse harmed. I could have turned him around at the base of the gully.'

TR didn't argue with her. 'Yes, you probably could have ... had you both got there in one piece.'

Queenie didn't answer, turning instead to watch the horse following them. But still she was conscious of the hard muscle of TR's arm cradling her and the warmth of his skin through his shirt.

Back at the stockyard TR dismounted and took the reins from her, leading the stallion back into the yard where he began to rear and snort. As Queenie slid down from TR's horse, he steadied the animal and tied it to the railing, then turned to Queenie.

'Just what were you trying to prove?' asked TR in a quiet voice.

Queenie stared at him, confused and angry, suddenly longing to rush into her mother's arms.

She turned away from him and fled back towards the house. Her breath was catching painfully in her chest as she rounded the corner to the kitchen garden. Near the old water tank was a tiny garden plot which Rose had nurtured, struggling to keep a bed of flowers alive.

Seeing the flowers that Rose had tended with such care — carrying a bucket of bathwater to them when water was scarce, singing to them as they bloomed — Queenie suddenly felt she would burst. She rushed at the flowers, snatching them up and pulling them from the ground. She kicked the tall stems of the stocks and poppies, snapping and crushing them; then flung herself onto the ground and lay there sobbing in the dry earth of the ruined garden.

It was there that Millie found her, and taking Queenie in her arms, stroked her hair and dirt-streaked face, murmuring a murri song — the only fragment she recalled from the time when her own mother held her as a baby.

Through her tears Queenie gazed beseechingly at Millie. 'Why Millie ... why? I miss her so much ...'

Millie felt her heart breaking and promised herself she would care for and love and defend this girl with all her heart and strength.

Gradually Queenie stopped crying and Millie helped her to her feet. Together, arms about each other's waists, they walked back to the house. Without a word being said, Queenie knew that this solid, and good-hearted woman, who had cared for her since she was a baby, would continue to do so and beneath the hurt and sadness, a calmness crept into her tired body.

The sense of loss never went away, but after a while the pain became a dull ache and there were times when Queenie caught her breath and found herself looking for her mother as if she was just out of the room for a minute. Over the weeks Patrick found he could begin to talk about Rose, but Colin, who was home on university vacation, didn't share his feelings or thoughts with anyone.

Sarah began to visit Queenie more often than she had in the past — although the Quinns' property was next door, it took an hour to get from door to door.

On one of her visits they were sitting in the music room as the wind howled outside. The girls were playing Monopoly with Colin and Patrick was reading the newspaper.

'Colin, you're cheating,' said Queenie, throwing the last of the paper money at him.

'Don't be a spoilsport — I'm just being a smart businessman,' sneered Colin, snatching up her money and adding it to his fat pile.

'Really, you are infuriating, Colin,' sighed Sarah. 'You don't have to win *every* game. You've bought up all the good places, so there's no way Queenie and I can beat you. Let's call it quits and talk about the Endurance Ride.'

'No, let's play it out till the bitter end,' replied Colin.

'In that case you can play alone,' Queenie said, getting up from the games table.

'How about making a pot of tea, and I wouldn't say no to some of Millie's cake,' Patrick muttered from behind his paper.

'Colin, you do it, it's your turn and the winner can afford to be generous,' said Sarah good-naturedly.

'Not on your life,' growled Colin.

'Colin . . . ' came Patrick's warning tone.

'I'll see if Millie's around,' said Colin sourly.

'Oh, never mind,' snapped Queenie. 'Leave poor Millie and Jim be. Come on Sarah — let's make it ourselves.'

As they waited for the kettle to boil on the ever-burning Aga cooker, Sarah turned to Queenie. 'Y'know, Queenie. I've been thinking . . . why don't you come overseas with me next month? It would be such fun. There's three of us going. We could visit all those Monopoly places for real!'

'I don't think so, Sarah,' Queenie replied, heaping teaspoonfuls of black tea into the warm china pot. 'Colin is going back to uni and I couldn't leave Dad on his own.'

'But TR is working with him now and I think it would be good for you . . . to forget everything, to get away and have a few adventures.

If you don't do it now, when will you ever go?'

Queenie grinned at her friend as she poured the boiling water from the old black kettle into the teapot.

'Just what sort of adventures did you have in mind, Sarah Quinn?'

Sarah giggled. 'Who knows... it will certainly be more fun than living out here in the middle of nowhere with friends miles apart. My parents won't let me go to the city and try and work but they will let me take a trip away. Broadening my horizons, or something like that — I just want to have a good time.'

Queenie handed Sarah the teapot covered in its knitted tea cosy and picked up the tray filled with the tea things.

'I have no desire to leave Tingulla. I like the bush, Sarah. I'm happy with my horses and I'm learning a heck of a lot about running the place.'

'But what for?' persisted Sarah, as she followed Queenie down the hall. 'Colin will end up running Tingulla, isn't that what he's supposed to be learning at uni, and you'll probably marry a man with his own place.'

Queenie didn't answer as they returned to the cosy room where Colin sat fiddling with the battery-operated wireless, trying to find a voice or music over the static.

'Mr Hanlon, I've been trying to persuade Queenie to come overseas with me. What do you think?'

Patrick lowered his paper and folded it as Queenie poured the tea. Colin glanced up quickly.

'Why, Sarah, I think that's a splendid idea. Do you good, Queenie, what do you say?'

'I don't think so, Dad,' she said, handing him his cup.

'I'd go like a shot,' remarked Colin.

'Yes, well, you have to graduate first, son,' said Patrick drily.

'Dad, I don't want to leave Tingulla, there's still so much I want to learn and things I want to try. What about our stockhorse breeding programme?'

'TR can help Dad run that,' said Colin.

'No!' said Queenie more sharply than she intended. She wouldn't admit it, but she was jealous of TR's ability with horses, especially since he had now been hired by her father to work at Tingulla. 'I'm not dropping something halfway through. I am not leaving Tingulla — ever!'

Sarah handed Colin a plate with a slab of cake on it and laughed nervously at the vehemence in Queenie's voice.

Colin snapped, 'Well one day you will ... '

'Why?' demanded Queenie.

'You don't *own* Tingulla, Queenie,' Colin replied.

'Now, now, let's drop it,' said Patrick, picking up his cup.

But as he sipped his tea he eyed Queenie thoughtfully.

Chapter Three

———— ❧ ————

The annual McPherson Endurance Ride came as a welcome relief from the sadness of the past month — like rain breaking a drought. It was more than a horse race — it was a test of horses' and riders' endurance, covering many miles along often difficult ground. Vets attended checkpoints along the way to monitor the fitness of each horse before allowing it to continue in the ride.

The race was started in an informal way by Dingo McPherson, one of the greatest bush riders in Australia. A legendary stockman and drover, he had made a fortune from mining gold and tin, then lost it all and returned to the bush he loved. He was a man loved and respected by all who knew him personally or by reputation.

In his fifties he took up oil painting, boldly illustrating the scenes, people and places he had encountered over the years in the outback.

The pictures found their way to the city and he was hailed as a success all over again. His paintings were in great demand and fetched high prices, which amused Dingo no end.

'Money for jam, I reckon!' he'd laugh, for he enjoyed his art and the special memory each picture recalled.

It was around a campfire one night when men bet 'my horse is tougher, smarter and faster than your horse!' that Dingo and a few mates set out to prove who really had the best. Over the years the ride had grown into an event which attracted riders and their horses from all over the country.

Tingulla station was one of the seven checkpoints along the ride and the Hanlon family had always participated. Queenie had come close to winning over the years but the 'Dingo Cup' had eluded her. She didn't feel so confident this year because she hadn't spent much time preparing Nareedah. She'd been too busy helping run the station.

Colin was riding Patton, his big bay gelding; and Sarah had entered her devoted Soldier. TR had entered at the last moment on a station stockhorse.

Patrick would act as an official at the Tingulla checkpoint and Millie would take Rose's place in providing hot soup, tea, coffee and sandwiches to the weary riders as they came through. The ride generally took about twenty hours, including a one-hour stop at each checkpoint, and covered one hundred and fifty miles.

A little before midnight the riders began

milling at the start — an old racetrack — where a string of white triangular flags had been strung across the course. Friends, helpers, the press and spectators lined up on either side, ready to send off the contestants into the freezing night.

Holding a mug of hot rum, Patrick stood talking to Dingo who looked fit and exhilarated, his trademark hat squashed on his white hair.

Now in his late sixties, Dingo suffered from a bad back and hip, the result of a fall several years before, and he'd missed competing in the last couple of Endurance Rides. But he was always there to present the cup which carried his name, although Dingo had always made the point that the Ride honoured all the men and horses of the bush who had opened the way for settlement in the vast outback.

The current member of parliament, a local grazier, was helped onto the back of a truck where the organiser with the aid of a bullhorn ordered the entrants to form a line.

It was a heaving, impatient line-up — both riders and mounts were anxious to be on the move. The breath of the horses and their riders was like jets of white steam visible in the spotlights.

The parliamentarian fired a rifle shot and the ride began. Horses sprang into the night to face the challenge of often unknown terrain and gruelling distances. Riders knew they had to travel at speed without straining or jeopardising the fitness of their horse. There was no point in racing to a checkpoint to be 'vetted out' with an exhausted horse.

But for those first moments, as the crowd cheered, each competitor felt the thrill of undertaking a personal test, surrounded by the thudding hooves of more than a hundred horses. They all broke into a wild and exciting gallop before disappearing into the darkness. In seconds the crowd raced for cars, horse floats, trucks and horses to reach the next vantage point.

Within an hour the field had spread out, headed by a fast-riding bunch. Colin was among the leaders, pushing his thoroughbred, Patton, confident he could stay with the leaders. Colin hoped he would win, but to him it was more important to beat Queenie, to prove he not only had a superior horse but was a better rider.

Queenie held back; Nareedah trotted surely, picking her way as if it were broad daylight. Some horses had a natural ability to see well in the dark, and a good 'night horse' was essential when droving in case of a 'rush' of stampeding cattle.

A large shape on the side of the hill caught Queenie's attention in the dimness. The moon was high but frequently obscured by clouds. The dark mass didn't look like rocks so Queenie steered Nareedah up the hill to take a closer look.

She suddenly recognised the bulk: a rusty old stamper battery used to crush rocks during gold mining days. Her father had brought her here once when she was a little girl and told her some of the history of the area. She vividly remembered the story of the Chinese gold prospectors and how they dug round shafts instead of square ones like the white men, so that no evil spirits could lurk in the corners. Patrick had told her tales of murder and intrigue, when men went crazy in their fight for gold.

After showing her the stamper, Patrick had taken her to the top of the hill and shown her the terraced stone walls built by those long-ago adventurers which formed a winding path on the precipitous hillside. It had been a short cut for the prospectors to the gold field. Queenie now realised that it was also a short cut down to Checkpoint Two in the Endurance Ride.

If she could find that track down the hill in the dark, she'd cut her time to the next checkpoint in half. Or she could get lost.

Queenie urged Nareedah forward, deciding to take the risk.

Soon the hill was falling away steeply beneath her in almost a sheer drop, and just as she was thinking she should turn back, Nareedah stumbled to the side and landed on a small track made by wandering stock. Here Queenie found the neat tier of stones, laboriously placed in layers so many years before, supporting a narrow path now used only by wild goats and straying sheep.

Nareedah walked on lightly, finding the route easy to follow, as it corkscrewed down the hillside. In the distance Queenie could see the lights from the fires at the next checkpoint. The horse pricked up her ears and lifted her head, then Queenie heard it too — footfalls and snapping twigs. A little further ahead of her she glimpsed the shadow of a horse.

As she drew closer she recognised the rider and with a surge of excitement she called out, 'Rider behind. Can we ride together?'

'Come join the party. Who is it?' came the friendly reply.

'Hello, Dingo, it's Queenie Hanlon — Patrick's daughter. I see you know the gold track, too.'

'Not much I don't know about this district. Clever of you to find it in the dark. You must have a good horse there, girl. This will save us a whack of time. Nothing in the rules says you can't take a short cut.'

They rode companionably side by side — the famed bush horseman and the slim young woman who was thrilled to be 'going down the track' with a living legend.

'Y'know, Dingo, I've often wanted to ask you, how did you come by your nickname? What's your real name?'

'Well, if you promise to keep it quiet, I was christened Oscar Braxton McPherson,' winked Dingo. 'So you see why my mates soon gave me an easier moniker. First job I had as a teenager was riding the dingo fence, making repairs so the dingoes stayed on one side and the stock and me stayed on the other, and that's where I got my name.'

After a pause he added, 'Amazing really to think of a fence running for a thousand miles across empty land to keep wild dogs out of the State. I used to lie in my swag at night under the stars and listen to them howling in the distance. Used to sound like a baby crying. Eerie really. But, you know, it's a wonderful place, the bush at night,' remarked Dingo quietly. 'Never be frightened out here. Once you know what's about and who's about, there's nothing to be afraid of — provided you've got a sure-footed horse. Some dopey horses can't see a yard in front of them or shy at the silliest things in the dark. You're a lot safer out here than crossing the road in the city, eh, Queenie?'

She was tempted to tell Dingo of that fearful night alone in the bush, a little girl alone in a storm — the night she had put down her beloved Gus — she knew he would understand as few people could. But instead she answered, 'I don't know. I've never spent time in a city. Just into Longreach, and once to Rocky, and to the Agriculture Show in Brisbane.'

'Ah, you haven't missed much — it's too fast, and men waste their time agonising over such fiddling problems. Makes you laugh, really. I'd like to see some of those "executives" cope with real problems — like drought and dying cattle, and bloody bushfires, and diseases that can wipe a man out quick as spit.'

He turned to the thoughtful girl who rode beside him. 'That's not to say you shouldn't give the city a go some time. I've had some bloody great times in the big smoke,' he chuckled.

Queenie smiled in the dark, remembering the stories she'd heard of his womanising and gambling. He'd also organised hundreds of farmers to ride into the nation's capital and camp outside Parliament House to protest against unfair taxes for the men on the land. They'd won the hearts of the country, and Canberra had caved in on the issue.

'Mind you,' continued Dingo, 'that's not to say I haven't had some pretty good times in the bush. An old chap once said to me, "If you don't stop and pick the wild flowers, when you come back they'll all be withered and gone!"'

He chuckled again and Queenie laughed with him, thinking, 'I bet old Dingo stopped to pick a few "wild flowers" in his time!'

They rode in silence a little distance and as they passed some old gold diggings now overgrown with blackberries at the side of the trail, Dingo remarked, 'Must have been quite a place in the old gold days.'

'My father told me there were thousands of people swarming over the district, and the town had dozens of pubs. No wonder it was called the roaring days!'

'You know "The Roaring Days"?'

'I know my Henry Lawson!'

'Off you go then . . . '

Queenie grinned, and as the lights of the checkpoint shone in the distance and the smell of welcoming fires drifted towards them, she began to recite —

> The night too quickly passes
> And we are growing old,
> So let us fill our glasses
> And toast the days of Gold;
> When finds of wondrous treasure

> Set all the South ablaze,
> And you and I were faithful mates
> All through the Roaring days!

Queenie never forgot the exhilarating feeling of breaking out of the dark bush to be greeted by a circle of eager and admiring faces as she and Dingo rode into camp, chorusing the final lines of Lawson's poem —

> Those golden days are vanished,
> And altered is the scene;
> The diggings are deserted,
> The camping-grounds are green;
> The flaunting flag of progress
> Is in the West unfurled,
> The mighty Bush with iron rails
> Is tethered to the world.

Dawn came, widening arms of soft light that swiftly embraced the crisp bush, turning hard needles of frost to limpid dew. It sneaked under tree tops, touching boughs and branches and the tips of feathered wings. Birds sang and warmth seeped into the cold ground.

Queenie rode alone and, like her, each rider experienced a private joy as the sun rose. Spirits lifted, smiles broke out and horses stepped forward with renewed energy.

By midday most followers of the race had gathered at Checkpoint Five, the Warrigal shearing shed, where a big barbecue was being prepared. Sleeping bags and blankets were spread in a row under a makeshift canvas shelter where tired riders could snatch a brief sleep. A row of temporary dunnies had also been built, facing the open country and commanding a magnificent view, the 'thrones' screened from the public by hessian sacking nailed to saplings pummelled into the ground.

Queenie was starting to feel a bit bruised and she knew she was going to have to judge the rest of the ride carefully, pacing and conserving her energy as well as Nareedah's.

Sarah hurried up to Queenie and handed her a hot sausage sandwich dripping with tomato sauce and fried onions. 'Thought you might be hungry, I saw you come in. How are you doing?'

'We're a bit tired but our time's good. What about you?'

'Vetted out,' said Sarah ruefully.

'Oh, Sarah, that's too bad. How's Soldier?' said Queenie, munching the leaky sandwich.

'It was my fault. I got lost. In daylight too. I missed one of the flags and went around the spur which took me ages and put me over the allocated time limit. Disqualified. But I was kind of glad because Soldier was bushed,' explained Sarah.

Queenie wiped her sticky fingers on her pants before removing Nareedah's saddle and rubbing her down with liniment and massaging her legs.

'Where's Colin? Is Dingo still in?' asked Queenie.

Sarah frowned. 'Colin is still up front but he's pushing too hard. At the rate he's going I doubt he'll get Patton through the next vet check. The poor horse is shot, he's run the Melbourne Cup twenty times over.'

Queenie looked angry. 'Colin is stupid. It's not fair on the horse.'

'Dingo McPherson is still in, but only just. The horse is fine but apparently Dingo took a spill, busted two ribs and hurt his hip, but he just got himself strapped up and off he went again. They almost had to lift him back on his horse — he's determined to ride it out.'

Queenie smiled. 'I think he just wants to finish more than anything. Who knows how many more chances he'll have to do this.'

Queenie linked her arm through Sarah's as they moved towards the rest area, 'Oh, Sarah, it was such a thrill to ride alongside him . . .'

With just one checkpoint to get through before the race to the finish line, Colin was charged with excitement, adrenalin and a few mugs of rum. He kicked Patton into a faster trot but the horse's rhythm was out of step, showing that the punishment and weariness were telling. He slowed to a walk and shook his head, sending droplets of sweat into the air.

'Damn you, Patton, don't give in on me now,' cursed Colin.

Reluctantly he allowed the horse to rest. He checked his watch — his time was still good.

Colin tied Patton to a tree and looked around him. Then leading the horse by the reins, he scrambled down a slight incline to a small creek. There had been very little rain this season, but in between the stones of the creek bed were pools of icy water. Colin stuck his hand in one, feeling his fingers go numb with cold.

Taking off his hat Colin began tipping hatfuls of the freezing water over the sweaty horse. Patton flinched and began to shiver before Colin led him up the bank.

Swiftly he reached inside his jacket and unwrapped a small package. Colin dropped the pink coloured sugar cubes onto the palm of his hand and held it out to the horse. 'There you go, Patton. This will make you feel good!'

He smiled to himself as the horse licked the sweetness from his hand.

The vet ran his hands over the thoroughbred, casting a wary glance at Colin who stood with his arms folded, a confident smile lurking at the corners of his mouth.

'Well, his pulse is extraordinarily slow. He hardly seems to have expended any energy at all.'

'I took it a bit easy on this leg.'

The vet eyed him. 'You made bloody good time for taking it easy.'

'Perhaps I took a short cut,' shrugged Colin.

'Well, I'd like to know it then,' muttered the vet, who knew the area well.

'Look, is this horse fit to finish or not?'

'All right, sonny, don't be in such a rush. I just want to confer with someone. You go rest and get something to eat, and we'll take care of your horse.'

'I'd rather you just finished this and give me the okay and then we won't bother you further.'

'Oh, it's no bother,' said the vet, taking Patton's rein. 'I just want to walk him about a bit and check his legs. Don't panic, mate.'

Cursing under his breath, Colin watched as the vet led the horse to the rear of one of the trucks where a pair of dusty boots dangled out of the window. The vet tugged at one foot. 'You still 'sleep, mate? You haven't got much longer.'

The boots disappeared and a sleepy TR sat up and peered out of the window.

'Time to go, huh?'

'Come and have a cup of coffee and look at a horse with me, TR.'

TR stepped out of the truck and stared at the horse beside the vet. 'That's Patton, Colin Hanlon's horse.'

'I'm aware of that. He's just come in making extremely good time, but this fellow looks like he's been on a Sunday stroll. He must have put the pressure on him, yet the horse isn't exhibiting any signs of exertion. If anything he seems to be running a bit slow, like he's been in the deep freeze. I might have a suspicious nature, but young Hanlon seemed a bit too anxious, if you know what I mean. You've been working over there at Tingulla for a while now — what do you make of it?'

TR brushed his fingers through his hair as he walked around the horse. 'Mmm... he's a good strong horse, but it doesn't sound right, and from what I've observed about Colin...'

TR ran his hands over Patton then leant down and pressed his ear against the horse's ribs.

'Y'know, an old jockey who used to know my father told me some stories about the race game in a pub once... I wonder... Open his mouth, Doc.'

As the vet held the horse's jaws apart, TR peered into the mouth then sniffed Patton's breath. 'I reckon that's what it is ... it's known as pink sugar. I don't know what drug it is, but here... you can see traces of pink still in the saliva on his teeth.'

As they led the horse back to the fire, TR continued. 'Apparently they can dose a horse up so their metabolism and body functions slow right down in the early stages, then as it gets into the blood stream it gives them a heck of a wallop and they go like the clappers for a short time, then just fold up. You have to be careful of the dosage, I believe. That old jockey told me he rode a horse once who'd been given pink sugar but they timed it all wrong and the horse fell down and passed out inches from the finish!'

'I'm only a country vet, I'm not up on racing tricks, but I figured something like that. I could possibly identify the drug from a blood sample but there's no way I can do a test here. Well, I'll just pull him in based on my observations. I can't prove the horse has been illegally interfered with.'

'Bloody foolish thing to do, I wonder why he did it?' mused TR.

'You will keep this to yourself, TR?' said the vet as they saw Colin watching them from the far side of the campfire.

'Sure,' TR nodded, and headed for the coffee pot.

Colin finished his rum, put the metal flask back in his pocket, then approached the vet who was making notes on a pad. The vet looked up and handed Colin the reins to his horse. 'Sorry mate, you're out.'

'What do you mean?' exclaimed Colin, his face reddening in anger.

'Do I need to give you a reason?' answered the vet quietly.

'What's TR been telling you? What's he know about this? Get the officials over here,' blustered Colin in a loud voice, causing several people to turn around and stare.

The vet spoke in a low but forceful tone. 'Look, if you want the reason officially made public that's fine by me. You and I know this horse can't go on and if you want everyone else to know, just give me the nod. If not, then drop out quietly and be thankful I don't report you to the committee. If it wasn't for your family, believe me, I'd bloody well tell everyone.'

The vet turned and strode away as Colin tore his hat from his head and kicked it in fury.

It was sunset and a crowd had gathered at the finish line. A rope draped with colourful cloth triangles was strung across the 'main street' of Lachlan. Once a thriving gold rush town it was now a ghost town, visited by occasional tourists who wandered through the few decaying buildings still standing.

For a brief time, it almost resembled a town again, with a large bonfire crackling, and horses, trucks and cars parked along the dirt street. Small children, woollen beanies pulled around their ears, kept running excitedly to

the fringes of the town to peer into the gathering dusk in the hope of being first to spot
the winning rider.

Queenie was tired and Nareedah was slow-
ing down, as if each leg was weighted with
lead. Every part of Queenie's body ached. Her
mind was focused on each few yards ahead
of her. When she had covered that, she concentrated on the challenge of the next hundred
paces before her.

She had no clear idea of where she stood
in the race, though she knew she must have
been keeping among the fastest of the remaining riders. She walked beside Nareedah, leading her for a spell; then mounted and trotted
on, standing in the stirrups to take the weight
off the horse's back. Nareedah had thrown
a shoe, but it didn't seem to bother her.
Queenie patted the horse beneath her.

'Nearly there, Needa... No matter what,
we've finished and that's something, old girl.'

The beginning of the old road was just visible — two grassy ruts which led into the
remains of Lachlan. Queenie slowed to a walk,
saving Nareedah's energy for the last sprint
to the finish line.

Suddenly she cocked her head, listening
intently. She pulled Nareedah up, calmed her
and listened again. Nareedah heard the faint
sound too and her ears pricked.

It was coming from the left. A low growl
— no, more of a groan. Queenie slipped from
her horse and walked slowly into the bush.

Off the track, slumped against a tree was
Dingo, clutching his side, his eyes closed in pain.

Queenie hurriedly knelt beside him. 'Dingo, are you all right? What happened?'

He opened his eyes and started to speak, catching his breath in pain.

'Take it easy, Dingo. Where's your horse?' asked Queenie.

'Okay. Took another spill... he's feeding. Whistle him,' Dingo managed to gasp between painful breaths.

Queenie ran her hands over Dingo's legs and arms feeling for broken bones.

He winced when she touched his ribs. 'I guess I fell asleep,' he murmured.

'Passed out, more like it. Dingo, you shouldn't have got back on after that fall, why did you keep going?'

He peered into her concerned green eyes. 'You have to ask that? And I was so bloody close.' He closed his eyes and the look of pain was as much from disappointment as discomfort.

'You dopey old thing, Dingo,' said Queenie fondly. 'Come on, let's see if you can stand — put your arm around my shoulder.'

In a businesslike manner Queenie snapped a branch from the tree and handed it to Dingo who draped his arm across her shoulders and supporting himself with the stick, managed to push himself upright.

He stood shakily leaning on the stick, and grinned at her. 'Thanks, Queenie. Send one of my boys back here and tell them I'm waiting. Now move along, girl, you can win this if you don't hang about with a silly old geezer like me.'

'No way, Dingo, you're still in this race too. Do you think if I gave you a boost you could get back in the saddle?'

He looked at Queenie, the light coming back into his eyes. 'I dunno. Let's give it a go.'

Dingo gave a shrill whistle and his horse trotted obediently to him. Queenie linked her fingers together and braced her legs as Dingo grasped the pommel and placed one foot in Queenie's hands. 'One... two... three... ' Dingo dragged himself up while Queenie heaved with all her strength, and somehow he managed to throw his leg over the horse. He slumped into the saddle as Queenie stumbled and fell to her knees.

'You okay?' asked Queenie, scrambling to her feet.

Dingo didn't answer. He bit his lip in pain, settling his feet into the stirrups and taking the reins from Queenie.

'Go on, Dingo — just hang on, mate. You'll get there.'

'Well, come on girl, let's not fiddle about.'

Queenie smiled up at the old man in the saddle, a dark figure silhouetted against the last rays of the day. 'I'll be right with you, just got a minor adjustment to make.' She slapped Dingo's horse on the rump shouting, 'Go!'

The startled horse broke into a canter and sped through the trees. Without turning to look over his shoulder Dingo lifted an arm in salute.

Queenie watched him disappear as she fondled Nareedah's ears. 'We'll just take a bit of a rest, old girl.'

*

The cry rang out from the edge of the town. 'Rider approaching! Who is it? Who is it?'

In the falling darkness the crowd peered at the luminous white number pinned to the rider's chest.

A cheer went up to greet Dingo, cantering steadily, holding his hat aloft and waving it in the air, a broad grin across his face, his pain forgotten.

And as Dingo approached the strip of dirt road, another shout went up. The second rider was in sight. 'Forty-nine — that's TR Hamilton!'

'And here's another rider... what a finish!' they yelled.

'It's a white horse... hey, it's Queenie Hanlon, she'll take out third place.'

'No she bloody won't! She's going for second, look at her go!'

Queenie and Nareedah broke from the trees onto the road, hot on TR's heels.

TR had been cantering easily behind Dingo but there was no way he was going to overtake the grand old man. Suddenly he looked over his shoulder to be greeted by the sound of thundering hooves bearing down on him. He kicked into a gallop — but too late. Queenie overtook him just when Dingo broke through the finish line to the cheers of the crowd.

Queenie flashed in seconds behind the winner with TR at her tail. The crowd went wild.

Dingo was helped down and he pushed his way through the happy throng to Queenie who was dismounting from Nareedah.

Dingo went to her. 'You took your time getting here, girl. If you'd ridden like that all the way you would have got in way ahead of me.'

Queenie smiled at him. 'I don't think so, Dingo. You won fair and square.'

Dingo leaned forward and brushed his lips against her cheek, speaking for her alone to hear. 'You're a winner, Queenie Hanlon. I owe you one. When you want a favour, call me.'

Dingo was swept along in a flood of well-wishers and Queenie turned to find TR grinning at her. He held out his hand to her and winked. 'I can see I'm going to have to watch myself when you're around, Miss Hanlon. Congratulations.'

Queenie laughed, her eyes dancing. 'Why thank you, Mr Hamilton. Now the score is even.'

Patrick pushed through the crowd and hugged his daughter, his heart gladdening to see the joy and laughter in her face. His only regret was Rose was not here. And Colin hadn't even bothered to turn up to see the Tingulla team take second and third place.

The celebration of the end of the Endurance Ride continued late into the night. Sipping drinks around the campfire, Dingo and Patrick were joined by TR.

'Dingo, do you know TR? He's started working for me at Tingulla. TR, you know who this is of course,' said Patrick.

TR shook hands warmly. 'It's an honour, Dingo.'

'TR, eh? I've heard about you. Pretty good with wild horses, aren't you?'

'Well ... I've made a fair living dealing with horses one way and another.'

'You wouldn't be interested in making some fast, big money in America, would you? Sorry Pat ... don't want to steal your boy, but he might be just the kid I've been looking for.'

Patrick shrugged. 'Can't blame a man for trying, and I can't blame another for taking a better offer. We have no written contract.'

'We have a handshake, Patrick — and that's a contract in my book. But what are you talking about, Dingo?' asked TR curiously.

'I visit the States a bit and a mate of mine runs the biggest rodeo circuit in North America. They're always looking for new blood and he asked me if I could find him a hotshot "Aussie cowboy" to ride a few wild ones round the circuit for him. It's good money — provided you don't get busted up.'

TR laughed. 'I can't see myself in one of those fancy satin shirts with fringes all over it and a ten gallon hat!'

Dingo slapped him on the back and winked at Patrick. 'Well, if old Pat here gives you a hard time you can tell him you've got an offer in America any time you want it, TR!'

Queenie had settled Nareedah for the night and planned to head back to Tingulla at first light. She was stiff and weary and began looking for Patrick's truck, planning to wrap herself in a blanket in the back and get some sleep.

Suddenly she spotted Colin sitting on the ground by one of the Tingulla Land Rovers.

He was leaning against a wheel, holding his flask of rum and looking morose.

'Hey, Colin, where've you been? Dad and I were looking for you. Did you see the finish?'

'Maybe I did. Maybe I didn't. If I hear one more person tell me how fantastic my sister is, I'll vomit.'

Queenie sighed and sat down beside him. 'Colin, what's up? Why do you have to turn everything into a deadly competition between us? I thought you'd be pleased for me.'

'Why should you care how I feel? You've got Dad patting you on the back every minute of the day telling you how bloody wonderful you are.'

'Colin, don't be like this. Dad is just as fond of you. But you make it so difficult for him to get close to you. You push everyone away all the time. I know you miss Mum — I do too — so we've got to stick together and help each other.'

'You and Dad can't help me. I'm stuck down in Sydney at boring uni while you stay at Tingulla running everything with Dad. Why do you want to try and run the place, Queenie? What am I supposed to do?'

'Colin, when you graduate we'll run Tingulla together — as a family. Like a board of directors. I always want to be involved in Tingulla. I love it. It's my home.'

Colin struggled to his feet. 'Yeah, well one day one of us is going to have to leave . . . and it won't be me.'

Queenie watched him go, staggering slightly from the rum. She knew his words were spoken out of maudlin self-pity, but his resentment worried her.

The spectre of her future loomed ahead. The thought of ever leaving Tingulla was anathema to her. Yet... what if she did fall in love with someone who wanted to live elsewhere? She didn't want to even begin contemplating such an idea.

Queenie yawned and pushed the thought to the back of her mind. She couldn't think straight when she was tired. She wrapped a blanket around her like an Indian, and headed for the truck.

Chapter Four

The weeks spun slowly into months, and although a new routine ensured the smooth running of Tingulla, the days seemed empty.

Walking through the deserted rooms of the house, Queenie would sometimes pause, listening for the soft humming of her mother as she went about her tasks, hearing her light footstep on the stair or her sweet voice teasing Patrick. The house always seemed cold, and the warmth and laughter of Rose hung in the air like a fading echo.

Millie kept the house spotless, and wholesome meals appeared with quiet efficiency. She even dotted small bunches of flowers in the house as Rose had done.

Looking at the neat posy in the centre of the dining room table, Queenie remembered her mother's deliriously vivid arrangements scattered about the house — pottery jugs filled with fresh gum tips and wattle blossoms;

trailing lengths of jasmine entwined around the bannisters; stems of bush orchids, and massive bird-of-paradise lilies springing from a large bowl.

Colin had returned to university and never wrote. Queenie and Patrick worked together with the station hands, moving sheep to better grazing paddocks as the drought continued. In areas where feed was scarce, they chopped the lower branches from trees for the sheep to eat. They were forced to sell some stock to reduce numbers, but the market was depressed — other graziers were selling too.

At night Queenie and Patrick went through the paperwork, planning for the coming shearing season and balancing the books. TR had proved to be a great asset and Patrick began to rely on his opinions, involving him more and more in helping to keep the property running smoothly.

Occasionally TR would join Patrick for a beer at the end of the day and they would talk about the prospects of breeding a strong line of stockhorses. TR talked of crossing the thoroughbreds with some good bush stock. But although he listened with interest, Patrick was reluctant to commit himself to the venture.

Queenie never joined her father and his capable new right-hand man. As Millie prepared the evening meal she would sit in the kitchen talking to her about supplies and the care of the men on the station, or simply making small talk. TR didn't join them for dinner, but ate with the station hands and returned to the shearing quarters where he shared a room with one of the jackaroos.

As they worked together, Queenie watched her father, noticing how his attention would wander and how he would stop and stare into the distance; or would become distracted and let little details slip past him — something he would never have done before Rose died.

Queenie was worried, and she and Millie talked at length on how to shake him from his lethargy.

'Maybe a trip to Sydney to see Colin?' suggested Millie.

'Yes, it's been a long time since we've been to the big smoke, I could ask him,' said Queenie.

Patrick said he'd think about the idea and didn't mention it again.

Queenie kept up her early morning ride, taking Nareedah for a gallop through the sparkling air before returning to eat breakfast with Patrick.

One morning as she washed Nareedah down, she heard wood being chopped and, peering around the stable, she saw TR swinging the axe into a log, making wood chips fly.

'Working up an appetite for breakfast?' asked Queenie.

TR straightened up. 'No, Jim is having a tinker with that old Land Rover I bought myself — so in exchange I said I'd chop the wood for him.'

'Oh, I see.' Queenie paused. 'How's the horse in foal coming along?'

TR's face lit up and as he leaned on the axe, the muscles of his suntanned arms strained against his shirt. 'Terrific. I think she'll deliver any day.'

'I'll be interested to see that foal,' smiled Queenie.

TR returned her smile. 'I'll be sure to get you the minute it's born.'

Kevin Hooper, the Flying Doctor, whose practice extended for fifteen hundred miles around the northwest section of Queensland, sat at the controls of his new Cessna, enjoying its smooth manoeuvrability. The plane hummed through the midday heat, a silver speck glinting in the endless blue.

Seven thousand feet beneath him there stretched ripples and waves of red sand dunes. It was a wind-made lunar landscape almost devoid of wildlife, its flatness broken by the occasional hiccup of rocky outcrop, or deceptive dirt track made by geologists carrying out surveys for possible oil exploration sites. From the air these rough roads could be seen running in squares and geometric patterns leading nowhere — a desert maze with no signs and no distinctive landmarks.

Kevin rarely flew over this particular remote stretch of land, tending to hop directly between the sprawling properties. Earlier in the morning he'd been called out to an isolated droving camp where one of the men had been badly trampled by bullocks during a 'rush' at night. They'd finally got a message through to the Flying Doctor Service on the two-way radio after one of the Aboriginal stockmen had ridden for two days back to the nearest homestead.

The injured man, suffering badly fractured ribs and a dislocated shoulder, was now lying on the specially fitted stretcher along the length of the cabin behind Kevin.

As he headed towards Cloncurry Hospital, Kevin glanced at the ground where something had caught his eye. He looked again, seeing a flash of sun reflecting off a shiny object. Near a rocky rise he saw a truck, so dusty it was almost invisible, camouflaged by the bull dust and sand around it.

Kevin banked the plane and swung around in a right-hand arc for another look. The truck doors were open but no figures were to be seen. Obviously it had been there some time because its tracks were completely covered by the bull dust. He circled, wondering where the driver had gone, why the truck had been abandoned and, more curiously, what was it doing there in the first place. It certainly wasn't a prospector's rig. The driver had obviously been lost as he was on no recognised road or track.

As Kevin flew lower he whistled softly in surprise — lying beside the open door, almost underneath the truck, was the body of a man.

He called over his shoulder to the sedated drover. 'Hang on, mate, we're going to make a bit of an unscheduled stop, won't take a tick. Nothing to worry about.'

The drover didn't open his eyes but lifted a limp hand in acknowledgement.

The Cessna slewed slightly as it skidded in a thick layer of dust before bumping to a stop on the crude road. Kevin jumped down from the plane, reeling as the solid wall of heat hit him in the face. Two hundred yards away the truck seemed to shiver in the dancing heat haze.

The four-wheel drive had been there many weeks and there were two badly decomposed bodies — both men. The one lying beside the truck probably died of dehydration, the second body was slumped across the front seat, a rifle beside him.

'Poor bastard took the quick way out,' thought Kevin as he picked up the dusty rifle. They had obviously been totally lost and unprepared for the harsh environment into which they'd driven.

Kevin shook his head as he saw the inadequate and impractical gear they had carried with them. Picking up the bags that contained their personal possessions, he reached into the glove box for any papers that might give a clue to their identity.

In the eerie silence of the outback where death had come so hideously to these men, Kevin unfolded the registration papers. The Land Rover was registered to Patrick Hanlon, Tingulla, RMB 427, Queensland.

Sergeant Dick Harris returned once more to Tingulla. He drove down the road leading to the massive log entrance where he saw Queenie riding ahead of him, the kelpie sheep dogs trotting beside her.

He tooted and pulled up. Still in the car, he quietly broke the news about the discovery of the truck and the two bodies. They had been escapees from a New South Wales prison — Rose must have disturbed them as they stole food and gear.

Queenie listened as she fiddled with Nareedah's reins, her throat dry, her heart pounding, then she leaned down from the horse to shake the Sergeant's hand. 'Thanks for coming out to tell us in person, Sergeant Harris.'

She turned the horse and rode away from him.

The Sergeant continued up the tree-lined drive to the main house and waited on the verandah, twirling his broad-brimmed hat in his hands while Millie went to fetch Patrick.

He gave him the details briefly. Patrick listened, not speaking, chewing the edge of his lip, his arms folded tightly against his chest.

'So it's all wrapped up now, mate. At least we know they didn't get away with it. God has his own method of retribution, I suppose. We can arrange to get your vehicle back, though it'll take time. It's to hell and gone out there.'

Patrick dropped his arms. 'Don't bother, Dick. Close the book. How about a cold drink or cup of tea?'

Calling to Millie, he turned indoors and the Sergeant sunk into one of the cool and comfortable squatter's chairs, sorry to have reopened the painful wound of Rose's murder.

*

In the quietness of the night Jim stepped softly into the kitchen where a kerosene lamp burned on the sideboard. Queenie dozed in the bentwood rocker by the Aga stove.

Jim poured the remains of the tea into two cups as Millie, wrapped in an old chenille dressing gown, joined him. Even though the days were hot, the land chilled quickly after sunset; and although Millie and Jim had their own quarters, they all liked the cosy warmth of the kitchen.

'Look at that girl,' whispered Millie. 'Tired out, she is. I don't know what we're going to do with her and Mr Patrick. Work and work, it's all the pair of them think about. It's not right, Jim. She's a young girl — she should be having some fun in her life.' Sipping her tea, she added quietly, 'There's no laughing in this house any more.'

'Give it time, Millie. They got to work it out in their own way.'

'I blame her Dad. He's pushing her too hard. Like he's trying to teach her everything all at once. I can't make him out. He's getting older by the day — and thinner. I'm worried, Jim. He doesn't seem to care about anything any more.'

'Millie, stop worrying about everyone or you'll get run down too, and then where will we be? Come on, I have to get up at daybreak.' Jim yawned and placed his cup on the sink.

Millie bent over Queenie and tapped her shoulder. 'Queenie, go on up to bed.'

Queenie stretched, settled more comfortably into the chair, and without opening her eyes murmured. 'G'night, Millie. I'll go up-stairs in a minute'.

Half an hour later she was still sleeping soundly in the rocker when there was a knock at the kitchen door. Queenie didn't stir. TR opened the door and stepped inside. He stood looking down at Queenie — her head tilted to one side, her face shadowed by the curtain of her hair which tumbled over her shoulder. The yellow light from the lamp cast a shine through the coppery gold tints of her glossy locks. TR leaned forward and gently smoothed a silky strand from her face.

She stirred and a smile curled about her mouth as her eyes fluttered open.

Seeing TR standing there she sat up with a start. TR drew back, embarrassed.

'Sorry, Queenie, didn't mean to startle you. I thought I'd see if you were still awake. The mare is in labour, I thought you might like to be there.'

Queenie relaxed and jumped to her feet. 'Yes, yes, of course. I'll get my jacket.'

In silence they hurried through the frosty night to the stable. The mare lay breathing heavily, her eyes wide as she concentrated on working the bulk of the foal out of her body.

TR crouched by the horse's tail as Queenie sat by her head stroking her and talking softly.

Twenty minutes later the horse grunted as a muscular spasm began forcing the foal in its placental bag from her body. However, instead of dropping from her body in a swift easy movement, the foal seemed to be obstructed. The mare whinnied and panted and began struggling to her feet.

TR moved swiftly. 'Hold her still, Queenie — it's breeched.'

TR slipped out of his coat, pushed up a sleeve and inserted his arm into the vaginal opening, slowly turning the small body around. As he adjusted the foal in the birth canal, the mare heaved and with TR gently easing it out, the bloodied foal flopped onto the straw.

Queenie and TR exchanged a worried look. For a second it lay there, then calmly the mare turned and began licking away the birth covering. The tiny horse lifted its head and stared with dark brown eyes at its new world.

Queenie felt tears spring to her eyes as she looked at TR who was watching the mare and her foal with a happy grin. 'How wonderful! Good on you, TR. I was worried the poor thing was going to suffocate.'

'She might have managed okay on her own, but it was probably a good thing we were here. Pretty little thing, isn't he?' said TR.

They sat there watching for a while longer, as the mare cleaned up her foal which was already attempting to unfold its wobbly long legs.

Queenie glanced at TR in the dim light shed by the lantern hanging from the rafter. She had never seen this tender side of him before and realised she knew very little about him despite the fact they were often in daily contact. She had only ever discussed day-to-day issues, reluctant to get too familiar with him. She had never forgotten the powerful emotions he'd aroused in her at her birthday party, and because the memory disturbed her, she had kept him at arm's length.

TR stood up and stretched. 'I think they'll be fine. I've got some coffee brewing at my quarters, do you want some?'

Queenie hesitated, she hadn't been inside the shearers' quarters since TR had moved in to share with Ernie, the sixteen-year-old Aboriginal jackaroo and rouseabout. 'All right, thanks.'

Ernie was asleep in his bunk, screened by a small partition. Through the doorway to TR's section Queenie could see a neatly made bed and a shelf of books. Between the two sleeping sections was a table and two chairs set before an old wood-burning pot belly. TR lifted the coffee pot from the stove and poured strong black coffee. Opening the stove door, he threw in a few more pieces of wood.

Queenie curled her hands around the steaming mug. 'So what are you going to call the foal?'

'I reckon that's your job, Queenie. It's your Dad's horse,' replied TR.

The smile faded from Queenie's face. 'Yes, but he seems to be taking so little interest in anything these days . . . ' Her voice trailed off and she took a sip of the coffee.

TR pulled up the other chair and leaned back in it, sticking his booted feet on the box of wood by the stove. 'Yeah, I've noticed. I've been trying to interest him in building up the horse stock. There's a big herd of brumbies roaming Blue Hills and the scrub country. If we could cull any good ones, and crossbreed them with the thoroughbreds and existing stockhorses, I think you could start building up a good line. There's still money in horses — despite Henry Ford.'

'How many brumbies are out there?' asked Queenie with interest.

'Apparently the Flying Doc spotted them the other day and radioed back that there were several dozen.'

'If you picked the best of them for breeding and broke some of the others — if they were any good — you could sell them for a quick profit,' said Queenie thoughtfully.

TR grinned at her. 'And who's going to do the breaking?'

Queenie blushed slightly and couldn't help smiling back. 'Okay, I'm happy to admit you're good with horses. You're the breaker.'

'We could do it together if you can persuade your father it's a good idea for Tingulla.'

Queenie stared at him. 'I'd want to be there to muster them as well as break and sell them,' she said firmly.

'Oh, I figured you would,' said TR, his mouth twitching in a half-smile.

Queenie handed him her mug. 'Thanks for the coffee. I'll have a word to Dad.'

As she rose she nodded towards his bookshelf. 'You like books? What are you reading?'

'Oh, everything. Technical stuff on horses at the moment and a bit of escapism. My Dad was a hopeless Irish romantic so I inherited his love of the blarney. Though I'm fond of the Welsh neighbours — Dylan Thomas . . . ' he stopped, looking sheepish. 'I read Henry Lawson too, y'know.'

Queenie tried not to look as surprised as she felt. 'Well, if you ever want to borrow a book from Tingulla's library, you're welcome.' She smiled at him. 'Good night, TR. And thanks.'

'Good night to you, Queenie. I'm glad you were there.'

Chapter Five

———— ❧ ————

Several days later TR was watching the foal frolicking by its mother when Sarah pulled up at the home paddock gate in her father's car.

'Hello, TR! And goodbye!' she called, hanging out the window.

'Where are you off to, Sarah?' TR climbed over the gate and strolled to the car.

'England, the Continent, the world! I sail in a couple of days but I'm going down to Sydney tomorrow. I just came to say goodbye to Queenie.'

'I guess you'll be gone some time?' TR took off his hat and leaned against the car.

Sarah thought again what an incredibly good-looking man he was. 'Well, at least a year. Not worth going if you don't see everything. I still wish Queenie were coming with me, it would have been such fun. Her Dad thought it would be good for her, too,' added Sarah, her bubbly enthusiasm stilled for a moment.

'I think she's happier here, working things out in her own way. She feels secure at Tingulla.'

'I guess that's true. But before she settles down she should see a bit of the world. Maybe she might come over in a few months and join me in my search for Mr Right,' smiled Sarah.

TR grinned at her. 'Mr Right?'

'Oh yes, ever since we were little Queenie and I decided we'd both marry tall dark handsome men with slight accents who we'd meet in the Alps or on a rocky island in the Mediterranean!'

'Dreamers!' TR held out his hand to Sarah. 'Good luck and take care, Sarah. If you don't find Mr Right remember you've got some good-hearted blokes hanging around here you might consider.' He winked at her as he squeezed her hand.

'Right, TR, I'll keep that in mind. But seriously, do keep an eye on Queenie. Colin is away, and so selfish anyway, and it seems Queenie is looking after her Dad more than the other way around these days.'

'I will, Sarah.'

She revved the car and waved. 'Goodbye ... and good luck with the horses!'

Queenie and TR confronted Patrick in his study. They'd been talking about horse breeding for months. Now they wanted a decision.

'Look, Dad, it's a good opportunity. Those brumbies are going to move on soon. There could well be some excellent horses amongst the hacks. They're wild and inbred but some might have come from good stock.'

'And to survive out there means they're tough and that's the quality we want to breed into our strain,' added TR.

Patrick leaned back, looking at the two earnest faces appealing to him. Queenie's deep green eyes and TR's vivid blue eyes stared solidly at him.

'It could be dangerous.'

'I wouldn't allow Queenie to take any risks,' said TR firmly. Queenie flashed him a defiant look, but she bit her tongue.

'I can't spare any of the boys. I don't like the idea of the two of you alone out there. If it was anyone else, TR, I'd say no... but —' Before Patrick could finish Queenie rushed to hug him. 'Thanks, Dad. You won't regret it. We'll come back with some good horses, I just know it! After all, you've got the two best horse people in the district on the job.'

'That's the only reason I'm allowing this mad venture.' Patrick knew his daughter was more than capable of handling herself and wild horses in the bush. He was also happy to see her bursting with enthusiasm and high spirits. This was his Queenie of old. How could he refuse her? He had to admit it could be a profitable exercise.

Queenie excused herself to break the news to Millie.

TR stood as Patrick studied him. 'I don't have to tell you of the responsibility I'm handing to you,' said Patrick quietly. 'I am trusting you with my daughter, TR.'

'She'll always be safe when I'm around. I promise you that.'

Patrick nodded and as he shook the younger man's hand he clasped it briefly in both his hands before turning away.

TR and Queenie squatted on their haunches in the sparse shadow of a gum tree and studied the group of wild horses grazing calmly in the valley below them. Flinty ironstone cliffs glinted in the sun on either side, sheltering this narrow and protected gorge.

The brumbies were spread out in a mass of colours and sizes, their manes and tails long and matted, their legs muscled and strong. As the mob rested, one horse stood apart, his black head lifted alertly.

'Don't they look proud and free. It seems a shame to break them up,' whispered Queenie to TR who was studying them through a pair of binoculars. 'How many are there?'

'Maybe fifty. Look at the stallion, the big black fella. I bet he's the leader.'

'He looks as if he's a bit suspicious, but he wouldn't know we're here — we're too high, and anyway, we're downwind. Maybe he just senses something is amiss.'

TR handed her the glasses. 'There are some nice horses in that mob. A few runts, but they look pretty fit.'

'Wonder where they came from,' mused Queenie.

'All over the place, some escaped from properties, some have probably been breeding out here for years. They travel for miles and miles to find each other, and then form big mobs.'

They continued to watch in silence, sharing the binoculars and studying the horses individually. Occasionally TR would nudge Queenie and point out a particular horse.

A loose rock suddenly dislodged from the opposite cliff and crashed down the cliff face, startling the horses who dashed into a tight group behind the black stallion.

TR and Queenie grinned at each other. 'He's the boss, all right. We get him where we want him and all the others will follow,' whispered TR close to her cheek.

'He looks a mean sod. You can break him, TR.'

'Thanks a lot. This isn't going to be easy with just the two of us and the dogs. It'll be hard riding, Queenie. And risky.'

'I can see that. And I'm not nervous. I know what we're doing.'

'Okay, don't bite my head off. Let's go work out how we're going to corral them.' TR slid back from the precipice where they were perched.

Silently they moved back to where they had hobbled their horses and, mounting them, turned back towards camp. Their quarry had been found relatively easily. Catching them would be a lot more difficult.

Queenie relit the small campfire and TR poured water into the billy from a water bag.

'So, how do you think we should round them up?' asked Queenie.

'If we get them down into that dry river

bed and herd them up the ravine to the dead end we can pen them and pull out the ones we want. We'll have to build a bit of fencing and a slip rail gate, but that won't take more than a few hours if we both swing an axe.'

'I can swing an axe, TR. I'd figured we'd have to do that anyway.'

'Just checking that I know what I'm doing, huh? I'm not worried, I have great faith in the dogs,' grinned TR.

Queenie gave him a slight push, causing him to sit hard on the ground. 'Dogs indeed. They're sheep dogs, they'll do as I say,' she said, throwing the black tea leaves into the bubbling water, determined TR would not get the upper hand.

Queenie lifted the blackened billy of tea off the fire with a stick as TR sliced a chunk of corned beef and slapped it between two pieces of damper.

'We'd better leave camp at daybreak and hope we get to them before they hear or smell us,' said TR, munching through the hunk of bush bread. 'This afternoon we build the pen.'

They rode back to where the ravine began, taking the packhorses with them, and worked their way down to the floor of the valley. The river bed began at the base of the cliffs where a waterfall would plummet in the rainy season.

It took most of the afternoon to build the trap. Although the spot they'd chosen for the stockyard looked narrow, they still had to erect almost one hundred yards of fencing to stretch along both sides of the valley to the sheer cliffs formed by a glacier in some distant age.

Queenie and TR worked side by side, each knowing what needed to be done without discussion. They swung axes, hauled saplings, lashing them to trees, and used the packhorses to drag fallen trunks along the fence line.

The heat was stifling as the sun rose above them and not a breath of wind drifted down to the floor of the ravine. The birds were silent as if singing was too much effort. Down in the sandy river bed the dogs dug holes in the shade of the bank and lay there panting.

TR dropped his shirt onto the ground. The sweat made his tanned body shine like polished brass. He swung the axe with the rhythmic skill of a bushman and Queenie noticed the iron-hard muscles in his arms that powered the steel blade into the logs needed for the fence.

Queenie worked just as hard. She too, used an axe, mainly on the saplings for the rails. She had a good eye and made a clean cut, though her muscles and back screamed and the perspiration ran in streams down her body and soaked through her shirt. Blisters began to form on her hands, but she didn't complain or pause. Strangely, she found it bearable and realised she was enjoying the silent companionship that came from working alongside TR.

The sun was setting as they finished the slip rails that would make the gate and cleared away the scrub at the entrance of the trap so the horses would have a clear run in.

They saddled up to ride back to camp. 'Well, what do you think?' said Queenie, critically eyeing their work.

'Some of your bits look a bit dodgy, but I reckon it'll do the job,' said TR with a slight grin.

'Thanks. You do dinner then,' said Queenie turning her horse so he wouldn't see her smile. She knew he had paid her a compliment in the backhanded way of bushmen. If any part of that fence was weak, they'd still be working on it.

Queenie sat by the campfire nursing her cracked and blistered hands. She stared thoughtfully into the darkening sky.

'The sky seems a different colour and there is a strange smell in the air. Surely we couldn't be getting rain after all these months,' she said.

TR glanced up. 'Chance'd be a fine thing. But I see what you mean. This drought has gone on long enough. Let's hope rain is on the way.'

He handed her a mug of tea, noticing her sore hands — but he knew Queenie better now, so said nothing.

At piccaninny light, the pearly grey light before the dawn, TR rolled out of his sleeping bag and poked the fire. It flared and he put a billy of water on to boil then checked the hobbled horses grazing nearby. Ten minutes later, holding a mug of steaming tea, he nudged Queenie in her swag with the toe of his boot. 'Time to move, Queenie.'

Sleepily, Queenie took the tea and sipped it. TR pointed to the sky. 'Take a look. Your premonition could be right.'

Smudges of black cloud hung above the first streaks of the sunrise.

'We've had a few false alarms. The clouds

could disappear by midday. It happens a lot,' said Queenie.

They had worked out their plan of attack, the signals to each other and the possible loopholes and dangers. They knew their key player was the black stallion — where he went the others would follow.

In the dawn light, as the edges of the sky began to run with lilac pink and gold, they started their slow circuit. Moving in quietly behind the brumbies, they followed slowly as the mob began to graze their way along the ravine.

Timing of their charge was crucial. They had to position themselves behind the group so they would head up the ravine into the narrow mouth where there was no exit and their trap waited.

The tail-enders among the brumbies knew there were two strange horses behind them but took little notice as the horses moved softly and held back. The dogs were out of sight awaiting their call.

The stallion was becoming edgy. He shook his head and whinnied. Picking up his feet he trotted forward, stopped and turned, facing the rear of the mob. Queenie and TR stilled their walking horses. They wouldn't be able to hold the brumbies back if the stallion turned them and charged at Queenie and TR.

The stallion hesitated, deciding whether to charge towards the strangers or retreat. In that split second TR lifted his stock whip, snaking it through the air with a shrieking crack that bounced off the cliff walls like a ricocheting bullet. At the same instant he kicked his horse into a gallop shouting, 'Now!'

On the left flank, Nareedah broke into a gallop as Queenie let out a piercing whistle to the dogs who bounded forward and raced up the ravine.

The sudden noise and movement galvanised the wild horses. The stallion reared and snorted, thudding his hooves on the dry earth of the river bed. He charged into the mouth of the ravine with the rest of the horses strung out behind him as they blindly followed.

In seconds a cloud of dust enveloped them, but sitting firmly and easily, Queenie and TR raced their horses forward, their stock whips cracking and snapping, the dogs barking and circling the brumbies at the rear.

It was a mad headlong dash into the unknown, and Queenie's excitement mounted as Nareedah sidestepped ruts and holes, leapt boulders, and swerved to avoid overhanging branches that threatened to slap Queenie cruelly across the face, possibly ripping out an eye, or dislodging her from the saddle.

She glanced across to where TR charged ahead, swinging his whip as he closed in on the stragglers to one side.

Then, like a tidal wave parting, the horses streamed on either side of the black stallion who had suddenly balked and swung about to face his pursuers. The mob slowed, reluctant to charge without their leader. In this moment of truth it seemed to Queenie the stallion was glaring defiantly into her eyes.

Queenie didn't hesitate. She spurred Nareedah forward, running straight at the great black horse, daring him to charge her. With the dogs barking shrilly at her heels and as she brought her whip down in a powerful crack, Queenie was unaware she was shouting at the top of her voice. Nareedah didn't flinch but surged forward, obeying Queenie's command.

Confronted with this fearless and frightening charge, the stallion swung about and raced on up the ravine.

Above the noise of the pounding hooves Queenie heard TR shouting, 'You little beauty!' The slip rails were down, open and waiting, and the stallion raced in, followed by the fastest of the brumbies.

Too late they realised there was no way out. By the time they had turned, and in the confusion of the others following on their heels, TR and Queenie were down on the ground racing to lift the rails in place. Some of the horses hadn't made it and they paused, unwilling to abandon their leader but fearful of the strangers in their midst. Then they crashed away as Queenie and TR lashed the ropes around the slip rail gate.

Some of the brumbies, including the stallion, reared and smashed their hooves against the confines of the pen, but the yard held firm. TR slapped Queenie on the back as he looped the last of the rope in place. 'Well done. I thought that black bastard was going to try and run you down.'

'Another second and he would have!' Exhilarated, Queenie surveyed the two dozen trapped horses. It had taken less than an hour.

Carefully, they inspected all sides of the pen. 'It'll hold okay. The horses will settle down soon.' TR wiped his forehead and pointed to the ground. A trail of ants were leaving their nest, climbing in single file up a tree. 'Rain.'

Queenie glanced at the glowering sky and back at the nervous horses in their makeshift pen.

'We'd better get the horses on the move before it starts.' TR pointed beyond the cliffs to where a dark grey curtain was suspended between clouds and the ground. 'Already raining over there by the look of things.'

'Dad will be pleased — the dams are practically empty.'

'Let's go eat. We'll let them settle down and tomorrow we'll pull the ones we want and let the rest go. We should be able to keep them with us once we chase away the rest of the mob and the leader,' said TR.

They spoke little as they unsaddled the horses at the end of the day, lit a fire and prepared their simple meal. In the afternoon they had broken camp and moved closer to the pen in the ravine. Both were almost too tired to talk or eat.

'I reckon we've got about six good horses in that lot,' said TR. 'It'll be a long hard ride back with them. You going to be okay?'

'Of course,' said Queenie.

They ate silently, occasionally looking skywards where the stars were fast disappearing behind clouds.

TR checked their horses tethered to a rail rigged between two trees near the camp. Taking another worried look at the sky he rolled into his swag.

Echoing his thoughts Queenie muttered,

'Let's sleep while we can, I feel the rain could hit sooner than we think.'

It was shortly before midnight when the rain began. It came with a great gust of wind — a solid sheet of water as if from a bottomless, upended bucket. The storm brought an incredible cacophony of sounds — thunder, lightning, wind and rain.

Pulling on oilskin coats, they rolled up blankets and swags.

TR grabbed the saddles. He bent close to Queenie's ear and shouted through the rain, 'Follow me, I remember where there's a cave. We'll take the horses.'

Queenie and TR led their horses with the packhorses tied behind. TR scrambled ahead, moving up to where the ground began to rise steeply towards the cliffs. The wet dogs tagged along behind the horses.

It took a while in the dark but eventually they found the opening to a small cave. They tethered the horses and ducked under a rocky overhang and into the welcome cavity that dulled the noise of the storm.

In the thin beam of light from TR's torch it looked dry and safe. 'No snakes, wallabies or ghosts,' said TR with satisfaction.

'Shine the torch back near the mouth,' said Queenie. 'There's a dead tree branch, it's still pretty dry. We can use it for a fire later.'

Together they dragged the gum branch into the cave, pulled their swags from the packhorses and unrolled their blankets.

'Dry enough for me,' said Queenie, stretching out on the floor of the cave. 'I'm beat.

I just hope there aren't any bats in here. Hate the things.' She was soon asleep, breathing evenly, curled in her swag.

TR leant against the wall of the cave and dozed uncomfortably, while the dogs crouched out of the rain under the overhang at the mouth of the cave, their noses between their paws.

Some hours later TR stirred, feeling cold and stiff. He cocked his head, listening for the sounds of Queenie's soft breathing. Switching on his torch, he swung its beam around the cave. Queenie wasn't there. Shining the light on his watch he saw it was three o'clock. It was still pouring with rain and he wondered if Queenie had needed to step outside. Then he heard it.

Above the sound of rain came a steady roar. He knew immediately what it was and where Queenie had gone.

'Damn her,' he muttered, 'why didn't she wake me?' Angry and alarmed he called the dogs and headed out into the wet, dark bush.

As he slipped and stumbled down the rocky slope he could hear more clearly the sound of rushing water. The once dry river bed was now a fast rushing torrent of water. Queenie had gone to the brumbies, knowing they would be trapped.

The dogs raced ahead of him and he could hear them barking.

'*Queenie*!' he shouted. 'Where are you?' His words were whipped away in the wind and rain, and he knew shouting was useless. He broke into a stumbling run, tripping on the undergrowth, fearful for Queenie's safety.

Sheet lightning illuminated the sky like a crazy neon sign as he reached the pen at the end of the ravine. The water was gushing down the hillside from the waterfall and swirling around the flanks of the frantic horses. Queenie had loosened some of the ropes around the sides of the pen and was waist-deep in the water, her oilskin coat swirling about her as she struggled in the dark.

TR could see that the horses would spring straight through the gap and knock her over if she did manage to drop the barrier.

He waded through the water and grabbed her arms. 'What the hell are you doing? You're going to get trampled,' he shouted.

'They're going to drown unless we get them out,' she yelled back.

'So are *you*! Here — take this and cut the ropes from that tree.'

TR unsnapped the pocket knife from his belt. 'I'll clear it down here. Then stand back. They'll rush through the gap.'

She took the knife and splashed through the river to the bank and began hacking at the ropes around the tree. TR, cursing at his previous thoroughness, began fumbling with tight wet knots.

Queenie cut through the rope and began to wade back across the foaming river to TR. When she was halfway over, the ropes and submerged slip rails were pulled free by the force of the water.

The panicked horses seemed to sense there would be a way out if they followed the water. The stallion was first to splash and kick his way through the opening, missing Queenie by inches.

'Look out,' shouted TR as he raced back to the river, grabbed Queenie and pulled her out of the water.

She handed him his knife as her knees gave way and she sat trembling on the ground. TR cut the last rope and it was swept away as the mob of horses, half swimming, half running, kicked their way along the river and up on the bank.

'You're bloody mad. Why didn't you wake me up?' demanded TR. 'I'm responsible for you, and you nearly got yourself killed.'

'I can look after myself,' shouted Queenie.

'No you can't! Come on.'

Grabbing her roughly under the arm, TR pulled her to her feet and began leading her back up the hill. His grip on her arm didn't lessen until they were back in the cave where Queenie sank to the floor hugging her knees, her teeth chattering.

Silently, still angry, TR stripped off his sodden jacket and hastily began pulling the leaves and twigs from the old tree. In minutes he had a fire crackling by the entrance to the cave. As the smoke swirled out into the wet night the rain began to ease. He turned and looked at the miserable, soaked figure in the firelight.

Queenie's wet hair streamed down her back and puddles were forming under her boots.

'Get out of that coat,' said TR, as he reached for her foot and began tugging at her sodden boot.

Queenie took off her outer layer. Her

moleskin pants were wet, but her shirt and jumper above the waist were fairly dry.

TR built up the fire and took off his own wet boots and socks, while Queenie held her hands out towards the fire. Her face looked pale and she was still shivering.

TR handed her a blanket. 'Get your pants off — they're soaked. Wrap up in this.'

Queenie hesitated, looking at the blanket he held out to her, but TR turned his head away as she wriggled out of the dripping pants and wrapped the blanket around her shoulders, folding it over her bare legs.

'Do you want some hot tea?' asked TR, sounding less annoyed with her.

She shook her head. 'I just woke up and heard the water and thought of the horses and knew I had to get there fast to see if they were all right. I didn't think of anything else,' said Queenie defensively.

'It's all right, Queenie, I understand. But it was still bloody stupid of you.'

'Don't call me stupid!' she blazed at him.

'I apologise.' TR threw the thick branch into the fire. 'There, that should last us till daylight.'

'I guess we won't see those horses again,' sighed Queenie.

'I'm afraid not,' said TR. Then, seeing Queenie's disappointed face added, 'but they'll turn up again. Or others will . . . and we'll get those.'

'Is that a deal?' asked Queenie with a small smile.

'You bet.' TR reached out and formally shook her hand. Clasping her chilled fingers he realised how cold she was. He picked up his blanket and moved next to her. 'Here, get under my blanket, our body heat will keep us both warm.'

Queenie didn't argue. She felt frozen to her bones. Gratefully she snuggled up to TR as he draped his arm and blanket about her shoulders, drawing her close to his side.

They sat in silence watching the fire as Queenie felt the warmth of his body seep into her own. Involuntarily she shivered.

'Still cold?' asked TR huskily.

Queenie shook her head, biting her lip, unable to speak. The closeness of him had caught her unawares and she was trembling. She felt again the tumbling sensations she'd experienced when she'd danced with him. She wanted to pull away but seemed unable to move. She lowered her head, hiding her face behind her damp hair.

'Queenie . . . ' It was almost a whisper and he leaned anxiously towards her, smoothing her hair back with his other hand. She turned and gazed at him. His hand lay still against the side of her face.

In the gold of the firelight a spark seemed to smoulder in the depths of Queenie's green eyes. She stared intently into the deep blue pools of his eyes, and her lips parted. But still she made no sound.

A pang shot through TR and he closed his eyes, his hand gripping her hair. As he gazed into her sweet upturned face a small moan escaped from him. He gently drew her face to his and softly brushed his lips against hers.

For a moment she didn't reject him or respond to him. Her eyes were open wide as his mouth touched hers.

He drew back swiftly. 'No, I can't... ' he turned away, dropping his hand from her face.

Queenie touched her mouth, feeling the tingle of her lips where he'd kissed her. Slowly she took his hand, turned it over, and lifted it to her lips, dropping a kiss into the palm of his hand.

They stared at each other with a dawning realisation of the chasm closing between them. TR leaned forward and kissed her tenderly, both their lips curving into smiles as they touched. Then he drew her to him, wildly kissing her eyelids, her face, her ears, the nape of her neck. He nuzzled his face in her hair and Queenie felt she was melting as she wound her arms about him.

Breathing in short gasps, they slipped down on to the old sleeping bag, and lay together, staring deep into each other's eyes.

'Are you sure?' whispered TR.

Queenie nodded, and in a swift movement pulled her sweater and shirt from her body.

TR caught his breath at the sight of Queenie's full firm breasts and tapering waist, the firelight dancing across her creamy skin. Queenie smiled shyly as he studied her beauty, waiting for him to lead her to a place she'd never known; but she knew this was the time, the place and the love she'd waited to find.

He softly cupped her breasts in his hands, delicately kissing each nipple. Queenie closed her eyes as her body quivered and responded to his touch.

TR was gentle and loving, arousing and awakening her body until her passion matched his and with a cry of pleasure she gripped his body to hers with her long lithe legs, straining to hold him deep within her.

She moaned with joy, her fingers grasping his back as his hands tangled in her hair and he clutched her to him.

'Queenie... my love...'

'TR, don't let me go...'

'Never...'

They clung together, hearts beating against each other. Finally TR reached for his shirt and gently wiped away the film of sweat shining on Queenie's skin. Then he threw the blankets across them as they settled to sleep, their bodies entwined, the light flickering on the walls of the cave, the fire cracking and snapping companionably.

They slept as the fire burned down to a dull red glow, while outside their warm cavern, the dark bush dripped as the rain eased and stars began to shine through the disappearing film of cloud.

During the night they stirred and kissed sleepily; and as Queenie curled up on her side, TR pulled her to him and made love to her again. Then spent, they slept, he still inside her, one hand circling a breast, their fingers locked together.

TR knew he would never let this girl out of his life, and Queenie felt safe, and loved and secure. This was where she belonged — in TR's arms.

Chapter Six

———— 🦢 ————

Relentlessly the rain fell in a bruising blanket that smothered the land. Trickles between trees became swelling torrents, creeks overflowed and joined with others to flood over paddocks and form lakes. The once-dry broad river beds now bulged and roared. All was swept along in the path of the water which raged over the parched earth.

Tingulla homestead was safe on its hill, but as their small creek flooded and the main river further away broke its banks, Patrick knew he would have to move the merino sheep with their valuable fleece to higher ground.

All the station hands, including Jim, had worked without break through the daylight hours, moving stock, horses and equipment to safety. Bush legends were still told of the Big Floods — rare but devastating. On a neighbouring property the bleached skull of a dead cow hung high in a tree top, victim of one such flood. Locals liked to point it out as an indication of the height of the water, not mentioning that the tree had grown fifteen feet since then.

Patrick saddled one of the stockhorses and took supplies for several days, 'Just in case I get cut off,' he told a worried Millie. He took the long way round the property, checking the land as he went, before crossing the river at its safest point. Bluey, his blue heeler went with him, lopping easily beside his master as he rode. Bluey was devoted to Patrick and was the best cattle and sheep dog for miles around.

Returning from their ill-fated brumbie muster, TR and Queenie had quickly assessed the situation and headed straight to Tingulla.

'Your father is going to be worried about you, Queenie,' said TR glancing at her as she rode hard beside him.

She nodded and smiled reassuringly, blowing him a kiss. TR smiled back through the rain running from his hat, his face reflecting the surge of love he felt for her.

The pounding of the rain on the iron roof eased by mid-afternoon and Millie ventured down to the shed where Jim was working on the water-soaked generator. 'None of them are back yet, Jim.'

'TR and Queenie'll be on their way. I can't imagine how they're going to bring back those horses in this, though.'

'Mr Patrick said he'd be back by dark. Ernie said he heard the river is running real fast.'

'Don't fret, Millie. You'd better get the

lamps out and lay in plenty of dry wood. We might not have any power tonight if I can't get this thing going again.'

Millie splashed through the mud in her old gumboots back to the house.

With the aid of Bluey, Patrick had rounded up a sodden, miserable flock of seventy sheep trapped on low ground by rising water. Nipping at their heels, Bluey had shepherded them along, working them to higher pastures. Once on safe ground, Patrick left them and rode on.

The wet had struck just before shearing time when the full fleece on each merino was worth a small fortune. Patrick knew that most of the thirty thousand sheep scattered about the property would be all right, at least for the time being. It was still raining heavily upstream.

Ernie and Snowy had moved the horses and the few head of cattle. Now there was just Queenie to worry about. Patrick had great faith in her and TR, but these conditions were dangerous and unpredictable.

It was dusk when he reached the river. Patrick reined in his horse and gazed across the expanse of muddy, swiftly flowing water. He dismounted and snapped a branch from a tree, tossing it into the river. It was snatched up and swept downstream in seconds. Patrick walked along the bank to a bend where the water slowed and appeared relatively shallow. The horse might keep on its feet here.

He knew there was no easy way to cross the river, but he didn't relish camping in the drenched paddocks for the night and running the risk of being caught by fast-rising water.

Patrick squatted on the bank looking at the river, and Bluey stuck his head under his master's arm, seeking some recognition. Absent-mindedly Patrick patted the smooth head of the dog as he watched the rushing water. The rain was easing when he stood and glanced at the sky, where a watery yellow tinge of sunset light could be seen behind the dark clouds.

He remounted, walking the horse down the slippery bank.

The horse shook its head as it felt the mud give way beneath its feet. In two strides it was out of its depth and forced to swim in the raging torrent. Patrick slid off the saddle and hung on to the pommel, as he was pulled along through the water. Without hesitating, Bluey plunged in behind them.

The current moved them downstream but the horse swam strongly in a diagonal line across the river. Patrick spoke gently to the horse whose eyes were firmly fixed on the opposite bank.

He didn't hear the distant roll of thunder as the billowing storm clouds moved east. The passing of the rain had come too late — the water, from a fan-like network of gullies and creeks, had created a flood on top of a flood. A wall of water like a tidal wave, was crashing down the river, taking everything in its way, at times tearing out trees that had survived a hundred floods.

Patrick heard the roar and turned to see the new flood peak, with its mass of debris hurtling downstream towards him. They were only halfway across. An eighty foot gum tree rolled down the river, swung sideways at the bend, and surged towards him.

In the last light of the day, the horse struggled up the bank, limping and bleeding. Bluey lay like a rag further along the broken river bank. Stumbling a little, the dog got to its feet and stood staring at the river. He sat and patiently waited for Patrick, his brown eyes focused on the span of muddy foaming water.

Suddenly, gathering his strength, the small dog hurried back to the bank and flung himself into the swirling water, paddling valiantly, his ears and snout pointed resolutely above the flood that sucked at his stumpy legs. His eyes searched the river in the fading light. Loyalty to Patrick, not reason, sent him on this brave and hopeless mission.

Bluey was about midstream where the current eddied and raced in a tangled surge of water. His legs thrust forward in a frantic struggle for survival but in seconds the small shape was pulled down and swept from sight.

Millie moved through the house, lighting the kerosene lamps and trying to make the house as cheerful and warm as possible. The log fire crackled in the sitting room and although there was no power she had a stew simmering on the Aga and hot water heated in large kero tins for a warm bath. She heaved a sigh of relief as she heard the jingle of stirrups and saddlery and a horse's hooves clattering on the flagstones at the front entrance.

Picking up a lantern, she hurried to the double front doors and pulled them open.

In the yellow light at the base of the steps stood a horse, reins dragging on the ground, its head bent with exhaustion and a trickle of blood running from a gash on its leg.

Her cry brought Jim running.

'It's Patrick's horse,' said Jim grimly. 'See if Snowy is here; we'll have to look for him.'

Jim and Snowy set out, with the Aborigine acting as tracker, using his ancient tribal skills to retrace the trail of Patrick's horse.

They had barely gone any distance before being hailed by two figures riding out of the damp darkness. 'We spotted your torch light. What's up?' asked TR as Queenie reined in behind him.

His expression changed as he saw Jim's tight face and the way Snowy glanced at Queenie.

'Patrick's horse has come in without him. He must have had an accident.'

'Oh God, no. Where was he, what was he doing?' demanded Queenie.

'Moving the last of the sheep.'

'But they were across the river!' exclaimed Queenie in sudden fear.

'The river will be running a banker in this rain. Let's go then,' said TR. 'Queenie, wait here for us.'

'No! I'm coming with you.' She turned Nareedah fiercely.

'No, Queenie. *No!*' TR spoke harshly. 'For once in your life do as you're told!'

'You can't speak to me like that. I'm coming.'

'Queenie, it's because I love you. I don't want you to come. Please. *Go back.*' TR kicked his tired horse and the three men moved off into the night, leaving Queenie confused and frightened behind them.

Since no more rain had fallen, Snowy easily followed Patrick's tracks to the river. They began their search where the horse had clambered up the bank, and from there spread along the river searching and occasionally calling Patrick's name.

Soon Snowy led TR back up the river and pointed to the torch–lit muddy ground. 'Look, — dog come out, sit, then go back in river.'

'Bluey,' breathed TR, his chest tightening.

'He tried to get Mr Hanlon, I bet. He gone now.'

It was TR who found him. The massive gum tree which had charged downstream knocking Patrick away from his horse, was wedged across the next bend in the river, Patrick's body clutched in its leafy arms.

Queenie was standing waiting for the sad procession by the front steps. She was wearing her father's old army overcoat, hugging it to her body, her hands disappearing in its sleeves, her hair blowing about her still face.

His horse plodding, TR was first. Patrick's body lay face down across the saddle before him. TR held the reins in one hand, the other held onto Patrick's jacket. Jim and Snowy walked their horses respectfully behind.

Queenie didn't move as TR dismounted and went to her. He reached out his arms, wondering how he could comfort and help her cope with this second cruel blow in so short a time.

She ignored his outstretched arms and caring face, and went to her father, reaching up to touch him, resting her face against the cold wetness of his shoulder.

Jim went to Millie who began weeping softly. TR stood helplessly by, his heart breaking for Queenie.

Snowy handed TR the reins of his horse and approached Queenie, touching her shoulder lightly. As she turned to him, her legs buckled and Snowy caught her up and carried her indoors. The old Aborigine, his hair a shock of white against his black skin, recalled the small girl he'd carried to her father the night of the storm after she'd put down her horse.

He knew bad spirits were hovering over Tingulla. Somehow they would have to be sent away.

Patrick's funeral was a brief, subdued occasion attended by the few friends and neighbours who could make it through the still high floodwaters.

Colin kept to himself leaving Queenie and Millie to organise the sad event. Reverend Peters was in Sydney and so the new young Reverend from the next parish flew in to conduct the service.

'It's not right. He didn't even know Mr Patrick,' said Millie to Jim. 'Still, I hope he and Mrs Rose rest in peace now. He's lived in the shadows ever since she went. Now there's just them two young ones. And Queenie is carrying it all on her shoulders.'

Queenie remained strong, handling matters in a businesslike manner. She kept to herself and spent long hours in Patrick's study going through his papers, or simply staring dry-eyed out of the windows over Tingulla's grounds.

At the graveside she stood erect and motionless beside Colin, no flicker of emotion passing across her face. At the conclusion of the short service, Colin stepped forward and sprinkled a handful of red soil on to the coffin.

Queenie then moved forward and gently placed Patrick's favourite battered bush hat on top of the rosewood coffin. It was buried with him, for, in Queenie's mind, no one else had the right to wear it.

Queenie went through the next three weeks in a trance — functioning but not feeling. She refused any comfort from TR and although it hurt him, he kept quietly in the background.

Colin wandered about the house and said little. Millie desperately tried to keep the household running as concerned friends and neighbours came and went in a constant stream.

Millie wheeled the traymobile set with the best china and silver teapot into the library where Queenie and Colin sat before Mr Hamish Barton, the family solicitor. A conservative and colourless man but a thorough lawyer, he was well respected among the old families of the region. He was a model of discretion and quiet competence.

Queenie poured the tea as Millie softly clicked the door shut. 'Milk and sugar, Mr Barton?'

'Please. Do you mind if I sit behind the desk, it might be easier with my papers.'

Colin slumped into a leather chair. Queenie pulled up another and they sat watching Mr Barton shuffle through the sheaf of papers from his attaché case.

He adjusted his gold-rimmed glasses, cleared his throat and lowered his voice a pitch, assuming his professional role. 'As you know, we are here for the reading of your father's will. It is a straightforward document he drew up after ... your mother's sad death. I will just read it through and after that if you have any questions, we'll discuss them.'

He began to read. Queenie sat looking down at her hands, paying little attention to the droning voice, but at a gasp from Colin she looked up.

Colin was glaring at the solicitor. 'That can't be right. Read it again, Mr Barton.'

'Colin, let him finish.'

'Oh, you'd like that ... just let him read on without saying anything! Just because you're getting everything!'

'Colin! What are you talking about? I'm sorry Mr Barton, I wasn't paying attention, could you repeat that.'

The solicitor read through the brief but specific will. Tingulla estate and Patrick's undeveloped property, Cricklewood, were left to Queenie. Colin would receive a large cash settlement, put in trust until he was twenty-one and spread out in several payments, along with a block of flats in the expensive Sydney suburb of Double Bay. The income from this was to go into Colin's estate but he could not sell the building for five years.

Patrick's personal possessions were left to Colin, Queenie inherited those of her mother. Other bequests went to Millie and Jim; Rose's nephew in England; the Flying Doctor Service; and small personal mementoes were to go to good friends — amongst these was Patrick's favourite stock whip which was to go to Snowy.

Queenie was stunned. Colin turned on her angrily. 'So that's what you were up to while I was away at uni... conning Dad into making you the boss of Tingulla. I'm his *son*! I should own this place!'

'Colin... I had no idea...'

The solicitor held up a hand. 'Please, please. When your father came into town to lodge this with me, he left a letter to each of you explaining his reasons. I will give them to you now, perhaps you would care to read them in private later. I can make no comment about the contents of this document — it was made at your father's discretion. I would like to say, however, that I would like to offer my services to you and advise you about managing your inheritance. You will need financial advice, Colin, and, Queenie, you of course will need to find someone to manage Tingulla for you.'

'That won't be necessary, Mr Barton,' said Queenie. 'Colin will finish his studies and we'll run it together. I can manage quite well as we are in the meantime.'

The solicitor looked thoughtfully at the beautiful, pale young woman sitting very straight in the chair before him. 'You are aware of the magnitude of Tingulla, Queenie. Your father was also beginning to develop some new ideas, I understand. Surely you don't think ... '

Queenie cut him off. 'I am fully aware of my father's plans for Tingulla.'

'*You* might be, but what about me? You don't expect me to stay down there in Sydney sitting for lousy exams while you play mistress of the manor!' exploded Colin.

'You have to graduate, Colin. Dad wanted and expected you to.'

'You're not telling me what to do just because you're two years older than me.'

'Well, Queenie is twenty-one and of legal age. Which means she has the right to make decisions, Colin. Look, I know you're upset, why don't you come and see me in my office in town in a day or so?'

Colin rose to his feet and slammed his cup down. 'I'll do that. And I intend to fight this. It's not right.' He banged the door behind him.

'Oh dear, I'm sorry he's taking it like this. It is a little unusual for the daughter to inherit the property. But I'm sure it's all explained in these letters.' The solicitor pushed Patrick's letters across the desk. 'I wish you too would think carefully about your future, Queenie, and come and discuss it with me. I'm sure I can be of help.'

'Thank you, Mr Barton. If I need advice I'll call you.'

Queenie rose and opened the library door. 'Millie will fetch your coat and hat. Thank you again.'

Queenie turned and hurried upstairs, her composure crumbling as she clutched her father's letter.

Colin sat in a far corner of the verandah and ripped open the letter from his father. Patrick had written brief, casual letters to him at university. Rose had been the letter writer and had kept him up to date on all the news and daily activities of Tingulla.

Biting his lip Colin read:

> My dear Son,
> I had hoped you would be a grown man, settled with your own family, before this day came. It is probably hard for you to accept and understand my leaving Tingulla to Queenie.
>
> Over the years I have watched you both, and I have come to the conclusion your heart is not with the land. I know you are proud and fond of Tingulla and what our family has built here. But in order to continue that, whoever runs Tingulla must put it first — before all else.
>
> I know Queenie feels this way and her devotion and capabilities, and the fact she is older, swayed my decision. How she will manage her own life and Tingulla should she marry, will be her decision. I feel you are still unsettled in your outlook. Perhaps in time, when you finish your schooling and have travelled, you will come to learn to love Tingulla and understand more fully what it means — as Queenie does.

*I have seen to it that you are financially cared
for, but again I have exercised restraint in view
of your youthful streak of irresponsibility. In
time I hope you will understand my caution.*

*I want you to know — although I might not
have always expressed it openly — that I am
proud you are my son and I hope you will
continue to make me proud. Calm your hot
temper, curb your aggressions and learn to show
love and tolerance. Give your sister support and
strength — she has a big job before her. I pray
you understand what I have done and that I have
your love.*

As always, I am your Dad.

Folding the letter quickly, Colin thrust it in
his jacket pocket and hurried across the lawn,
his hands deep in his pockets, his shoulders
hunched.

In the solitude of her room, Queenie turned
her letter over in her hands then opened and
smoothed the thick paper covered with
Patrick's familiar writing.

My Dearest Queenie,
*I am assuming your circumstances haven't
changed as I write this, for had you married I
would have made appropriate adjustments to my
will. However, rest assured that it has always
been, and always will be, my intention that you
hold the fate of Tingulla in your hands. I know
your deep love for our land and home and all that
it stands for, and I can rest easy knowing you
will continue to cherish it. I feel sure no matter
what the future holds for you and your own*

family, Tingulla will continue as it is. I hope my grandchildren will grow up at Tingulla and learn to love it too.

Which brings me to Colin. He is still youthful and headstrong with a reckless streak which worries me. Painful as it is, I cannot convince myself his feelings for Tingulla are the same as your mother's, mine and yours have always been. I know you will make a place for him at your side at Tingulla, but I want you to be the one to make decisions concerning Tingulla. Trust your instincts and your knowledge, but I know you, Queenie — so don't be too proud to seek advice and help.

I hoped I would be around for a long time to spare you this burden, but I pray you will find happiness and joy in your life. Watch over Colin. You are strong and beautiful and I am so very proud of you.

I hope you know how much I love you.

Dad

These words stabbed through the protective wall Queenie had built around her heart. Running from her room, she went out of the house, through the gardens and past the sheds and stables to the shearers' quarters. She hammered on the wire mesh door.

TR was reading at the rickety table, but seeing Queenie he stood quickly, tipping over his chair, and held out his arms. She clung to him, sobbing, while he smoothed her hair, his arms wrapped about her tightly, shielding and loving her.

Chapter Seven

TR walked along Hudson Street in Charleville, past the stock and station agent, and past the grain store, to the Empire Hotel on the corner. The giant boab tree with its bulbous trunk and spiky fronds shaded the side of the pub's open verandah where a few drinkers lounged with their frothy beers.

He walked up the front steps, past a utility truck and a tethered horse and into the cool interior. On his left were the creaking stairs which led to the basic bedrooms above with their sagging brass beds, pine wardrobes and dressing tables. He headed past the public bar and through the ladies lounge until he reached an oak door with frosted glass panels featuring an etching of an emu, and gold lettering announcing that within lay the dining room.

TR glanced at his watch — it was eight-fifteen. Breakfast was still being served. He took a table, upending his hat on the floor by his feet. The only other diners were a commercial traveller and another man — possibly a grazier, thought TR, glancing at the uniform of tweed jacket, woollen tie and riding boots, and noting the squatter's hat hooked on the back of his chair. They nodded and exchanged a brief 'G'day'.

Through the swing door to the kitchen where TR could hear the sound of pots banging, came a peroxide blonde with over bright lipstick and tired eyes. She placed a typewritten cardboard menu in front of TR.

'What'll it be, luv?' she inquired, taking a stub of pencil and a notepad from the pocket of her grubby apron.

'I've been up some time, guess I'll go for the full breakfast and a pot of tea,' said TR smiling and handing back the menu.

'Mixed grill; steak and eggs; bacon, eggs and sausages; or ham and tomato?'

'I'll try the mixed grill, but leave out the liver would you please.'

'Righto, luv. I'll give it to the dog hanging round the back door.'

TR was spreading a layer of Robertson's marmalade on his second slab of toast as the chair opposite was scraped back from the table. TR got to his feet. 'G'day, Dingo. Good to see you. I'm afraid I started without you,' he said as they shook hands.

'Don't stand on ceremony, TR. Trip took a bit longer than I expected. So now ... you've changed your mind about the rodeo job? I figured with Patrick gone, you'd be needed at Tingulla.'

'It's a bit awkward, to tell you the truth. I was working on a special project with Patrick for breeding up some better horses — we even talked about maybe getting into breeding quarter horses for sprint racing — but that doesn't seem practical for the moment. Queenie has enough on her plate just keeping the place running. They're about to start shearing.'

'Queenie? She's running that big property on her own?'

'Well, she still has all the old hands about the place, and Patrick had already contracted for the shearing team, but I just felt it put me in a bit of an uncomfortable position... for several reasons. I'd like to know if the offer is still open to ride the rodeo circuit in America.'

'Just tea and toast please, luv,' said Dingo to the waitress. 'Yes, it's still open. You have to pay your fare over there, they'll take care of all the expenses once you're signed up. I reckon you could make yourself a fair old packet, TR. And the ladies are going to take a fancy to you too, I reckon.'

'The fare will take everything I've saved, and it's a bit of a gamble, but heck, if you don't take a risk or two you'll never know, will you?' grinned TR.

'That's right, mate. My bet is, in a year you'll be a celebrity with a fair old bankroll, no strings attached. Then you can come back here and marry any girl you choose... that's if you get away from those Yankee ladies. Hell, they might even put you in the movies!'

'I don't want to know about any of that stuff. I just want to make enough money to put a down payment on a place of my own.'

It hadn't been an easy decision for TR.

Queenie had taken over the reins of Tingulla with a vengeance. She was determined the shearing would go smoothly and that Tingulla's wool would fetch a good price. Colin had sulked back to uni and Queenie was up at dawn each day for a fast ride on Nareedah before facing the decisions of the day.

TR had watched her dealing with the men, and with Millie and the house during the day; aware of the paperwork and business details she was probably wrestling with at night.

One morning he rode out after her at daylight and found Queenie sitting on a rock gazing sadly into the distance. He dismounted and let his horse graze as he went and sat beside her. They sat in silence for a few moments then TR gently took her hand between his own. He stared at her long slim fingers with their oval nails then lightly kissed her hand and squeezed it between his own strong suntanned hands.

'Queenie, we must talk. I can't bear to see you carrying everything on your shoulders. You must share some of the load.'

'I can manage.'

'I know you can, and you're doing beautifully. But it's not right that you tie yourself down like this. Please consider getting in a manager ... at least until Colin finishes at uni.'

Queenie's lips tightened but she didn't answer.

'Queenie... there's something else... what about us?' said TR softly.

She turned to him, her face expressionless. But the struggle not to give in to her emotions wavered, and her huge emerald eyes grew moist.

'Oh, Queenie... I love you.' TR wrapped his arms around her. 'Please tell me the truth... do you love me?' He held her by the shoulders, his fingers burning through her shirt as he stared into her uplifted face.

Unable to speak, Queenie nodded her head and closed her eyes as a tear slipped from under her lashes.

Tenderly TR drew her to him once more. 'That's all I wanted to know. Queenie, I want to marry you. I love you with all my heart and I'll never, ever stop loving you. But we have to wait...'

He took her hands in his, suddenly shy. 'I can't marry you when I'm a penniless nobody and you're the mistress of Tingulla. Everyone will think I married you for your money.' A rueful smile crossed TR's face.

'I don't care what people think,' said Queenie fiercely.

'Queenie, you must. Think of me.'

'I am thinking of you — you said you want us to be together. We know we love each other, it doesn't matter what silly gossips say!'

'Queenie, that's typical of your stubborn, impetuous nature. Grow up, for goodness sake. Think about it. It might not seem important now but in years to come it could begin to be a problem, with you owning the property and me feeling like just a hired hand.'

Queenie exploded, pulling away from him. 'Don't tell me to grow up, and if that's the way you think... then stay a hired hand and forget about sharing your life with me and Tingulla.'

'Queenie, I'm going away to America... to make some money... for us. Give me a chance — a year. That's all I ask.'

She scrambled to her feet and threw over her shoulder. 'A year! I thought you loved me...'

She flung herself back into Nareedah's saddle and galloped off, leaving TR shaking his head and muttering, 'Queenie, Queenie... I *do* love you...' Then suddenly angry at her, he shouted after the disappearing white horse, 'You don't make loving you *easy!*'

TR and Queenie avoided each other for the next two weeks and before Queenie knew it, he'd left.

When Jim came back from driving TR into town to catch the train down south, he handed her a letter.

In the quietness of the sunny study Queenie slowly opened it.

> *My darling Queenie,*
> *I couldn't bear to say goodbye. I am on my way to America to take up an offer to do some rough riding round the rodeo circuit. I understand there's a chance I could make some big money*

*pretty fast. I have several ideas for developing a
career of my own back there with you, but I need
capital and I need to be able to stand on my own
two feet so I can claim you fair and square.*

*I love you, Queenie. I always will. And I still
want to marry you. I think we are rushing
things a bit, though. You need time to adjust to
the sadness you have suffered. I don't want to be
just a shoulder to lean on. I want you to love me
for my sake. But I will be there should you need
me.*

*I promised your father I would look after you,
and I always will. But I want us to be equal
partners in life. I hope you will wait for me, my
beauty. I promise to write. I've never been much
of a letter writer, so give me a few weeks to settle
in — wherever that may be — and I will write
regularly. And remember there'll be a kiss in
every letter.*
TR.

Later Millie placed a cup of tea on the desk
beside Queenie who was working on the
accounts. 'Too bad TR has gone away to America. I thought he wanted to stay at Tingulla.
Got used to him round the place.'

'He wants to make a life of his own and
earn more money than he makes at Tingulla,
Millie. I don't wish to discuss it. Thanks for
the tea.'

Millie left the room with raised eyebrows
and a small sniff.

Inside, Queenie was desperately sad and
lonely. She agreed that saying goodbye to TR
would have been painful, but she was sorry

they had parted on bad terms after a silly argument. She longed for his strong arms and soft voice, she'd miss his laughing blue eyes and dry sense of humour. She had come to rely on him more than she realised. Just knowing TR was about the place gave her strength. She felt very abandoned and a little sorry for herself. 'Damn him,' she cursed, sipping the strong refreshing tea. She'd show him. She could manage — with him or without him.

Queenie flung herself into the shearing season, hovering around the shearing shed to make sure the sheep weren't badly cut and that the fleeces were properly graded and baled.

It was Jim who took her to one side, suggesting she keep her distance and do her checking up after hours. 'The men don't like a woman bossing them around, Queenie. They're starting to grumble a bit . . . you being so young, too.'

'I understand, Jim. But I want them to know that I'm still keeping tabs on them even if I don't show my face in the shed.'

'Or your pretty backside in those tight pants,' thought Jim, knowing full well the sort of remarks being tossed about by the rough and tumble working men. Maybe he'd better get Millie to talk to Queenie. She'd didn't seem to realise the effect she had on men, especially the kind who'd been in the bush, away from female company for months.

Queenie worked herself to the point of exhaustion. It was getting more difficult to rise at dawn each day to go riding, but it cleared her head. She found herself longing to spend a day in bed just resting and reading, something she had never been tempted to do before. She felt as if her energy was being drained and she worried over accounts and delays with the shearing.

Finally the wool clip was ready for sale and Queenie hoped it would fetch a good price.

Colin arrived home from university for the mid-term break but refused to take any interest in the business affairs of Tingulla.

'But it's your future too, Colin,' said Queenie in exasperation.

'You own it — you run it. If the place goes bankrupt it's no skin off my nose,' he retorted and stormed from the room.

Queenie packed a small bag and left for Brisbane for the wool sales. She felt she needed a break as she hadn't been into a town in several months. Wearing a dress for a change and strolling down the street, her spirits lifted and she began to feel more positive about her future. She hoped she would hear from TR soon.

The sale took place at the Wool Exchange and she stood nervously at the back of the stuffy crowded room as the Dalgety auctioneer opened the bidding.

Back at Tingulla, Colin sat at Patrick's — now Queenie's — desk, rifling through papers and account books out of idle curiosity. Grudgingly he had to admit Queenie seemed to have things well under control.

Colin was bored. He wished Sarah was still around. Most of his friends were busy working on their parents' properties.

He strolled out to the verandah in time to see a cloud of dust on the road leading to the driveway. Five minutes later the mailman on his weekly round pulled up by the front steps.

He handed Colin a fat bundle of letters, newspapers and a couple of magazines tied with string. 'You looking after things for a bit, are you? Have you heard what the wool prices are like?'

Colin shook his head. He was not inclined to gossip with the mailman who carried news from station to station.

'Well, I'll be on my way. Give my best to Queenie. Tell her I'll see her in a week or so.'

The mail truck disappeared behind its own dust storm and Colin ambled inside, sorting through the mail. Three letters addressed to Queenie caught his eye and he turned them over to find they were from TR with a return address of a post box in Oklahoma.

Colin went back into the office and sat turning them over. Curiosity soon got the better of him and he walked cautiously into the kitchen. Millie was upstairs sweeping. Colin pulled the kettle of hot water back over the heat and carefully steamed open the flap of the first letter.

As he read he felt angry, hurt and betrayed. The letters were the first TR had written to Queenie; full of love, amusing anecdotes and a promise they would be together soon. He was making top money already and he was investigating some business prospects for their future. Colin read,

> ... Queenie, darling, I know how you feel about Tingulla and I know you don't want to leave. So I'm thinking I might be able to buy a property nearby and run a horse breeding and training business from there while we live at Tingulla — after we're married. What do you think? I miss you so much ...

Colin crumpled the letter in a clenched fist. If TR married Queenie and moved in here he'd never stand a chance of becoming boss of Tingulla. Colin suddenly realised with great force how much he wanted to own Tingulla. He didn't want the daily grind of running the place — he'd hire a manager to do that — but he did want the status and pride of owning one of Australia's grand properties.

Let Queenie and TR go off and breed horses, or whatever they wanted to do. Tingulla rightfully belonged to *him* — his father was wrong. He did care about Tingulla. He wanted it.

Queenie walked from the Wool Exchange well pleased with the price her nine hundred bales of merino fleece had fetched. After a year or more of hard work it had been sold in a matter of seconds. She wondered where Tingulla's wool would finally end up — perhaps in a Saville Row suit or European couture dress. She recalled her conversation with the beefy and jovial Dalgety wool agent who had predicted wool prices would continue to rise due to the overseas demand.

'This country rides on the sheep's back, Queenie, don't you forget it.'

Queenie decided to treat herself to some new clothes even though it would be weeks before the wool cheque was deposited in the bank. Trying on a skirt in a cramped dressing room of Fletcher Jones, a sudden feeling of nausea swept over her. A nervous reaction to the tension of the sale, she supposed. She quickly dressed and headed outside, turning into a small Greek café and milk bar. She sat in a booth and ordered a pot of tea and raisin toast and soon felt a bit better.

She hoped Colin would at least be pleased she had managed so well. Queenie began planning how some of the wool money would be spent around Tingulla. The shearers' union rep had been a bit militant and threatening when she had talked about next year's shearing contract. The woolshed with its prewar equipment needed updating.

That evening Colin sat at the long dining room table with a glass of Scotch beside his untouched dinner.

Millie clattered angrily in the kitchen dishing up Jim's dinner, muttering, 'Waste of good food. I'm not going back in there — he snapped my head off.'

'Just leave him be, Millie. Come on, where's my steak?'

Colin shoved his plate to one side, took his glass and went into the office. Pulling writing paper from a drawer, he began to write in swift, determined strokes, sealed the letter and addressed it. He then picked up the three letters from TR and threw them in the ashes in the open fireplace and dropped a lighted match on top. Quickly they caught fire, curled and disintegrated.

Far away on the coast in Brisbane's Grand Hotel Queenie eased herself into the creaking iron bed. She lay there as the light from the small bedside lamp with its dusty fringe threw shadows around the room. For a while she stared blankly at the fly-spotted ceiling, unconscious of the noise from the bar downstairs.

Clicking off the light, Queenie curled on her side hugging her knees, overwhelmed by the enormity of the realisation that she was pregnant.

Chapter Eight

·❦·

For several weeks Queenie tried to blot out of her mind the knowledge of the child growing within her — as if by ignoring it, the reality would go away. She was not prepared to feel happy or defeated by it. Had there been news from TR she might have felt differently, even though they had parted on angry terms.

She couldn't understand why he hadn't contacted her. She didn't want to believe she had slipped to the fringes of his mind as he was swept along in the excitement of rodeo riding in America.

At first she was puzzled by his apparent silence, but as the weeks passed she found herself becoming annoyed, then angry. She vented this anger by flinging herself into a frenzy of reckless activity, exhausting herself by taking physical risks. She rode unbroken horses and took Nareedah on wild gallops, jumping over fallen trees and charging through the bush in pursuit of big kangaroos just for the release it brought.

One quiet Sunday when most of the station hands had gone into town and Millie and Jim were resting in their own quarters, Queenie wandered through the empty house brooding about her plight. She walked up and down the verandah pausing to look across the peaceful grounds in the hope of spotting a rising cloud of dust that might signal the arrival of a visitor... anyone. She suddenly wanted to see TR, and badly. She closed her eyes as anger, desire and loneliness spread through her like a wind fanning a bushfire.

Soon she found herself on Nareedah, racing wildly through the scrub country. She had no memory of saddling her but now the fire in her heart began to subside, quelled by the exhilaration of the ride and the eucalypt-scented air.

Suddenly a grey kangaroo, as tall as a man, appeared from behind a growth of shrubs where it had been grazing. Startled by the galloping horse it veered and bounded away and Queenie nudged Nareedah after it.

Within seconds the frightened kangaroo was almost at top speed, slowed only by the thickness of the scrub and its swerving changes of direction. The white horse kept close to its zigzagging course, urged on by Queenie's low voice — 'Faster, girl, faster...'

The roo stretched out, increasing its speed and heading in a straight line. It took huge leaps powered by the immense force of its back legs, its extended tail providing perfect balance. Queenie had eyes only for the giant kangaroo and was oblivious to all else. It was for this reason that she didn't see the fence.

The kangaroo had cleared it with an effortless bound and had kept going. Nareedah balked and swung to the left, but still slammed into the taut wire strands. Queenie, off balance, flew out of the saddle and over the wire.

She came to, unaware how long she had blacked out — seconds or minutes. Faithful Nareedah was still standing on the other side of the fence, picking at the thin coarse grass. Slowly Queenie sat up and felt her head, but apart from a headache and slightly bleeding lump on her forehead she seemed to be in one piece. She tested her legs — no breaks — then crawled to the fence post and leaned against it.

Still dazed she rested for a moment, when it suddenly struck her — perhaps she had harmed her child. She touched her stomach lightly, undecided as to whether losing the baby would be a good or a bad thing.

Slowly she began to realise what she had subconsciously been doing to herself. She had no right to force the situation. What if TR suddenly walked in the door that afternoon and found she had deliberately caused a miscarriage?

But there had been no news from TR. A thought hit her like a blow — perhaps he'd had an accident. Maybe he'd taken a bad fall in a rodeo and was lying injured in some strange hospital. This possibility hadn't crossed her mind before; she'd been so selfishly wrapped up in her own problems. Scrambling to her feet she painfully eased her bruised body back into the saddle and headed for Tingulla at a sedate pace.

Queenie clattered into the rear courtyard and slid from Nareedah, shouting for Ernie to stable her horse. She plodded wearily through the kitchen, tossed her hat on the sideboard and sank into a comfortable chair.

Millie appeared, took one look at her and tutted, kneeling to pull Queenie's riding boots from her feet. 'What are you trying to do? Kill yourself? Go have a hot bath, girl, and stop trying to be two men around here.' Millie watched her go with a puzzled and worried expression.

Silently Queenie trudged upstairs.

Inhaling the sweetness of the rose oil, Queenie lay back in the steamy water and closed her eyes, trying to visualise the tiny form inside her womb. A smile crept to her lips and slowly the tension flowed from her body as she relaxed and began to accept what was happening to her.

Everything would be all right.

Alone in the study and eating a hearty meal for the first time in days, Queenie thumbed through the *Brisbane Courier Mail*.

She turned a page and froze, dropping her fork with a clunk. She pulled the paper to her with both hands. There, staring up at her from the feature photograph was the smiling face of TR, surrounded by admiring girls in cowboy hats and fringed blouses.

The local-boy-makes-good story related how TR Hamilton had won the Texas Triple Rodeo Crown for buckjumping and bull riding, pocketing a hefty pile of American dollars for beating all comers. *Down Under Cowboy Comes Up Tops* boasted the banner on the picture.

The initial shock gave way to a flush of pride, but after skipping through the article in which TR told how much he was enjoying the North American rodeo scene and his success, she looked again at the photograph. The girls had their eyes on TR, not the camera. No wonder he hadn't written. Too many distractions, no doubt. She threw down the paper and stomped from the room.

Queenie sat under a silvery satin-smooth ghost gum on the bank of the creek not far from the homestead and trailed pointless patterns in the sand with a stick. After the first flash of anger, Queenie had found her head clearing as she walked across the paddock to the creek. Now she could see everything clearly. No longer was she confused and concerned about the path she had to take. It wasn't going to be easy, and she would need help from the only person close to her whom she could trust ... Millie.

She bit her lip and thrust the stick deep into the sand. Millie would not be happy with her solution, but her mind was made up.

Queenie found it hard to take her friend aside and speak to her. There were long silences as they sipped their tea in the kitchen before going to bed.

Despite the fact TR had gone out of her

life, Queenie was not ashamed of having loved him. She was sad and scared at being pregnant, and if she was totally honest, more annoyed at herself for getting into this predicament.

She felt like a foolish, ignorant and simple girl. She knew the kind of remarks that would be passed around the woolsheds and pubs — 'Miss Queenie Hanlon's up the duff', 'she's got a bun in the oven', or 'she's no better than the gins who sleep with drunken white men for a couple of quid'.

Millie knew it too. She could imagine the gloating laughter and comments in the bars proving gleefully that the Hanlons were no better than the rest of them. Her first and immediate reaction was to go around the table and wrap her plump arms about the young woman who gripped a tea cup in both hands, stiff with tension.

'So that's how it is, Millie. I'm not saying anything about the father. Don't ever ask who he is. Please. But I'll need your help.'

'Of course, Queenie love. One more little mouth to feed around here is no problem.'

Queenie pulled away and reached for the teapot. 'I'm not keeping the baby, Millie. I'm putting it up for adoption.' Queenie spoke softly but with determination.

Millie blinked back the tears and bit her lip as an exclamation sprung to her lips. She wanted to shake Queenie, to shout at her not to be so silly. But it was not her place.

She stared at Queenie's set face. 'Why, Queenie? We can all love and look after it. I think it would be a good thing. I brought you up with your mumma. I know about babies ... even though Jim and I never ... had one.' The tears slid down Millie's dusky cheeks.

'Please don't cry, Millie. This is hard enough. I will need your help with the practical details. I have to think of Tingulla. I don't want to look like a silly young girl. I can't deal with the business of running this place and appear a responsible adult when I obviously can't even look after myself. Think of the embarrassment and shame it would bring to Mum and Dad ...' Her voice faltered.

Millie sat down and folded her hands. 'So what do we do?'

Queenie smiled slightly at the loyal Millie accepting the news as her problem too. 'I'm going into town to see Doctor Miller. He'll advise me on how I go about ... everything. I'll probably go to Brisbane, maybe even Sydney, to give birth. But in the meantime I plan on moving over to Cricklewood to start work on that property.'

Queenie had thought it all through. She spoke matter-of-factly.

Millie was still struggling to take in all the details. 'Cricklewood? There's nothing there. Just a rundown old property that's been untouched for years and years.'

'That's true, Millie. Dad and I did talk about developing the place one day ... to run a few cattle and maybe start our horse breeding programme there. He left it to me in his will and — well — I'm just going to start work on it a bit sooner, that's all.'

Millie nodded. She understood Queenie

would want to be as far away from prying eyes as possible.

'I would like you to come with me. I'll take Snowy as well. Jim will have to stay here to keep an eye on things. Obviously he can come over to visit when he has time. It's a good day's drive. But I'll need you with me, Millie. Ruthie will have to take over here. She's young but you've trained her well.'

Millie blinked. This was all going too fast. 'But who's going to run Tingulla? Colin hasn't graduated yet.'

Queenie stood. 'I've put out feelers and made a few enquiries for a station manager. I have explained to everyone, including Colin, that I am tired and need a change and a rest. If anyone asks, I'm taking a holiday.'

She had mulled over the idea of confiding in Colin, wishing she could open her heart to her brother, now her only family. But instinct warned Queenie that revealing the truth to Colin would not be prudent.

Queenie drove into town late the following morning and parked in the middle of the broad street divided by a row of trucks and dusty cars. A cattle dog lay on the road, idly scratching its fleas. Queenie turned into a doorway where a wine-red glass box with a light in it hung above the entrance, with *Doctor* painted on it in gold lettering.

Doctor Miller was understanding and sympathetic and maintained a detached professional manner. Queenie was brisk and businesslike as she informed him of her plans.

He didn't try to persuade her otherwise but

simply asked in a steady voice, 'Are you absolutely sure, Queenie?'

She answered firmly, without hesitating. She'd done her soul and heart searching. 'Yes. You know I have no other choice. And termination is out of the question.'

Looking down, the doctor lifted his pen. 'Very well then. I will write you a reference to my colleague Doctor Reese in Charters Towers who will take care of matters discreetly. I don't know that your idea of staying on that undeveloped property during your term months is such a good thing, though.'

Queenie shrugged. 'You say I'm fit and healthy. There's a homestead there, although it's run down — but it's quite liveable. I'm taking Millie, my housekeeper and the senior stockman to work with me.'

'There is the matter of regular medical checkups, Queenie.'

Queenie looked concerned, wondering how she was going to get around that problem. She couldn't appear anywhere in the district while she was pregnant.

Understanding her difficulty, Doctor Miller smiled at her. 'Well, I suppose I could drop in and see you at Cricklewood every couple of weeks. I make rounds to the outlying districts on a regular basis. A month before time you'll have to go to Charters Towers.'

Queenie looked relieved. 'Thank you, Doctor Miller.'

Queenie did some shopping, stocking up with baggy men's shirts and loose workmen's overalls, and by the time she set off back to

Tingulla it was dusk. She didn't want to stay in the pub in town or drive late into the night. So after several hours driving she pulled off the track and lit a campfire, opening the sandwiches and thermos of hot tea before rolling into her swag on the ground by the car.

She lay there thinking about the day. Even though her plan was now in place, she hated all this deception. She felt she was being pushed along a path she didn't want to follow. Trying to think through all the possibilities and the final outcome was hard. She sighed, telling herself to cope with each day as it came along. Why, oh why, had TR been so stubborn? Things could have been so different. She stared at the sky, a deep black dome inlaid with shining sparkles and pinpricks of silver. She remembered looking at these stars with her father, finding the Southern Cross and trying to count the Milky Way.

Out here, far from any town, the night sky seemed close and comforting. An image of TR's brilliant blue eyes flashed in her mind, and her heart lurched.

Softly she began counting the stars, longing for sleep to come and obliterate the memories.

At Tingulla the next day, Queenie sat in her office and wrote letters to stock and station agencies, advertisements for the *Land* and *Country Life* newspapers and, on the spur of the moment, a quick note to Dingo McPherson.

During their morning smoko Jim looked solemn as Millie blurted out the news about

Queenie. 'Now you keep it to yourself, Jim. But I just don't think it's right. Her giving away a baby to strangers. A baby we could all love. But that's Queenie's decision.'

Jim gave Millie a sympathetic smile. They had no children and Millie longed for a large family. She had faint memories of her own sisters and brothers, an extended family of cousins and kids who seemed to belong to everyone. Until they were taken away to the mission schools. She'd lost touch with all her family now. In their place she had, in her secret heart, replaced them with the Hanlons.

Slowly the muddled pieces of Queenie's life began to fall into place. It was Dingo who came to her rescue with the name of a possible manager. The man who would be the 'boss' of Tingulla had to have a variety of skills — knowledge of farming and grazing, and accountancy and managerial abilities. He would need the respect of the men working on the station; foresight and business acumen in planning sales of wool and stock; and the ability to keep everything in running order. Above all, Queenie wanted someone who would recognise and continue to nurture the spirit of Tingulla.

A married couple would have worked out well, but Dingo wrote in glowing terms of a single man, Warwick Redmond, whom he knew from his days in the Kimberleys in Western Australia.

. . . He's young still, about thirty, I think, but he's been around big stations in the West. He is

exceptionally personable, has all the right qualifications and is keen to move to the other side of the continent. His family had some money and he hoped to get a place of his own but they did their dough on some wild oil exploration deal, I believe. He has four sisters who all married quite well. He was the baby of the family and unfortunately the money had been lost by the time he was ready to set himself up in the world. But he's been a hard worker, done a variety of things, even worked in the city for a bit. He ran one of my mate's properties for a couple of years and he was real pleased with him. I think Warwick's been kicking round the city for a bit and he's dead keen to get back on the land.

Give the bloke a go, Queenie. I think it could work out well. I'm glad you contacted me, that's what mates are for. Remember, I'll always be there should you need me. And I'll never forget our ride in the dark with the ghosts of the roaring days! You're doing real good, girl . . . don't feel you're handing over the reins of Tingulla 'cause you can't manage. You've been through more than many have to suffer in a lifetime. Go have some fun and see some different scenery. You'll be a new girl when you get back to Tingulla.
Fondly, Dingo.

The next week's mail brought a letter from Doctor Miller with some documents for Queenie to sign and details of what the procedure would be when she moved to Charters Towers to await the birth of the baby. She would spend the last weeks in a Catholic-run hostel. Doctor

Miller explained that the nuns ran a private service to assist girls and to prevent abortions. They worked with the welfare authorities to place the babies with adoptive parents.

Doctor Miller added that he understood a family had been selected and her child would be fortunate in going to a very good home. Naturally he was not told any details — the 'transaction' would be conducted between the mother superior, state officials, lawyers and the adoptive family.

Like a blowfly buzzing in a summer room, thoughts hummed at the edges of Queenie's mind. She tried to push away the knowledge that she would never see the baby now growing within her body. Vaguely she understood the child would never be able to trace her, nor she it. She was finding it hard to follow the doctor's advice to try not to think about it, and when it was all over, to put it behind her.

She began the preparations to move to Cricklewood while giving the impression to Sarah's parents and other neighbours that she was taking a holiday in Sydney and might even go overseas. The Quinns urged her to try and link up with Sarah, although they were a bit vague about her exact whereabouts in Europe.

Queenie just smiled, thanked everyone and went about her tasks.

After a few days she received a letter from Warwick Redmond saying he'd heard from Dingo McPherson that she might be looking for a manager, and enclosing some details about himself.

His references and experience were excellent. From his letter he sounded keen and resourceful with a sense of humour. He'd apparently travelled round the world a bit, but realised he was best on the land and he hoped she'd give him a chance to prove himself. He had done his homework on Tingulla — no doubt much picked up from Dingo — but in Queenie's mind his biggest asset was the fact Dingo had recommended him. She'd make a few enquiries, and talk it over with Hamish Barton the solicitor, the Quinns and Jim. But already in the back of her mind, she knew, unless something negative turned up, Mr Warwick Redmond had a job.

Chapter Nine

❧

Queenie and Jim had finished drenching the new lambs and decided to stop for a smoko.

Jim lit a small fire as Queenie filled the battered billy from the canvas water bag tied to the front bumper bar of the Land Rover. 'I think I've found a manager, Jim. A bloke Dingo McPherson recommended.'

'Well, if Dingo put you on to him, he'll probably be all right.'

'He's from the West but worked all over the place. Grew up on the land but apparently his family lost their money and property. He arrives next week. I'll spend a week or so with him covering all the paperwork, and take him into town and introduce him around a bit to the accountant, bank manager and the stock and station blokes. Then I'll hand him over to you. Okay, Jim?'

Jim nodded, then reached into his shirt pocket for tobacco and papers and methodically went through the ritual of 'rolling his own', paying close attention to every detail.

Queenie watched and said nothing.

The water began to boil and she threw in a handful of tea leaves and stood the billy can in the white ash at the edge of the fire. Jim lit his cigarette with a burning stick from the fire and as he tossed it back, their eyes met, and for a moment there was a wordless communication between them.

Queenie knew that the veteran station hand could not express his trust and loyalty in words, but the look in his eyes made her throat tighten and she felt tears welling up.

She wiped an eye with a dusty hand and reached for the billy. 'I don't have to tell you I feel I'm really leaving Tingulla in your hands, Jim.'

'Don't worry, lass. I'll keep an eye on things... and this new bloke. You just look after yourself.' He reached for his mug. 'Ta... good brew,' he said brightly, signalling that there was nothing left to discuss.

Queenie knew that Jim would be unofficially running Tingulla. However, his cursory schooling didn't equip him to manage accounts and the administrative work and he had no interest in the business side of the property. Jim was a hands-on, nuts and bolts, practical man of the land — and a mechanical whiz. His love and loyalty for Tingulla and Queenie's late parents were worth far more than any university degree.

*

Queenie stood on the platform where a dozen people waited for the arrival of the passenger train from Rockhampton. She exchanged pleasantries with the Station Master who treated the event as a social occasion and made a point of talking to everyone, sifting out bits of news and information from one to pass onto the next person.

Queenie smiled. By the time the distant whistle of the approaching train was heard, everyone on the station would know she was waiting to greet the new manager of Tingulla.

It was probably the day's hottest bit of news and gave everyone an added interest in the train that for some minutes had been a smudge of smoke on the horizon — the only feature on the great brown expanse of sunburnt grass and the huge, blinding blue sky. Everyone squinted into the heat haze and watched the steam engine emerge as a solid shape from the mirage down the track.

The driver gave an extravagant blast on the whistle and with much hissing of steam and clanging and crashing of iron and steel, brought the train to a stop.

Stockmen threw out swags and saddles, women lined up suitcases. Some had straw baskets or string bags, each topped by the inevitable thermos flask, long emptied of the tea which had sustained them through the journey across the outback.

Queenie sized up the passengers and saw two men who might be Warwick Redmond.

One was short, ruddy and muscular. The other a tall rangy man, thin but wiry. She hoped it would be the well muscled man. Both gazed around the platform, but it was the tall thin fellow with a mop of black curly hair who grinned at her and picked up his bag. 'You must be Miss Hanlon.'

'I must?'

'Dingo described you. He said you had terrific long hair. I'm Warwick Redmond.'

They shook hands and turned towards the gate. 'Thanks for coming in to meet me personally. I didn't expect it.'

'I had to come to town anyway. I thought we might go over to the Crown Hotel for a bite to eat before we face the long drive to Tingulla.'

'Suits me. I had a stale meat pie for breakfast and I couldn't get a sleeper so I've been folded up in a second class seat for hours.'

'I guess long legs can be a bit of a problem in cars and trains.'

'And on horses. Hope you've got an eighteen-hander or thereabouts, otherwise I wear my boots out dragging my heels on the ground.'

Queenie laughed. 'I think we might be able to find one big enough for you.'

She watched Warwick Redmond carefully over lunch. He was affable, easy–going, but had a certain panache. Although he didn't name-drop or boast, it was obvious he'd travelled abroad and seen more than the inside of bars.

He contrasted the train trip with one he had made on a quaint steam train through the French Alps and compared the stale meat pie with French bread, wine and cheese. 'Top tucker... travels well too,' he observed. 'Reminded me of a painting I saw in the Louvre, a still life of wine bottles, bread and cheese.' Then, as if embarrassed at the recollection, he flashed a big smile and added, 'Reckon someone ought to paint a damper served up from a bush oven with a mug of tea and treacle.'

They laughed and Queenie felt herself warming to her new station manager.

He turned the conversation to Tingulla with polite but pointed questions.

It was a pleasant lunch but eventually Queenie indicated they had to get on the road. 'So many questions! We have a long drive ahead. I'll fill you in on the family history and what we're doing as we go,' smiled Queenie.

Gallantly, Warwick extracted the bill from her fingers and insisted on paying.

The hours passed easily as Queenie drove and answered Warwick's questions about the state of the land, the stock, and descriptions of everyone working at Tingulla.

Queenie began to relax. He didn't talk about changes or what he'd like to do at the property. He treated her respectfully but with a certain friendly humour, and seemed unfazed that his new boss was a slip of a girl ten years his junior.

Warwick, however, was glad Dingo had pre-pared him for Queenie and told him about the tragic deaths of her parents. He had expected her to be tougher. She was dressed in a skirt, a large man's shirt and jacket with riding boots and broad-brimmed hat, and he saw immediately that she was extremely pretty. Her shining hair cascaded loosely down her back and she seemed rather vulnerable. Obviously running a station as big as Tingulla was too great a task. It needed a manager at the helm.

Over the next few days Warwick's self-confidence wavered slightly as he saw the scope of Tingulla and began to realise how capably and efficiently Queenie ran everything. She maintained a friendly but business-like attitude and occasionally quietly tested him as they travelled about the property.

Warwick insisted on looking over every part of the property with either Jim or Queenie. It was a thoroughness that made everyone feel confident the new boss was 'fair dinkum' about the job.

It seemed the magic of Tingulla was already starting to grip the newcomer. 'It's a beautiful property,' observed Warwick softly one day, when with Queenie, he was looking over one of the remote paddocks from a slight rise in the plain.

They were standing up in the front of the old Land Rover, its canvas top down, and leaning on the windscreen. After a pause he went on, 'I understand now why everyone here seems so devoted to it. A lot of love has gone into it over the years.'

The remark surprised Queenie, but she showed no reaction. It wasn't the sort of emotion bushmen expressed openly. Manliness in the outback didn't encompass such pronouncements.

'It's not all that perfect,' she countered. 'I reckon this part needs something to give it a kick along.' The remark was said lightly, but she was probing and testing him.

Warwick scanned the area, taking in patches of scrub, a few stands of trees, the lay of the low, rolling hills, and what passed as a watercourse. 'Needs a bore, I'd say. Too far from water for stock to make much use of it.'

'Well then,' said Queenie with concealed satisfaction, 'we'd better do something about that.' She slipped down into the seat, and swung the Land Rover towards the homestead.

She had settled him into the main guest suite and found him a suitable stockhorse. It was a massive unbroken animal, strong and stubborn. Warwick knew as a point of honour he'd have to break it in himself and it was a frenzied tussle of two strong wills.

The men watched, cheering him on as he took a fall then remounted. Queenie stayed quietly in the background watching Warwick fume and struggle with the big tough horse. In her heart she felt she could have bent the animal to her will with far subtler methods, but she said nothing. Warwick had to prove himself in front of the men.

Warwick had grasped the book-keeping system and stock management programme immediately and had a good knowledge of the wool industry.

After dinner one evening Queenie offered Warwick a port in her study and outlined her future plans for breeding a line of strong stockhorses. Warwick listened and watched her as she talked. He had reassessed Queenie and found her to be more than equal to the job of running Tingulla. He knew she was twenty-two years old, but she was an intriguing contrast — a poised and knowledgeable businesswoman who also showed flashes of the daring young horsewoman he'd heard about. So far he had only seen Queenie trotting sedately on Nareedah but he was impressed by her skill with horses. Sometimes he sensed a fragility about her beneath her assured exterior. He supposed the turmoil of the past months had taken their toll, and she was simply holding herself in check until she could get away and fall apart, then gradually renew her emotional strength.

His respect for her grew and he wondered how he would have coped with the tragedies which had befallen Queenie. She never talked about her personal life, although she referred naturally to her parents in the course of conversation. She was a strong young woman, feminine too, despite dressing like a man most of the time.

Millie tapped on the door and brought in coffee and more cake.

'Millie, I couldn't eat another thing. But I'm sure Mr Redmond will. You'll find Ruthie bakes almost as well as Millie, Warwick,' she said, as he reached for a slice of fruit cake.

'Not for me thanks, Millie. I'm rationing my cake intake,' said Queenie, as Millie ignored her initial rejection.

'You should be eating up hearty, Queenie.'

'Thank you, Millie. That will be all.'

Warwick glanced in surprise at the curt tone in her voice.

Warwick faced his first small crisis over a disagreement with Jim.

A new bore had to be sunk and choosing its location threw both of them into a headlong collision. Warwick studied the geography and geology and indicated where he thought it should go, subject to the opinion of the drilling crew. Jim insisted they call in the district's water diviner, known far and wide as Donald the Diviner — or Divine Donald to the wags.

Queenie listened politely to Warwick's reasoning, agreeing it seemed the logical choice. However, Warwick sensed she was simply humouring him and had already made up her mind to let Jim have his way.

'These water diviners can be unpredictable blokes. Some have the knack, or gift, or whatever you want to call it; but if they get it wrong you can spend a lot of money and end up with a useless hole in the ground,' advised Warwick.

'There are some charlatans about, but Donald is a local and has a pretty good reputation. Jim will keep an eye on him.'

Warwick had turned away from Queenie with a tightened mouth and angry step. That evening at dinner Queenie spoke quietly to him. 'I didn't wish to usurp your authority, Warwick, and I don't want to make things difficult between you and Jim. As manager, naturally the final decision on matters will rest with you, and Jim will abide by what you say.

However, where possible weigh Jim's opinions carefully. He knows Tingulla inside out and seems to operate on some sort of instinct which is rarely wrong. You'll find him a strong ally, don't make him a thorn in your side.'

Warwick smiled at her across the table. 'Message received loud and clear. The last thing I want is a split in the camp. I want all the men to feel we are on the same team. Don't worry, Queenie, I won't rock the boat.'

Queenie relaxed, mentally thanking Dingo once again for sending this sensible, capable man to her. They finished their meal and Millie brought in the pudding, smiling fondly at Queenie. Warwick watched the warm but wordless exchange between them and wondered at the relationship between Queenie, the half-caste Millie, and Jim.

At the end of the month Queenie knew she would have to make the move to Cricklewood soon. So far she had been able to disguise her condition under the baggy overalls and shirts she wore but the strain of constantly being the lady boss of Tingulla was telling. She had confidence in Warwick Redmond and knew Tingulla would be well looked after.

Queenie now had to face her own ordeal. She could feel the baby moving more each day and it was difficult to stop feeling joyful and awed by the knowledge of TR's child making its presence felt.

Queenie decided to give herself a send-off party and introduce Warwick to neighbours, friends and business acquaintances. She asked Colin to come back from Sydney for a few days, and to her surprise he grudgingly agreed. 'I'm supposed to be cramming, but I might as well spend the study week up there. Besides, I miss Millie's cooking,' he confessed.

For the first time since Queenie's twenty-first birthday party, Tingulla looked festive and the sounds of laughter rang through its beautiful rooms. Warwick, dressed in an elegantly tailored Harris tweed jacket, charmed the women and won the approval of the men. His dark, curly head towered above most of the groups of guests as Queenie watched him circulate with ease.

She breathed a sigh of relief. He was going to fit in well. Watching some of the women and their daughters flutter about him it suddenly occurred to Queenie she knew little about his personal life. He had simply referred to his marital status in his letter as 'unattached' but she wondered if he had ever been married. An attractive, thirty-two year old bachelor who knew the land, was a welcome addition to the area. Queenie smiled to herself. Warwick wouldn't be short of invitations to tennis, the races, dinners and dances.

Queenie was especially pleased, although at first surprised, at how well Colin and Warwick hit it off. Colin's initial caution and hint of resentment had faded, and they quickly became friends. It seemed from snatches of conversation she overheard, that they had visited the same nightclubs in Sydney and Warwick had given Colin several tips about places to go and people to look up. Although twelve years older than Colin, the pair behaved like a couple of larrikin schoolboys. Queenie hoped Warwick would be able to advise Colin should the need arise. She suspected he'd listen to Warwick Redmond rather than his 'bossy sister'.

Out of her earshot the guests talked about Queenie doing the right thing and finding the right man for the job. All agreed that running Tingulla was too big a job, even for Queenie, who was looking tired and rundown and obviously needed a rest. Everyone had a suggestion of where she should go, from the Barrier Reef to Europe.

'I mightn't get past Brisbane,' laughed Queenie. 'I'm not making any plans.'

Late that night she fell into bed telling herself she just had to hang on several more days and then her secret journey would begin. She gazed about her room, filled with mementoes of her childhood. The next time she returned to this room she would be a mother. She buried her face in her pillow — she had to put that thought out of her mind. She had a trial to face and then it would all be over. But she wished she was bringing her baby back here to where she had enjoyed such a safe and happy childhood.

And, oh, how she wished TR was lying beside her.

Donald the Diviner arrived the day before Queenie was due to leave and introduced himself to Warwick along with his mate, a grinning but shy old Aborigine who had worked with Donald for twenty years. Whenever there was divining to be done, Nugget came along.

177

It was quite an expedition to the distant paddock — Queenie, Warwick and Jim all went along. At the site, Donald took a flexible, green forked stick, grasped the ends of the fork and then bent them outwards, giving the stick a tension that balanced it delicately. Then he started walking, the Aborigine at his side.

Jim rolled a cigarette and said nothing. Warwick watched their progress, referring to his own scribbled map on a scrap of paper. Queenie was watching Nugget study the ground as he walked beside Donald.

Two hours later Donald stopped and thrust the stick into the ground. 'Here,' he announced, and demonstrated how the tensioned stick swung downwards, almost as if it had been pulled by an invisible force. 'What do you reckon, Nugget?'

'Sure thing, boss. Plenty of water bilong dis place.'

'There'll be water there,' said Jim firmly.

Warwick was checking his own calculations and turned to Queenie in triumph. 'Well, he's only a few yards off where I figured to dig anyway.'

'You're both wrong,' laughed Queenie. 'I bet you ten dollars, Donald's mate Nugget is the true diviner. That old Aborigine knows where the water is. I don't know how, but I just know he does.'

Warwick started laughing too. 'I think you might be bloody right, Queenie! Well, I hope he pays him a bonus.'

*

Queenie finally managed to coax the reluctant Nareedah into the horse float and slammed the little door on her rump. The Land Rover was packed and Jim would bring more gear and supplies over to Cricklewood in a few weeks.

Queenie gazed at the stately entrance to the homestead with its airy verandah, elegant columns and beautiful gardens. She felt a lump come to her throat as she climbed into the driver's seat, telling herself she wasn't leaving Tingulla forever.

Warwick stood in the mauve shadows of the front step under the drooping, heady wisteria blooms, wondering why Queenie seemed so sad at leaving. He had done his best to assure her all would be well. He had hoped he'd won her confidence. She'd told him she was spending a few weeks with Millie at the other property, Cricklewood, before leaving on her holiday trip.

Ruthie had taken over Millie's duties and Warwick promised Queenie that everything at Tingulla would continue to run on oiled wheels.

Jim pulled off his hat and leaned forward. He gave Millie a kiss on the cheek and dropped his arm around her shoulders, giving her an affectionate squeeze. 'G'bye, old girl. Look after yourselves. I'll be over to visit, but send a message if you need anything or if there's any ... problem.'

'We'll be right, Jim. Don't worry. Snowy is already there,' said Queenie.

Millie pulled herself into the seat beside

Queenie, tying her straw hat under her chin. 'Well, let's be off. Hooroo, Jim.' She fluttered a hand out the window.

Taking a deep breath, Queenie turned the ignition key. The throaty engine roared to life and the sturdy vehicle rolled down the grand drive.

The house behind them was empty. But for Queenie it was filled with memories.

Chapter Ten

Cricklewood was a vast change from Tingulla.

Patrick Hanlon had bought the property for its development potential not long after the War. The previous owner hadn't returned from the front and his widow and young family had sold, leaving a rundown homestead which had been slowly deteriorating ever since.

Patrick had periodically made running repairs but Queenie and Millie faced a big task to make the house liveable.

Queenie, however, enjoyed the physical activity of scrubbing and washing and wielding a hammer and saw. 'I'm not much of a handyman I'm afraid, Millie,' muttered Queenie, with nails clenched between her teeth. She was struggling to lift floorboards.

'You're doing real good, Queenie. Leave the hard jobs for Jim when he comes over. Or Snowy could help.'

'Snowy has his hands full with fencing and repairing the sheds. One day I'll get around to turning this place into a decent sort of home. Who knows, maybe Colin might want to work this property some time.'

'I thought your Dad left Cricklewood to you.'

'That's true, but I was thinking if I ever get my horse breeding programme developed or get into beef, Colin might like to go into partnership with me.'

Millie didn't answer immediately. 'Better wait till he graduates.' Millie couldn't see Colin readily agreeing to live at Cricklewood, no matter how well it was fixed up. He was too much of a snob to give up living at Tingulla.

The last weeks of her pregnancy dragged slowly. Queenie gave up riding and took long walks about the property, taking sandwiches down to Snowy at lunchtime. Gradually she familiarised herself with the layout of the land, mentally mapping the terrain for future development.

Heading up towards a rocky outcrop one morning, Queenie was startled by a sudden noise. Catching a glimpse of a low, dark shadow crashing through the undergrowth, Queenie turned swiftly back towards the homestead. She took her .303 rifle from a rack in the kitchen, checking the safety lock, and put it on the shelf behind the seat of the Land Rover.

The vehicle bumped across the paddocks close to where Snowy was splitting logs, fitting the strainers and stays together with wire to make a sturdy fence. Queenie stuck two fingers in her mouth and leaned out of the window, whistling to Snowy.

The Aborigine sauntered up to the car with a questioning look. 'Hop in, Snowy. There's a decent old razorback boar up on the hill. I disturbed him while I was walking.'

Once they reached the hill Snowy checked the ground and quickly found the animal's tracks. With the rifle held ready, Queenie walked carefully beside the old man as he silently moved through the scrubby bush. She wished she had one of the strong dogs with her, and kept her finger close to the trigger, ready to fire.

After a few minutes Snowy halted and pointed to the scrub about fifty yards ahead, then whispered, 'Mebbe better I kill him. You give the rifle to me, Queenie'.

'No, Snowy,' she said softly but firmly.

'He's one big fella. Mebbe dangerous.'

She shook her head and motioned him on.

A rustle from the prickly clump of scrub brought them both to a halt again. They exchanged a quick look and Snowy circled downwind to get on the other side of the animal now screened by the bushes.

Steadily Queenie raised the rifle and braced her legs, feeling off balanced by the bulge of her belly. She moved one foot slightly behind the other to steady herself and as she did the baby fluttered. Flashing into her mind came a kaleidoscope of confused images; images of the blood and horror she had seen when wild pigs attacked and disembowelled stock with their deadly tusks. The vision blurred, and so did reality.

The scrub ahead went out of focus. 'Oh, God.' The rifle suddenly felt very heavy and her knees weak, the barrel of the rifle pointed toward the ground and it seemed as if the whole world was coming to a stop. The bush had gone quiet.

The sharp deliberate snap of twigs by Snowy sounded like a gunshot. Sensing danger, the startled wild pig tensed, lowered its head and charged towards the threat it could smell upwind — Queenie.

The angry black razorback rocketed out of the bush. Queenie instinctively raised the rifle and aimed at the blur but couldn't pull the trigger. She knew she had time for only one shot, and it had to kill, not wound.

On its short legs the pig surged forward with tremendous speed, powered by two hundred pounds of muscle, squealing demonically, its nostrils flaring.

There was barely ten yards between them when Queenie's vision cleared and she fired. Momentum carried the huge pig almost to her feet where it crashed to the ground, blood gushing from a hole between its eyes.

'Good tucker,' commented Snowy.

As they dragged the carcass towards the car, Queenie was shaken by a sudden spasm. She leaned against the side of the engine as cramps crushed her lower pelvis. Closing her eyes, she took deep slow breaths as the pain washed over her. Lifting the heavy pig had been too much.

Snowy stood stoically by, saying nothing. He had asked no questions nor made any comment about Queenie's condition or why she was at Cricklewood. In the depths of his dark eyes there sometimes flickered a question but now he gazed at her sympathetically, waiting till she spoke.

'Whew,' Queenie smiled weakly at him as the pain subsided and she opened her eyes. 'That's one big pig. Let's get it back to Millie. You can butcher him and we'll have wild boar for weeks!'

But Queenie couldn't face eating the game meat. She felt queasy and unsettled and was anxious for the next visit from Doctor Miller. She had only one more week to go before moving to Charters Towers to spend the final weeks there before the birth.

Two days later the cramps returned and when she noticed spots of blood, Queenie called Millie and told her she was going to Charters Towers. 'I'm not waiting. I'll drive myself. Take care of things here, Millie. As soon as I can I'll be in touch.'

Millie shook her head. 'You're not going there by yourself. I'm coming too.' She marched from the room and began putting clothes in a small suitcase.

Queenie didn't try to dissuade her — she knew it would be pointless. Millie would follow her anyway. And she was glad to know Millie would be close by. She didn't like to admit it, but she was a little scared, wondering what giving birth would be like. How was this bulge ever to get out of her body?

They drove mainly in silence, Millie wishing

she could drive properly, casting anxious looks at Queenie who gripped the wheel as ripples of pain caught her unawares.

Queenie concentrated on driving and the physical event she was facing. She tried not to think about the consequences.

Doctor Reese was surprised to see Queenie sitting white-faced in his office with a concerned half-caste Aboriginal woman hovering beside her.

'Problems?'

Queenie nodded and followed him into the surgery.

While Queenie got dressed, Doctor Reese approached Millie. He felt uncomfortable speaking to the housekeeper, unsure of her role in Queenie's life. 'She'll have to go into the private hospital where she can be monitored until the birth — probably only days away. There's nothing drastically wrong, but she needs to be watched, just in case. She tells me she had a bit of a fracas with a wild boar. Not a good idea in her condition.'

'That's Queenie,' said Millie philosophically. 'No one can tell her what to do or not to do.'

'Well, I'm afraid she's going to be under the thumb of the Sisters of Mercy. They run a tight ship over there.'

Millie and Queenie stopped at a milk bar in the centre of Charters Towers — a thriving outback town — and bought thin white bread sandwiches and bottles of coloured fizzy soft drinks which they shared sitting on the grass in the town's park.

Magpies carolled in the trees and two kooka-burras sat overhead, silently watching in the hope of picking up some tasty scraps. Beds of cultivated flowers were set in the lawns and a bougainvillea vine smothered in scarlet flowers covered the austerity of the public toilet block.

'Nice place,' commented Millie.

'You can take walks here, Millie. The guest-house is only a block away.'

'I will. There's a good spirit feeling about this place.'

Queenie saw Millie was half smiling, look-ing into the distance. 'Spirits, Millie? You can find spirits even in town?'

Queenie threw a piece of ham onto the grass and a kookaburra eyed it carefully before swooping down to pick it up in its large strong beak and carry it to the branch above. She remembered how, when she was a little girl, Millie would tell her stories from the Abo-riginal Dreamtime. The stories always involved trees, creeks, rock formations and the shapes of the landscape.

'Sure, Queenie. The land is our mother. The Dreamtime spirits own the land and we people belong to the land. We don't own the land, it owns us. You feel it at Tingulla. You call it love. You say you love Tingulla, that's because it's your spirit place. It's your mother land.'

Queenie nodded. Despite her mission upbringing, Millie had never forgotten the first lessons she had been taught as a child about her complex heritage. These had been handed down by word of mouth for tens of thousands of years.

Millie didn't say it, but she knew that same spirit would be in Queenie's child — whatever happened to the baby, Tingulla would be its spiritual home.

Leaving Millie at the Blue Lagoon Guesthouse, Queenie caught a taxi to the small private hospital run by the Sisters of Mercy.

The mother superior was brisk and matter of fact, and Queenie felt she was being censured. Under other circumstances Queenie might have reacted imperiously, but she realised that to the nun, she was just another silly girl who had unwisely got herself pregnant.

She stared at the white wall above the mother superior's shoulders as she rattled through the adoption procedure. 'It's best you don't see the child, but rest assured the baby will go to a good home. We are very particular about the families we select. I assume the doctor has gone over the formal details with you and that you realise this is a final step you are taking.'

Queenie nodded.

'Very well, then. During your stay here you will observe our routine. When your time arrives you will be taken to the hospital ward.'

The mother superior rose with a starched rustle and Queenie silently followed her down the dim corridor to a cell-like cubicle. 'This is your room. I hope all goes well for you. God bless you, my dear.'

Queenie let her bag drop onto the straight-backed wooden chair and flopped onto the thin iron cot, burying her face in the hard little pillow. What was she doing here? She wanted to be back in her room at Tingulla while her mother played the piano in the drawing room and Patrick's cheerful voice called to her to come for a ride.

Running through her thoughts came the soft murmur of TR's voice... 'Queenie, I love you. I always will. Never forget that.'

Angrily Queenie punched the pillow. 'Who forgot, TR? So much for your promises.'

Darkness crept into the little room where Queenie lay undisturbed until a soft tap at the door roused her. Wiping her red eyes, Queenie opened it to find a young nun holding a kerosene lamp, and smiling sweetly at her.

'Hello. I'm Sister Claire. I brought you a lamp. We don't have power in this wing. If you want to wash there's a bathroom at the end of the hall and then I'll show you the chapel, dining room and kitchen so you'll be able to find your way about.'

Queenie thanked her and took the thin, white towel from the small dresser and followed the little nun down the hallway. After splashing her face with cold water — there wasn't any hot water — Queenie felt better. Sister Claire chatted easily and Queenie found herself smiling at the nun's sense of humour.

When they found they both shared a love of horses and the bush — Sister Claire had grown up on a remote station — they began talking like two young girls, sharing anecdotes and stories. A friendship developed and Queenie was grateful she had someone to talk to, for she missed Millie.

Despite doing little, Queenie fell into bed at night physically drained, cursing TR and herself for getting into this situation. She would think twice before allowing her emotions to run away with her again.

She felt like a drudge, her body pushed obscenely out of shape. Her thick long hair had lost its lustre and her eyes their sparkle. She longed to see Millie and began to wish she could escape from this prison.

In the early hours of the morning Queenie awoke and threw back the covers, shivering as her feet hit the icy floor. She hurried down the dark hall, groping her way towards the bathroom when she felt a trickle of warm water down her thighs. She realised the baby was on its way. Fear, excitement and loneliness swept through her.

She tiptoed down a flight of stairs and tapped lightly at the far door. She was a bit taken aback to see Sister Claire dressed in a white cotton shift, her face childlike in the light of the candle she held. Her bare head was covered in a fuzz of cropped brown hair, topped by a nightcap.

'Is it time, Queenie?'

Queenie nodded, shivering, her arms holding her tightly distended belly.

'Go back to bed. I'll be with you shortly. And don't worry.'

Queenie lay in her bed watching the wavering shadows on the ceiling from her small lamp. She began to feel flickering waves of muscle contractions across her abdomen.

Sister Claire, dressed in her familiar habit, appeared quietly beside her. 'Doctor Reese will be on his way soon. He'll be here in plenty of time. You have some time to go yet, my dear.'

The next hours passed slowly. The mother superior came and went but Sister Claire stayed beside Queenie, arranging the pillow to make her more comfortable, wiping her brow and murmuring encouraging words. The contractions were stronger and Queenie could see them rippling across her belly.

She pulled up her knees, and tried lying on her side, but could find little relief from the rushes of blinding pain. 'I want to get up and walk around,' insisted Queenie pacing around the tiny room counting the steps and breathing deeply.

'Mother Superior doesn't allow patients to do this, Queenie,' worried Sister Claire.

Queenie kept pacing, then returned to the cot exhausted and parched.

Sister Claire gave her a damp wash cloth to suck. The grey light of a rainy day seeped into the room and Sister Claire blew out the lamp.

A few hours later Queenie looked at the tired face of the little nun and in the brief minutes between contractions gasped, 'Go and eat, Sister Claire — I'm fine. Leave me for a little while.'

Sister Claire nodded and left the room to take some hot tea and toast. The doctor telephoned and said he'd be on his way shortly. The nun sighed — so much pain and no joy for it all. Indeed, little did Queenie realise the real pain would begin after the baby was taken from her.

Sister Claire's concerned face swept in front of Queenie's eyes as she felt herself being lifted onto a mobile bed which had metal sides raised and snapped in place. Queenie felt like she was being put in a cage and she kicked out with a foot against the metal bars.

'Take her to the labour ward and do not lower the sides of the bed. And watch her, Sister Claire.'

'I want Millie ... please ... get Millie!' cried Queenie fiercely.

Her bed was wheeled into a clinical white room where a black crucifix hung on the wall. Queenie closed her eyes and retreated into her body, breathing through each bolt of pain, the few moments' relief, then the next one. She thought no further ahead than the next second.

The gentle voice of Doctor Reese brought her back to what was happening about her as he examined her. Queenie caught the look and small shake of his head directed at Sister Claire.

'Millie. Get Millie,' demanded Queenie in a firm voice.

'She'll be here when it's over, Queenie. Hold on for a bit longer,' said Doctor Reese. 'I'll be back to see you in a little while.'

Queenie turned her pleading eyes to Sister Claire and with a mammoth effort said, 'She's all I've got in the world. Millie Nicholson, she's staying at the Blue Lagoon Guesthouse.' Tears soaked into her pillow and she began rocking herself and murmuring in pain.

Sister Claire looked at the pale girl lying on the bed, struggling so hard and refusing to let the pain overwhelm her. Rising from the chair beside Queenie she left the room.

Millie had watched the rain drip from the sky, knowing Queenie needed her. She sat stolidly in the small public room at the guesthouse with her hat and coat on, waiting. She'd been there since daybreak. Hearing the telephone jangle in the office she was already halfway to the phone before the caretaker called her.

Sister Claire opened the outside kitchen door and let Millie inside. 'Guests are supposed to wait in our vestibule or in the sister's office, but I think Queenie needs you. It's been such a long hard time for her.'

'I hope you don't get into trouble for this. Thank you,' said Millie following the nun upstairs.

Queenie smiled and relaxed slightly when she opened her eyes and saw Millie smiling down at her. Millie leaned over and smoothed the damp hair from her forehead. 'You're doing real good, Queenie.'

When Doctor Reese returned he found Sister Claire sitting by as Millie rubbed Queenie's back. Queenie was in a squatting position on the bed.

She glanced defiantly at the doctor. 'Millie's not leaving.'

'All right, Queenie. I'll try to keep Mother Superior at bay.'

Things happened quickly when the baby began to thrust insistently into the world. Sister Claire and Doctor Reese took over, preparing Queenie for the delivery room. At the last moment Sister Claire took Patrick's watch from Queenie's wrist and slid Rose's engraved gold wedding band from her finger and handed them to Millie.

Millie waited, alone in the room. Forty minutes later Sister Claire came in and whispered. 'It's all over. She's very tired. Would you like to see her?'

'The baby?'

'The baby is fine. I'm sorry she can't see the child. She has to put this from her mind and heart now.'

Millie nodded, her own heart aching as she went to Queenie's side. Queenie's green eyes were hollow and so dark they looked almost black. Millie took her hand and patted it, unable to speak. She took the watch and buckled it back on Queenie's wrist and slipped Rose's ring back on her finger.

Millie sought Sister Claire and took her aside. 'Please let me see the baby, just for a moment. I can't have kids. Queenie's my only family.'

Sister Claire stared at the kindly woman, a mix of race and cultures, who obviously cared deeply for the beautiful young white woman who had suffered so much. 'Stay here. I shouldn't — but just for a moment.'

Sister Claire returned holding a tiny bundle

in a simple white blanket. 'I'll be back in two minutes. I have to speak to the doctor.'

She shut the door behind her and Millie looked down at the sleeping child. Gently she unfolded the blanket and touched the small pink hand. The little hand curled around Millie's dark finger and held on. Softly she ran her finger along the baby's chubby legs then stopped, staring at the infant's upper thigh. 'Well, I'll know you if we ever meet again.'

At that moment the baby opened its eyes and stared up at Millie.

Millie smiled. 'If I ever wondered who your Dad was, I know now. There's no mistaking who *your* father is, little one.'

Chapter Eleven

TR awoke with a start, alert and tense, thinking a voice had shouted to him. Queenie's voice. He heard it so clearly and felt her presence so strongly. It was as if she was in the room. He could smell the lingering fragrance of her hair and skin. Instinctively he reached beside him, finding the bed cold; and when he clicked on the bedside lamp, the room was empty.

He thought he had been successful in pushing the memory of Queenie to the back of his mind, hoping to ease the pain. Yet in seconds he was enveloped by an immense longing for her. Why had he felt her presence so forcefully?

TR swung his legs out of bed and reached for his wallet in his jacket hanging on a chair in the motel room. His lean and muscular body had lost its tan, and bruises shone on his naked hip where he'd taken a fall. Pulling a piece of paper from his wallet he unfolded the letter Colin had written with such malice — the letter TR believed was from Queenie.

> ... and so, TR, I think it best we part company and forget the brief time we shared. I'm too young to think of settling down. I want to travel and get away from all the sad memories here. I'm arranging for a manager to run Tingulla and I plan on going overseas indefinitely. Forget me. It's best.
> Queenie.

Again the anguish he'd suffered on reading the letter surfaced. He simply didn't understand. TR looked at his watch, it was midday in Australia. He reached for the phone and asked for the overseas operator.

Hearing the friendly nasal accent of the Australian country operator putting the call through from town to Tingulla, TR could see the study where the radio telephone sat by Patrick's old desk.

A man's voice he didn't recognise answered as the operator told TR to go ahead. 'I was trying to reach Miss Queenie Hanlon,' said TR, hearing his own voice reverberate back to him.

'I'm sorry, she's not here. Is this personal or business?' came the strange voice.

TR hesitated. 'Personal. I'm a friend. I'd like to talk to her. When will she be there?'

'I'm sorry, mate. Queenie has gone away on a trip. I'm Warwick Redmond, the manager here. Can I pass on any message if she gets in touch?'

'No ... thanks. No message.'

TR replaced the receiver and sat on the edge of the bed staring about the Superior Room of the Lone Star Inn. There was no way he was going to sleep now. He pulled on his jeans and boots and denim jacket and strode from the room.

His hands thrust deep in his pockets, shoulders hunched miserably, TR wandered down deserted Pennsylvania Street where neon signs flashed and an occasional car cruised by. Tomorrow he would move on to another Midwest town, another 'thrill-packed' rodeo, where hungry young cowboys were anxious to knock the Aussie from his pedestal.

TR was tired. His body was sore and his heart ached. The excitement and gratification of proving himself a top-liner had worn thin. The cheering crowds, the acclaim, the money — none of it filled the emptiness in his life. In every town there were girls who sighed over the handsome Australian with the sky-blue eyes and lopsided grin. His elusive and reserved manner made him all the more appealing. There had been several one-night stands — soft bodies, a physical release — but the longing and the loneliness never left him.

The other riders on the circuit couldn't figure out why TR never took more advantage of the women and girls who flung themselves at him. 'I have a girl at home,' said TR evasively.

Home. Maybe he should go back to Australia. He missed the clear sharp air, the intense blueness of the sky, the song of the birds, the solitude of the bush. TR turned into an all-night drugstore and sat on a stool and ordered a coffee from the sleepy young black man behind the counter.

'Out late,' he commented, as he splashed the hot coffee in TR's cup.

'Couldn't sleep, mate.'

'Where you from?'

TR sighed. No one ever guessed Australia. They generally thought he was English or confused Australia with Austria. Little was known about Australia other than kangaroos and tennis players. 'Australia.'

'Is that right? Well hang me. I'm just reading 'bout one of your famous authors.'

TR blinked. 'That makes a change. Most people think I speak English well.'

The young man laughed and poured himself a cup of coffee. 'I'm a student, doing a comprehensive lit course.'

'Lit?'

'Literature. Learning about writing, writers, communication. I've been reading Morris West.'

'Who?'

'Shoot. Whereabouts in Australia are you from? He's one of your best writers, man. Along with Patrick White!'

TR shook his head. 'I'm from the bush. Ask me about horses.'

'Ask him who won the Melbourne Cup last year . . . he'll know that one,' came a hearty voice with a deep Southern accent.

TR turned around to see a tall and bulky man behind him.

The man pushed his broad stetson back on his head and extended a hand. 'Howdy. Clayton Hindmarsh.'

TR shook hands with a bemused smile.

'An Aussie, eh? I've been down under several times,' said Clayton Hindmarsh, indicating he wanted coffee.

'This is all a bit much in the middle of the night in a little town in Idaho, to find two people who know Australia,' said TR.

'That's life, sonny. As a matter of fact, I even know you. You're Hamilton. I watched you ride this afternoon. I check out the rodeo circuit whenever I can.'

'What were you doing in Australia?' asked TR.

'Usual thing. Lookin' at horses. And riders and trainers.'

'You're in the horse business?'

'Y'might say that. I run one of the biggest horse studs in Kentucky. I move round the country seeing people, lookin' at horses. Must say, I was mighty impressed with the way you handled them cranky cattle out there today.'

'Thanks. But the novelty is starting to wear off.'

'Is that so? What are your plans, boy? Going back home?'

'I've still got another month of my contract to ride out. I really don't know. I had planned to go home and breed, break and train some decent stockhorses.'

'Whaddya know about racehorses, Hamilton?'

TR laughed. 'Not much.'

'Wanna learn?'

TR drained his cup. The fascinated student refilled it and leaned on the bar, following the conversation closely.

'I'll come clean. I checked you out. I talked to a few people and I heard you're pretty good with horses. Not just riding 'em, I mean. So . . . let's talk turkey here,' said Clayton Hindmarsh, slapping his stetson on the counter top. 'I'd planned to run you to ground one way or another. This chance meeting is fate at work, boy.'

Two days later TR flew to Kentucky to meet Clayton Hindmarsh III on home ground. TR had done a little checking himself and was still somewhat stunned at the extent of the Hindmarsh spread. It was one of the showcase studs in the country, producing some of the top racehorses. Hindmarsh was considered a bit eccentric, but he'd made his millions by sheer hard work, shrewdness and a few lucky gambles.

'Racehorses are a different breed of horse — high strung, strong, yet fragile. It doesn't take much to ruin a horse's racing career.'

'So they end up here at stud?'

'Only the best, TR. I have an old guy who can't read or write but is magic with horses. He's even fixed up some horses and got them racing again. Tommy's gettin' on, he has to pass on some of that magic, before it's too late.'

'Maybe it's his own gift and talent and can't be taught,' said TR, thinking of the skills of some Aborigines.

'I'd like you to try to learn what you can. I sense you could develop into a helluva horse trainer. It takes a certain way with horses to get them to respond. I think you've got it. Finish your rodeo contract and come back here and see what you think. The job's open any time you want.'

'I'll have to think about it, Clayton. It's a big step for me. It's not how I saw my life working out.'

'Life seldom does go entirely to plan, TR. Let me know when you're ready. I got where I am today 'cause I know horses and I know men. I think you're the right man for the job.'

He slapped TR on the back. 'Let's go back to the ranch house. Them women have been cookin' up a mess of fine stuff all day.'

The Bon Vite stud homestead was an elegant Southern mansion surrounded by manicured, lush green lawns and neat white fences. Two men were employed full-time painting fences, stables and equipment sparkling white. It reminded TR of a picture he'd once seen of a wealthy stud in Ireland. So green, so neat, so expensive looking.

The Southern women were the same. Soft lilting flirtatious voices, neat hairdos, feminine dresses and smelling of money. They all made a fuss of TR, which had him blushing awkwardly, much to their delight.

Clayton introduced TR to his family, friends and business associates. TR had mint juleps and bourbon pressed on him and he found it difficult to follow the drawling accents and to keep track of everyone he met.

*

The next morning a pre-breakfast hunt was arranged and TR was astounded to find everyone dressed in traditional British scarlet coats riding to the hounds.

He tugged at his tweed jacket. 'I'm sorry, Clayton, I didn't come prepared for this.'

Mrs Hindmarsh eyed TR from the tips of his shiny riding boots to the top of his Akubra. 'Honey, you look more than just fine, believe me. Here, have an orange blossom.' She lifted a crystal flute from a silver tray held by a black waiter in formal attire, even to white gloves.

TR sipped the amber liquid, stifling a sneeze as the champagne bubbles went up his nose.

'See you at breakfast, TR,' said Mrs Hindmarsh, giving him a knowing smile and fluttering her eyelashes.

TR gulped the rest of his drink.

TR rode easily with the field, preferring not to be at the front — he thought it a bloody stupid sport and was longing for a pot of tea.

As the braying dogs, giggling women and loud men reassembled two hours later, Clayton muttered to TR, 'Don't get the wrong idea, life ain't like this all the time. This weekend is to humour Mrs Hindmarsh. She loves to party.'

'Pleased to hear it. I don't think I could last the distance,' grinned TR, eyeing the breakfast spread in the specially erected marquee.

Breakfast turned into brunch, which turned into tennis, which turned into billiards, which turned into late afternoon cocktails, which turned into a massive barbecue where servants sliced smoked ham and roasted sides of rare beef.

A social photographer clicked away, promising Mrs Hindmarsh she'd make the Sunday colour supplement. TR found himself being frequently posed alongside cooing young women.

The pictures caused much ribald comment at the next rodeo event. The other riders gave TR a hard time, either teasing him about the girls — 'Watch those Southern belles ... ring-a-ding-ding!' — or accusing him of being a snob — 'Our company not good enough for you, huh?'

He didn't mention the job offer from Clayton Hindmarsh to them, but TR longed to talk it over with someone. He made some international calls, eventually tracking down Dingo McPherson.

Dingo roared with laughter over the long distance line. 'You wouldn't read about it! Of course I know who Clayton Hindmarsh is! Listen, TR, I know it seems a strange and foreign world over there — well it is! And they have some funny ways of doing things. But Clayton's word is good and if you work with him for a couple of years, you'll be able to write your own ticket when you come back to Australia.'

This cheered TR. He could look on this job as a sort of apprenticeship, learning what he could to set up his own business back home. In his heart he had been considering it a means of escape, rather than having to face returning to the memories of Queenie.

'You're right, Dingo. I reckon I'll take it. Any other news?'

'Need bloody rain, but that's nothing new, mate. No, everything is fine. Let me know how things work out. If I'm in the States, I'll come visit.'

After he hung up it occurred to Dingo he could have passed on the news of Warwick Redmond managing Tingulla. He dismissed the idea. TR won't be going back to work at Tingulla, or anywhere else when he comes back. He'll be setting up his own place. 'And good luck to him,' thought Dingo.

So TR called Clayton — no one seemed to write letters in America but used the telephone instead — and accepted the job as assistant trainer for Bon Vite, the Hindmarsh stud. He would be under the wing of old Tommy and Clayton's job instructions were blunt: 'Pick the old buzzard's brains clean, TR.'

In a month he would go South, to a new life and a new beginning. Australia, Tingulla and Queenie were the past.

Chapter Twelve

It was all over.

Queenie stood on the quiet, tree-lined street outside the anonymous walled grounds of the convent where her child had been taken from her. The street was deserted and only an occasional car splashed through the water-filled potholes. Drivers, intent on the road ahead, ignored the lonely figure with bag at her feet, sheltering from the drizzling rain under a maple tree, waiting for a taxi.

She felt utterly desolate. She was guilt-stricken because she hadn't fought to see her baby, but knew in her heart that had she seen and held it, the wrench, the sense of loss, would be even harder to bear. Large drops of water fell from the clouds onto her hair and washed wisps over her forehead and eyes.

Queenie looked up at the tree — an imported species — and stared at the dripping leaves, so foreign to her outback eyes. 'You don't

belong here,' she thought. 'And neither do I.'
She closed her eyes and let the rain run over
her face.

'C'mon, luv. Hop in and get out of the bloody
rain, or you'll start sprouting.' She hadn't even
noticed the taxi pull up.

The taxi dropped Queenie at the Blue
Lagoon Guesthouse, and Millie met her and
hugged her on the verandah. 'Come on up
to my room and we'll dry you out. Lord, you
do look a wreck.'

In the spacious, high-ceilinged room with
Victorian furniture and shiny brass bedstead,
Queenie towelled her hair while Millie put on
the electric jug and spooned instant coffee into
cups. 'How are you feeling?' she asked over
her shoulder.

'Fine.'

Millie turned and looked at her.

'Lousy,' Queenie corrected and tried to
smile. Instead tears began to slide silently
down her cheeks.

Millie smoothed them away. 'Well, that's
not surprising, is it? But there's no time for
tears, Queenie. You've got to get on with life
— and there's a lot of it to come. Now, what's
the next step?'

Queenie drew a deep, shuddery breath. 'I
don't honestly know. I thought I'd go further
north. Maybe see the Barrier Reef. A tropical
island sounds like a good idea for a bit.'

She smiled wanly, took the coffee and sat
in a cane chair. She wouldn't admit it but she
felt physically and emotionally drained. She'd
been having nightmares that some beast had

attacked her, ripping the baby from her body and taking all her insides as well. She felt hollow, shell-like and haunted.

After recovering some composure under Millie's sure hand, Queenie took a room at the Blue Lagoon, and next day they both went to the railway station where Millie caught a train back to meet Jim at Cricklewood. Queenie was feeling much better. A long night's sleep after a good meal in the company of relaxed guests at the Blue Lagoon had helped dispel some of her gloom, and fussing around getting Millie packed and booked on the express gave life a new sense of purpose.

When Millie was settled in her train seat she let down the window. They exchanged smiles. 'Enjoy the trip, Millie. I'll keep in touch.'

'Quite looking forward to it really. You have a good rest, now.' There was an awkward silence. 'Me and Jim will pack up everything at Cricklewood and head back to Tingulla at the end of the week. Don't you worry about anything, luv. You go off and have a nice holiday.'

There was a shrill whistle from the platform attendant, the guard waved a green flag, doors banged shut, the engine whistle blew; and with a rattle the train slowly began to move.

Queenie and Millie quickly exchanged a kiss, held hands briefly, then let them slip apart as the train picked up speed.

They waved to each other until the carriage passed the end of the platform and swung away. Queenie turned and walked into the crowd.

*

Two days later Queenie was in another world. She lay on her back on soft silver sand, the warmth of the sun seeping into her bones. The harsh sunlight was filtered by the swaying fronds of a palm tree and a book lay discarded by her side as she dozed.

Gradually the sun moved and began burning her legs. She stirred and sat up, gazing along the deserted strip of beach. Past the breakwater she could see the splashing white spume as waves crashed on the narrow strip of reef with a faint rumble.

Queenie pulled up the straps of her swimsuit and ran to the water, slipping into the aquamarine coolness. She swam underwater with lazy strokes, her hair fanning out around her like drifting sea ferns.

Drying off in the sun once more she saw Alf, the leaseholder of Neptune Island, strolling towards her in his uniform of torn shorts, faded singlet and battered straw hat. 'G'day.'

'G'day,' replied Queenie, taking off her sunglasses.

'Flat out like a lizard drinkin', I see. Guess you're copin' with the pressure.'

Queenie laughed. 'I'm coping, but how are you standing up to the executive stress of management?'

'Oh, getting by. Doing my best to ignore the Dow-Jones Index and the price of gold in London.'

Queenie was enjoying the banter. Such exchanges had become part of the daily routine. Alf seemed to be perpetually ambling around his island on foot, or on a rusty old bicycle, chatting up guests, or doing the odd repair job.

'What executive decisions have you made today, Alf?' Queenie asked with a wry smile.

'Whether to put sea perch or bream on the menu for lunch. Which reminds me, lunch is on — the others are already tuckin' in.'

'What is it, bream or perch?'

'Both . . . and prawns I caught last night.'

'I'll be right along.'

Alf had been a beachcomber who had lived for years on Neptune, an island in the Whitsunday Passage off Queensland's north coast. He was almost a recluse, barely making ends meet, until one day on a trip to the mainland he'd bought a lottery ticket and won a small fortune.

Alf had simply expanded his simple cabin-style accommodation on the beach, bought a bigger boat and taken in a handful of guests. It was an almost primitive, peaceful paradise and relatively few people knew about it.

Alf didn't advertise, but word of mouth recommendations guaranteed him a steady flow of like-minded guests who weren't too demanding.

Queenie found it a healing time. She took each day as it came. The biggest task was deciding on which side of the island to swim and sunbake; or whether or not to go out to the reef and snorkel, and to lose herself in the jewelled world beneath the surface, where a myriad of multi-spangled fish darted through the rainbow coloured coral and grottoes.

Some mornings she rose early and joined Alf in his fishing boat, enjoying the challenge of bringing a fighting tuna alongside. Other days were spent swinging in a hammock between palm trees, or reading in the cool shade of the rocks on the shore where the sea breeze turned the pages.

Her body quickly returned to its slim firm shape, her skin bronzed, and her hair shone with streaks of sunlight.

Queenie lost track of time and stopped caring about it. Until one morning when Alf came strolling up the beach to her personal hideaway behind some rocks and squatted down for a chat. Over the weeks he had become quite interested in the attractive young woman who kept to herself so much and seemed to be guarding her privacy.

He pushed back his ragged-rimmed straw hat, took his pipe from the hip pocket of his shorts and went through the silent ritual of lighting up. Satisfied with the flow of smoke he ran his eye around the white sandy foreground and two-tone blue horizon and announced decisively, 'Beaut day'.

'Like every other day,' said Queenie, rolling on her stomach so it would be easier to talk to him.

'Yep. Get more than our fair share of good days, I reckon. But it'll rain one day. Storm like hell. Cyclone will come screamin' in from the north-east and practically flatten everything. You can bet on it happening but you can't predict when. But that's life, isn't it?'

Queenie turned her head slightly to look

at the weather-beaten face. 'That's life?' she repeated.

'Well, what I mean is,' and he paused to puff on his pipe for a few seconds, 'what I mean is, life's calm followed by a storm, followed by calm, isn't it? The thing is, not to let the storms flatten you. That's why these palm trees here are so old and still standing despite the storms. They bend with the wind, and when it's all over they carry on as usual.'

Queenie thought for a while. 'I guess you're right, Alf . . . calm, storm, calm.'

'You been in a storm lately, Queenie?' asked Alf casually.

'Why do you ask that?'

'Cos you looked like a refugee from a big blow when you arrived.'

'How do I look now?'

Alf looked down and grinned. 'Calm . . . dead calm.'

They looked at each other for a few seconds, saying nothing. Then Queenie rolled over and sat up. They both gazed at the empty horizon. 'Then I guess I'd better get on with life, Alf.'

'Yep. That's what we've all got to do — get on with life. And I'd better check on lunch. See ya.'

He knocked out his pipe, stuffed it in his shorts and set off back down the beach.

Queenie knew it was time to move on.

The next day she paid Alf and he ferried her across to one of the bigger islands nearby where she caught a seaplane back to the mainland. Her car was still parked under the mango tree where she'd left it, dotted with splotches of rotting fruit.

Queenie picked a dozen edible mangoes from the ground and put them on the seat beside her. She drove back down the coast but didn't feel she was ready for Tingulla. She kept going south, through Brisbane to the resort city of Surfers Paradise.

She marvelled at the towers of twinkling lights looming along the beachfront and decided to check into one of the new luxury hotels. Staying above three levels was a novelty and Queenie asked for the highest room available.

'I feel like a bird in its nest,' she thought, peering down from the fifteenth floor.

Queenie eyed the mystery of the bulky television set in her room. In a while she was sitting transfixed, laughing aloud at the antics of the Lucille Ball show.

Later, Queenie bathed and sprawled across the deluxe queen size bed, flipping through the *Women's Weekly* magazine. She stopped and slowly sat up. In the coloured pages of the 'People Overseas' section was a picture of TR.

The photograph was taken at the famous Kentucky Derby and there was TR holding the winning horse. The picture was headlined, *Australian Aids US Winner*. The caption told of the success TR Hamilton was having with top stud and stable, Bon Vite, owned by Clayton Hindmarsh, pictured with his daughter, Miss Virginia Hindmarsh.

Queenie studied the picture. TR had moved into another world as well, working for an

American millionaire who owned champion horses and who had a pretty blonde daughter.

Slowly she closed the magazine, placing it neatly on top of the TV. She smoothed the bed and pulled out her bag, opened the built-in cupboard and began folding her clothes.

Queenie realised the holiday had come to an end. As though finishing a book, she snapped her mind shut to TR, past joys and lost dreams. She was ready to go back to Tingulla and start life anew.

The next morning she checked out of the hotel and flung her bag in the back of the car. She drove with her back to the sea, away from the overindulgent blues and greens of the coast, heading towards the great inland plains, the austere red heart of Australia and the land she knew and loved.

As was her way, Queenie didn't tell anyone she was returning to Tingulla. It was in the back of her mind to see how things were functioning under Warwick's guidance without alerting him that she was coming home.

The sight of the familiar landscape as she approached Tingulla filled her heart with happiness, and a calmness settled over her. The land worked its magic and soon Queenie's mind was running over with plans and ideas for carrying on her father's dreams for Tingulla.

Queenie parked the dust-coated car in front of the grand entrance to the homestead, noting with pleasure the well-kept gardens, the repaired fences, some fresh paintwork and an overall air of well-being. After an absence it struck her forcefully what a showplace this was and what a responsibility she held. The heritage and beauty of Tingulla Station had to be preserved.

With Millie back at the helm the house was spotless, although lacking Queenie's personal touch. Queenie sniffed appreciatively at the smell of baking which led her to the kitchen.

Sitting at the large pine kitchen table, watching Millie pull a batch of scones from the Aga oven, was Sarah. Both girls squealed in delight and ran to hug each other, making Millie jump. 'My goodness, Queenie. You didn't half give me a shock. You might have told us you were coming back. And so soon,' exclaimed Millie, as Queenie gave her a hug.

'What for, Millie? Everything looks great, the tea's made, scones are ready and you've got my best friend sitting here!' Queenie turned to Sarah. 'So... ? Tell me *everything*.'

Sarah didn't say a word but simply held up her left hand, dangling it in front of Queenie's nose. A sapphire and diamond ring glinted in the light.

'You're not! Engaged! Oh, Sarah... who, who, who?' demanded Queenie, examining the ring.

'You don't know him... but he's wonderful.'

'Of course! Don't tell me... he's a Swiss banker, an Austrian ski instructor... a Venetian gondolier!'

'No, he's a Sydney boy now, but originally from Inverell and his name is John Maxwell.'

'A bush boy from sapphire country... no

wonder you have such a lovely ring. What's he do?'

Sarah settled down for a long chat, extolling the virtues of her fiancé, John. He had worked in real estate in rural NSW, selling farms and houses, but made the move to Sydney where he had built up a reputation as a top salesman. They had met on the ship when Sarah sailed for England, and met again in London. The smitten John had followed her to Europe and proposed under the Leaning Tower of Pisa.

'Oh, Sarah . . . it's like a fairy tale,' laughed Queenie. Impulsively she hugged Sarah. 'I hope you'll be so, so happy.'

Millie turned away, her eyes filled with tears. Seeing Queenie so ecstatic for her friend when Queenie had not only lost a love, but a child as well, was too much for Millie.

Millie crossed her fingers and muttered a silent prayer that Queenie, too, would find a man to make her eyes shine like Sarah's.

'So when is it to be? What do your parents think?'

'They like him. Dad has given up the idea I'll ever be a career girl, so I think they're rather pleased. Mum isn't too happy that I'll be so far away in Sydney. She's hoping John will move up here one day and sell big stations and stuff, but he won't. Oh, Queenie, he is so bright, and he just has a way of getting on with people, and he's honest.'

Queenie suddenly grabbed Sarah's hand. 'Get married here at Tingulla. Oh, Sarah, let me give you the wedding as a present . . . would your parents mind?'

Sarah's face lit up. 'That would be wonderful. Tingulla is so beautiful and so... special. Are you sure?'

'Of course. We can put up John's family and friends if you like, and you can marry in our church here on the property. We'll make it the loveliest wedding ever! Won't we, Millie?'

'My word we will. Don't you worry about that, Sarah.'

As the two girls talked excitedly and began making plans, Millie went quietly about her work. She thought how good it would be to see the church used for a happy occasion.

An hour passed and Millie replenished the teapot, enjoying the sound of Queenie laughing at the endless stream of amusing tales Sarah related.

'You should travel overseas, Queenie. You'd adore Europe. Now that you've got a manager, why not?'

'One day, Sarah. I have too many things I want to do here. Tingulla is my career.'

'What about Colin?'

'We won't know what his plans are until he graduates.'

'With Colin back here it will almost be like old times.' Both girls were silent for a moment, knowing things would never really be the same again.

Before embarking on plans for Sarah's wedding, Queenie invited Warwick into her study after dinner. 'Warwick, your trial basis is up and I'm very happy with what you've been doing. I'd like to extend your contract... if you're interested.'

Warwick paused. 'Yes, I would be interested. But frankly, Queenie, I'd like to take on a bit more than a caretaker role here. You did mention you had plans to develop a stockhorse breeding programme and I think you could upgrade the overall quality of Tingulla's wool. There are a few people starting to get into goats, too, you know, for the cashmere and angora.'

'Goats! Oh, Warwick! They're such stupid things and they have to be mothered a lot from what I hear. They sound like far too much trouble. But I'm pleased you're thinking along the same lines. I can't afford to go mad, though I would like to expand, it's just . . .'

'You need a bit of advice along the way, that's all,' said Warwick, realising Queenie found it difficult to admit she might be getting out of her depth.

One Sunday, Queenie arranged a barbecue for the hired hands, the jackaroos, the stockmen, Jim, Ernie the rousabout, and Snowy. Warwick kept quietly in the background as Queenie told them Warwick would be staying on and that she had plans to improve and develop the property. The men appreciated being put in the picture and each felt a special pride in working at Tingulla. They all wanted to see Queenie succeed.

Privately though, they were glad Warwick would stay boss. Queenie was too much of an attractive woman and sometimes too stubborn and hot tempered, to be giving the men orders on a daily basis. It also irritated some of them, especially the young jackaroos, that she could do their jobs so much better than them, as well as outride and outshoot them.

So Warwick settled into life at Tingulla. Although he stayed in the main house, he was gone at dawn and only ate an evening meal with Queenie on occasional nights. The rest of the time he ate with the men. Sundays he went socialising, playing tennis at the Quinns' or visiting other friends. Queenie didn't question him about his private life and was glad she didn't have to entertain him.

Queenie also received invitations to functions but turned most of them down. However, she keenly accepted an invitation to dinner at the Quinns' to meet Sarah's John.

It was a large gathering of family and friends, a kind of engagement party, and Queenie liked John Maxwell the moment Sarah introduced them.

He shook her hand warmly. 'I feel I know you, Queenie. Even though I'm taking Sarah away to Sydney I hope you'll consider our home yours, too — any time.'

Queenie thanked John, feeling a tug at her heart as she watched Sarah, holding John's hand, manoeuvre him around the room to meet everyone. He was a sandy-haired, solidly built man, with flecked hazel eyes that always seemed to be smiling.

Queenie could see why he was so successful. He had a friendly country style, which she realised sheltered a shrewd business mind. His father was a bank manager in Inverell, and John was financially comfortable. Sarah told

Queenie he had bought them, 'An adorable little house in an area John says is the best kept secret in Sydney. It's going to double in value really fast'.

Queenie laughed. 'You're already sounding like the wife of a successful real estate agent!'

'Sarah's done all right for herself,' commented Warwick to Queenie as he passed by looking for the hors d'oeuvres.

Before leaving, Sarah and her mother talked over the wedding plans with Queenie: the number of guests, the food, the wedding attendants and the logistics of getting the interstate guests settled at Tingulla.

'Queenie, I want you to be my bridesmaid, nobody else, just a flower girl and pageboy,' said Sarah.

'I thought you were going to have a traditional wedding with six groomsmen and six bridesmaids,' laughed Queenie.

'Just kidding. You're my best friend. I want you beside me for this big event in my life,' said Sarah.

When the decision about where to go for a honeymoon came up, Queenie clapped her hands. 'I know just the place. My friend Alf's!'

Queenie told Sarah and John about her stay on Neptune Island and they both agreed it sounded perfect.

Perfect. That seemed to be how things were working out for Sarah, and Queenie was determined to make the wedding perfect too. Her life, it seemed, would not follow the same ordered path as Sarah's seemed to be following

— with a supportive family, a loyal and loving man, and a secure future.

Queenie wasn't jealous, she was relieved and happy for her childhood friend. She knew Sarah would always be there to call on if she needed her. But Queenie couldn't help wondering when she, too, would find happiness.

Chapter Thirteen

&

If Queenie had written a list of exactly what she wanted for Sarah's wedding day and sent it to heaven, things couldn't have been more perfect.

The sun blazed in a cloudless sky, but a soft breeze kept it from being too hot; it rustled the gum leaves and lifted the edge of Sarah's embroidered veil. The little church, which Queenie had decorated with bowers of wattle and heavy branches of scarlet bottlebrush, overflowed with people.

Nareedah, brushed so she shone, with her mane and tail braided with ribbons, and a garland of flowers over her ears, pulled the tiny sulky bearing the bride and groom from the church to the homestead.

The verandah and drawing room were transformed with flowers. Millie and Mrs Quinn had excelled themselves with the lavish buffet spread along one side of the verandah.

Tables and chairs were set on the front lawn, shaded by a canopy of branches covered in lemon-scented gum leaves. The natural perfume drifted over the guests beneath, and dappled light danced on the table tops.

Queenie had continued Sarah's green theme by dyeing the tablecloths a pale apple green, with centrepieces of creamy gardenias. The triple-tiered wedding cake was decorated with iced gardenias and topped with a bouquet of fresh lily of the valley. White roses with green ribbons trailed about the poles holding the leafy canopy over the dance floor.

Extra staff had been brought over from the Quinns' and everyone working at Tingulla was included in the wedding festivities.

Warwick agreed to act as master of ceremonies. 'It's all very informal, anyway,' said Queenie, 'but it is good of you.'

Warwick turned out to be a witty and charming choice, adding just the right note of joviality and sentimentality where needed.

As dusk drew in, the torches in the garden were lit and the band changed from discreet background music to romantic dance tunes.

Looping up her train Sarah led John to the dance floor followed by Queenie and Warwick. Unlike the bridegroom, who shuffled through the basic steps, Warwick waltzed Queenie around the floor in sweeping style to much applause.

'You dance as well as you make speeches,' said Queenie. 'What other talents have you been hiding from me?'

'Wait and see,' teased Warwick, tightening

his grip a little to pull Queenie closer to him. He wanted to tell her how beautiful she looked in the deep emerald green silk dress that matched her eyes. Her hair was piled on top of her head, with a gardenia posy tucked in one side. Circling her throat were the opals her parents had given her. She looked sophisticated and very elegant.

Warwick had almost gasped when he'd first seen her just before the ceremony, remembering how she had dressed when he'd arrived at Tingulla. Out of those baggy shirts, he found Queenie had a showgirl body.

'I'm glad you don't dress like this all the time. I'd never get any work done,' said Warwick provocatively.

Queenie blushed, but enjoyed the compliment.

During a break in the dancing Sarah took Queenie aside and pressed a small box into her hand. 'A little present from John and me to say thank you.'

Inside were a pair of dainty emerald earrings. 'Oh, Sarah ... you shouldn't. This is too much.'

'Nonsense. We wanted to give you this for making my wedding so utterly wonderful. I'll never forget this, it's the happiest day of my life.'

Sarah and Queenie hugged each other as Warwick approached. 'My turn to dance with the bride. And the groom is looking for you, Queenie.'

Queenie enjoyed herself more than she could remember. Millie and Mrs Quinn had everything running smoothly, the food was lavish, friends and families mingled happily, and Queenie found Warwick made her laugh and relax. If there was a subtle shift in their relationship from boss and employee to good friends having fun, Queenie put it down to the social circumstances.

She was intrigued by Warwick, whom she had never considered the sort of man whose company she would so enjoy. He told her stories of living abroad, his escapades in Sydney, his two failed love affairs and how his once-rich parents had fallen on hard times. 'So, I'm making my own way in the world, Queenie. I admit I'm ambitious — but not at the expense of others. I'll probably never be as rich as my Dad was — I don't have the killer instinct.' They both smiled and their eyes met. As they stood in silence for those few short seconds, each sensed that their friendship had taken a new direction.

Several weeks later Warwick came to Queenie and asked her about Cricklewood.

Queenie looked up in surprise. 'Why?'

'I understand it's not being utilised. Jim mentioned Snowy had repaired the fences and there was reasonable feed there a few months back. I was reading about these new strains of cattle, Brahmans and Charolais which are big tough beasts and carry a lot of meat. Why don't you run some up there?'

'Oh, Warwick, I'm stretched to the limit at the bank. I'd have to hire more men, and the stock wouldn't be cheap.'

'The returns can be phenomenal, Queenie.'
Warwick pulled a chair round the desk to sit
beside her, spreading out the papers on the
desk.

Together they studied stock prices and pro-
jected financial returns. Queenie, deep in
thought, chewed the end of her pencil, and
Warwick was suddenly aware their heads were
almost touching as they leaned over the documents. A warmth spread through him and
he breathed in the sweet smell of Queenie's
hair.

'Well? What do you reckon?'

Queenie sat back. 'I must say it all sounds
pretty good. It's the outlay of capital that worries me.'

'I'd like to see Cricklewood. Couldn't we
take a couple of days' break and drive over
there?'

'It's been very dry, I suppose the roads are
okay. It'd be a bit of a rough trip,' mused
Queenie.

'C'mon, boss,' cajoled Warwick.

'I guess so ... I've been feeling restless since
the wedding. We'll leave in two days,' said
Queenie finally, pushing back her chair.

They were half a day's hard driving from Cricklewood. They'd taken the shorter back road
to save time, but it was in poor condition. The
few vehicles that had gone through during
the last wet season had left deep ruts, now
dried to cement hardness while the rest of
the road was axle–deep bull dust, as fine as
red talcum powder.

Warwick was driving and Queenie dozed in the heat, a rolled jacket under her head, cushioning her face against the window as the Land Rover lurched along.

The sun-baked landscape looked bloodshot, the red afternoon light bouncing off the orange and ochre rocks. Warwick rubbed his eyes and in the split second his attention wavered, a giant red shape loomed in front of them.

He swerved, instinctively wrenching the wheel to the side as the left fender crashed into the body of a huge kangaroo. There was the sound of bending metal as the roo staggered and the Land Rover veered into the loose dirt, the back wheels spinning as Warwick fought to stop it rolling. He spun the wheel and the car slid to a halt, crunching into a low boulder. The wheel lifted and buckled, leaving the tyre spinning uselessly in the air.

Warwick cursed and turned to Queenie, who was gripping the handlebar on the dashboard with one hand, the other covering her eyebrow which had been split. Blood dribbled between her fingers.

'Christ, are you okay, Queenie? I hit a roo — couldn't do much about it.' He bent forward lifting her hand away to examine her face.

'You did well. I thought we were going over. Thank God these are solid vehicles.'

They got down and examined the damage. Queenie took the first aid kit from under the front seat.

'Here, let me.' Warwick helped her to sit in the shade. Leaning against the side of the car, he swabbed her cut with antiseptic, crossing two bandaids over the cut. 'It doesn't look too bad, hope it doesn't leave a scar.'

'Thanks, Warwick. Well, step one in the outback emergency list is to boil the billy, I believe,' said Queenie.

She watched Warwick gather dry wood for the fire. Already a dull throb was hammering at the back of her head.

Warwick leaned down and snapped a solid small branch from a log then peeled off some dry bark. With a sudden exclamation, he leapt back and dropped the wood, cursing and holding his arm.

Queenie scrambled to her feet.

'Get the gun. It's a bloody snake!' shouted Warwick, not taking his eyes off the bronzed snake, curled tightly, its head lashing from side to side as it poised to strike again, its tongue flicking swiftly in and out.

Queenie aimed the gun and fired. Most of the snake disintegrated in the blast. 'Got it. A king brown snake... damned dangerous. Good thing it didn't get you, Warwick.'

Warwick held out his wrist with two red punctures. 'I'm afraid it did.' The laconic remark and casual grin hid the fear beginning to burn in the pit of his stomach.

Queenie caught her breath but spoke calmly. 'It'll be all right. Don't panic. Come back to the truck.'

The first-aid kit was basic. Warwick reached for the razor blade and made a small incision, letting his blood run onto the ground.

'Don't suck it, you might swallow the

poison,' said Queenie, quickly pushing the pile of twigs together, lighting the fire and putting on the billy of water.

'You think tea is going to help?' asked Warwick.

'I need boiling water. I'm going to make an Aboriginal antidote for snakebite. It's a long shot but Snowy told me about it years ago, and showed me the plants.'

She saw Warwick's raised eyebrow. 'Look, I know most people knock Aborigines, but they've survived out here a long time and Snowy knows a lot about the bush. I'm going to give it a go. We haven't much alternative, anyway.'

Warwick's eyes were closed. He opened them slightly. 'Okay.'

Queenie gazed about the bare landscape in the fading light. 'Warwick, breathe slowly, keep the arm down and stay as quiet as possible. I'll be back in a few minutes.'

Taking a small-handled axe from under the front seat, Queenie broke into a sprint, heading for the hazy, distant green-grey clump of scrub.

She found what she was looking for and using the axe, stripped papery bark from a small tree, and pulled spiked leaves from a nearby shrub, heedless of the thorns which ripped at her skin. She ran back to the car, her breath rasping in her chest and sweat running down her shirt.

Warwick was lying down, his eyes closed. He had been vomiting and was drowsy. The venom was taking effect.

Queenie built up the fire, shredded the leaves and dropped them into the boiling water. She put the bark at the edge of the fire to smoulder.

When the water in the billy had cooled she lifted Warwick's head, encouraging him to drink. He looked at her with glazed eyes and didn't seem to understand what she was saying. Gradually he managed to swallow, and struggled to focus on Queenie.

'Don't try to speak. Relax. Just sip. It's going to be all right.'

She then took the charred bark and rubbed it into a powdery ash. This she spread over the puncture wound on his wrist then bound it firmly with a bandage from the first-aid kit. Warwick closed his eyes again, beginning to drift into a feverish world suspended between reality and nightmare.

Queenie next turned her attention to the vehicle. She examined the wheel and axle sitting on the rock. The wheel looked out of alignment, but the suspension and axle looked in reasonable shape. She got out the jack and put it under the front bumper bar and cranked it until it would go no further. The axle had only lifted about half an inch off the rock.

'That's enough,' thought Queenie. 'If I can get it going in reverse, with luck it should slide down the rock.'

She climbed into the cabin very carefully, started the engine and slipped it into reverse gear, her left foot holding the clutch to the floor, her left hand on the handbrake.

'Right . . . let's go!' she shouted, and simultaneously let out the clutch, hit the accelerator and plunged the handbrake down.

The Land Rover's wheels dug into the bull dust, the vehicle shook, then suddenly moved backwards. The jack fell away, the axle came down with a thump, and with a crunching slide settled on its four wheels, swerving back onto the road.

Queenie didn't stop to rest. Dragging Warwick to the car she lifted him into the passenger seat with enormous difficulty. During the struggle he became semiconscious and was able to take some of his own weight, but collapsed across the seat once she had got him into the cabin.

Queenie fell into the dirt beside the car, her head throbbing. She sat panting for a few seconds, then dashed to the fire, smothered it with dirt, grabbed their gear and scrambled back into the car.

She slid behind the wheel, lifted Warwick's head onto her lap and started the engine.

They arrived at Cricklewood just before dawn. It had been a slow and cautious drive. The Land Rover limped and rattled on its damaged wheel and Queenie could feel the heat from Warwick's fever burning into her lap.

The homestead was as Millie had left it two months before — orderly and, apart from some dust, clean. Swiftly Queenie lit a kerosene lantern and by its light dragged Warwick from the car. He was still unconscious and Queenie knew she couldn't lift him into the house. Stripping a blanket from one of the beds, she wrapped it around him, then pulled off her belt and buckled it over the blanket and under his shoulders. She used the belt to drag him inside.

She raced to the two-way radio, then stopped in shock. It was gone. On the radio shelf was a note from Millie. *Radio faulty. Jim taken to Tingulla to repair.*

Queenie looked at the shelf and the note in stunned disbelief. She raised the lantern, as if more light might make the radio materialise, then lowered it again, and turned and walked dejectedly back to the kitchen. Warwick was lying helpless on the floor. There was no way she could contact the Flying Doctor or call in any help. Millie knew they'd be gone several days, so wouldn't miss them.

Warwick began to toss about, muttering incoherently. Queenie poured the dregs of the liquid from the billy into a mug and brought it to Warwick's lips.

He gagged then swallowed, his eyes fluttering open briefly. Queenie dragged him to a bedroom and onto the bed, then collapsed on a mattress she put on the floor beside him.

The sun rose and blazed down on the tin roof of the homestead. Queenie sat by Warwick, bathing his face with cool water. He was soaked with sweat, his skin was pale, his pulse rapid.

She sponged him down regularly with cold water from the tank at the back of the homestead, and spent hours sitting by his bed.

Eventually Queenie nodded off, her chin sinking onto her chest.

'Queenie,' called Warwick in a loud voice, and she awoke with a start. He was delirious, thrashing about on the bed. 'Queenie!' he called again.

'It's all right, Warwick, I'm here.' Struggling to keep him on the bed she lay across him, pinning him flat, and murmuring calming words.

Slowly he relaxed and finally slept. Straightening up, Queenie looked at him for a minute or two, then went to the kitchen to make some tea.

He slept fitfully but deeply, and his breathing slowly began to return to normal. Queenie smiled and leaned over to smooth a damp curl from his forehead, tucking the sheet around his shoulders. The crisis had passed.

He slept through the rest of the day and in the early evening Queenie heard him faintly call her name again. Hurrying to the bedroom she saw he was awake.

'You're here. What the hell happened to me?'

'Sshhh, take it easy. Don't you remember the snake? You've been a bit crook. We're at Cricklewood. Don't move. I'll make you some tea.'

'Christ, I feel like a truck has run over me. How did I get here?'

'No more questions. You're not better yet.'

Warwick didn't answer. The effort had tired him.

Warm weak tea revived him a little. 'I don't

think I want to go through that again. I guess I owe you one, Queenie. You saved me.'

'Thank Snowy for teaching me some bush medicine years back,' she smiled.

They stayed for several days, Warwick slowly regaining his strength. The poison had left him dehydrated and debilitated. The first time he got out of bed he fell over, and Queenie helped him back into bed admonishing, 'You don't realise how weak you are still. Take it slowly.'

On a cheerful sunny morning two days later, Warwick announced he was going outside. Queenie took his arm, supporting him, as they walked a short distance, both taking deep breaths of fresh, clear air. They didn't talk much, enjoying the sun and the companionable warmth of their linked arms.

Warwick slept most afternoons, moving into a chair in the kitchen as Queenie prepared their simple evening meals from tinned supplies.

'Like playing house, isn't it?' he laughed.

Queenie laughed with him. But she was conscious of him watching her and she was glad she didn't have to bathe his face or care for him so intimately any more.

One morning she woke up to the sound of banging metal and saw Warwick had rummaged in the shed, found some tools, and was working on the damaged wheel of the Land Rover.

'It's a bit makeshift, but it will get us where we want to go, I think.'

'All the way back to Tingulla?'

'No. You promised to show me over Cricklewood... so let's go.'

They took a packed lunch and Warwick drove, with Queenie guiding him over the property.

'You should certainly do something with this place, Queenie. Running some of those new breeds of cattle here could be a big money-making exercise.'

'I've already been through this with you, Warwick. They're expensive. I've had to outlay a lot of money at Tingulla.'

'So... bring in a partner — an investor.' He hesitated. 'If I could raise some money, would you consider taking me in with you?'

'Could you? Raise the money?'

'Possibly.'

They faced each other and Queenie suddenly felt that Warwick was about to say something else. He leaned towards her, but she turned away, confused and unsure. 'Let's talk about it when we get back to Tingulla. Do you think you're up to the trip?'

'Yep. Shall we make a move tomorrow?'

That night Queenie lay awake in the main bedroom unable to sleep. Warwick was either dreaming or aware she was awake, for he softly called her name. 'Queenie?' And again. 'Queenie...'

She hesitated. Was he dreaming or did he need her? Wrapping a blanket around herself she padded quietly into his room. Faint moonlight shone through the narrow, curtainless window. She could make out Warwick's shape in his bed.

She was about to turn away when he spoke. 'Queenie. Come here a minute.'

'Do you feel all right?' she moved closer to his bed.

'No.'

'What's wrong?' Concerned, she sat at the edge of his bed and reached out to touch his forehead. He grasped her hand and pulled her closer to him, encircling her shoulders with his other arm.

'Queenie...' He pulled her head down and pressed his mouth to hers. For an instant she began to kiss him back then wrenched upright and jumped to her feet.

'Warwick! What do you think you're doing?'

'Queenie, I've wanted you for so long...'

'No!' She ran from the room and slammed her door.

It was a restless, unhappy night, and she finally fell asleep at dawn. She slept with blankets and pillow over her head, hiding from the world.

Warwick tapped her lightly on the shoulder and Queenie angrily flung back the covers and sat up.

Warwick was dressed and silently holding out a mug of steaming tea. 'Tea. The porridge is cooking. I've packed up all the gear. We can hit the road as soon as you're ready.'

She said nothing, but drank the tea, staring at him with brittle green eyes dancing with angry sparks. Her hair was tousled and clothes rumpled. Warwick thought she looked adorable.

She handed him the empty mug. 'Thanks. I'll get dressed then.' Her tone was cold and Warwick left the room.

She washed in cold water, changed her shirt and joined Warwick in the kitchen where he had breakfast set out. They ate in silence. Warwick seemed relaxed and unconcerned as if the previous night had never happened.

'Maybe he's going to pretend it was all a dream, that he was delirious and didn't know what he was doing,' she thought. She turned furiously away from the sink, dropping her bowl with a clatter. 'Warwick, about last night . . . '

He held up his hand, ignoring Queenie's icy voice. 'I'm sorry. I shouldn't have tried to con you. But it's so hard to get through that defensive wall you've built around yourself. I don't apologise for the fact I find you a desirable and appealing woman, though.'

Queenie looked down, disarmed but not totally mollified.

He leaned down and peered into her lowered face and made no move to touch her. 'What I was saying yesterday about going into partnership with you — I'd like to do that. I can raise the money. But I don't want us to be just partners. I want you to marry me, Queenie.'

A small gasp escaped her and she looked up at him. A hopeful smile hovered at the corners of his mouth and his grey eyes were full of love and longing.

She turned away. 'I don't know what to say . . . Warwick, this is all wrong . . . '

'Why, Queenie? I think we're well suited. Couldn't you love me?'

'I don't know... I... ' Flustered, she began washing the breakfast bowls.

Warwick dried them and replaced them in the cupboard. 'Think about it. I won't pressure you. We can go on as before.'

'Oh no, we can't!' exploded Queenie. 'It would be impossible.'

Why was life so complicated? Things had been going so smoothly. Why did people's emotions keep getting in the way? She didn't want any part of this. She had a job to do and a life to get on with. 'I'm not ready to get married. I don't know you... as a man, I mean.'

Warwick reached out and grasped her by the shoulders, slowly turning her around. Gently he touched her cheek. 'So get to know me, Queenie.'

She stood motionless and Warwick softly kissed one cheek, then the other, then the top of her head. 'Let's go home.'

Chapter Fourteen

Millie knew something was up the moment they returned. She fussed over Warwick, cooking him big meals to build up his strength, but was aware of the tension in the air between him and Queenie.

At times Queenie was aloof or coolly businesslike, but Millie would catch her eyes following Warwick. He, on the other hand, seemed unperturbed by her fluctuating moods, and sometimes teased her gently, making her smile despite herself, and a swift look would pass between them before Queenie turned away.

Warwick was true to his promise and made no demands on Queenie, although he did go out of his way to be attentive, charming and witty. He then announced he wanted a couple of weeks off to return to the West to see his family and business associates about financial matters. Queenie agreed, and Warwick flew to Perth.

Queenie didn't like to admit it, but Tingulla seemed very quiet and empty without Warwick about the place. Riding Nareedah one morning she came across Ernie, the young rouseabout, and one of the jackaroos riding along the northern boundary fence. 'Everything all right, Ernie?'

The boys touched their hats with one finger in respect as they reined in their horses. 'Gotta problem with some of them pregnant ewes down by the new bore. Have to talk to the boss when he gets back.' Ernie gave her a cheery broad grin showing large white teeth.

'What's the problem? Maybe I can help.'

'S'all right. I'll talk to Warwick 'bout it. See ya.' They nodded and rode off.

Queenie wheeled Nareedah about. 'Talk to the boss! I'm still boss of Tingulla.' She kicked Nareedah unnecessarily firmly and galloped away.

Within days the monotony was broken by the arrival of Sarah, flushed with happiness and bubbling over with the details of life as a new bride in Sydney. Queenie spent a day with her at the Quinns'.

'John's away for a week looking at property up the coast so I thought I'd come and visit Mum,' she explained. 'Oh, Queenie, I'm so happy. Married life is such a ball! Come and stay with us in Sydney. We can shop and go to the theatre — and John has some lovely single friends,' she teased.

'Sarah, stop matchmaking. I'm doing just fine.'

'Why don't you go overseas? You could find yourself an exciting man,' persisted Sarah. 'You'll never meet anyone but boring old bushies staying at Tingulla.'

'They're not all boring. And I don't need to go away to catch a man, Sarah... in fact I had a proposal just a couple of weeks ago.'

'Oh, sure. Who? Dreary Michael O'Rourke, I suppose.'

'No, actually. Warwick asked me to marry him.'

Sarah's jaw dropped, then a grin spread across her freckled face.

'You're kidding?'

'No. And why should that be so funny?'

'Oh, Queenie... it's wonderful. I mean, it's so obvious. There he was, right under our noses... handsome, fun, smooth, and knows the land too! He's perfect for you! I just thought Warwick was the type to stay a bachelor for years. Have you said yes?' bubbled Sarah.

Queenie suddenly regretted mentioning Warwick's proposal. 'Well, no. It came as a bit of a surprise to me too. I'd never thought of him other than a business partner and friend; and he is a bit older than me.'

'That makes him perfect for you! Queenie, I don't want you to get mad, but as a friend I have to mention this... he's not marrying you for your money, is he? I mean, managing Tingulla is one thing. Marrying the owner is another.'

'It had crossed my mind,' confessed Queenie. 'But he's gone back home to talk to his family. Apparently there's some money due to him from what was left of his inheritance. And he says he can raise a lot of capital. He wants to go into partnership to develop Cricklewood ... to run cattle.'

'Well then, that proves he isn't worming his way into Tingulla. You'll be partners and that's what marriage is all about.'

Queenie laughed at Sarah's pontificating. 'It's all right for you, you have the perfect man, the perfect marriage, the perfect life.'

'I know,' said Sarah seriously. 'Queenie, there's one important thing you haven't mentioned. Do you love him?'

Queenie's smile faded. 'I don't know, Sarah. It's not the love I ... imagined. But I like being with him, he makes me laugh a lot. I respect him, and I've missed him while he's been away in Perth. Is that love?'

'Only you can answer that one, Queenie,' said Sarah gently. 'Don't get married for the wrong reasons. Let's see Mum — I think lunch is ready.'

Sarah turned away, suddenly unsure about advising Queenie. She could see Queenie was lonely and vulnerable. Sarah liked Warwick but she wished Queenie was head over heels in love and had no doubts about him. Sarah sighed. How lucky she was to have found John. If only Queenie could know what deep, passionate love was really like. Not everyone was lucky enough to find it.

That night Queenie drove home through the starlight, thinking similar thoughts. Sarah didn't know it, but Queenie had once found

242

true and passionate love, and all it had brought her was pain and unhappiness. Perhaps settling for life with Warwick would be the answer. They understood each other, she knew they would get along smoothly, and they shared a lot in common. She even had to admit to herself that she did find Warwick attractive. The brief moment their lips had touched tingled in her memory. She had forgiven him for his devious attempt to kiss her that night. He had behaved impeccably ever since, although he didn't stop casting longing looks in her direction, his grey eyes clearly betraying his intentions.

He wanted her, she knew that. On occasions when their arms touched or hands brushed, Queenie felt her own body responding to the magnetism of his physical appeal.

Sarah's comments about him marrying her for Tingulla had struck a chord in Queenie. She would wait and see what he had to say when he returned.

In America TR continued to learn and develop his horse training skills, proving to Clayton Hindmarsh that his decision to hire the handsome Aussie had been a good one. Clayton insisted on treating TR as a member of the family, not just an employee.

Although TR appreciated his privileged position, he felt uncomfortable. He preferred the way they did things at home, where the working men led their own lives away from the homestead and the boss's life. The racial situation also bothered him. Aboriginal stockmen were treated with respect for they were skilful bushmen and great horsemen. In town they mightn't drink at the same pub or mix socially, but around the campfire they were equals. The blacks working about Bon Vite were servants — treated well, but regarded as inferiors. And Clayton had taken TR aside and explained that, 'It just wasn't seemly for him to mix with the coloured folk'.

TR tried to keep to himself as much as possible and spent many hours with the horses and talking to old Tommy about races, remedies and training tips. Clayton kept telling TR he seemed keener on horses than girls, which according to the American, wasn't healthy.

Privately, TR did prefer horses to the fluttering, empty-headed females who attended Mrs Hindmarsh's endless parties. Clayton's 'baby daughter', Virginia, had visited from the expensive ladies college she attended, and while she was very sweet and pretty, TR found conversation with her ran dry very swiftly.

'Ginny' was twenty, blonde, tiny yet buxom, with china blue eyes that reminded TR of the little dolls on top of the sticks you won at the fair. After she had listened to him in rapt attention while he talked about several of the horses, TR suggested she might like to go riding with him.

'Well, I'd love to see them darlin' horses, but I wouldn't care to go riding them, thank you all the same,' she answered sweetly.

'Young ladies get past that horsey stage, TR,' trilled Mrs Hindmarsh, overhearing him.

'But Ginny would love to watch you work out the horses, TR. Wouldn't you, Ginny?'

'If you say so, Mamma,' replied Ginny.

TR stiffened. 'Aw, I reckon that'd be a bit boring for you. I'll see you round.' He excused himself and slipped away before Mrs Hindmarsh could come up with another suggestion for more tennis or croquet followed by drinks and a few friends dropping by.

A vision of Queenie galloping across the manicured grounds of Bon Vite flashed into his mind and tugged at his heart.

Clayton noticed TR seemed a little despondent. 'I fancy you're a bit homesick, TR. How'd you like to make a quick business trip back to Australia for me?'

'Hey, I'd really like that. What kind of business?'

'I'm looking for property. I want to set up a base in Australia and run cattle, train racehorses ... so I'll need two places. I looked at that Scone area once — nice land. But if I go out there and start nosing around, the property values are going to treble. But if you made a few inquiries ... that'd be a different matter. Frankly, TR, I'm hoping you might eventually run the racing side of it for me — if it all works out.'

'Sounds great to me. I'll look around for cattle property first — I realise I still have a lot to learn about the horse training side of things.'

'You're a fast learner, TR. You've got a natural gift — I'm not worried.'

*

It was a lazy Sunday afternoon and the heat had been bothering Queenie, so she had slung a string hammock between two shady trees in the garden and retreated with a pillow and a book. The gentle swaying in the dappled light soon sent her into a light sleep and the book fell from her hand.

She was dreaming that hundreds of butterflies were alighting on her, and in a half-awake state she flicked at her face and felt something in her hair. She opened her eyes to find Warwick staring down at her.

'Oh! Hello.' She tried to sit up and was suddenly aware of being covered. Queenie looked down to find she was completely smothered in paper. Warwick was holding a wad of money and continued to sprinkle the notes over her.

Queenie burst out laughing. 'What are you doing?'

'You looked cold... I told you I was going to get some money. We can start looking at Brahman bulls any time...'

'Warwick, there's thousands of dollars here...' A fresh breeze suddenly lifted the money off Queenie's legs and it blew over the grass.

'Warwick... you're crazy!'

Laughing, they skipped about the garden picking up the bills.

Queenie handed him the money. 'Here, put this in the safe and we'll talk business tomorrow.'

'It's yours... partner,' said Warwick, pushing the money back at her. He stared at her then picked up his hat, 'I need a cup of tea. Been a long trip.'

When Queenie came to a decision she acted on it without delay. That evening, as Millie took away the dessert plates, Queenie pushed back her chair. 'Millie, please bring us coffee in the study. Come along, Warwick — we have a business deal to talk over.'

Warwick settled into the comfortable leather chair, crossing one foot on his knee and watching Queenie with an amused expression.

Queenie stacked papers in a neat pile on the desk. 'I've read as much as I could find about these new cattle breeds, I called a few people and I think it's a good idea. I spoke to the bank and Frank will see us any time we can get into town. He likes the idea. You're right, Cricklewood is an asset that's not being utilised. I'm willing to take the plunge and try and make it a profitable cattle run, and I accept your offer to come in as an equal partner.'

She paused, trying to remain businesslike and keep her face expressionless. 'As to your other offer... I accept that, too. I think we could get on well together and make it work.'

Warwick's amusement suddenly faded. He hastily stood and leaning over the desk, looked at her intensely. 'You're accepting my proposal of marriage, Miss Hanlon?'

'The offer is still open, I take it?' she teased.

'Oh yes,' said Warwick quietly, moving around the desk and taking her hand to help her to her feet. Queenie gazed steadily up at him.

He took her in his arms and lowered his face to hers, murmuring, 'May I?' He kissed her long and hard, tightening his arms about her, pulling her to his body.

Queenie felt nothing.

Warwick drew back and stared at her, his eyes hard and hurt. Dropping his arms he turned on his heel and left the room, flinging over his shoulder, 'You're a bloody challenge, Queenie. I'll give you that.'

Queenie didn't answer. She closed her eyes, swallowing hard.

No more was said about getting married. They went into the bank manager and also saw Hamish Barton, Queenie's solicitor, who drew up a partnership agreement; and they deposited an equal share of money in the new Cricklewood account.

Over a sandwich and a glass of beer at the pub they discussed how they would begin to crossbreed the new Brahman bulls with Hereford cattle.

'There's a stud down in Victoria who started importing Brahman bulls. Took him years to get them in and established, but he's now selling. That's where we go,' said Warwick.

'Those bulls will be costly and we'll have to buy a decent mob of Hereford breeding stock.'

Warwick drained his beer. 'You end up with a tougher beast and more meat to the pound. It'll be worth it, Queenie.'

*

The next morning Millie came to Queenie in her study. 'The generator's conked out. Sounded like something blew up, Queenie.'

'Better get Jim to look at it quick smart, Millie.'

'There's not a bloke around the place. They're all out.'

'Always the way,' sighed Queenie. 'Can it wait?'

'We were pumping water into the house tanks from the creek. The generator smells like it's burning.'

'I'd better have a look at it.'

An hour later Queenie was still tinkering with the generator motor. She'd burned her hand, oil was smeared on her clothes, face and hands. She worked noisily with a spanner, stripping down parts and cursing aloud.

She didn't hear Warwick approach. At the moment he walked through the door the spanner slipped, and her knuckles slammed against metal, tearing at the skin. She yelped in pain, and kicked furiously at the machinery.

'Temper, temper,' admonished Warwick.

Queenie stood, rubbing her bleeding hand. Warwick picked up the spanner and looked at her angrily. 'Why the hell couldn't this have waited? Why do you have to do everything yourself, Queenie? You don't have to keep proving you're better at everything than everyone else — we all know that.'

'Don't you shout at me!'

'Why do you try to be so tough all the time?' Warwick stepped forward and shook her by the shoulders. 'God, you make me mad. Wake up to yourself, Queenie. Stop fighting the world.'

An expression of such hurt and sadness flashed across Queenie's face that Warwick's anger evaporated. 'I'm sorry, Queenie. Did you hurt yourself?' He turned over her wrist and impulsively kissed her where she was cut.

Wordlessly Queenie reached out to him and Warwick gently wrapped his arms about her, holding her close to him. He stroked her hair and knew at last he'd broken through to the real Queenie. She lifted her face to his and kissed him willingly.

Queenie told Millie privately that she was marrying Warwick. She made no fuss about the blunt announcement and it seemed to Millie she could have been telling her to stock up the larder. 'Nothing will change, Millie. This will make things much easier for me. Warwick will continue to help me run Tingulla, and he's invested in Cricklewood so we can get that property operating too.'

'You going to be happy?'

'Well, I hope so, Millie,' smiled Queenie.

'You love him?'

Queenie turned away. 'What's love, Millie?'

'I thought you knew that, Queenie.'

'Maybe I did, once. But I'm choosing companionship, friendship, trust, and a man who'll stick by me and share the load life brings along. I think that's more important.'

Millie reached for the kettle. 'It's your life, Queenie. Warwick's a good bloke, that's for sure.' There was a small silence as she filled the kettle. 'So when do I start cooking for the big day?'

'We're not having a big Tingulla wedding, Millie. I don't want any fuss. We're just going to have a quiet ceremony.'

'You're not getting married at Tingulla? Your mumma wouldn't like that. Why, Queenie?'

'I did that for Sarah. I don't have any family, Colin never contacts me . . . it wouldn't be the same, Millie. I just couldn't face all that. We're going into the registry office in Brisbane, then somewhere nice for a bit of a honeymoon.'

'Sounds like you're running away to me.' Millie slammed the kettle onto the Aga hotplate with a loud bang.

Queenie put her arms around her. 'Oh, come on Millie. I'm being sensible for a change. I thought you'd be pleased.'

Millie hugged the slim young woman with the girlish shiny braids. 'Queenie — all I want is for you to be happy. You deserve some happiness and I hope Warwick will be good for you.'

Millie bustled about making tea but her heart ached. She knew who Queenie should be marrying, and she wished with all her heart that she could change the way Queenie's life was working out.

Warwick went to Sydney on business, details of which he didn't reveal to Queenie. While there, he broke the news to Colin of their planned wedding. He explained that he and Queenie were also entering a business relationship as well as a personal one. 'I'm investing in a scheme to breed Brahman bulls at Cricklewood. Some new blood is needed in the beef industry.'

'We've always been in wool. Sounds a bit of a gamble,' said Colin non-committally.

'I just want you to know I have a few plans of my own. I'm not marrying Queenie for Tingulla.'

Colin sipped his beer. 'Not much, mate,' he thought to himself. But the knot of anger in the pit of his stomach eased. Warwick was not the threat TR would have been. He knew Warwick's weakness and he knew a man like Warwick would never change. His trump card was the fact Queenie didn't know Warwick like he did. He'd bide his time — a leopard doesn't change its spots. Forcing a smile, he put out his hand. 'Congratulations.'

'I'm glad you're pleased. I hope you'll always consider Tingulla your home too, Colin.'

'Oh, I do, I do,' laughed Colin. 'But for the moment, Sydney is my town.' He chuckled again, a bitter cynical laugh which made Warwick look at him with a puzzled expression. He ordered two more beers. Colin had taken the news better than he thought.

Queenie was surprised, then pleased, at Colin's attitude and impulsively asked him to be a witness at their wedding.

'I'm not going all the way to Brisbane for a five minute ceremony in a registry office.'

'I suppose it's not very practical.' Queenie tried to hide her disappointment.

'What are you doing with yourself?'

'I get my results soon. Then it's bye-bye

Australia. I'm going abroad with some friends for a while.'

'How are you paying for that?'

'Don't tell me you've forgotten your little brother's birthday? I collect some of the money Dad left me next birthday.'

'Don't fritter it all away, Colin ... '

'Don't you tell me what to do, Queenie. You'll soon have a hubby to boss around, so leave me alone.'

Queenie hung up the phone in exasperation. Colin hadn't changed at all.

'Colin won't be able to make it to the wedding,' Queenie said that evening. 'He's right. It's a long way to go for such a brief ceremony. I was going to ask Sarah to come... but I suppose if we're keeping it simple, then let's not tell anyone and just do it.'

'We'll elope. Just the two of us. Then everyone will say, "how romantic!" Warwick hugged her. 'Let's do it soon. This waiting to make love to you is driving me crazy.' He nuzzled her hair.

Queenie squirmed out of his arms. 'Just a little while, Warwick. Be patient.'

TR stretched and breathed a deep sigh. It had been a long and tiring flight but he felt exhilarated. As soon as he stepped out of Kingsford Smith International Terminal he looked up at the Sydney sky — bright clear blue, even in the city. He grinned and headed for the domestic departures to get on a flight to Brisbane.

He had a rough idea of the areas he wanted to look at but decided to drive to Longreach, talk to stock and station agents and find out which properties were on the market, and who might consider selling if the offer was good enough.

As soon as he parked the dusty rental car in the familiar street in Longreach, TR felt at home. People strolled along at a leisurely pace, always finding time to stop and talk a while.

He was greeted warmly by the plump, balding publican when he checked into the Empire Hotel, his favourite pub. 'Long time no see, TR. You stayin'? Or going back to Yankee land?'

'Just staying the night for the moment. Going bush to check out a few things.'

'Right you are. Room eight. Buy you a beer later.'

TR picked up the keys and his bag and headed upstairs.

He was tired, but he pulled out a map and began studying in detail the areas he planned to look over. He was drawing a ring around several properties when the name Tingulla leapt out at him. It would be so easy to just stop by and see Millie and Jim... Who was he kidding? It was Queenie who drew him to Tingulla. He could see the homestead in his mind and imagined Queenie riding out to meet him on Nareedah. He leaned back in the cane chair staring at the timber-lined wall of his room.

He felt Queenie's presence so strongly. She must be back from overseas. She was back at Tingulla, he felt it.

If he could just see her — confront her once and for all — then maybe she would stop haunting him. Or perhaps he could even convince her they were meant to be together.

He looked at the map again, then folded it up, realising that he had always intended to visit Tingulla. TR ran through the scenario in his mind — he'd see Queenie and simply take her in his arms and they'd never be apart again.

Whistling, he headed for the bathroom. He needed a shower and a good sleep.

Queenie and Warwick decided not to tell anyone they were getting married until they returned from the wedding. They were postponing their honeymoon for a while because Warwick had promised to show Queenie his favourite parts of Europe in the northern spring. They swore Millie to secrecy and made their plans.

Warwick went ahead to Brisbane to make the official arrangements and buy a ring. Queenie drove into Longreach and checked into the Empire Hotel, planning to drive on to Brisbane the next day.

That evening she walked into the dining room to be greeted with a cry of welcome. Sitting at the next table was Dingo McPherson. They hugged each other warmly and Queenie joined him.

'I was going to give you a yell since I was in the neighbourhood. Thought I'd stop by and see Warwick.'

'He's in Brisbane.'

'Well, what luck running into you instead. How are things going, girl?'

'Dingo, you're just the man I want to talk to... what do you know about Brahman cattle?' Briefly Queenie explained her plans for Cricklewood and found Dingo, as always, a source of information, wisdom and helpful advice.

They chatted and laughed their way through dinner, enjoying each other's company. Dingo delighted in the presence of a beautiful young woman and his respect for Queenie was immense. He understood the deep love she held for her land and admired the way she cared for and planned to develop Tingulla.

To Queenie, Dingo had always been a hero, a living legend she had come to know as a trusted friend. She loved his battered face topped with thick white hair, and his merry blue eyes. What an old charmer, she thought as he paid her compliment after compliment.

'So... are you pleased I sent you Warwick Redmond? He's working out okay then?'

Queenie grinned at him. 'You might say that. We're getting married.'

Dingo tipped back in his chair, roaring with laughter. 'Well, I'll be blowed... that's bloody marvellous. Now listen, Queenie, I swear that was the last thing on my mind when I suggested he go to Tingulla!'

'Mine, too. But well... it just seemed to work out that way.'

Dingo stuck out his great paw of a hand. 'I hope you'll both be very happy. When's the big day? I hope I'm invited.'

Queenie looked down. 'Well, actually ...
we're not telling anyone. I didn't want a lot
of fuss ... I'm driving over to Brisbane in the
morning. We're just going to be by ourselves.
Now don't let the bush telegraph get hold of
our news. Keep it to yourself.'

'I understand. I'll keep it under my hat. Give
Warwick my best. Good luck to you both. Now,
how about a drink in the bar to celebrate?'

'No thanks, Dingo. I'm tired and I have
a long drive tomorrow.' She kissed him and
went upstairs, down the narrow hallway past
Room Eight, and turning the key in the door
of Room Eleven she closed the door behind
her.

TR slept off the effects of his jet lag and the
long drive and, feeling refreshed, headed into
the bar. Several people nodded to him, but
it was Dingo that TR spotted and sat beside.

Dingo slapped him on the back. 'Struth! A
man can't have a quiet beer without running
into every man and his dog. How's it going?'

The hours passed and the empty glasses
stretched along the bar in front of them as
TR related his experiences in America and
revealed the real reason he was back.

'Few good places about. Pricey, but not to
someone like Hindmarsh,' said Dingo. 'So, he
might end up in racehorses, eh? You're moving
out of the brumby days, TR.'

TR downed the last of his middy and didn't
answer, remembering the brumby roundup
when he realised he'd fallen in love with
Queenie. 'Yeah, I guess so. Queenie and I

never did bring back the brumbies that time,'
he said aloud but more to himself.

'Queenie... by God, do y'know she's getting
married? And you can thank me,' Dingo
laughed, his words slurred, his promise to keep
the news to himself forgotten.

Slowly TR placed his glass on the bar. 'Married? She found some bloke overseas then?'

'No bloody fear. She's marrying Warwick
Redmond, the fellow I sent to manage Tingulla... I'd say he managed very well!' Dingo
hiccupped over his joke.

'Who is he?' TR could hardly speak.

'What's that?... Oh, don't worry, TR, he's
got a few bob of his own. He's going into
business with her, he's not a penniless nohoper. Don't you worry. They're going to do
real well. Struth, I'd better shut up, no one's
supposed to know.'

'Another drink, gents?'

'A double Scotch,' said TR.

He threw back the drink in a gulp and turned
to Dingo. 'I'll be seeing you, Dingo. Got to
hit the road early.'

They shook hands and TR walked from the
noisy bar, his shoulders sagging, seeing no one.

Despite a slight hangover TR checked out
early the next morning, paying his bill and
handing over the key.

'Be seeing you, TR. Good luck in America.'

'Thanks... Oh, hell, I've left my jacket in
the room. I'll just race back and get it.'

He dumped his bag by the desk and sprinted
up the stairs.

As he disappeared from sight Queenie came in the front door, her cheeks pink and her hair windswept. She stood beside TR's abandoned bag without noticing it. 'Morning. Gorgeous morning out there. There's a cool breeze, but it's going to be a scorcher later. I went for a walk. Not many people up yet.'

'No, you're an early bird. Breakfast's on if you're ready.'

'You bet. Thanks.' Queenie turned and walked into the dining room.

As the glass doors swung shut behind her, TR reappeared with his jacket hooked on his thumb over his shoulder. He picked up his bag, nodded to the man behind the desk and walked into the street.

II

1970s
Cricklewood

Chapter Fifteen

The piebald pony trotted obediently round the stockyard and the tiny figure in the saddle bounced joyously up and down, shrieking with laughter.

'More, Snowy . . . more . . . ,' pleaded the little girl, as Snowy stepped forward to lift the four-year-old down from the horse.

'No more, Sassy. Millie's got your lunch ready.'

He sat the child on the railing and turned around. She jumped onto his back, linking her arms around the old Aborigine's neck to be piggy-backed to the house.

Millie smiled when she saw Snowy jogging past the herb garden to the kitchen with the child cajoling him to go faster.

She opened the screen door. 'Saskia, you little monkey, you're going to wear poor Snowy out. Come and wash your hands, your mum and dad are waiting for you.'

Snowy grinned at the tiny streak of energy who dropped from his back and charged past them, her dark curls bobbing as she ran.

'She loves the horses. Just like her mumma.'

'Don't I know it, Snowy. You have to watch her every minute or she's down there in the yards. I daren't turn my back on the little devil.'

Saskia skidded to the doors of the dining room, wiping her wet hands on her shirt and shaking her curls before stepping sedately into the sun-filled room.

'And about time, Miss. We've been waiting for our lunch. I hope you've washed your hands.'

'Yes, Dad,' she replied earnestly, slipping into her chair opposite her mother.

Queenie smiled fondly at her across the table. 'I bet I know where you've been.'

Warwick passed a thick slice of Millie's home-baked bread to his daughter. 'You spend too much time with the horses. I think you should start some schoolwork.' He spoke seriously, but burst out laughing at the immediate interest and enthusiasm this generated. 'Oh, Saskia, everything is an adventure to you, isn't it?'

Queenie joined in the laughter. 'Sas, perhaps we could start proper lessons, maybe an hour a day. I'll start you off, then you'll be ready for School of the Air next year. We'll practise reading and writing.'

'Just Saskia and Mummy?' asked the young girl.

'Just the two of us, but it's work time, not play time,' said Queenie firmly.

Satisfied, the child nodded and began eating her pumpkin soup.

'She learns a lot from Millie,' said Warwick. 'She was helping her in the kitchen shelling peas and learning sums.'

Warwick watched his daughter devote her attention to her meal. How like Queenie she looked. She had his dark curls and large grey eyes, but her mother's features. She was going to be tall, like him, and a beauty, like her mother.

He saw Queenie gazing fondly at Saskia. 'What are you thinking, Queenie?'

'How lucky we are to have Saskia.'

Warwick leaned over and ruffled the child's hair. 'Luck had nothing to do with it. She's perfect, like everything else you do, Queenie, I knew you'd have a gorgeous baby.'

'I'm not a baby,' said Saskia firmly.

'No, you're not any more,' said Queenie, with a sigh as Millie appeared with the cold lamb salad.

Where had the years gone? Queenie had become pregnant a few months after she and Warwick married, which meant they had never taken their honeymoon trip to Europe. However, Saskia had brought them both so much joy. Queenie and Warwick had a calm and happy existence. If at times Queenie longed for some passion, excitement or adventure in her life, she pushed the thought away. She had to keep reminding herself how lucky she was to have a husband who cherished her, adored their child and, apart from periodic business trips to Sydney or Brisbane, shared each day with her.

Maybe that was what niggled at the back of her mind. Warwick never took her away with him, telling her it was all boring business meetings and paperwork. She knew he saw Colin when he went to Sydney, but she often wondered what he did do when away from her.

They had taken two trips back to Neptune Island with Saskia, who had learnt to swim like a fish in a matter of days and had won the heart of Alf, who still ran his island kingdom. Yet . . . always in the bottom of Queenie's heart there was a question mark. What would her life have been like had she married TR? What did their child look like?

Queenie shook her head, her long thick hair tumbling about her shoulders — she mustn't revive such thoughts. Instead she headed for the stables. 'Nareedah, you fat lazy old girl. Let's go for a ride.'

Colin had settled into the Sydney social scene once he returned from his eighteen-month sojourn around the high spots and flesh pots of England and Europe.

He had no desire to look for work on the land. He had scoffed at Queenie's suggestion of running Cricklewood, and was not going to be 'a hired hand' at Tingulla. He refused to consider working at someone's property, no matter how prestigious. 'I have a general degree which I can use for anything. Maybe I'll look for a job in the city.'

In fact, being a playboy had a lot more appeal.

One night in Chequers Nightclub in Sydney he was introduced to a darkly voluptuous and exotic Italian woman called Andina.

Colin guessed she was several years older than he, and was immediately attracted to her sexy looks, sophistication, and worldliness. He quickly learned she came from a very wealthy family. She was there at a family birthday dinner and her parents, Signor Alfredo and Signora Maria Camboni, made no attempt to conceal their wealth. They were flamboyantly dressed, and mother and daughter had arrived with lush fur coats slung casually over their shoulders. Any patch of bare skin had a piece of jewellery draped over it.

Colin and his companion, a friend from university days who knew the Cambonis, were invited to join their table. As soon as politeness allowed, Colin asked Andina to dance.

'Please, I prefer to be called Dina,' she replied, extending her hand as he rose to lead her to the dancefloor.

As they danced, he enjoyed the sensation of her soft fullness in his arms, and he pulled her close to his body while they talked casually. He told her he had just returned from Europe and now found Australia, especially the bush, boring.

'You are a farm boy?'

'Not exactly. My late father owned one of the biggest properties in Queensland.'

'And you do not want to go back to ... the bush?'

'I'm having too much fun here.' He tightened his arm about her as he twirled her round the dance floor.

'Ah, you are a playboy!'

'What about you? Do you like to play too? Or are you married, or ... spoken for?'

'No. The family are hoping I will marry a family friend in Rome, but I am not interested, so I lead a busy social life here. My father spoils me. However, my mother would like to see me married — to her I am almost a spinster!'

'You are a very glamorous spinster — you must have admirers all over Sydney. If I were you, I'd make the most of it. Unless your parents are very strict?'

They were talking light-heartedly, but a different conversation was happening between their bodies — each felt the physical pull of desire as they touched.

'I am an adult woman; I lead my own life. I have a very nice apartment at Vaucluse. My father is very generous.'

Colin leaned closer to murmur in her ear. 'Perhaps I'll come and visit you — I live in Double Bay. Could we meet some time?'

Dina pulled away and gazed at the handsome young man. A smile curved at her dark red mouth. 'There is no time like the present. Shall we leave now? Your place or mine?' she laughed.

They excused themselves and left separately, meeting outside. Dina handed him the keys to her convertible parked at the kerb saying, 'My place, I think.' All pretence dropped away and she rested her hand on his thigh as he drove. Once in her plush apartment, they fell into bed and made love, and slept, and made love again, then arose at midday and went out for lunch.

From then on the two began exploring the thrills of hedonistic living and the seamy side of Sydney's high life — as well as living it up in the city's favourite nightspots and expensive restaurants — the bills paid by Andina's indulgent father.

'He never asks what I do with his money, so long as I am happy. He knows I'll eventually have to settle down and be a good Italian wife. But for the moment I am a liberated Australian girl.'

Colin moved into Dina's plush penthouse. He kept his flat in Double Bay as a private bolt hole, but rarely used it, although officially he still lived there.

'Why not rent it out? You spend all your time with me, anyway,' suggested Dina.

Colin laughed, telling her he kept a secret mistress there and besides, he didn't need the money.

'Then you pay some of these restaurant bills,' snapped Dina, throwing the sheaf of dockets at him. 'This month my father is complaining I'm spending too much. He wouldn't like to know I am keeping a lover-boy.'

That struck Colin's ego. He flung himself on Dina, pinning her across the rumpled satin sheets on the bed. 'You tell your old man you're not playing house with some gigolo, but the son of Tingulla Station.'

'What is Tingulla... some chunk of dirt in the middle of nowhere?'

'Listen, Dina... one day I'll own Tingulla and then I'll show you what class and style and money can do.'

'Darling, I couldn't live in never-never land! Stay here and play with me... ' She wound her arms about Colin, not liking the hard angry glint in his eyes. 'If you really are a rich country boy... maybe you should come home and talk to my father so he can approve of you.'

'And then what?' asked Colin suspiciously.

Dina began nuzzling his ear. 'Then Papa will know you're not after my money and he will keep paying the bills, *caro mio* ... '

The fortunes of Bon Vite — the beautiful and elaborate horse stud which was one of Kentucky's finest, in a state renowned for its prestigious and profitable estates — had gone from rich to megarich.

The classic white colonial mansion with its columns and elegant portico, was set at the centre of the land. A circular drive swept up to it through manicured lawns and gardens studded with ancient, imported English trees. Several full-time black gardeners kept the grounds immaculate. Bent double in the heat of the day, they plucked out the first shoots of a troublesome weed or an unsightly drooping flower.

As far as the eye could see, rolling green fields, neatly hemmed by freshly painted white fences, housed beautifully groomed horses.

These costly but money-making animals and their keepers lived in stucco Spanish-style stables whose bright red roofs added a splash of colour to the green and white landscape.

Water was abundant, spilling from fountains, shining in ornamental lakes and special horse ponds, or sprayed from the hoses constantly washing out the cobbled floors of the yards and stables. The property looked and smelled of success, money and permanence.

Clayton Hindmarsh had included TR in his largesse, giving him bonus payments and a share in the profits of the horses he helped train.

TR found these payments difficult to accept graciously. He knew he had worked hard and struck it lucky with several of the difficult horses, getting them to perform and win when no one else could. But he sensed the money and gifts lavished on him were binding him to the family in the hope that he would propose to their daughter, Virginia.

Ginny had blossomed from the coquettish student he'd first met, into a demure young woman. However, beneath her pliable and soft exterior, TR suspected, was a will of iron. This was a girl used to getting her way with feminine guile.

Ginny was sweet, gentle and amiable. While she played the coy Southern belle, TR had no doubts she'd leap into bed if he suggested it. He'd taken her to several social functions to please Mrs Hindmarsh and from her exuberant necking in the car — something she had instigated — TR suspected Ginny, by all appearances a sweet and innocent virgin, would be a demanding and insatiable bed partner.

Wisely, TR kept her at bay. On one hand, it kept the girl and her mother frustrated but still keen. But on the other hand, Ginny frequently caught him unawares, visiting him when he was alone, and he was sorely tempted to take advantage of her teasing and flirting. Instinctively TR knew if he fell into her creamy perfumed embrace, he'd be snared firmer than a rabbit in a trap.

Ginny was fascinated by TR. He was so different from the other men with whom she came into contact. In his unpretentious, easy way he exuded a tough sexiness. She knew TR was a man who could survive in the wilderness, a man who would protect a woman, a man other men respected and didn't challenge; yet there was a shy vulnerability about him which caused Ginny to feel faint with desire.

He became an obsession which she cleverly disguised, but her longing for him never abated. In her mind this was not an infatuation — TR was a prize she ardently wanted to possess.

The game lasted two years and at the age of twenty-three, Virginia Mae Hindmarsh had to find a husband. Clayton took TR aside and spoke to him.

'My intentions towards Ginny? She's sweet — I like her — but to be honest, Clayton, marriage is the last thing on my mind.'

'Why, TR? Let's not horse around, here.

You could do a lot worse than Ginny. She's an affectionate little thing, her mother has taught her the niceties of being a good wife, mother and hostess; and frankly, TR, having you in the family would be a sensible business arrangement and we'd be right proud to have you. And I know Ginny is very, very fond of you.'

'I'm fond of her too, Clayton. But that's all. Fond. I'm not ready to settle down.' He was evasive, giving little away.

Clayton sensed his discomfort. 'I feel I'm not getting the full story here, TR. But I won't pry. That's your business. But don't throw your life away on a lost cause.'

TR glanced at him quickly, but then realised he wasn't referring to Queenie but to Martine Hoxburgh, an attractive divorcee he had been seeing. Martine was a sleek, well-groomed redhead who ran a fashionable boutique in Louisville. TR had been having a discreet but casual affair with the former beauty queen without commitment from either side. Martine would have liked to make their relationship permanent, but she recognised TR carried a scar and so didn't push or rush him. She was a worldly and sophisticated woman, and TR liked her class and style as well as her company.

Ginny was unaware of his involvement with Martine as they kept their meetings and outings as private as possible, spending weekends at Martine's luxurious ranch. She had done exceedingly well financially from her second divorce, and coupled with her family's money and a successful fashion business, she was considered a great catch.

She didn't allow TR to guess how determined she was that he be husband number three, for she knew it would frighten him away. Like a fisherman playing a shy trout, she just kept stalking her quarry. She was not prepared to wait forever, however, as she had decided that in the next two years she'd like to have a child. Preferably one with TR's sky-blue eyes.

TR had ambivalent feelings about American women. Charming, always attractive, they made him feel ten feet tall, yet beneath the glossy surface he suspected a barracuda-like force that could strip the flesh from his bones in minutes.

Clayton's voice brought him back from his musings. 'You're a talented man with horses, TR,' he sighed. 'And I'm too smart to let a woman get between me and business. Even if she is my daughter.'

'Clayton, Ginny is one of the most eligible debutantes in the whole South, she has a string of suitors to choose from! She can do better than a simple Aussie cowboy,' smiled TR.

'There's a heap of hopefuls hanging round the porch, that's true. But I was kinda hoping she'd get herself a real man. Well, TR, I think it's time I made my move into Australia. You ready to start operating that land you bought for me?'

TR chose his moment to confront Ginny who had pouted and flounced away each time she sighted him. He waited till she was alone, swinging morosely in a fringed loveseat in the garden.

He sat beside her, pushing the swaying seat to and fro with his boot. 'Ginny, I guess your Dad has told you I'm going back to Australia to work for him there.'

'You don't have to go, TR. But I guess there's nothing here to hold you.' She turned and looked away from him.

'Listen to me, please don't feel hurt that I'm not asking you to come with me. My life there is not for you, truly, you wouldn't like it out there where it's lonely and wild . . . '

Tears welled in Ginny's large blue eyes. 'But TR, I'd be with you . . . '

He wrapped his arms about her in a comforting hug. 'Trust me, Ginny, it wouldn't last. One day you'll thank me. And don't think I don't find you terribly attractive and desirable . . . because you are.'

A smile hovered through her tears. 'You think so?'

TR nodded. 'And, Ginny, you know you have a dozen blokes just panting after you. You just have to snap your pretty little fingers . . . '

'But I don't want them!'

TR imagined if Ginny had been standing she would have stamped her foot. 'Ginny, we don't always get what we want in this world. And sometimes it's better to hold onto the dream than find the real thing is not what you'd imagined. Let's stay good friends.'

'You're more like family, TR.'

'And I think of you that way — like my sweet little sister.' He picked up her hand and kissed her fingertips. 'Goodbye, Ginny ... be happy.'

Ginny didn't look at all happy. 'I'll be seeing you some time, TR, won't I?'

'Of course. I have to come back and see your father regularly.'

Ginny got up from the swing seat. 'Then I'll wait for you, TR.' She gave him a mischievous smile and sauntered away, her hips swaying provocatively beneath the summer dress.

TR groaned. But he suspected Ginny would get over him quicker than she thought.

It hadn't been so easy breaking the news to Martine, but she managed to be gracious and understanding. 'Maybe I'll come and visit you ...' They left the promise hanging between them as a possibility. TR knew she could well afford the trip but he didn't know quite what she'd make of the harsh Australian bush after the luxury and spoiled life style of the South. The thought of the glamorous Martine in the outback made him grin. To Martine's chagrin he didn't insist she come to visit.

There was only one woman TR wanted to see.

Clayton shook his head at the speed with which TR tied up loose ends and settled business matters.

'You are leaving with indecent haste, TR,' teased Clayton as they discussed their plans for Guneda, the proposed racehorse stud in northern New South Wales. 'There ain't no fire on your tail to get the place up and running. Take your time — be thorough, pick the right men, the right animals. I'll come out whenever you say.'

'I'll keep in regular contact, but I'll miss seeing you, Clayton. I'll do my best for you. Guneda will be a showcase in no time — you'll see.'

'Remember, you have a stake in this too, TR. You get a share of the profits. I'm glad you're anxious to get started. Good luck to you ... mate.'

TR laughed at his pronunciation of the Aussie expression, and shook his hand warmly. He was more than anxious to get started on this new chapter of his life.

He was returning to the vast open land he loved and to be near, yet so far, from Tingulla and the only woman he loved.

Chapter Sixteen

&

Colin and Dina strolled through the warm spring sunshine streaming onto Macleay Street in Kings Cross, laughing as spray from the giant dandelion ball of the El Alamein fountain misted over them. They cut through the lane leading to Kellett Street, avoiding the lingering daytime transvestites, prostitutes and pimps patrolling the clubs, bars and delicatessens of Darlinghurst Road.

Signor Camboni had asked the couple to join him for lunch along with a few of his friends.

'Why does your father want me to come?'

Dina shrugged. 'He knows I've been seeing you regularly...'

'Regularly! We're together nearly twenty-four hours a day, my darling!'

'Well, he probably just wants to check you out a little bit... he is very protective of me, you know.'

'Still concerned I might be after your money?'

'Pappa can be very old-world Italian at times. Don't worry, enjoy the lunch, Natalino is an old friend and always cooks something special.'

They were greeted effusively by the owner Natalino, who took them through to the tiny ivy-covered outdoor terrace. Six large men in dark suits sat around the table where two empty places waited. Signor Camboni rose to greet them, kissing his daughter on both cheeks and shaking Colin by the hand. The signori were introduced, although Colin found he couldn't remember a single name. He felt like an extra in a European movie.

Most of the conversation round the table was conducted in volatile Italian punctuated by bursts of laughter. Dina squeezed Colin's knee and gave him encouraging smiles.

Shouts of greetings and cheers suddenly interrupted the small trattoria as Australian boxing champion, Rocky Gattellari, and his entourage entered. Rocky came to their table where he was greeted warmly and introduced to Dina and Colin.

The handsome young Italian fighter kissed Dina's hand and winked at Colin. 'You don't mind?'

'Not at all, champ. Great to meet you,' said Colin, gripping the small but lethal fist.

He wished he could have joined the noisy Gattellari table where Rocky was eating with his minders and a group of journalists. Dutifully Colin turned his attention back to Signor Camboni.

At the end of the meal Colin rose with Dina, farewelling her father's business associates. He thanked Signor Camboni for the lunch, explaining they had an afternoon appointment.

Signor Camboni extended a manicured hand. 'You are welcome to visit with our family any time. If ever I can be of assistance...' The offer hung in the air accompanied by a faint shrug.

Dina took Colin's hand and they left the men sipping their short black coffee. 'Pappa thinks you are *simpatico*. It is true what you told me... about your Tingulla.'

'How do you know?'

'Pappa has friends everywhere. He told me it is all right to continue our relationship. You are a wealthy young man in your own right, apparently.'

'One day, I'll have Tingulla for my own, then no one will need to ask who Colin Hanlon is.'

'What about your sister? You said she lives there.'

'For the moment. For the moment.'

Dina linked her arm through his. 'You are plotting something, eh, Colin? Come, we have an appointment... back at my apartment.'

Colin leaned back on the pillow, his arms behind his head, and kicked a foot out from the sheets. 'I'm bored...'

Dina rolled on her side to face him. 'Well that's a wonderful thing to say after we've just made love!'

'You know I didn't mean it like that! I just think maybe I should look for some sort of job.'

'Here in Sydney?'

'Of course. Unless you want to come to the country with me,' he joked.

'Ugh! You need a job to suit your talents ... not riding around on smelly horses and ruining your hands digging fence posts or whatever you do.'

'I'm good at biting off sheep's balls.'

'You don't!'

'I do. Like this ...' He buried his face beneath the sheets, diving between Dina's legs as she squealed and jumped from the bed.

'Colin, I will speak to my father. He will find you a job.'

'I don't want you telling your old man I need a job. I just want something to give me a bit of a challenge, with a touch of class that will make me oodles of money!'

He slipped from the bed and began pulling on his clothes. Dina watched him, noting with satisfaction how elegant he now looked. She had made him throw away the remaining casual clothes he'd worn in the country. The well-worn riding boots, the broad-brimmed hat that shouted 'country' and the Harris tweed jacket were tossed out. She took him to her father's tailor for European cut suits and insisted he buy soft slip-on leather shoes and fine silk socks.

Colin balanced on the dainty boudoir chair. 'Y'know, these shoes wouldn't last a week in the bush,' he remarked, eyeing his fashionable foot.

'Forget the bush, darling. You are a sophisticated city man now.'

'Thanks to you, hey?' Colin pinched her rounded hip. 'Dina, why don't we get married?' The remark slipped out without thinking, but it suddenly seemed like a good idea.

'That is not a romantic proposal, Colin. You must court and woo me.'

'Flaming hell, Dina. We've been living together; you've been running my life; we know we get on. Why not get married?'

Dina was adamant. No casual Australian proposal for her.

'I'm a man of the land, I'm not into flowers,' said Colin gruffly.

Colin thanked his lucky stars Queenie couldn't see him ordering roses in a florist shop, picking out expensive jewellery, and footing the bill for Dina's betting spree at the races. He now accepted this was the best way to win Dina, and he devoted long afternoons to lovemaking, pleasuring and indulging her fantasies.

Despite the last idle year of high living, Colin was still youthfully lean and muscular. Dina, now thirty, was less firm but full, ripe and soft. Colin sucked and nibbled at her dimpled white flesh as if attacking a plate of rich pasta.

Queenie had just returned from her ride on Nareedah and walked into her study when the phone rang. 'Hi, it's Sarah. How's life at Tingulla?'

'How lovely to hear from you. It's a bit dry,

warming up, though we had a frost this morning.'

'This is no time to talk about the weather. Don't you have some news to tell me ... some family news?'

'Sarah, what are you talking about?'

'I wondered if you knew. Listen, I just picked up the Sunday paper and Colin is all over the social pages. With his fiancée.'

'His what? Who is she?'

'It says here that Colin Hanlon of famed Tingulla Station in Queensland has announced his engagement to Signorina Andina Camboni, formerly of Lake Como, now of Vaucluse.'

'Why didn't he tell me — or discuss it? He doesn't even have a job, Sarah! What's she like?'

'You know Colin, Queenie. The signorina is very glamorous, she looks older than him and luscious looking in that dark Italian way. Apparently her daddy is very rich, though John tells me he has dubious connections — if you get my drift.'

'I am hurt he didn't tell us. I suppose he figured we'd try and talk him out of it. I hope he knows what he's doing.'

'I'm sure you'll get an invitation to the wedding. Sounds like it's going to be the wedding of the year.'

'Thanks for letting me know, Sarah. Talk to you soon. Love to John.' Slowly Queenie replaced the phone.

When the ornate invitation arrived from the Cambonis, Queenie was tempted to refuse.

Warwick gently chided her. 'Don't react badly. Just because he didn't come to our wedding. You are his only family, Queenie. It wouldn't look good. You know Colin is just a little thoughtless.'

Queenie thought that was putting it mildly, but reluctantly she agreed to go to Sydney.

'We'll leave Saskia here with Millie and we can spend several days in Sydney and go shopping and party a bit after the wedding. You'll enjoy it, Queenie.'

The wedding festivities passed in an agonising blur for Queenie. She felt as if she had been caught up in an Italian art film which had a cast of deported immigrants from Calabria and was set amidst the ugliest of the *nouveau riche* social scene.

She and Warwick sat in the middle section of St Mary's Cathedral as the High Church ceremony dragged on, complete with choir, harps and the twelve attendants escorting Dina, who was buried beneath a mountain of beaded tulle and a long lace train.

After the service the crowd milled around the lawns as the bridal party posed on the steps in front of the historic sandstone church for the formal photographs.

'Colin looks quite pleased with himself,' whispered Warwick. 'And no wonder — Dina's a sexy looking lady.'

'I hope he realises he has also married the family,' added Queenie, looking around at the predominance of short men in dark suits and sunglasses, and women who wore either widow's black or were outrageously over-dressed in cocktail outfits, hats, furs and jewels.

A procession of long black cars glided to the front of the church to bear the wedding party away to the reception at a private club.

'This looks like a wake rather than a wedding,' said Queenie stepping into their rented American Chrysler.

The photographer from the society pages trailed them to the Mandotti Club and continued his frenetic clicking of candid shots. He left before the lavish food — seven courses — appeared and the many speeches were given. The wine, imported from Italy by Alfredo Camboni, gushed from tall dark bottles and the music, dancing and laughter became louder and faster.

Within a few hours the formal reception resembled a drunken village festival.

'Warwick, I can't take this dancing on the table tops and all the men singing and dancing together any more. I can't talk to these women, and Colin and Dina left hours ago,' said Queenie stifling a yawn.

Warwick had been rather enjoying himself. 'If you insist. But we must say goodbye to the Cambonis.'

Mrs Camboni, her blue rinsed hair set in corrugated waves, her bulk encased in cyclamen satin, held out a bejewelled hand, and in a heavy accent thanked them for coming from so far away.

'She makes it sound like we came from the moon,' hissed Queenie as they approached Signor Camboni to bid him good night.

'You cannot leave yet! I have not had a dance with the beautiful sister-in-law of my daughter.'

Before Queenie could protest she was swept onto the floor as Camboni clutched her against his crushed carnation buttonhole. 'I hear you have a very magnificent property at Tingulla. But far from everything, no?'

'Depends what you want to be near, Signor Camboni. I don't feel at all isolated.'

'Please, call me Alfredo. And you make good business at Tingulla? Perhaps we can do business together, now that we are all family?'

Queenie pulled away to study the ever-smiling face and suddenly wondered if he dyed his jet black hair. 'What exactly is your business ... Alfredo?'

He tightened his grip around Queenie's waist and executed a fancy turn. 'Import and export. A little of this, a little of that.'

'Well, unless you're importing bull semen I don't think we can do business together.'

She smiled sweetly and Camboni smiled unsurely back at her. 'Bulls? I thought you kept sheep?'

'I run both, Signor. Perhaps you and Mrs Camboni would like to visit Tingulla one day?'

A broad smile creased his face. 'That I would like. Mrs Camboni ... I don't think so. She doesn't go out much.'

'Thank you for your hospitality. I'm sure Colin and Dina will be very happy together.'

'If he doesn't make my daughter happy ...' Grinning, Alfredo Camboni made a slicing gesture across his throat and laughed at his joke.

'Good night ... Alfredo.'

'Good night, bella Queenie. I look forward to seeing Tingulla one day.'

They waited outside the club for their car to come around to the front. 'I hope Colin knows what he's getting into. Thank God they're not interested in the land. Can you just see all those heavies in their black suits and patent kid shoes tramping around Tingulla!' Queenie laughed. 'Alfredo has promised to visit ... one day. Somehow I think it will be a long time coming.'

'I think it could be fun. We could show them what country hospitality is all about. Camboni could be useful though. He has contacts all over the place.'

'Not the sort we need. The Hanlons have always managed their own affairs quite well on their own,' remarked Queenie tartly, sliding across the leather seat and kicking off her high heels.

The following day the wedding party had been invited to the Spring Carnival at Randwick Racecourse as guests in the Cambonis' private box. Warwick told Queenie the family had racing connections and they were guaranteed a few 'sure things'.

'You go. I couldn't face it. I'm going to laze by the pool with a book. Or maybe go shopping.'

'Don't be a spoilsport. Come on, Queenie, this is one of the big social events of the year. It'll be fun. Just for the first couple of races. Maybe I'll win a packet and you can go blow the lot in town in the shops. Dress up and show those gaudy women what class is all about.'

'Warwick, I'm not even a starter in the fashion parade stakes,' laughed Queenie.

'Why not? I thought you'd give anything a go. You'd walk off with the best-dressed prize, y'know.'

Many heads did indeed turn to admire the slim, strikingly beautiful young woman in the tailored suit and hat with a sweeping brim which offered the merest glimpse of high cheekbones and luminous green eyes.

Queenie slipped away from the noisy drinkers in the Camboni's box and stood by the saddling enclosure, enjoying the sight of the thoroughbred horses.

Warwick stopped by and squeezed her arm. 'I'm not having much luck with Camboni's tips I'm afraid. But I'll come good, don't worry.'

'Warwick, if I were you, I'd put some money on number eleven over there.'

'Why, did someone give you a tip on it?'

'Warwick, for goodness sake, just look at the animal — unless he's carrying a ton of lead, he's twice the strength of the other horses in this race.'

Knowing her knowledge and judgment of horses, Warwick didn't argue. He hurried towards the bookmakers, deciding to place a large bet to make up for his losses.

Out of interest Queenie stood by the winner's circle and watched the race, won, as she predicted, by number eleven. She grinned to herself. It certainly was a beautiful horse, prancing in to have the winner's sash draped around its neck as the owners and trainers clustered around for a photo.

Suddenly Queenie froze and gripped the white painted railing. Standing in the group smiling his lopsided grin, was TR.

At the same instant TR glanced at Queenie and their eyes met. He walked straight towards her, ignoring the pleas from the group and the photographer.

She stood immobile as he came towards her, their eyes never leaving each other's face. Electricity crackled between them, drawing them together.

He reached her, staring into her eyes. No movement crossed her features until he rested his hands on hers.

'Queenie... ' his voice was low.

She didn't trust herself to speak. They stood staring at each other, the years gone, the force of their attraction as powerful as a physical blow.

TR was conscious of people staring at them. He ducked beneath the railing, took her elbow and led her away from the crowd by the winner's ring. 'We have to talk.'

She still hadn't spoken. Her high heels stumbled slightly and he steadied her as she put up her other hand to hold her hat in place.

He smiled at her. 'I like your hat.'

Queenie suddenly halted and shook her arm free. 'TR... please...'

Before she could continue, her name was called and Warwick hurried towards them, a broad grin on his face. 'Hey, you're a real whizz, girl. Number eleven romped home!' He brandished a pile of banknotes.

'You backed my horse?' TR raised a quizzical eyebrow.

Queenie's voice was low. 'I didn't know. Warwick, this is TR Hamilton. My husband, Warwick Redmond.'

The two men shook hands. 'Of course, TR Hamilton. You used to work at Tingulla, it's a wonder we haven't met before. The men often mention your name. So now you own racehorses. You have done well.'

'I don't own them, just help them to win.'

'This calls for a drink. Come on Queenie, let's go back up to the box.'

Queenie shook her head, avoiding looking at TR. 'I'd rather not, Warwick. I have a headache, I want to go back to the hotel.'

'Are you all right? What's wrong?' asked Warwick solicitously.

'Nothing. I'm fine. Really. You stay. Give me the key and I'll see you back at the hotel.'

'Well, if you're absolutely sure you'll be all right.' Warwick handed her the key with Chevron Hotel emblazoned on its plastic tag. 'The car is waiting over there. Come on, we'll walk you over.'

'Nice to see you again, TR.' She held out her hand which he grasped tightly until she pulled away.

TR stood back and observed Warwick — handsome, dressed in a fashionable suit Colin had persuaded him to have made — as he helped Queenie into the back of the expensive car while the chauffeur held the door open. Queenie had married well.

As the luxury car pulled out into the traffic

on Anzac Parade the handsome young driver eyed Queenie in the rear view mirror. 'Where-a you wanta go, Signora?'

'The Chevron Hotel please.' Queenie slid her dark glasses on and turned away, staring blindly at her reflection in the tinted glass — a beautiful sorrowful face with trembling lips.

She gripped her handbag with icy fingers, trying to stem the flood of feelings swirling inside her.

In the solitude of her suite Queenie ripped off her jacket, throwing her hat on the bed and pulling the pins from her hair so it fell about her shoulders. She felt as if she had been violated. The protective wall she had built around her heart over years had been penetrated in an instant.

She stripped and stepped into the shower. Damn TR for causing her such pain, such sadness, such longing. The hot water soothed her. She let the pinpricks of water tingle over her skin.

Stepping out of the shower, she wrapped her wet body in a thick white towelling bathrobe and coiled her hair in a white towel turban. Feeling better she lifted the phone and ordered a salad and a pot of tea from room service.

She began pacing about the large sitting room with its floor-to-ceiling windows looking out over Sydney's glorious harbour. Across the bright blue water the 'old coathanger' spanned the city's north and south sides, while yachts and ferries floated past the soaring white shells of the new Opera House. She pushed the TV on and off, flipped through a magazine and tossed it aside, then stood and gazed at the activity on the harbour.

The door buzzer made her start, and tightening the belt of her robe, she went and opened the door.

TR stood there holding a tray and smiling hesitantly.

Queenie was frozen in shock.

TR moved past her into the room placing the tray on the table. 'I met the waiter at the door, so I tipped him and sent him on his way.'

'What are you doing here?'

'Queenie, we have to talk. Can I sit down?'

'Where's Warwick?'

'He's still at the track. Don't worry, he doesn't know I'm here.' TR rose to his feet again and moved to face Queenie. 'I haven't been able to forget you, Queenie. Not for one moment . . . '

'Stop it, TR! There's no point.' Queenie turned away, her voice harsh and hurt.

'No point! Goddamn it, Queenie. You owe me this, at least!' TR's voice was raised and equally angry.

'I owe *you!* That's a laugh.' She longed to scream at him — why hadn't he written? She wanted to kick him, beat her fists against his chest.

They stared at each other, churning emotions flickering between them.

'Why didn't you wait for me, Queenie?'

'How long was I supposed to wait, TR?'

'You could have given me a chance . . . '

'I gave you a chance . . . it's too late now.'

So many misunderstandings, the lost opportunities, the truth neither knew about the other. Once again, they were at cross purposes.

'This whole situation is too painful for me, TR. It's over.'

But her face belied her words. TR reached out and took her in his arms and lowered his lips to hers. For an instant their passion was rekindled, as fierce and strong as the first moment they'd touched.

Queenie wrenched herself out of his arms with a forceful push, knowing if she lingered for a second and kissed him, there would be no turning back. 'TR ... I've made a new life. I'm married.'

'So, unmarry. I'm not letting you out of my life again.'

She sat down sadly on the edge of the sofa. 'It's not that easy. I have a child. A little girl. I couldn't bear to hurt her. I am quite happy.'

TR knelt beside her looking earnestly into her face. 'Quite happy. Is that what you want from life? I can make you deliriously, ecstatically, wonderfully, gloriously happy. Queenie, don't do this, don't throw this chance away. It will be difficult, but it will be worth it. We *must* be together.'

A slight smile softened Queenie's sad face at his impassioned plea. 'I can't do that to Warwick and Saskia. And I can't leave Tingulla. No, TR, we've lost our chance — for whatever reasons. I'd like us to be friends, but for the moment it's too upsetting seeing you.'

TR jumped to his feet, hurt and angry.

'Friends! Upsetting! God, Queenie, I'm dying inside.'

Queenie was fighting back the tears. 'Just go, TR... please... just leave me alone.'

TR strode towards the door. 'I'm going. But I'm not giving you up, Queenie. I know you love me. I'll wait.' He closed the door behind him.

Queenie sank into the sofa, her shoulders shaking as sobs tore from her heart. Eventually she was able to draw a shaky breath and, lifting the phone, she dialled Ansett Airlines.

She needed to go home to the tranquillity of Tingulla. To try to forget.

Chapter Seventeen

The stockhorse cantered easily to the crest of the hill overlooking the boundary paddock at Cricklewood. Queenie reined in the horse and pointed at a herd of cattle.

'Look at them, Sassy ... down there by the dam,' she said to her daughter who was perched on the saddle in front of her.

'They're big. The bulls won't chase us, will they?'

'No, the Brahmans are pretty placid beasts. They've certainly gained a lot of weight. They'll soon be ready to breed with some Herefords and hopefully we'll have lots of good new calves.'

'Like Bessie?'

'Not quite. Bessie is a dairy calf. When she gets a bit bigger you can learn to milk her and Millie can make lovely cakes with real cream. Well, let's get back to the homestead and pack up. Time to go back home to Tingulla and tell Daddy how well the Brahmans have done.'

Queenie had brought Saskia over to Cricklewood for several days to check on the stock, and Saskia had loved sharing the days in the saddle and evenings by the log fire alone with her mother, 'playing house' and riding over the property.

Warwick swung Saskia high in the air. 'I've missed my little girl ... how was your trip to Cricklewood?'

'Good fun. And Mummy says the new bulls can start making babies soon.'

'That's good news.' Warwick kissed Queenie. 'I've also arranged to send a few thousand merino wethers into the woolcutters' sales next week. Prices are high at the moment.'

'Be good to have some money coming in, instead of going out.'

'Queenie, you're becoming conservative. That new bulldozer has meant we can clear and fence more paddocks. We're now producing a lot more stock feed which we can store in case we get a bad season or two. Or we can sell it. And our wool quality has improved since we introduced the finer fibre rams. There's a big demand for our nineteen micron fibre.'

'I know, I know. I just feel we're pushing ahead too fast. All this expansion. Why must Tingulla be the bunny and rush in first and set the trend?'

'Because, we put our money where our mouth is — experiment and develop. *And* reap the profits, my love.'

'There are a lot of cautious graziers waiting to see if we fall on our faces first, though; before they dash in and copy our methods.'

'That's their loss.' Warwick turned away. 'Let me worry about the accounts and paperwork. You keep your pretty eyes on the animals and the land.'

Queenie was tired. It had been several months since she had sat down with Warwick and gone over the accounts. She had a nagging worry he had stretched their resources too far. While he was away at the sales next week she'd go through the books.

She and Warwick had different methods of operating. Queenie was prepared to experiment and be adventurous, but not at the cost of putting themselves in financial jeopardy. Warwick was flamboyant and liked the world to know what they were doing. Tingulla had been written up in the magazines and metropolitan newspapers as well as the agricultural press. He claimed publicity increased the value of their stock at auctions.

Queenie tended to follow the tight-lipped tradition of men on the land who kept their business to themselves, and revealed no more than was absolutely necessary to remain civil and friendly. She had heard farmers and cattlemen who had suffered heavy losses during a drought remark laconically, 'Been a bit bloody dry lately'. Others who had made huge profits in a good season would stand a round of drinks in the pub, casually remarking they'd 'done orright'.

Tingulla was certainly a star on the map

of large, prosperous properties. There was a contingent of permanent workers about the place, they'd doubled the number of sheep shorn over the last four years and more land was being developed with the establishment of bores and dams.

Over at the smaller property, Cricklewood, there was a full-time manager, stockmen and a jackaroo now that it was running cattle. The Brahmans, with their solid bodies, doleful eyes and rolls of meaty flesh had adapted well and, when eventually put over the local Hereford stock, they hoped for a heavy, sturdier crossbred beast.

Nevertheless, Queenie was quietly worried.

Queenie and Saskia waved farewell to Warwick as he drove down the sweeping drive, heading for the stock auction at Roma. He also planned to spend a few days in Brisbane socialising with some of the agents and buyers and 'picking up a few things'.

'You should have gone with him, Queenie. You haven't had a break since Colin's wedding,' said Millie quietly behind her.

Queenie started, and turned around to see Millie moving the pots of geraniums around the verandah, wondering at her uncanny ability to voice her thoughts. But she didn't want to admit that she felt vaguely abandoned.

'Heavens no, Millie. I find all that mateship stuff tiresome. They sit in the pub and drink and spin outlandish stories. The sales are exciting, but it's all over in a few minutes.'

'What's happening in Brisbane?'

'I'm not sure. But Warwick has his reasons for making the trip. Perhaps he needs a bit of a break too.'

Millie didn't answer and lifted Saskia out of her miniature wicker chair. 'Come on, Sassy. Time for your bath.' She carried the girl away.

Queenie leaned against the verandah post, staring wistfully at the dissipating cloud of dust from Warwick's car.

Within forty-eight hours Queenie desperately wished that she had gone with Warwick. Problem after problem descended on her shoulders.

The first, and most worrying, was Jim, whose leg was badly crushed when the tractor he was driving overturned down by the creek where part of the bank had given way. He'd jumped clear but his leg had been pinned beneath the wreckage. He was lucky he hadn't been killed.

Ernie had galloped to the house calling for Millie, 'Jim hurt, Millie. Come quick!'

Millie had screamed for Queenie as she began running from the house.

Queenie grabbed the first-aid kit and they both scrambled into the Land Rover as Ernie clambered into the back. Queenie drove recklessly and the car bounced across the open land. Millie's face was grey and she wrung her hands, muttering in a near-forgotten dialect as Queenie tried to assure her he'd be all right.

Jim's leg had multiple fractures and he was in great pain. Queenie and Ernie hitched a wire from the winch on the four-wheel drive around a tree and onto the capsized tractor. Millie watched anxiously as Queenie prepared to move the vehicle up the slope.

Ernie hovered by the tractor ready to drag Jim free. 'Could be dicey for the Rover... if the wire breaks, you gonna go like a bullet. Big trouble is the ground no good. Bloody rabbits dug it all away underneath.'

'We'll have to take our chances, Ernie. Just watch yourself in case the tractor rolls.'

The engine began screaming and straining in protest as Queenie let out the clutch, pushing down on the accelerator to inch the vehicle forward. The wire rope squeaked as it tightened and for a moment the Land Rover skidded backwards. But Queenie jammed her foot hard on the accelerator and the wire began to bite into the bark of the tree, taking the strain. A tremor went through the tractor and Ernie grasped Jim under the shoulders, resting a foot hard against the restraining metal.

Ernie gave a shout as he saw the tractor move, wobble and with a thud, right itself. He dragged Jim away as Millie rushed forward.

Jim was unconscious but breathing steadily. Queenie gave him a pain-killing injection then drove to the homestead to radio for the Flying Doctor. Fortunately Kevin Hooper was only one and half hours away. When he landed the Cessna on Tingulla's airstrip Jim was lying in the back of the Land Rover with Millie squatting beside him, holding his hand.

Queenie helped Kevin lift Jim onto the stretcher and into the specially modified plane.

'Millie, go with him. We'll manage here. I'll send in anything you need.'

Millie ran to the house and returned in minutes with a string bag of clothes. She gave Queenie a quick hug and climbed into the plane.

'He'll be right as rain, before you know it,' said Queenie. 'Don't worry about anything. You look after Jim.' She looked into the plane at the groggy patient. 'Take it easy, old mate. You'll be right.'

The plane took off and Queenie drove back to the creek with one of the men to help Ernie get the tractor back up to its shed.

That night Millie rang her from Longreach hospital. Jim was resting as best he could with a leg and hip in plaster.

'Stay with him as long as you need to, Millie. Ruthie can take over here.'

'How is she?'

'Fine, I guess. I haven't seen her yet. Why do you ask, Millie?'

Queenie wondered at the strained tone in Millie's voice.

'She's bin having boyfriend problems.'

'Oh no, that's all I need. Well, she can't go mooning off over some lad. I need her to help in the house and look after Sas.'

'I didn't want to bother you with it. I hoped she would sort it all out.'

'Sort what out? Millie, tell me what's been going on.'

Queenie listened with her head in her hands as Millie told her that Ruthie was being courted by two young fellows. One, an itinerant half-caste stockman, the other, a full-blood warrior from Ruthie's traditional tribal home who had been seen staying at the blacks' camp which had established itself in the no-man's land between Tingulla and the township.

'Ruthie may be a full blood, but she's a mission girl, Queenie. She don't know anything about what to do. Them boys are filling her head with such nonsense. And one don't know about the other,' finished Millie.

'Right. I'll soon fix all that. Thanks for letting me know, Millie. Keep me posted on Jim. Cheers.'

Queenie hung up the phone. She'd better get Ruthie's love life straightened out. It had all the ingredients of a major conflict. The blacks had an incredibly complex social system, and relationships had strict rules. Anyone who broke tribal law was in for big trouble.

Nervously Ruthie sat in the kitchen twisting a corkscrew curl of her thick dark hair against her cheek. She hung her head, mumbling, and avoiding eye contact with Queenie.

'Now, Ruthie. Look at me. Which of these two boys do you like?'

'Both good fellas.'

'I'm sure they are. But you can't have two boyfriends. How serious is this? I mean, do you want to marry one of them? Have they asked you to marry them?'

Ruthie shook her head from side to side. 'They just want me go down the back with them.'

'Sleep with them, you mean?'

Ruthie's frightened face stared at Queenie. 'I know it's wrong. I ain't done nothin'. The nuns teach me. I'm a good girl.'

'I know you are, Ruthie. I think it best if you tell both of them you can't see them anymore. And they are not to come onto Tingulla land. Okay?'

Queenie rose, patting a miserable Ruthie on the shoulder. 'I know it's hard, Ruthie, but it's for the best. You'll soon find a nice man you'll like much better.'

The following night Queenie was awakened by dogs barking and raised voices at the rear of the kitchen. Pulling on her cotton robe Queenie grabbed the torch from beside her bed and hurried downstairs.

Ernie, who had graduated from rouseabout to stockman, was hammering on the door to Ruthie's small room by the laundry.

'What in heaven's name is going on, Ernie? Don't tell me you're one of Ruthie's boyfriends too!'

'No, no, Queenie. Them two fellas bin fightin' over Ruthie. Georgie got drunk and went and punched up Freddy at the camp and Freddy say he gonna spear 'im good.'

'Where is this Georgie fellow now?'

'He run away but I hear he coming to hide at Tingulla, so I tell Ruthie.'

'Thank you, Ernie. You go back to your quarters. I'll take Ruthie inside.'

Ruthie spent the rest of the night huddled on the couch in Millie's workroom.

In the morning Queenie visited all the men

on the property, telling them firmly that no strangers were to be sheltered at Tingulla — white, black or brindle.

She thought about putting in a call to Sergeant Harris but decided against it. In the sober light of day, she hoped Georgie, the half-caste stockman — now hungover — and Freddy the visiting Aborigine, would both have realised that courting Ruthie was inviting trouble.

There hadn't been serious trouble among the Aborigines in the district for years and Queenie hoped that was the end of it. Ruthie went meekly about her chores and Queenie settled down to going through the pile of account books.

That wasn't the end of it.

The following evening Queenie pushed the accounts to one side, feeling troubled and confused. She went upstairs to her room, searching in her bathroom for a headache tablet. She took the pill and glass of water onto the upper verandah off the bedroom and stood in the night air. The moon looked watery and faint, and the wind made the trees rustle and whisper. She was glad she wasn't out there, the night didn't feel friendly. She shut the french doors and returned to the cosy, softly lit bedroom.

Queenie wished Warwick was back. She needed to talk to him. The books weren't adding up correctly. They balanced, but there had to be something Warwick had overlooked. They couldn't be so deeply in debt to the bank.

She didn't even know where to contact Warwick. When she'd phoned his hotel they told her he had checked out. Maybe he was coming home early. Queenie pulled down the bedspread and shook her pillow. She certainly hoped so. She tiptoed in to check on the sleeping Saskia and wished she could sleep as peacefully.

While Queenie tossed and turned in her troubled sleep, a dream-like figure moved silently, stealthily, through the shadows and pale moonlight of the landscape.

It was the figure of an unearthly man. His skin was thick with grey clay paste, white and red ochre markings were painted in ceremonial patterns on his body. His face was obscured by a mask; and leaves and feathers formed a tall headdress and a brief covering around his genitals. His feet were shod with thick pads of soft grasses which left no mark as he ran swiftly and lightly, his spear balanced in his swinging arm.

Georgie rolled in his blanket by the embers of his campfire. He was well hidden in a small gully close to the eastern boundary of Tingulla. His few possessions were tied together ready to hit the road at dawn, seeking a stockman's job. He had contemplated sneaking close to the homestead in the hopes of finding Ruthie, but decided it was too risky. In any case, there were plenty of other girls about who would be only too happy to share his blanket.

His horse was hobbled nearby but it pricked

its ears and gently swished its tail as Georgie slept.

There was no sound, but Georgie opened his eyes and went cold with fear, his hair rising in prickles on his head. The ghostly figure stood above him with spear raised. Before Georgie could move or utter a sound, the spear flashed down, piercing his thigh.

He screamed in fear and pain, and his horse, now let loose, took fright and galloped into the night.

The figure withdrew the spear, turned and melted into the trees.

The next afternoon Snowy appeared at the kitchen door asking for Queenie. 'Some boys found a stray horse down the eastern fence. Me and Ernie back-tracked 'im and found that fella Georgie. He bin speared, cut up pretty bad.'

'My God ... I suppose it was the other man — Freddy. I was afraid something like this might happen.'

Snowy was shaking his head, his eyes wide and fearful. 'Not Freddy. Well, not exactly. He speared by kadaicha man. Now all the black fellas working here want to go away from Tingulla.'

Queenie was about to make a quick retort, but bit back the sarcastic comment. That was all she needed now — a walkout by the Aboriginal stockmen.

The mysterious kadaicha, or payback man, meted out justice as violently as deemed necessary. No one ever knew who was the unidentifiable member of the tribe who became the kadaicha man to revenge a wrongdoing.

Many believed the kadaicha man was a spirit called back to human form to carry out these deeds.

'Has someone called the Flying Doctor?'

'He no want white medicine. He get fixed up with Aboriginal medicine.'

'And then will he go away? Far away from Tingulla, Ruthie and Freddy?'

Snowy nodded. 'Yeah. He look for work some other place. He sorry he punched up Freddy. Now he mad at Ruthie.'

'Well, you tell one of the boys to get the message to this Georgie that Ruthie isn't having anything to do with Freddy either. The matter is finished. Okay, Snowy? Tell the men they have no need to fear staying here.'

Queenie went in search of Ruthie to tell her what had happened and found her at the clothesline unpegging the washing.

She knew all about it. Ernie was squatting by the large wicker washing basket repeating the story in graphic detail. A wide-eyed Saskia sat nearby pretending to play with the clothes pegs, but following the story as best she could with a frown of concentration.

Ernie rose to his feet and grinned as Queenie approached. 'Ruthie's famous. The kadaicha man came after her boyfriend!'

'He's not my boyfriend.'

'Ruthie isn't having anything to do with Freddy or Georgie or anyone else for the moment. She has plenty to do while Millie is away looking after Jim. Isn't that right, Ruthie?'

Ruthie dumped the last of the sheets on top of the washing basket, nodding her head in firm agreement. 'That's right. I got to work hard. No time for boys,' she answered emphatically.

Queenie turned away and headed back to the house so Ruthie wouldn't see the smile twitching up the corners of her mouth.

Ruthie pushed the mountain of washing down into the basket and grasped the handles.

Ernie sprang forward. 'Here. I'll carry that, Ruthie.' She was about to answer she carried that and more every washday, but seeing Ernie's eager face, she smiled shyly at him. 'Thanks, Ern.'

Warwick drove up to the front entrance and slapping his hat on his leg to shake off the dust, he flung it on the hat stand in the vestibule. It was two days since the spearing drama, and things had settled down.

'Queenie... where are you, my love? I'm home.'

He gave her an affectionate bear hug as Saskia clung to his leg, squeezing it tightly. 'So how have things been while I've been away? Nice and quiet?'

Queenie stood back and, folding her arms, spoke calmly. 'Jim had an accident and Millie is looking after him in hospital. We had a falling-out between two suitors of Ruthie's which was settled with a spear and the kadaicha man, half a dozen sheep have died with ticks and, according to your accounting, we are over our heads in debt — and you checked out of your hotel and disappeared off the face of the earth. What in heaven's name is going on, Warwick?'

Chapter Eighteen

--- 🦢 ---

Saskia perched at the desk before the bulky two-way radio unit, talking animatedly into the microphone. ' . . . And my horse is called Admiral and I ride him every day, and we have a cow called Bessie and lots of chickens. Oh, and sheep.'

She finished, but Queenie, who was sitting next to her gently prompted, 'Say "Over" and flip the switch'.

The teacher's voice crackled back from the fabric-covered loudspeaker of the old wireless. 'Thank you, Saskia, for telling us about your pets. That was Saskia Redmond of Tingulla. Now we're going to hear from Jason Browne at Barcoola.'

The School of the Air session finished and Queenie and Saskia walked hand in hand to the verandah for morning tea.

'I have to do a drawing for school, Mummy. I think I'll draw Bessie.'

'You can do that this afternoon. I think Tom, the mailman, might be round tomorrow and we can send it on to your teacher right away.'

'I like school, Mummy.'

'I'm glad, Saskia. But when you are older you'll have to go away to school. To boarding school.'

Saskia's lip trembled and tears sprang to her eyes. 'I don't want to go away.'

Queenie reached out and scooped her into her lap and hugged her. 'Oh, Sas ... it won't be for a couple more years. When you're a big girl. So don't worry about it. By that time I bet you'll really want to go and have fun with all the other girls.'

Saskia was now crying steadily into Queenie's chest but managed a firm but muffled response. 'I don't want to go away from Tingulla ... '

Queenie rocked her, wishing she hadn't mentioned it so early. She wasn't looking forward to that day either. 'Tell you what, possum. Dry your eyes ... I'll make you a promise.' Gently she wiped Saskia's wet cheeks as the child stared hopefully at her mother. 'When you're ready for big school, if you still don't want to go away, Daddy and I will get you a governess, a special teacher, to come and live here at Tingulla and teach you. How does that sound?'

'Good.' The little girl slipped down from Queenie's lap, her problem solved. 'I'm going to get Bessie so I can draw her.'

Queenie gazed through the window at the bleached, yellowing ground as Saskia scampered off. Six months with no rain. Feed was getting scarce. She and Warwick would have to help the men start hacking off branches of the mulga trees for the sheep to eat. She hoped it wouldn't get to the point of having to buy in feed. Warwick had explained away their huge debt at the bank as the cost of their expansion and 'investment' plans, which he confidently promised would more than be recovered at the end of the next shearing season.

Queenie had remained unconvinced. She was a risk-taker, but not a gambler. Patrick had cautioned her on getting into anything 'over her head'. Queenie well knew the vagaries of the outback climate and this drought had struck at the worst possible time for them.

She got to her feet and went towards the stables, kicking at the dust, leaving a trail of small ochre clouds at her heels. But they would weather it. They'd lose some sheep but it would take more than a drought and one bad season to knock Tingulla over.

She sighed as she saddled Nareedah. There always seemed to be a crisis lately. Perhaps Colin was the smart one, after all, swanning around Europe on his honeymoon without a care. It struck her again — she and Warwick had never taken their honeymoon trip abroad. Well, one day, when the finances were healthy again. Tingulla had to come first.

TR decided to concentrate his energies on setting up the horse stud at Guneda. He hired a team of workers who began repairing and painting the miles of fencing over the property. Some of the old sheds were torn down and plans for elaborate stables and training facilities were drawn up. It was by no means as fabulously over-the-top as the stud at Bon Vite in Kentucky, but TR combined the best of the new with the best of the old.

Some of the new buildings looked like colonial slab wood huts, with wooden shingle roofs; whilst others were built of slices of bush rock so they blended in harmoniously with the landscape. They were insulated and lined so they would be cool in summer and warm in winter, the interiors freshly whitewashed. The floors were concrete and each horse box was comfortable and well ventilated. The stablehands had a modern bunkhouse and a special room near the horses in case any needed to be closely monitored during the night.

A two-mile racetrack was carved out of the bush for training, and TR surprised the old hands by digging a special dam with a pontoon. As part of their fitness programme, the thoroughbreds would take their exercise in the dam, swimming up and down while the trainer walked around the pontoon holding the lead rope.

The old homestead was renovated and TR had plans to eventually add a wing of guest rooms for buyers and breeders. That would come later. First he had to buy his horses.

He had hired two young stablehands — a couple of hopeful bush jockeys who had grown too big to race, but still wanted to ride. They would exercise and care for the horses. He also hired two Aboriginal horsemen to help with the horse-breaking. He wished he could find a couple like Millie and Jim to manage and run the house and oversee the property, but settled instead for Mum Ryan, a capable, no-nonsense widow who had raised ten children and buried two husbands. There wasn't much Mum hadn't seen in her days as a 'bush-wife'. From giving birth at home alone, to bushfires, and snakes in the bed. Mum cooked, washed, cleaned, and bossed everyone about.

That left one more man TR wanted to find — Bobby Fenton, the legendary strapper who had cared for some of Australia's greatest race-horses back in the 1930s. Now in his sixties, Bobby had retired quietly and dropped out of the racing world. TR remembered his father telling him about Bobby. How he had special ways with horses, that he was considered a bit unorthodox, especially with his feeding methods, but the horses he cared for were strong, with enormous stamina and heart.

After a lot of letters and phone calls TR found him living in a Brisbane suburb with his daughter. TR wrote to him, phoned him and finally visited him, to persuade him to come and work at Guneda.

TR and Bobby sat on the lattice-trimmed verandah of the old Queenslander house, built on stilts to catch the afternoon breeze. TR outlined his offer. Old Bobby scratched his head. 'I dunno. I'm a bit old for that sort of caper now. Though I do miss having horses around.'

'What do you do with yourself, Bobby?'

'Aw, do a bit of gardening. Go to the pub occasionally. Do the crossword in the paper,' and with a grin added, 'and follow the nags a bit. Have the odd bet.'

'I reckon you could be really valuable to me and teach me a lot, Bobby. Be a shame to take all your knowledge with you.'

'Yeah, I got a few secrets,' grinned the wiry old strapper. 'So, your old man used to ride, and you're setting up as a trainer. Where'd you get the money?'

TR laughed. 'It's all above board, Bobby. I'm working for a rich American horse breeder who wants an investment out here. I'm in it because I love good horses and I want to make a quid or two.'

'Fair enough. You seem an honest sort of a bloke. I'll think about it.'

'Come out and look around before you decide, Bobby.'

A few weeks later Bobby turned up at Guneda unannounced. He stowed his 'port' packed with his special possessions under his bed — 'for the moment' — and never left.

He and Mum Ryan quickly engaged in open but friendly warfare, each constantly contradicting the other. 'Keeps you on your toes, stops the brain being addled if you stir her up a bit,' Bobby confided to TR.

Mum referred to Bobby as 'that silly old fool with his whacko ideas' but always managed to drop the tenderest bit of steak on Bobby's plate or the last of the treacle pudding would turn up for his morning smoko. TR relaxed when he realised the two were actually developing a firm friendship through their cracks and digs at each other.

One morning TR strolled into the stables

telling Bobby, 'Righto, get yourself ready. Tomorrow we're leaving for the thoroughbred sales. Time we started getting some up-market bloodstock for the place.'

The yearling sales, held in Sydney, were becoming a bit of a social event.

A special pavilion was set aside near Randwick Racecourse with padded seats placed around the centre ring where the expensive animals were paraded. Prospective buyers could study the horses beforehand in their stalls, reading their pedigree posted on the box door or in the sale catalogue. If requested, a trainer, owner or stablehand, might take the horse out and walk it about for closer inspection.

Gossip and rumours flew about the stable area, passed on from the boy who swept out the stalls, to the head of an owners' syndicate... stories that a certain horse was going to fetch a fortune... that the progeny of a famous sire was really up the creek.

Fashionably dressed women went to be seen at the sales, fanning themselves with their catalogues in the steamy heat. Lavish luncheons were held in private tents around the grounds. The social column writers and sports page journalists ensured everyone and everything of consequence or interest got reported.

Bobby was in his element. He found some old mates, some still working, others retired like himself, who enjoyed the exhilaration of the auction and couldn't keep away. Bobby knew breeders and owners, their successes and failures, and could recite the genealogy of most horses. His advice was invaluable and TR listened to and noted his comments.

His tweed cap pushed back on his head, cigarette stuck to his lip, hands clasped behind his back, Bobby strolled up and down the horse stalls, looking and listening. TR scribbled in the small notebook he kept in his checked shirt pocket, and estimated his limit on each of the four horses he planned to buy. He and Bobby had mutually agreed they would all be solid investments. Fit, fine-looking horses with good pedigrees. Nothing flashy, not big 'stars', but all with the potential to produce possible winners.

Late in the afternoon the day before the major auction took place, when the bars were crowded with the hybrid collection of racing and breeding identities, Bobby tugged at TR's arm. 'Let's go get a meat pie.'

They left the noisy bar and went to one of the small stands outside selling meat pies, sausage rolls, salad rolls, sweet buns, tea and fruit juices. Carefully lifting the pastry lid on his pie, Bobby squirted in a liberal dash of tomato sauce and headed for a bench in the open air. TR sat beside him, biting into a flaky sausage roll.

'I spotted another one I think you should look at, TR.'

'I can't afford another horse, Bobby. Clayton has set me certain limits. Unless you think we should get this one instead of one of the others?'

Bobby shook his head, wiping the red smear of sauce from around his mouth with the back of his hand. 'Nope. I reckon you should buy this one for yourself. To race.'

'Come off it, Bobby. I can't afford to get into the racing game. We're here to buy horses for stud purposes. With someone else's money.'

'He's only a young fella. Going up in the yearling sales after the big auction starts. You'd get him for a thousand dollars. I know a bit about his background.'

'Sounds like a bit of an expensive gamble to me.'

'Horses are always a gamble, TR. But some of them have something about them. Strike me, I'd be prepared to sink my savings into this bloke and go you halves!'

'You'd be willing to risk the lot on this unknown, untried colt?'

Bobby screwed up the paper bag which had held his pie, and grinned at TR. 'Hell, I've taken a punt before today and lost. Won some, too. Keeps life interesting.'

'You'd better show me this wonder horse.'

Bobby led the young stallion from its box, nodding to the boy lounging on a chair reading a magazine. 'Just going to walk him out to the water troughs and back, Ginger.'

The boy shrugged. 'Sure, Bobby, go ahead.'

'Knew his Dad,' commented Bobby as he patted the horse. 'Come on, Blinky Bill.'

'God almighty! What sort of a name is that for a horse?'

'Didn't you ever read *The Adventures of Blinky Bill* when you were a kid . . . wonderful book. Blinky was a very wise bloke.'

'He was a fat little koala who got into trouble a lot.'

'You're right. Well, this fella's grandfather always ran in blinkers. Went bonkers if he didn't. Was called Sir William of Orange or some such rubbish but was always known as Blinky. This is his grandson, Sweet William. I'll tell you his lineage later... take a good look at him.'

Bobby walked the horse around in a circle in the sun-drenched paddock by the stalls, watching his legs and feet.

TR sighed. 'Struth, he's not an attractive horse, Bobby. In fact, he's quite ugly with those long spindly legs. And his head's too big. How old is he?'

'Ah, he's still growing into his feet, aren't you Bill?' The young horse stretched forward and sniffed Bobby's hand curled in his pocket.

TR walked around the horse, running his hands down its legs, lifting its hooves, then feeling the pectoral muscles and the horse's heartbeat. The horse sidestepped away.

'Easy, Bill,' murmured Bobby. 'He's going to be a big strong fella.'

'Bloody great drink of water,' muttered TR looking up at the horse. 'I agree he's big for his age and since he's still growing, he'll be a monster. Will he be a runner, though?'

'He's got a big heart, TR. That means he's got stamina. And he's got personality — not pretty, but smart.'

They walked on either side of the horse, heading back to the stables.

'I don't know, Bobby,' said TR dubiously as

he unlatched the half-door of Bills' box. As he spoke, the horse dropped his head and gave TR a heavy butt in the centre of his back, sending him sprawling into a pile of hay.

The horse whinnied and Bobby burst out laughing. 'Think you're pretty clever do you?' said TR to the horse, as he dusted the straw from his clothes.

'He's got spirit hey, TR?' said Bobby as they walked away.

'Mmm.' TR was deep in thought and Bobby kept silent, rubbing a plug of tobacco in the centre of his palm, a cigarette paper stuck to his bottom lip.

The bidding during the main auction for the good horses kept everyone entertained as prices rose, voices were raised and the crowd gasped and applauded as the auctioneer's gavel banged.

TR recalled some advice Dingo had once given him, and sat to one side with an offhand manner, keeping out of proceedings until what seemed like the last bid, then he came in quietly and confidently. It was a tactic that tended to close out the opposition. His manner didn't invite a bidding challenge and since the horses he wanted weren't major 'stars' of the day, TR got them for below the price he'd set himself. Bobby waited in the rear of the pavilion, finding it far too nerve-wracking an experience.

Later in the day TR and Bobby watched the yearling sales where offspring of Melbourne Cup winners and other well-known race-horses, fetched high prices.

Bobby snorted under his breath as one nervous young horse was sold for a record price. 'Just because his sire and dam won a couple of big ones doesn't mean he's ever going to win a race,' he sniffed. 'They're lookin' at the paperwork not the bloody horse.'

TR smiled at the old man, thinking he was probably right in that case. But as Sweet William was led out he wondered how good Bobby's judgment really was. This horse seemed a bit of a long shot and TR wasn't surprised when the bidding was half-hearted.

To TR's shock, Bobby suddenly jumped up and shouted. 'Four hundred!'

'Sit down and keep quiet, Bobby. If we're going to buy him, let me do it.'

'What do you mean, *if*?'

Several people around them grinned at the wild bid from old Bobby. One owner, knowing Bobby's record, leaned forward to whisper in his partner's ear. He raised his hand and the bidding went up again.

TR kept a restraining hand on Bobby's arm as two more entered the bidding and like a ping pong match the auctioneer turned from one to the other as the price went up in hundred dollar lots.

Bobby was squirming and muttering, but TR remained calm and disinterested.

'Seven hundred...'

'Going once... Going twice...'

'Eight hundred.' TR spoke quietly but it stilled the auctioneer's hand.

'We have new blood, ladies and gentlemen. Do I hear any advance on eight?'

'Nine,' came from the other side.

'Nine. Thank you, sir.' The auctioneer raised an eyebrow at TR.

TR nodded. And smiled. Bobby was looking down, twisting his gnarled hands together.

The opposing bidder looked at TR then shook his head. The auctioneer banged his hammer. 'Sold. At one thousand to Mr Hamilton.'

'Sweet Mary, Joseph and Jesus! You had me sweating, TR.'

'I told you not to worry, Bobby. I didn't decide to buy him till the six hundred mark anyway.'

'Well, you've done it now.'

'You mean we've done it, Bobby. You still want to go fifty-fifty? Or have I just bought myself a horse?'

'No flaming fear. Count me in. Sweet William is going to be a winner.'

'Bobby, let's get this straight — we call him Bill, OK?'

'Whatever you say, TR. But I'll still think of him as Blinky.'

TR laughed. 'Let's go get a beer. I'm still not sure if I should be celebrating or having my head read.'

Before leaving Sydney TR was invited to the races with a group of acquaintances and friends who had several horses running. He was anxious to return home, but decided it might be wise to maintain contacts and let them know he was planning to breed and train on a large scale.

It was a wise move. Several owners were interested immediately, asking if they could look over Guneda. Others were prepared to send horses to him for training simply on the basis of his and Bobby's reputation.

Towards the end of the day, TR decided to place a bet, his first for the meeting. He'd been too busy socialising, talking horses and watching them run to think about betting. He strolled over to the crowd around the course bookmakers who shouted from beneath their bright umbrellas; cash bag around their neck, odds chalked on a board beside them.

He stood in line, silently debating his choice, when a slight commotion broke out at the stand next to them. 'What's up?' TR asked the man beside him.

'Some bloke arguing about the odds. My bookie mate told me he's lost a packet.'

TR glanced over at the unlucky punter and caught his breath. Warwick was angrily tearing up his betting tickets.

He hesitated. Should he greet him or pretend he hadn't seen him? It was TR's turn to place his bet. By the time he'd done it, Warwick had disappeared in the crowd.

TR returned to the exclusive Members' Stand, ordered a coffee and moved around the club room, his eyes roving for one particular man — Freddie the Fly, famous for knowing all the course gossip. He was like the proverbial fly on the wall — seeing and hearing everything.

Spotting the effusive, balding Freddie, TR drew him aside and, ordering a round of drinks, listened to Freddie's latest gambling and business conquests before asking idly, 'You know Warwick Redmond from Tingulla?'

'Struth, yes. See him out here whenever he's in Sydney. And I ran into him at the Doomben track in Brisbane once.'

'Bit of a punter is he?'

'A bit! He'll bet his shirt on two flies walking up the wall.'

'I guess he knows what he's doing.'

'I've seen him shout the bar when he wins. You don't hear about the losses, of course. But I know he bets heavy.'

TR wondered if Queenie knew Warwick was a wild gambler. If he was losing heavily she'd know it — unless he gambled his own money. Nonetheless, TR was troubled for Queenie's sake. He'd seen too many men lose everything they owned at the racetrack.

It had been a bad week for Warwick. The bank's head office in Sydney had not been at all helpful in the matter of extending his loan. A sure thing he'd been tipped at Rosehill had been beaten by a nose and he was running up a staggering account with the illegal SP bookies. Without cash he'd resorted to placing his bets through the off-course bookmakers. And now his problems were fast becoming public.

Although Colin and Dina were still away on their honeymoon, Warwick decided to call Alfredo Camboni to say hello.

'My dear friend. You must come and eat with us. I insist.'

Between the *veal parmigana* and the *insalata mista*, Warwick had hinted he was having financial difficulties, that Tingulla was a tremendous drain on cash resources.

Alfredo patted his arm. 'I have very shrewd business advisors, I'm sure they might be able to offer some assistance. Shall we meet tomorrow, at my office? Say, about eleven? Now ... *mangia* ... the food, is *magnifico*, no?'

Chapter Nineteen

Colin and Dina returned exhausted from their long and expensive honeymoon. They locked themselves in Dina's newly decorated apartment and slept through several days, arising for late afternoon coffee and pastry at the outdoor tables of the Cosmopolitan Café in Double Bay. Here the wealthy European and Jewish community gathered to gossip and examine their latest status symbols — jewellery, cars, clothes, wives, mistresses.

Dina felt at home in this crowd; Colin did not.

'I thought you adored Europe and all that culture, darrrling,' goaded Dina.

Colin waved away a drift of cigar smoke from the table beside them. 'I do, but this mob are just rich refugees. It's a club. They don't mix with anybody else.'

'You're jealous because you're not a member.'

'Don't want to be. Give me your noisy Italian friends or bushies any day. At least you know where you stand with country people.'

'I must meet some of these famous "bushies" one day. So, dear husband, what are you going to do to keep me in the manner to which I am accustomed?'

It was a thought that had been troubling Colin. 'I could always sell one of the flats in my apartment block. But I need some sort of career. Something with a bit of prestige — that's interesting — that makes me money. I don't want to work like a dog on the land, nor do I want to slave away in an office from nine to five.'

'Dear me. Perhaps you should marry a wealthy, older woman!'

Colin grinned at her. 'I know how I'd keep her happy, too.'

Dina stood as he slipped several notes into the leather folder on the table to cover their bill.

'What are you waiting for then?'

Ever accommodating, Dina's father had a suggestion. He arranged for Colin to meet some business friends at the European Mercantile Merchant Bank. Colin, with a degree, good looks, social contacts and solid background — coming from 'the famous Tingulla estate', as Alfredo Camboni put it — had the necessary qualifications. He was taken on, given a vague title and a substantial salary, and sent out to hunt down potential investors and clients.

It was Sarah who, once again, during their

periodic but lengthy telephone calls, passed on the news to Queenie about the activities of her young brother.

'I'm pleased to hear he's got a job at last. But banking! What does he know about it?'

'I think he's like a salesman, Queenie — a front man, drumming up contacts for the real numbers men. He's obviously being quite diligent. He contacted John to ask him about any rich clients who were buying or selling property.'

'It certainly seems as though he's turned his back on everything Dad built up.' There was a wistful note in Queenie's voice.

'Frankly, Queenie, I think things have worked out for the best. You never saw eye-to-eye with Colin.'

'I did try, though, Sarah. I don't know how or where, but somewhere along the line we seemed to fall out.'

'Put it down to sibling rivalry. He always resented you, Queenie.'

'And that makes me sad. I never wanted things to be this way.'

'Give it time. Maybe one day Colin will grow up.'

'I suppose you're right. When are you coming back home again?'

'Queenie, this is my home now. Why don't you come down to the city and visit us? Bring Saskia to play with young Tim.'

The two girls began exchanging stories of their children. Queenie had seen Sarah and John's two-year-old, Timothy, only a few times, and she would have enjoyed taking Saskia to visit her godmother Sarah in Sydney.

'But I just can't get away, Sarah. The station is quite a problem at the moment. We keep hoping for rain and we're stretched to the limit financially. I'm really quite worried about it all.'

Later, Sarah poured John his pre-dinner drink and told him about her conversation with Queenie. 'I can't imagine that Tingulla would be having financial problems. Sure, they need rain, so does Mum and Dad's place, but that's part of life on the land. You calculate for that.'

'You think Warwick has gone overboard a bit, do you? I can't see Queenie allowing things to get out of control,' mused John.

'I just sense Queenie is more worried than she's letting on.'

Warwick yawned as he turned into the stretch of dusty road leading to Tingulla's gates. God, it was dry. The countryside was like a tinderbox — one spark and the lot would burn like fury. For most people on the land the fear of bushfire in dry seasons was a constant worry.

Water was scarce and the dams were low. The sheep he passed had a thick coating of dust on their cream wool so that they matched the dun-coloured earth. They stood in pathetic clusters in whatever spindly shade was available. At least he would be able to tell Queenie they would be all right financially, thanks to Alfredo Camboni. The meeting with his associates had gone well. They wanted to see some details of Tingulla's earning capacity and had assured him they had investors who would be willing to put up additional funds.

He put off revealing these details to Queenie until he had showered, rested and made love to her. She was distracted and uncommunicative so he took her in his arms. 'Queenie, love, don't fret about things. I know you've been worried about the money situation. But I've taken care of it. We're going to be fine,' he said soothingly.

'How's that, Warwick?'

'I had some business meetings in Sydney and we've found some investors willing to put money into Tingulla to tide us over.'

'What sort of investors? What did you put up as collateral? People don't give you money without getting something in return.'

'It's more of a profit sharing arrangement. Besides, I haven't actually done anything about it. It's there if we need it.'

'There won't be any profits to share at the rate we're going. How did you find these people? Not through Colin, I hope.'

'Not exactly. Alfredo introduced me to a few people. Wealthy men who have tax problems. They need to shuffle money around, to appear to make a loss. Creative accounting deals.'

Queenie sat upright, swinging her feet over the edge of the bed. 'Warwick, I can't believe what you're saying. You'd allow cronies of Camboni to put money into Tingulla? They're probably laundering Mafia money!'

Warwick laughed. 'Don't be melodramatic. Just because they're Italian . . . '

'They're Calabrian! And frankly, I've been

nervous of where Cambonis' money comes from. Sarah and John told me he has a very unsavoury reputation.'

'Rubbish! Look, Queenie, it's just like taking out a loan to see us over the rough patches. But if you feel like that I'll tell Alfredo to forget it.'

They got dressed in angry silence. Warwick watched Queenie furiously pulling the hair-brush through her long hair. He sighed and wrapped an arm about her shoulders. 'Maybe it will rain and we won't have to worry.' He smiled at her reflection in the cedar-framed mirror.

Queenie stared at him, put down the brush and walked silently from the room.

The days ran together like blue and gold elastic stretched to the point where any minute it must surely snap. But no rain came. Nervous tension simmered behind tense faces, tempers sizzled, arguments flared over small issues, energies were sapped, and the animals began to suffer and die.

As food became scarce with the withering of the bush, creatures from the wild began to move in closer to the homestead, much to Saskia's delight. But this soon changed to something more dramatic. She had been build-ing a doll's house under the cool shade of the water tank by the kitchen. When she returned from lunch she found a large brown snake coiled in her makeshift house.

Her shouts had brought Millie running. 'It's a brown snake, Millie. That's poisonous.'

'You bet. Go get your Mummy — I'll stay here and watch it. Remember, never take your eyes off a snake, Sas... they move off real quick, then it's big trouble if you don't know where it's gone.'

Her short little legs churned up the dust as Saskia streaked for the house shouting, 'Mummy, Mummy, come quick! A big snake!'

Queenie bolted down the stairs heading for the kitchen. 'Where is it, Sas? It didn't bite you, did it?'

'No. But it's a big brown one on my dolly's house. Millie is guarding it.' The little girl was breathless but her eyes sparked with excitement.

Queenie grabbed the rifle from the kitchen wall, saying, 'Maybe the axe would be better.'

Saskia hurried at her heels. 'Oh no, Mummy, you might break my house.'

They came round the side of the house to find Millie walking backwards, her eyes wide in horror.

'What's up Millie... where is it?' Queenie strained towards the doll's house.

'I thought I heard one of the men coming and I turned around to call out and the bugger slipped out... he was so quick.'

'Saskia, don't move,' commanded Queenie. Millie leaned down and lifted the child into her arms, fearfully searching the ground. 'I think he went under the house, Queenie.'

'Damn — we'll never find him.' She crouched and peered into the shadows.

'I have an idea, Queenie. There's a dead rat in the trap by the pantry. I heard the trap go off not long ago, so it'd still be pretty fresh. It might lure him out if he's hungry.'

'Worth a try, Millie.'

Holding the still-warm rat by the tail and at arm's length, Millie placed it in a patch of sun in the dust by the tank stand.

'Okay, Saskia,' said Queenie, 'we'll take it in turns to stand rat watch. Be very quiet and still.'

It only took half an hour for the snake to slide out and investigate the motionless rat.

Saskia was sitting patiently on the steps, her chin in her hands resting on her knees. Keeping her eyes on the shining brown snake slowly edging closer to the dead rat, its tongue flicking in and out, Saskia calmly called, 'He's here . . .'

Silently Queenie appeared behind her small daughter and fired the rifle. The snake flipped once and lay still.

Millie edged around the door. 'Sure its dead? They play doggo you know, and just pretend.'

'No more snake, Millie. Mummy shot him right in the head,' said Saskia proudly.

A car came speeding towards the house with Jim and Warwick in it, looking anxious. 'We heard a rifle shot . . . everything okay?' Warwick called, as he jumped out.

Saskia ran to him. 'We had a big brown snake . . . right in my doll's house. Mummy shot it.'

Warwick scooped her into his arms. 'You be careful, possum. Brown snakes are deadly, you know.'

'I know. But I'm all right. Mummy looked after us.'

Warwick let her slide to the ground, watching Queenie go back into the kitchen to put the rifle away. 'Yes, we're very lucky to have such a clever Mummy aren't we,' he murmured coldly.

Millie looked over her shoulder in surprise as she hung the snake over the garden fence.

Jim, still limping from his injured leg, leaned on the heavy stick he was carrying. 'You'd better carry a stout stick wherever you go, Millie. You could find a snake in your washing basket one day.'

'I can manage all right. You're the one who'd better watch out. You can't do any running with that bad leg.'

'It's taking it's time to mend, all right. I'm damned sick of hobbling about the place, Millie. I reckon I could get on a horse though, if you gave me a hand.'

'What for? So you can break the other leg? The doc said to take it easy.'

'I hate seeing Queenie taking on so much. She seems real worried about the place.'

'Hadn't you noticed we haven't had a drop of rain in over half a year?'

'I know that. But there's something else bothering her.'

'Warwick keeps telling her everything is going to be okay.'

'All very well to say, Millie. They've put a lot of money into the place and if we don't get rain we'll have a bad season — and I reckon Tingulla could have big troubles.'

Millie hooked a supporting arm around Jim as they turned back to the house, neither saying what they were thinking. Patrick and Rose had weathered some cruel years with careful management and Jim considered Warwick rash and foolhardy. Millie fretted at the strain showing in the set of Queenie's mouth.

Queenie was having a quick cup of tea in the shade of the verandah, one lanky leg flung over the arm of the squatter's chair, her hat resting on her other knee.

Millie appeared in the doorway. 'Ernie's at the kitchen door looking for you or Warwick. Trouble with some sheep in the western paddock.'

'Warwick went to check on all the bores and dams. I'll see what he wants. Thanks for the pick-me-up, Millie.' She handed the empty teacup to Millie and went through to the kitchen, opening the squeaky flyscreen door to where Ernie waited, looking worried. 'What's up with these sheep then, Ernie?'

'They're dead. It's dingoes. Killed real bad.'

'How many?'

'Six. The little ones too.'

'Bloody hell!' Queenie pulled her hat on her head, and headed to where Nareedah stood in the shade of the stables. 'Get Snowy to come with us.'

The slaughtered ewes and their young were easy to find: above them circled the crows, their black bodies gleaming against the blue sky, their harsh and mournful cries echoing across the cloudless horizon.

Flies buzzed over the carcasses as Snowy looked closely at the ground around them. 'Dingo all right. One big fella. See, he go for the kidneys, them juicy bits.'

'Bastard! If they want a feed, then why not take a whole sheep? This senseless killing of so many is bloody maddening.' Queenie was angry. The loss of expensive stock was one thing, and knowing the poor animals had tried to protect their young and probably all died a gruesome and painful death didn't help.

Now there was an efficient killer on her land that would strike again and again. She didn't like the idea of the wild dogs coming in so close. The house pets, the chooks, the ducks ... with a shudder she recalled how a dingo had attacked a baby sleeping in its pram or so the story went.

'We'll have to hunt it. There's probably a pack of them around the place, but the one that is coming in to kill ... I want its scalp.'

Snowy was studying the tracks in the dust. Ernie looked thoughtful. 'Jim told me he used to be a dogger in his early days. He got paid a bounty for wild dog scalps.'

'Hard to know where their lair might be. I reckon he's coming in from miles. He run through the night,' said Snowy.

'I'll talk to Jim.' Queenie turned her horse around and cantered away.

'No good, eh, Snowy?' remarked Ernie.

'No, mate. Dingo is a smart fella. Run quick, kill and run away. We have to set him a trap.'

The next day Jim concocted a foul-smelling brew in an old kerosene tin.

'Excuse my language, Jim, but that smells like shit,' remarked Queenie, wrinkling her nose.

'No, piss,' grinned Jim. 'Got sheep's urine in it. Among other things.'

Queenie gazed at the reddish goo swilling in the tin. 'Well, I hope the hell it works. Are you sure you don't want me to come with you?'

'I'll be right. Snowy and me'll take the four-wheel drive in close and I'll set me trap using this. We'll build a bit of a hide and sit it out for a few nights. If the bastard is around, he'll come in sniffing round, then one of us will shoot him.'

'I don't want any strychnine baits left about in case the dogs pick them up.'

'Don't worry, Queenie, this stuff hasn't failed me yet.'

Queenie refilled Warwick's coffee cup after dinner, two nights later. 'I wonder how Snowy and Jim are doing with their trap out there.'

'Hope they get the bastard. Once they get a taste for easy kills, a couple of dingoes can do a hell of a lot of damage.'

'We can't afford too many losses, either.'

Warwick sipped his coffee. 'Alfredo Camboni contacted me a few days ago. Said he had an interesting proposal for us.'

'Warwick! I thought we'd decided we didn't want them investing in Tingulla.'

'This is something entirely different. A way Tingulla could make some money for a couple of months. He has some Americans coming out on a project and Tingulla would be perfect for them.'

'For what? Are we going into the bed and breakfast business?'

'No, Queenie — they're interested in using the property as a movie location.'

'A *what*?'

Warwick shrugged. 'I told him I'd discuss it with you. They're making a film set in the outback and need a glamorous homestead, horses, horsemen, and a base location for accommodation and stuff. They'd pay a hefty whack for our setup each week.'

'You've got to be joking, Warwick! And what are we supposed to do? Go and live in a tent in the scrub and leave them and the stock to it?'

'No. They'd pay us — a large location fee each week and money to any men we could spare. They need horse wranglers, stunt riders and people to help with the logistics of filming and getting around, stuff like that — people we could help them contact. And I figured we could accommodate them in the shearers' quarters and hire Stan to feed them all. They'd pay bloody well for that.'

'You've thought it all out, then, have you?'

Warwick shifted uncomfortably at the icy tone in Queenie's voice. 'Of course not. They were just a few ideas that came immediately to mind. Queenie, this is a big American movie outfit. We're talking several thousand dollars a week.'

Queenie pushed back her chair. 'If they're prepared to pay that sort of money it must mean they cause a lot of trouble and expect a lot.'

'Sounds like money for jam to me, just the same,' retorted Warwick to Queenie's retreating back.

The next day Queenie rode Nareedah across

the patchy brown paddocks where tree branches sagged in the heat, their leaves already shrivelled and curled. The stockpile of feed for the sheep was diminishing rapidly and soon they would have to start buying it in. The drought had sent stock feed prices soaring. Their cash flow was almost non-existent, and this would have to be added to their already huge debt.

Maybe the money from the movie people would be useful. The thought of a stack of tourists, actors, city trendies and film phonies clambering over the place made her shudder. But then it would probably only be for a few weeks, and the money would certainly pay for the feed.

She cautiously raised the matter with Warwick. 'I'm certainly not agreeing to this mad idea, but just suppose we did say yes. I was thinking if they do pay well, it would cover the cost of feed for a couple of months.'

'For sure it would. Queenie, I'll look into it in more detail and find out exactly what's involved. It was just an idea. Camboni said they had some advance man out here scouting around for possible locations.'

The chartered Cessna trundled along the dirt strip at Tingulla raising an orange dust cloud. Warwick fanned the choking dust from his face with his hat and watched the pilot, dressed in blue shorts and casual shirt, unlatch the door and help the expensive-looking American businessman from the aircraft, taking out his smart luggage as Warwick stepped forward.

Warwick had spoken to Alfredo Camboni who had put him in touch with Roger Ambrose, the location manager for Mountain Pictures of Sunset Boulevard, Los Angeles. It had seemed logical to invite Mr Ambrose to visit Tingulla to see the homestead and surrounding countryside for himself.

The film executive was in his thirties, his hair cropped unfashionably short, very tanned, and dressed casually in cotton pants, a light golfing-style T-shirt and canvas loafers on his feet.

The three men climbed into the Land Rover and headed to the house. As they approached the imposing double-storey homestead Ambrose caught his breath. 'My God! It's beautiful! It's like a mansion in the South. Only more... relaxed, I guess. It suits the setting. Very impressive. I had no idea...'

Warwick smiled and looked again at the gracious facade that welcomed visitors to Tingulla. Drought or not, Millie still managed to recycle water onto the flowers and the brolga fountain splashed and sparkled in the sunlight. It was a magnificent home. No wonder Queenie was devoted to it.

'Built by my wife's great-grandfather. It's part of the country's history.'

'It certainly is lovely. It would be wonderful to share this with people around the world by putting it in our film. You could never build a set to create this sort of magic,' enthused Roger.

Warwick turned to Roger Ambrose. 'I should alert you to the fact that my wife isn't overly enthused about this idea. She's out with the horses right now, but we can drive over later on and I'll introduce you. I'm sure once you explain what it entails . . .'

'That's what I'm here for,' smiled the American smoothly. 'I'm certainly looking forward to seeing over the house.'

Millie served cool drinks, tea and sandwiches on the verandah, and afterwards the interested pilot tagged along as Warwick showed the American over the interior of the homestead.

Roger Ambrose had a soft accent and a gentle manner, and exuded enthusiasm without gushing. 'The rooms are spacious with so much natural light. Perfect for shooting interior scenes. What's the noise level like outside? Obviously there's no traffic. Many planes go over?'

'Not unless you ask for them or someone is lost,' said the pilot.

'Perfect, perfect.'

'Birds make a bit of a racket.'

'Indigenous sound effects. We can live with that. It's all looking very good, Warwick. I'd like to meet your wife and see if I can convince her to allow us to shoot here. From what I saw from the plane as we flew in, the surrounding area looks like it will fit the bill as well.'

They drove the pilot back to his plane and watched him take off. 'I'll take you for a tour around the property and outer paddocks. And you can meet Queenie at the same time.'

Roger Ambrose made notes as they spent the next two hours driving about the property.

'It's not looking its best because of the drought. Hasn't been this dry for years.'

'These red and orange earth tones are wonderful. If we wanted lush green we'd film in Ireland. How many sheep did you say you had?'

'We run fifty thousand on two hundred thousand acres. We have a smaller property a couple of hundred miles to the northeast called Cricklewood which we're still developing. Queenie is experimenting with breeding up a new strain of cattle over there.'

'Man, you're talking Texas figures! You don't have oil on this place by any chance?'

'Who knows? No one's ever bothered to look.'

Roger Ambrose shook his head. 'This country is amazing. Most Americans have no idea what's out here. We think it's all kangaroos and natives and pioneer towns. I was knocked out by Sydney, and now to see a place like this out here in, what did the pilot call it . . . "never-never land". Unbelievable.'

The afternoon was closing in, the sun sinking behind the blue hills. Warwick turned the Land Rover towards the stockyard where Queenie was working.

The big bay mare had proved an obstinate animal. Ernie grinned as he watched Queenie walk the horse about the ring talking to it softly but firmly. The horse tossed its head and its haunches quivered, disliking the light saddle buckled to its back.

Warwick switched the engine off and the two men sat quietly watching Queenie. 'Who's the black man?' whispered Roger.

'Ernie — one of our senior stockmen. Good man, does some droving too.'

'Why doesn't he break the horses?'

'You'll see.'

Queenie decided it was time to attack once again. She brought the horse to a stop, turned its head and had a foot in the stirrup, swinging lightly into the saddle before the bay realised what was happening.

The horse began bucking and propping, and although her hat was flung from her head, Queenie stayed firmly in place, managing to look in command, gracefully flowing with the violent movements of the bay mare. Within a few minutes the horse resigned itself and began walking, then — guided by Queenie — started trotting.

'See how she's giving the horse commands with the reins. Watch how she turns its head, but she's incredibly gentle with its mouth. When Queenie breaks a horse it stays a good horse. A badly broken horse stays bad,' commented Warwick.

Queenie slid from the horse, unbuckled the saddle and handed it to Ernie. She fished in the pocket of her shirt for a couple of sugar cubes which she gave to the horse. Then, without warning, she grasped the horse's mane and swung herself onto its bare back. 'Open the gate, Ernie. I want her to get used to the feel of someone on her, not just a saddle.'

He lifted the looped wire over the post and pushed the gate open. Holding the reins lightly, Queenie pressed her leg against the horse's flank and moved it through the gate.

She rode bareback easily, taking the horse into a slow canter, her gold-brown hair dancing around her head as it caught the last of the light.

The two men stepped from the car and walked over to Ernie. Roger Ambrose strained his eyes for a better look at Queenie. She had a superb figure and sat a horse better than any man he'd ever seen, but he wondered what she looked like close up.

Feeling pleased with herself, Queenie turned the bay back to the yard where it trotted obediently to the railing. She slid to the ground, looped the reins over the post and turned to face them.

Ambrose had seen some beautiful women in his time, but Queenie took his breath away. Her soft hair fell about her shoulders framing her heart-shaped face and vivid emerald green eyes fringed with thick dark lashes, her high cheekbones and glowing skin. Her wide, sensuous mouth was grinning with delight.

'This is my wife, Queenie. This is Roger Ambrose.'

'Hello. Welcome to Tingulla.'

'My pleasure to be here. You're quite a horsewoman. And very beautiful. You should be in the movies!'

Queenie laughed. 'Now, you're not going to win me over with flattery. But thank you, anyway.'

She spoke briefly to Ernie before turning back to the men. 'Shall we head back to the house? So tell me, Mr Ambrose, what do you think of my Tingulla?'

'Call me Roger. I'm completely knocked out by it — by everything.' He gazed at Queenie, including her in his comment.

'I'm pleased to hear it. But the best is yet to come. You haven't tried Millie's cooking yet.'

The food was delicious, but Roger Ambrose scarcely noticed. He wasn't listening to Warwick's talk, either. He was watching Queenie.

The stunning girl in the paddocks had bloomed into an alluring and sophisticated woman in the candlelight.

Roger Ambrose had made his decision. Tingulla had a lot more possibilities for *Red Jack* than he'd ever imagined.

Chapter Twenty

It was early morning and raucous bird calls rang through the bush. In the stillness a heavy, dead eucalypt branch crashed to the ground, causing the birds to shriek and with beating wings, sweep away. An immaculate magpie flew from the cover of the trees across the cleared ground to land on a smart white paling fence. It cocked its head at the sound of galloping hooves in the distance.

Carved from the natural bush setting was a neatly fenced, dirt racetrack, where a horse thundered around the circuit in the haze of morning light.

An old man sat on a log bench beside the track, his chin sunk on his chest. He was not dozing in the sun but watching the spinning second hand of his fob watch. He glanced up as the horse approached, striding broadly and easily as it neared the end of the two mile gallop. A frail Aboriginal boy was perched on its massive back like a dragonfly balanced on a charging rhino.

TR drove his new Range Rover past Guneda's tidy green paddocks to the racetrack and joined old Bobby on the bench.

Bobby looked back down at his watch and gave a soft whistle.

'Bill doing all right, hey?' asked TR.

'Going like the clappers. Bugger can run all right, TR. What we don't know is whether he wants to win every race.'

'Won't know that till he has some competition.'

'Yeah. He's strong. And big. But still a youngster. He's not ready yet.'

TR grinned as the horse slowed and the young jockey turned it towards them. 'I have to admit he's grown into a better looking fella than that gangling great dane we picked up at the auction.'

'It's all the attention he gets. He thrives on affection,' said Bobby.

The big russet horse lifted his head and turned at the sound of Bobby's voice, and trotted to the two men as they leaned over the railing.

'How's he doing, Mick?'

The boy slid down from the tall animal, unbuckling his hard hat, allowing the shock of blue-black curls to spring free. 'Good, boss. Still likes to have his own way a bit. But he's learning.'

'You both are. You're coming on real good, Mick,' said Bobby. 'You got a ride this week?'

'Yeah, for Donaldson at the Timbarloo picnic races. Don't think much of me chances. I'm waiting for the day I get to ride Bill here in the Melbourne Cup.'

'You may be a little kid, Mick, but you've sure got big dreams,' laughed TR.

The horse leaned forward, sniffing TR's jacket and giving him a disdainful nudge with his nose before turning his attention to Bobby, snuffling and forcing his way into Bobby's coat where he knew there was a treat waiting. Mick took the saddle and blanket from his perspiring horse.

Bobby ducked under the railing. 'I'll take him back and groom him. See you later, TR.'

'Mick, throw the gear in the Range Rover and I'll take you back to the stables.'

They drove off and Bobby strolled through the paddock with the devoted horse walking beside him unguided, his reins swinging free. The two of them spent a lot of time together, 'going for walks'. The old man would drag on his hand-rolled cigarette as he enjoyed the sight of the trees and the song of the birds; the horse beside him, occasionally pausing to sniff the ground or nibble a bush. It was always Bill who decided when it was time to go home, turning around and giving Bobby a gentle nudge just to make sure he got the message.

TR and Mick went into the stable set aside for Bill, and TR looked on as Mick began pulping Bill's feed.

'He's giving him pineapples and beetroot.' Mick shook his head. 'Never heard of a horse loving pineapples. Bill's crazy about 'em. Bobby has some friend in Queensland with a farm who sends down tons of them. Old Bobby sure got some funny ideas. Says Bill's never gonna wear shoes either.'

'Whatever he's doing, Bill seems to be happy. Well, I better go check on that temperamental mare of Sir Ashton Holloway. She won't let the stallion near her.'

'Them's women, hey, boss?' commented the worldly wise seventeen-year-old.

'So what exactly is this movie *Red Jack* all about, Roger?' asked Queenie as she poured the tea.

'It may surprise you. It's an Australian story but with universal appeal — a romance. It's loosely based on a poem by one of your old bush poets. Red Jack is a wild and beautiful young woman no man can tame. A woman who can outride any man — a real tomboy and rebel. Being Edwardian times, her behaviour is considered rather shocking. She lives with her poor widowed father who is in danger of being thrown off his land by the rich landowner next door. The landowner has a handsome son who thinks of himself as the best horseman in the district. The girl's father has a young racehorse and it comes down to a gamble between the rich son and his horse, and the poor father and his horse to decide the fate of their land. If the father's horse wins, he stays, if Benton the landowner's son wins, *his* father takes the land and Red Jack, and her father will be homeless. It all hinges on this race.'

'And naturally the girl rides her father's horse and wins,' said Queenie drily.

'Of course! But she rides disguised as a man. And naturally Benton falls in love with her and they end up together, so the father can stay on his land the rest of his days. There's a bunch of other stuff in there, like how Benton has to win Red Jack over. She's called Red Jack because of her wild red hair. You'd make a wonderful Red Jack.'

'I don't go to the pictures, let alone act in them,' replied Queenie. 'I hope you can find an actress who can ride well.'

'Oh, that doesn't matter . . . ' Roger paused, a smile spreading over his face. 'Say, you'd be perfect as Red Jack's double!'

'As what?'

'If we dyed your hair red you could stand in for the actress by doing all the actual riding scenes. Would you? We'd pay you well for it, of course.'

'Roger, I haven't agreed to this film being made here yet! I still have to run Tingulla. My time is very valuable.'

'Name a price.'

'I'll think about it. Warwick and I will discuss it all and get back to you.' Queenie cocked her head, hearing the distant drone of a Cessna.

'I can't thank you enough for your hospitality. These past couple of days here have been truly wonderful. It's too bad you couldn't take in paying guests. This is the Australia tourists should see.'

'Please! I have enough to contemplate — what with movie crews and stunt riding or whatever, without thinking of going into the tourist business.' Queenie shook his hand warmly. She had found the American charming, polite and practical. Not at all what she had expected from a Hollywood movie man. 'As I said, we'll think it over.'

'Can't ask more than that.' Roger Ambrose picked up his bag. 'Say goodbye to Warwick for me.'

'He's gone to collect two of our men who are out after a killer dingo . . . a wild dog. Hopefully they've got him. He's been slaughtering our sheep.'

Roger Ambrose nodded. He was still finding it difficult to adjust to this beautiful and authoritative woman. She was totally feminine but there was a capable toughness about her that he found fascinating. It was interesting to compare the helpless beauties he knew with this gorgeous woman who was utterly self-sufficient. He realised that if they were out there alone in this wild country he would be dependent on her for survival.

As the plane rose above Tingulla homestead he saw Queenie walking across the front lawn. She had a lot of qualities of the heroine of their film. If only she'd allow them to shoot there. It would solve a lot of their problems, but in his heart he knew Queenie was wise to be' cautious. He'd never allow a film crew anywhere near his home. It was like inviting a full-scale circus, an opera company, and the government of a banana republic to take over your life.

It took Warwick some time to locate Snowy and Jim from the rough directions they had given above the static of the two-way radio. It was late afternoon before he spotted the curl of blue smoke from their campfire.

Snowy had pegged out three dingo skins and Jim sat by the fire, his rifle and walking stick resting beside him. He lifted a hand in cheerful salute as Warwick drove through the trees.

Snowy poured tea from the old billy into a mug and handed it to Warwick. 'Jim's medicine worked real good. Them dogs come in sniffing after his brew quick smart.'

'Potted the first one, no trouble,' Jim said. 'The other two were more wary. But we reckon we got the bugger that killed our sheep.'

'Any more of them around?'

'Hard to say. Snowy can't find any fresh tracks. Think it was just one group. Haven't seen any elephants or tigers either,' grinned Jim, indicating their brush hide which had sheltered and hidden them for the last few days. 'We were beginning to feel like two biggame hunters. Started making up stories to pass the time.'

'I see you've been keeping busy,' said Warwick to Jim.

Jim lifted the strips of leather he was braiding into an intricately patterned belt. 'Roo hide. Thought I'd make a present for Queenie. I'm working her initials into it.'

'Looks good, Jim. Christ! What was that noise?'

Snowy and Jim exchanged a glance then Snowy reached under the blanket beside him and lifted out a fat golden-brown ball of fur. 'Dingo pup. We killed the mother. This little fella crawled into our camp.'

'Well, kill it. Bash it on the head. We don't want more full-grown dingoes about the place,' said Warwick.

Jim and Snowy looked uncomfortable. 'He put up such a fight we figured he'd earned a chance. I thought I'd take him back and give him to Millie to feed till he can manage on his own, then take him up into the hills and let him go.'

'What the hell for? You can't make a pet of these dogs, Jim. Their killer instinct is bred in too deep.'

Jim took the pup. 'If he puts a paw wrong, I'll do him in.'

Warwick shook his head and refilled his mug of tea. 'Reckon you blokes have been out in the sun too long. Pack up and we'll head back.'

'You ever hear the story of giant devil dingo?' Snowy asked Jim as they started gathering their gear together.

'Nope. Tell it to us, Snowy.'

Warwick helped the men break camp, throwing the dingo hides in the back of the truck, but found himself avidly following Snowy's sing-song recital of one of his favourite Aboriginal tales, and soon forgot all about the dingo pup.

Colin and Dina joined the Camboni family for their traditional Sunday lunch. Eighteen people were seated around the long wooden table under the grapevine in the garden. *Antipasto* of home-baked bread, olives pickled in the Australian sun, goat cheese and assorted salamis were spread on platters. Frascati wine in raffia-covered bottles was passed up and down the table, while in the kitchen the Camboni women prepared and garnished the main courses.

Included among the guests was Roger Ambrose who once again enthused about his visit to Tingulla. 'Colin, if you have any influence with your sister, please ask her to agree to letting us film there. It's perfect. The location, the house, the animals, extras who can ride — it's all there. I told Queenie she'd be a great double for the leading lady. Boy, can she ride!'

Dina turned to Colin. 'I must see Tingulla and your sister at home on the range, darling.' She turned to Roger. 'It's hard to imagine her like that. I've only seen her dressed up here in Sydney where she seems such a... ' She was going to say snob, but knew that wasn't right. What was it about Queenie that faintly irritated Dina? Her aloofness maybe.

'... a lady,' supplied Roger. 'Elegant and gracious one minute, then a sort of free spirit on horseback the next.'

Colin changed the subject. 'The film is definitely going ahead then? You've found all your investors?'

'The studio put up the distribution guarantee and half the budget so it wasn't too hard to persuade a few wily businessmen it was a worthwhile investment.'

'Gamble, you mean,' laughed Alfredo Camboni. 'Movies are always a risk unless you are prepared to lose money or have a clever accountant.'

'Surely if the film is a hit you can make a big profit,' commented one of the other men.

Roger leaned forward. 'Of course you can. And a film like this is sure to make money. It has American studio backing, it's got two major American TV stars in their first big film, it's a great script and the Australian setting is going to knock the socks off American audiences — and the rest of the world. They'll love it. Can't miss.'

'So where do I send my cheque?' laughed the old Italian.

Colin held out his hand. 'See me. I'm handling the financial side. I thought I'd even put up some of my own money, I believe in the project so much.'

Dina gave Colin a bemused glance but said nothing.

Colin later called Warwick and spoke to him privately. 'This *Red Jack* movie deal could be good. I've lined up several investors this end so, frankly, I think you should persuade Queenie it's a good idea. If you could scrape up some of the ready to invest yourself, Warwick, I reckon you'll make a killing too.'

The glamour and the novelty of a film being made at Tingulla meant nothing to Queenie. But the figures did. She sat at her desk working out the cost factors of time, facilities, food, availability of men, horses and vehicles, and weighed it against the income offered by Mountain Pictures. Tingulla came out in front.

'All right, Warwick, we'll do it. But I want you to keep tabs on the outgoing costs involved on a daily basis. I can just imagine they'll be changing their minds and asking for this or that which we hadn't allowed for, and if that's the case, it's to be charged to the film. This is a business exercise, not fun and games.'

Having agreed to *Red Jack* being filled at Tingulla, Queenie went about her business. Letters of agreement were sent to her from Mountain Pictures in Los Angeles which she read carefully, and passed on to her solicitors before signing. Roger Ambrose included a personal note saying how delighted he was and how he looked forward to 'working with her'. He also explained it would be at least two months before they came out.

Queenie pushed the film to the back of her mind and settled to the task of looking at ways to keep Tingulla and Cricklewood afloat. With the drought dragging on, the sheep had to have feed supplied to Tingulla, but there was still enough grass about for the hardy Brahman cattle on Cricklewood. Some graziers were selling what they could before prices sank lower. Queenie decided to hold off until their sheep carried a full fleece in the hope rain would come in time to improve their condition.

'It's a shame we can't buy stock while prices are this low,' said Warwick, as they discussed the problem in the study one evening before going to bed.

'It wouldn't be worth it. We can't afford to feed them.'

'What about cattle? I hear there are a lot being sold at the auctions. We are going to have to put those Brahmans over a heap of Herefords to start building up the numbers.'

'I know. But if the drought goes on, we could lose more than we save in buying cattle while prices are down.'

'We just have to hold on, huh, Queenie?'
Warwick smiled at her, wishing he could
smooth the worried expression from her face.
He reached out and took her hand. 'Why don't
you and Saskia take a little holiday? Go to
Neptune Island for a week.'

'Oh, Warwick, you are so impractical. We
can't afford it! But it was a nice idea. Thanks.'
Queenie rose and kissed him lightly on the
cheek; gently withdrawing her hand, she
headed outside.

Colin opened his crocodile skin briefcase and
drew out a folder of documents and put it
on the table.

Dina placed a glass of Scotch and soda beside
him. 'Bringing work home from the office. My,
my, I am impressed.'

'My commission from this little exercise will
be quite profitable, so don't sneer.'

'Enough for your wife to go shopping at
Mr Steiner's?'

'Jesus, Dina, haven't you got enough
jewellery?'

'A woman never has enough jewellery.
Besides it's an investment.'

'Crap. You have no intention of selling it.
If you want an investment, buy good stones,
put them in the vault for ten years, then flog
them. The stuff you wear morning, noon and
night would have to be surgically removed
from your body before you'd sell it.'

She nibbled Colin's ear. 'You like making love
to me when I wear nothing but my jewellery.'

'I'm not averse to a bit of sexy underwear

or high heels either. Now go away and leave me be. I have to sort out these *Red Jack* contracts.'

'You've persuaded people to invest in the film?'

'Yep. Even Warwick. He figured he should put some money in it as Tingulla will feature heavily in the film.'

'And what about you — are you putting money into *Red Jack* too?'

'No way, sweetheart. Films are too risky for me. I prefer commodities. Beef, wheat, wool.'

'That's your country background talking.' Dina curled her arms about his neck, running her fingers down his chest inside his shirt.

'Nope. It's my new insider trading talk.' Colin drew her head around and kissed her, the papers falling to the floor, forgotten.

Queenie felt as if she was in a holding pattern waiting for some change to the blistering blue sameness of every day. The days merged — an endless routine of feeding, checking the condition of the stock and anxiously watching the level of the water in the dams sink lower and lower.

There was no wind to turn the fans of the windmill, and petrol-driven portable pumps were used to drag the sickly yellow sulphurous water from far beneath the ground.

'There are minerals in this bore water that are making the sheep crook. We need a desalination plant,' said Warwick.

'We can't afford it. We'll have to make do as things are for the moment,' sighed Queenie.

The weeks were stretching out and Queenie

was so absorbed in her day-to-day problems that it came as a shock when Mountain Pictures announced their advance group would be arriving within a week.

'I don't know how we're going to manage with all these extra people about the place — what with the water situation being so desperate. And you know what city people are like — let alone Americans — they waste water without realising it.'

'Queenie, if the worst comes to the worst we'll have to buy in water.'

'That'll knock a big hole in our profits. God, Warwick, I should never have agreed to it.'

'There's no going back now, Queenie. You'd better start doing your rain dance.'

Warwick was joking but Queenie was thoughtful. At sunset she strolled down to the stables and stood rubbing Nareedah's velvety nose, watching the burning rays of the setting sun spread hot fingers across the twilight sky.

Softly as a shadow, Snowy materialised beside her. They stood in companionable silence, the elderly Aborigine and the beautiful young woman he'd watched over since a child.

'You got worries, eh, Queenie?'

'It's this damn drought, Snowy. Tell me, when is the rain going to come? I feel like I'm drying up, too. Like all the juices have gone from my body and I'm just a hollow shell. If another problem drops on me I'll simply disintegrate in a pile of dust and drift away on the wind. Pouff... that's the end of Queenie.'

Snowy didn't smile at this rhetoric but

nodded understandingly. 'Hold on, girl. Rain come in three, mebbe four days.'

Queenie studied his face, hope flickering in her heart. No teasing twinkle lurked in his black eyes, the expression on his deeply lined face was calm.

'You've read the signs, Snowy?'

'Some. Mebbe magic man been round. Mebbe time we helped the rain come.' His face was impassive and his eyes had a faraway look which didn't invite further questioning.

Queenie knew better than to probe further. There had been times in her life when events and incidents had happened because of Aboriginal intervention that simply could not be explained. She didn't try to understand but simply trusted and accepted.

In any other matter Queenie was forceful, the first to query, or demand an explanation. But when Aborigines were involved on a spiritual or mystical level, she became calmly fatalistic, flowing with events she could not control or fathom yet felt were preordained.

She drew a deep breath, feeling strength seep back into her bones, and touched Snowy gently on the arm. 'G'night, Snowy.'

'Sleep good. Watch for *mi-mi* spirits,' he grinned at her.

Queenie smiled as she turned away, flooded with memories. As a small girl, Snowy had told her the story of the strange spirits who appeared as dancing lights in the empty landscape, beckoning and leading those unwise enough to follow to their doom.

She wondered if Snowy had ever told Saskia

that myth. Snowy had replaced the grand-father figure in her daughter's life and the two spent a lot of time together. Between Millie and Snowy, Saskia was storing up vast and varied knowledge.

Thinking about her clever little girl, Quee-nie popped her head into the kitchen where she heard the hum of Millie's voice and Saskia laughing. Saskia was sitting cross-legged on the floor playing with the dingo pup, now a roly-poly bundle of mischief.

'What's going on here? I thought Devil was supposed to be living outside. He's not an ordi-nary dog, Sas, you understand that, don't you?'

'Oh, yes. Millie and Jim have told me. But I think he's special. And different. He talks to me, Mummy. I mean I understand what he's thinking.'

Queenie looked at Millie who shrugged. 'They get on good. I've told her to watch those teeth of his, they're sharp now.' Softly Millie admonished Queenie. 'She's never had a real pet of her own. The other dogs are working dogs and can't be petted. Remember the baby roo you raised for all those years.'

Queenie nodded. Her heart still lurched at the memory of that stormy night when she'd had to shoot her horse Pegasus and had brought home the infant kangaroo. 'And the day I had to let it go in the wild, I thought my heart would break.'

'Your mother wasn't sorry to see him go. He ate the garden, messed on the verandah and went silly looking for a mate. He was happier out in the bush.'

'The trouble is, if they come to depend on people, they can't manage so well when they have to go back to the bush.'

'I dunno, Queenie. Seems to me an animal's instinct comes back real fast.'

'I hope so, Millie. I've always wondered how my pet roo survived. I sort of think of him in a different way to the kangaroos that over-run properties. Come on, Saskia, put Devil back in his box and let's get ready for dinner.'

Queenie woke at piccaninny light and slipped quietly from her bed so as not to disturb War-wick. She wrapped one of Rose's crochet quilts about her shoulders and stepped out onto the upper verandah. There was a different smell in the air, and the sky was tinged with a faint sepia glow. Wisps of shredded cloud sat low on the horizon as the line between sky and land became more clearly defined.

As she sat in a cane chair watching the sunrise, she knew that Snowy's prediction would come to pass.

Two days later the advance crew from Moun-tain Pictures drove their convoy of hired vans and loaded trucks into Tingulla. They were the last people to get through for the next six weeks.

The rains came and Tingulla was an island speck in an inland sea.

Chapter Twenty-One

———— ❧ ————

Jim picked his way through trucks, vans, caravans and canvas chairs, stepping over cables snaking across the ground and dodging past young men in shorts and coloured T-shirts with hair hanging to their shoulders. He sidestepped a hurrying girl who was wearing a psychedelic print caftan. She was carrying a clipboard covered in flapping papers and had a stopwatch around her neck. She appeared not to see him.

Reaching the kitchen screen door, he sighed with relief to find it deserted save for Millie and Stan making a batch of scones and pikelets ready for the film crew's morning smoko.

'Looks like a flamin' blacks' camp out there. What do these people do? They all just seem to stand around.'

'They talk and eat a lot,' offered Stan, now upgraded from shearers' cook to film crew caterer.

'So where are these famous movie stars? When do they earn their dough?' asked Jim, dipping his finger in the pikelet batter.

'They spend all their time in their dinky little caravans. *She* doesn't want to go out in the mud and *he's* getting stuck into the grog.'

'Go on, Stan, is that right?'

Stan grinned. 'Seems the Yankee TV bloke has discovered Aussie beer. I wonder if anyone's told him it's strong enough to blow the arse feathers off a bald turkey.'

'He'll be blotto by midday. Thinks he's as flash as a buck rat with a gold tooth too. This film-making business is a load of old cobblers if you ask me.'

'Nobody is asking you, Jim. Now buzz off — Stan and me are busy.'

Roger Ambrose sat close to Queenie as they discussed business in her study. 'Because of the water and mud, shooting outside is impossible, so we'll do all the interiors first up. That will mean using certain rooms. We'd like to do scenes in the sitting room first off.'

Queenie waved a hand. 'Whatever is necessary to get on with it.'

Roger touched her arm and gave her his best smile. 'I know it seems chaotic, but things are actually all under control. Now, Queenie, about you doing some doubling work for us . . .'

The charm wasn't working, Queenie rose to her feet. 'Roger, I have several hundred bogged sheep to move from creek flats. I'm sorry — I'm just too busy.'

'I understand. But we won't be getting to

the horse-riding scenes until the conditions are better outside. Be two weeks at least, I should think. Would you please think about it, Queenie? We've located some guy who's an ace horseman to ride with you as Benton.'

'Who is he?'

'Can't remember his name. Casting dug him up in New South Wales. I'm told he's one of the best riders in the country.'

'I'll be interested to meet him. Now, if you'll excuse me.'

Ambrose smiled to himself as he watched her leave. He was beginning to get the key to Queenie. She liked a challenge. When he mentioned this hotshot horseman she hadn't said she wouldn't ride with him. He figured she'd do the doubling scenes as Red Jack just to see if she could ride better than the other fellow.

The film people swarmed into the house, carrying lights, cameras, boxes of sound gear, and miles of cables. While one man began building what looked like a miniature train track down the hall into the living room, another started tacking coloured plastic film over the windows. Two girls moved in and started rearranging the furniture, removing all the family possessions and replacing them with period pieces. Footprints of red mud congealed on the polished wood floors and Persian rugs. Tea mugs were placed on top of mahogany side tables leaving wet white rings.

Millie blew her stack and strode from room to room shouting above the din of set-making and rehearsing. 'All right, you blokes. No food or drinks indoors. Tea is served on the verandah and the cups are to stay out there, thank you very much.'

The rugs were rolled up and newspapers spread over the floor. Millie had all the personal possessions stored in a spare bedroom and kept an eagle eye on sixteen people at once.

She tugged at a man bolting the train tracks together. 'What's that for?'

'It's a camera dolly, luv. So we can run the camera smoothly alongside the actors as they walk into the room.'

Millie shook her head. She hoped they were paying Queenie a lot of money for this. She leaned down to a kneeling man with a mouthful of nails.

'If one nail goes into that floor I'll personally castrate you with a blunt knife.'

The storms stopped and the floodwaters began to recede. The truck carrying extra food supplies for Tingulla which had been bogged for the last week, could now get through. The driver had simply camped on higher ground near his truck and finished reading Henry Miller's *Tropic of Cancer* and started *Forty Thousand Leagues Under the Sea*.

Roger Ambrose had arranged for a vital piece of film gear to be flown in along with fresh fruit and vegetables. The plane carried the first cans of film to the processing laboratory in Sydney and from there they would go by Qantas to Mountain Pictures in Hollywood.

Around Tingulla the sun baked the boggy ground into crazy ruts and patterns. Stan regaled the film crew at mealtimes with tales of sheep and cattle carcasses hanging from the tops of trees, and flash floods ripping through the desert in seconds to sweep away a mob of a hundred cattle and two trucks with no warning.

After ten days of filming inside the house Roger went to Queenie. She had virtually taken up residence in her study, having given her bedroom over to the female star who had constant complaints about filming conditions. Queenie had breakfast at sunrise in the kitchen with Millie and didn't return till after dark to bathe, take her dinner from the oven and eat it at her desk while catching up on paperwork before stretching out to sleep on the leather sofa.

Warwick had moved into a smaller back bedroom off the verandah and spent most of his time assisting Roger Ambrose, helping to organise whatever station facilities were needed. He and Queenie were passing like ships in the night, and while she found the whole process wearing, Warwick seemed to find it stimulating.

Roger tapped at the study door late one evening and looked at Queenie bent over the account books on her desk. 'Can I interrupt? I bring refreshments.' He held aloft a bottle of Bollinger champagne and two glasses.

'That looks very welcome. Where did Warwick unearth cold Bollinger?'

'Courtesy of Mountain Pictures. The plane

came in today to collect this week's rushes and brought some goodies. Word is back from LA that what we've got in the can looks wonderful. They thought the flood scenes looked great. Seeing as it was all there we did some aerial shots of the water surrounding the homestead and the flooding all over the countryside. I think the executives think we arranged it all ourselves. Bigger than De Mille,' he laughed.

Queenie laughed politely and sipped her champagne. 'I'm glad things are going well, though how you tell I can't imagine.'

'You can never tell till it's up on the big screen. Queenie... we'd like to do the race sequences in a few days' time. The bloke doubling for Benton will be here on Friday. Warwick has the horses all set for us, and if you're willing, wardrobe and hairdressing would like to see you as soon as convenient.'

'I knew there was a reason for this,' smiled Queenie, holding up her glass.

'No ulterior motive, I swear. I thought you might enjoy a little pick-me-up and some company. You work long hours, too.'

Queenie pushed the books to one side as Roger topped up the crystal flute beside her. He was right, she did feel like some company. She began to ask him about his life in Los Angeles, trying to imagine the world he described, so vastly different from her own.

They finished the champagne and Roger bid her goodnight, kissing her lightly on the cheek. 'A Hollywood habit,' he explained.

*

What was supposed to be a quick visit to the wardrobe and hairdressing girls turned into several hours as Queenie was fitted for her old-fashioned riding habit and her long bronzed hair was rinsed a deep russet red.

Saskia and Warwick loved her new look. 'I want my hair coloured, too,' demanded Saskia, shaking her inky-dark curls.

'Not on your nelly. Don't you ever touch your beautiful hair. You're a lucky girl that you inherited Daddy's lovely locks,' said Queenie firmly, glancing at Warwick and noticing for the first time several silver threads sprinkled at his temples.

'That red hair makes your eyes look even greener, Queenie. You're much prettier than the star of this epic.'

'Thank you darrrling,' replied Queenie, with an exaggerated American accent. Kissing the air near his cheek, she said, 'a Hollywood habit, you know,' and swept out of the room in melodramatic style as Warwick applauded her exit.

Dressed in a looped skirt, an old-fashioned man's shirt and a hat with a fly veil, with her red hair crimped and in waves down her back, Queenie sat on a fold-up chair while the make-up girl patted orange powder over her face.

'Is all this necessary? Surely no one's going to see my face?'

'The skin tones have to match, even at a distance. The director likes every detail to be as consistent as possible.'

A further fifteen minutes were spent

discussing whether Red Jack would ride side-saddle or not. Queenie decided to weigh into the argument — no matter if she was right or wrong, some decision had to be reached or they'd obviously be there all morning.

'Women in those days did ride side-saddle on formal or public occasions. But you can't tell me that a spirited young woman who was such a good horsewoman wouldn't ride like a man around her own place or alone in the bush.'

'Queenie's right. That's just how Red Jack would think,' said Roger Ambrose. 'Dump the side-saddle.'

Roger explained the scene to Queenie. 'Now, what's happening here is the scene where Benton tells Red Jack that the fate of her father's property rests on the result of the horse race to be set up the next day. All we are seeing here in this scene are the two of them meeting on horseback, and riding together to fetch her father. The race sequences will be in a different setting and on another day in the story.'

'I see... I think,' said Queenie somewhat dubiously. 'Just tell me what you want me to do. Where is the fellow I'll be riding with?'

'He's gone with the wrangler to bring up his horse. If you'd like to mount and get into position we'll check the lighting.'

Queenie didn't see the necessity for extra lights in broad daylight, but said nothing as she lifted the heavy skirt up to pull herself into Nareedah's saddle. She patted the big white horse who had been groomed and brushed and looked magnificent.

'I see Nareedah gets a starring role, too!' The sky started to spin at the sound of that voice.

Queenie spun Nareedah around to see TR on a beautiful mount trotting towards her, a wide grin on his face. He too was in period dress, a scarf knotted at his throat, a straw cabbage tree hat shading his face which also had an artificial tan. His blue eyes and white teeth gleamed as he smiled at Queenie, and he looked incredibly handsome.

'Well, I should have guessed it would be you, of course.'

Roger Ambrose looked from one to the other. 'Do you two know each other?'

'Kind of,' muttered TR, not taking his eyes off Queenie. 'That's some get-up you've got on.'

Roger stared at the two on horseback, aware that there was some sort of chemistry between them. They made a far more charismatic pair than the actors they were standing in for.

Queenie hadn't seen TR since he had visited her in her hotel room after the races in Sydney. She knew Jim and Millie were in touch with him, and Warwick had mentioned running into him in Sydney once or twice. But Queenie never expressed any interest in news of TR, so no one ever discussed him in her presence. In her heart Queenie was interested, but she knew she couldn't begin to let anything chip away at the barrier she had cemented around her memories of him.

'Can we start now?' asked Queenie, coming out of her reverie.

'Right, we're ready. Let's push this shoot along today.' The director raised his voice. 'Okay everyone, stand by.'

Queenie concentrated on what she was instructed to do. Stand here, turn the horse there. Wait for TR to trot towards her. Turn around and wait. It was time-consuming and tedious. Whenever they changed position the camera and lights had to be moved.

'Hurry up and wait, eh?' muttered TR with his crooked grin. He and Queenie exchanged a look which said, 'What the heck are they doing? This has got to be a waste of time.'

To pass the time, they chatted quietly about horses, Brahman bulls, and the Quinns' quarter horses. Their conversation was as foreign to the crew as the technical film jargon was to them. But Queenie found she was relaxing and was now less defensive with TR. In this artificial setting, dressed as another woman, she no longer felt threatened by the past.

After several hours, they stopped for morning tea.

Warwick strolled over and shook TR's hand, greeting him before turning to Queenie. 'I'm going into town, be back tonight. I'm seeing the bank manager and stock and station blokes and will pick up a few more supplies.' He spoke briefly to Roger Ambrose, waved and left.

Queenie and TR did several more dry runs without moving the horses, then were told there would be a take.

Roger Ambrose repeated the details of the action. 'This one's for real. Your two horses ride off, trotting only, but keep side by side, neck and neck, or whatever. The third post is your mark where you turn around and break into a slow canter — still staying together. Okay?'

Queenie and TR nodded, grinning at one another. So much fuss and detail over a seemingly inconsequential sequence.

The crew fluttered about them, the camera assistant running a tape measure from the camera to Queenie, while the make-up girl asked TR to lean down so she could pat more powder on his face.

Queenie found the film crew an amusing group with their own jokes and strange sense of humour. And they were fun to be around. They called her Red, and she began to feel like another person. It was all unreal — a game.

With the two horses settled into position, the camera and the director and crew set up behind them, Queenie glanced across at TR. He winked at her.

'Quiet on the set... Stand by... roll camera... clapper... and... *Action!*'

They set off trotting obediently side by side as instructed and, at the given mark, broke into an easy canter. Queenie glanced down at the nose of TR's stockhorse, stretched forward, glad to be given a run rather than all the stopping and starting of the morning. She nudged Nareedah forward to keep even with TR. TR inched forward a step... Queenie matched him.

The cameraman watched the two horses cover the landscape within the frame of his viewfinder. They were approaching the point where they would stop and swing about.

The two horses cantered forward, seemingly picking up speed. They passed the stopping point and broke into a gallop, a dust cloud kicking up behind them.

'What the . . . ' the cameraman lifted his head away from the lens and peered around the side of the camera.

'Cut!' screamed the director. The horses were flat out and disappearing into the distance.

'What the fuck is going *on*!' shouted the director, turning in exasperation to Roger Ambrose.

Stan was watching on the sidelines, holding a giant teapot. 'It's a bloody race, that's what it is! Go, Queenie!'

The horses swung past the line of trees as they headed down towards the creek with Nareedah slightly ahead. A cheer went up from the assembled crew and the director kicked at a pile of horse dung with a fancy Texan boot, swearing out loud.

'Lunch,' bellowed a grinning Stan.

TR and Queenie were in a time warp of their own — a world of swift judgment and pounding hooves, the thrill and exhilaration of two fine horses surging forward.

They thundered down the hill towards the creek and instantly slowed as the horses hit the still muddy ground.

'Let's call it a draw,' called TR.

'Okay, I'll let you off this time,' smiled Queenie as they reined in their horses.

TR dismounted and went to her. She flung

both legs over the saddle and holding the bunched skirt in her hands, slid to the ground, supported by TR's strong arms. They walked to the shade of a willow and sat on the ground, leaning against the twisted trunk.

'So, Red, how's life treating you?'

Queenie touched her hair. 'I hope this stuff washes out.'

'Looks nice. But I prefer Queenie to Red Jack. How is this film deal coming along? They look like a bunch of chooks running around with their heads cut off. But I suppose they know what they're doing.'

'I wonder. I wish we were getting double the money. I had no idea of the inconvenience of it all . . . '

'How's Warwick feel about it?'

'He's loving every minute.'

'Maybe they'll offer him a job in Hollywood.'

Queenie laughed. 'Now, that I can't see . . .'

For a few moments they looked at the tree-lined creek where birds were singing and hunting insects, oblivious to their presence.

'I've spent a lot of hours down here. Ever since I was little. This was where I came when I was sad or happy. Every inch of Tingulla has a special meaning for me,' said Queenie softly.

A silence fell between them. Queenie closed her eyes as dappled sunlight drifted through the hazy green branches, warming her face.

TR leaned over and, without touching her, brushed her mouth with his lips. She didn't open her eyes but her lips parted slightly as TR slowly and softly kissed her top lip, then her bottom lip. Light as a butterfly touching her skin, he gently kissed her cheek, her forehead, the tip of her nose, and once again her lips, now lifted in a slight smile.

Queenie hadn't moved, hadn't even opened her eyes.

TR slid his arm behind her and lifted her face to his as he lowered his mouth firmly and possessively to hers. Her arms wound about him as she fervently kissed him back, lost in some dream, some memory of being in her rightful place, protected from reality as if by an invisible membrane.

A shrill whistle and shout pierced the shell around them. 'Coo... eee! Hey — you two! The director wants you back. He's furious.'

Queenie pulled away, shaking her head as though dazed. TR looked around to see one of the young men who operated as a gofer sitting on an old motorbike at the top of the hill and shouting to them.

TR lifted his arm in acknowledgement. He and Queenie stared at one another for a moment then silently rose to their feet. He helped her back into the saddle and they rode back towards the homestead without speaking.

Sundays were scheduled as rest days, but there was little to entertain the crew. They slept, drank and cajoled the stockmen into teaching them to ride. They'd learned that driving all the way into Longreach was a pointless exercise as the town was deserted and dry.

'Can't we even get a goddamn drink in the pub?' asked one of the young fellows.

'Not on a Sunday, mate. Town's as dry as a dead dingo's donger. This is Queensland,' explained one of the station hands.

'It *is* the twentieth century though, isn't it?' muttered the young man, wandering away.

To give the crew a boost, the production manager and Stan planned an evening barbecue. Stan slaughtered a lamb, the lawns at Tingulla were lit by kerosene flame torches and a band made up of crew and station hands provided some rough and ready, but loud and cheerful music.

For the first time, the stars joined the festivities rather than eating as usual in Tingulla's formal dining room.

Queenie said she'd be down later, and ate her meal in the kitchen with Millie and Saskia. She read Saskia a story and tucked her into bed, then reluctantly joined the rowdy party in the garden. She didn't feel like being bright, or smiling at endless stories about a show business world which she neither knew about nor cared for. She sighed. The men were well away, a knot gathered round the beer keg, shouting with laughter.

Warwick was deep in conversation with Roger Ambrose, who saw Queenie and waved her over.

'G'day darlin'. Roger is telling me we're going to have some more visitors. That'll make your night, won't it?' laughed Warwick, putting an arm around Queenie and slopping his schooner of beer.

'What do you mean?' Queenie didn't look pleased and turned to Roger.

'Some of the investors want to come up and have a bit of look at the glamorous and exciting world of movie making,' grinned Roger. 'I hope that's all right with you. I've assured Warwick it will only be an overnight visit.'

'These investors want to see where their money is going — and you're not worried? I would think it'd be better to show them something on a screen.'

'Hell, no. Never let investors see rushes, they don't understand disconnected, unedited grabs of film. Puts them off immediately. They like to see all the paraphernalia of lights, camera, action. Eat with the stars — that kind of thing. Believe me, I've been down this road before.'

Queenie shrugged. 'It's your film.'

'Anyway, Queenie luv, we know some of them. These are not the tycoons from America, these are Australian investors. Alfredo and a few friends,' said Warwick.

Queenie was annoyed but could say little in front of Roger Ambrose. She excused herself and went over to the young women who looked after continuity, hair and make-up. They were amusing and effervescent company and soon had Queenie laughing at their flow of outrageous anecdotes. For a while she envied these girls their adventures, their freedom, their lack of responsibility. But soon enough they were lamenting about how hard it was to find a decent man.

'The guys around here are terrific. *Real* men.'

'Shy, though... till you give them a bit of encouragement,' laughed one of the girls.

'Too bad they don't like the city.'

Queenie smiled at them. 'Maybe you should look for a job in the country. It's a lovely and very special life.' Feeling content she excused herself, bidding the girls good night.

TR wasn't at the barbecue. He had returned to Guneda to check on Bobby, the horses, and Mum Ryan who was anxious for news of what the movie stars were really like. TR didn't tell her the truth. He was due back on the set in a week and if it hadn't been for the presence of Queenie he'd have told them to shove it. Movie making was for the birds. There were too many egos hanging out, too much artificiality, too much panic and hassle over small things, too much chaos. Too many people.

'The suits have arrived,' muttered the focus puller to the cameraman.

'Look busy and say nothing,' sighed the old hand peering back down the lens.

The investors in *Red Jack* did look intensely out of place. Bundled into a chartered jet in Sydney, they were suddenly poured out onto red dirt in the middle of an outback station. The suit jacket slung over the shoulder and loosened tie really wasn't quite casual enough. Singlets, shorts, grubby moleskins and jeans were the uniform of the day — even for the girls. None of the city men wore hats, and their polished shoes were soon coated in a film of orange dust.

However, they looked happy to be there. Queenie came forward to greet Alfredo, relieved to see there were only four visitors. Her smile tightened when Warwick told her,

'The others went straight to the house to wash and have a drink.'

'Warwick, there are a couple of ewes in labour and having a hard time of it. I came across them in the dam paddock and I think we might have to help.'

'Queenie, I can't play midwife at the moment. Can you manage?'

'Of course.' She nodded to the men and strode away.

When she returned several hours later she was physically exhausted and spattered with blood, dirt and dung. Without thinking, she stepped out of the truck and hurried up the front steps wiping her hand across her forehead, smearing dirt on her face.

A tinkling laugh pulled her up and she turned to see the group gathered on one side of the verandah enjoying sunset cocktails as if they were in Double Bay.

Colin was stretched out in a squatter's chair; Dina, crisply elegant in white linen, sat in a cane chair holding a tall glass filled with ice cubes. Camboni, now dressed in casual white slacks and open-necked shirt revealing a gold medallion on a chain around his neck, rose to greet her. Warwick, too, was freshly washed and had changed into sports clothes.

Dina lifted her glass. '*Salute*, Queenie. You look like you need a drink. At the very least.' She smiled. 'I had no idea this place was so civilised. It's utterly charming.'

'You never believe a word I tell you,' complained Colin.

'We have had a most fascinating afternoon.

Won't you join us for a drink? Your maid makes an excellent gin and tonic,' said Alfredo with a gracious smile.

'Millie is not exactly a maid...' began Queenie.

Warwick stepped forward taking her arm. 'Queenie, darling, why don't you go and freshen up and join us? The others will be along shortly.'

'Yes, I have had rather a difficult day.' She smiled sweetly at Dina in her white dress. 'Pulling a stillborn lamb from a distressed ewe is always so wearing, don't you agree?' She turned on her heel and stomped indoors.

Warwick laughed lightly. 'Even with fifty thousand sheep she takes one bad birth to heart.'

'That's Queenie, all right,' remarked Colin without smiling.

'Ah, here come Roger and the others,' said Warwick with relief.

Queenie found the evening meal excruciating. Millie had outdone herself with a beautiful spread. The silver glinted in the candlelight, Warwick poured fine wine into crystal glasses and a faint breeze blew the scent of night flowers into the gracious rooms. The guests were thoroughly enjoying themselves and Queenie couldn't wait to leave.

She excused herself at the first possible moment, claiming tiredness from a day which had begun at sunrise. Her leather sofa in the study was firm and cool, and she was glad to be alone with her thoughts and weariness.

Colin and Dina settled themselves in Colin's old room. Dressed in a flimsy lace negligee, Dina stepped through the French doorway onto the upper verandah and waved her brandy at the expanse of stars shining on the quiet gardens. 'This is adorable, Colin. Why don't you want to live here? I could live here. Very easily.'

'You! You're the ultimate city slicker.' He laughed as he stood behind her, wrapping his arms around her and fondling her breasts through the sheer silk.

'I mean it, Colin. It would be a very nice life style to stay here, and when it gets too boring, we could zip down to Sydney or over to the coast.'

'And what do we *do* while we're here? I can't see you pulling dead lambs from a sheep's backside.'

'That's your job, darling. You know all about this land business. It's what you were trained for, after all. But don't people get managers to do all that sort of thing? Run the place?'

'Generally not while the owner is capable and living on the property. Let's not talk about it, Dina. Come to bed.' He nuzzled her cheek.

Dina wasn't ready to drop the subject. She linked her arm through Colin's and rubbed her head on his shoulder, saying softly. 'I think you were cheated, my love. This place should belong to you.'

Colin said nothing but picked her up and carried her to the bed. Dina let him make love to her but, although her body responded, her mind was elsewhere.

As Colin rolled over to sleep, Dina dropped a leg over his, murmuring, 'Tingulla will be ours one day, *caro*. I promise you.'

Colin grunted and fell asleep.

Chapter Twenty-Two

&

It was a country race meeting, but unlike the beery, boisterous events usually found on the bush circuit, the Scone Races were popular with high society.

The small town on the upper Hunter River was one of the prime horse breeding centres in New South Wales. Its annual cup day provided a showcase for horses and people. Everybody dressed to the teeth in gloves, hats and ties, and best boots polished to a waxed gleam. Picnic hampers were spread on card tables set with linen tablecloths, silverware and serviettes. Coolers were filled with ice to cool the abundant French champagne and local wine. Large bets were flamboyantly laid, big losses dismissed with a philosophical shrug.

Bobby, sporting a new wool jacket with his war veteran's badge pinned to his lapel, strolled among the groups picnicking by their cars, pausing to chat and accept a glass of beer.

He rejoined TR at Bill's stall and filled him in on the news of who was around and what the local graziers had to say.

'Bill ready to run the big one, then?' asked TR.

'As ready as he always is ... never seen a horse enjoy racing like this bloke does.'

'Y'know, Bobby, if he picks up this one and a few more, we could run him on the flat in the metropolitan circuit. And from there ... who knows ... maybe the Melbourne Cup.'

Bobby rubbed the chestnut's nose and Bill pushed his head inside Bobby's coat looking for the sweet that always nestled in a pocket. 'Wouldn't that be something, hey?' His voice was soft and TR glanced at the expression on his face as he stroked the big horse affectionately. He realised how much the horse meant to old Bobby and the pride and satisfaction it would give him to have the horse accepted to run in Australia's greatest race.

Bobby pushed the horse away. 'Go on, you big galoot ... wait till you've won the race, then you get your reward.'

While the jockeys were weighing in for the main event on the race card, the Fashion Fillies Cup was being held on the grass before the main grandstand. Elegant women, from teenagers to grandmothers, were decked out in special outfits, all wearing hat and gloves. Parading before several critical judges they slowly walked around a small ring marked by tubs of petunias. The winner of the Best Dressed would carry off a weekend for two in Sydney at a smart hotel with all expenses paid, plus a small silver cup.

Last minute bets for the main race were placed and the crowd began to gather at the fence and in the quaint old, but freshly painted, grandstand. The horses pranced and circled behind the starting gates. The race caller breathed on his binoculars, polished them, and tested the public address system.

Bobby helped Mick, their regular jockey, into Bill's small light saddle. The slight young Aborigine tightened the chin strap on his hat and adjusted the number nine tied to his back over the pink and navy silks — the colours owned by Riann Hamilton, TR's father.

'Let Bill go right from the start, don't hold him back. I reckon he can run the distance hell for leather, Mick.'

Mick flashed a wide grin. 'He's a bugger to hold back. He likes to be out in front all the time. Sees the finish and goes for it. Never have to touch this bloke with the whip.'

Bobby touched Bill's nose. 'Behave yourself. Don't give Mick any trouble, you do what he tells ya.'

The horse lifted its head, a twitch rippled through his muscular shoulders and he side-stepped daintily, anxious to get on with it.

'Off you go. Good luck, Mick.'

The young jockey tapped his whip to his hat and headed for the stalls across the track.

The new electronic gates clunked open and simultaneously the ten horses sprang free.

Bill rocketed to the lead and settled into a powerful but steady gallop. He didn't slacken, hesitate, or look to right or left as he thundered round the racetrack, oblivious to the swaying multicoloured blur of the crowd roaring on the sidelines.

The loudspeakers attached to poles and trees echoed around the lush green track as the horses streamed past the winning post... 'and it's Sweet William, number nine, by two lengths...'

Bobby and TR led the big chestnut into the winner's circle. 'Well done, Mick.'

'I didn't do nothin'. Just stayed on. Bugger led all the way. Did it real easy, I reckon.' He slid down to the ground and went in to be weighed.

Bobby and TR unsaddled the horse and led him forward to collect the green satin cloth fringed in gold with 'Scone Cup Winner' emblazoned on it. The watching crowd applauded and Bill lifted his head, nodding to his fans as Bobby led him around the ring in a lap of honour.

One of the wealthy farmers who also owned a couple of racehorses congratulated TR. 'You picked up a good young horse there, TR. If you find anything else that looks good, let me know. How's Guneda doing?'

'Real good thanks, Donald. We have two mares about to foal and either of them could produce a strong runner, and I've been training a little colt for Dan Westbaker which is coming along well. He could be bought for the right price at the moment.'

'I'll let you know. Cheers, TR.'

'Bill is the best advertisement we could have, eh, TR?'

'Yeah, thanks to you. I would never have picked him.'

'Rubbish. You've got the eye. Once you know all my training tricks you'll be able to turf me out.'

'You've always got a home with me, Bobby, for as long as you want. In fact I reckon I should speak to Clayton Hindmarsh about giving you a commission or some percentage deal.'

'Nah. Don't need money. My daughter is nicely set up, they don't need anything. Whatever I tuck away will go to me grandkids. What do I want more money for?'

'Buying another horse?'

'No fear — Bill's me mate and he takes all me spare time. Besides, the bugger would never forgive me if I started racing another fella.'

'Okay, Bobby,' laughed TR. 'But if you feel like taking a trip to America for the Kentucky Derby or England for the Grand National... it's on me.'

Bobby nodded, saying seriously, 'Thanks, TR. I tell you what, though — I wouldn't mind thinking about maybe going to Melbourne... wouldn't that be something?' Shaking his head, Bobby wandered off.

TR watched him go, his heart full of love for the man who had become a replacement for his father who had never made it in the race game. He muttered to himself, 'We'll get Bill to the Cup if it's the last thing we do, Bobby.'

Warwick and Queenie were celebrating their sixth wedding anniversary and Warwick insisted they get away from the chaos of the film set at Tingulla. 'The Quinns have asked us over to dinner. Sarah and John are coming up and it will be a party for us.'

Queenie sighed. 'That's nice of them. To tell you the truth, Warwick, it will be nice to get away. This film thing is all a bit much.'

'We're making money from it... you wait and see.'

'Are we?'

Warwick gave her a hug. 'You can't have your present till we come home from the party.'

'Warwick, you are being so mysterious about this present. What's going on? Saskia is going around like she's fit to burst with some secret. I haven't got you anything too exciting I'm afraid.'

'This is a present for all of us. Wait and see.'

TR returned to Tingulla to be on call for filming his final sequences, while Bobby returned to Guneda with Bill in the horse float.

The next day Roger Ambrose apologised to TR. 'Bit of a delay. Won't need you for several hours. Sorry, TR.'

TR nodded and didn't bother asking what this morning's drama was about. He drifted towards the homestead kitchen and tapped at the door. Millie and Saskia were in the kitchen. Millie greeted him warmly. 'Come and have a cup of tea, TR. Saskia has just made some Anzac biscuits.'

Saskia ceremoniously handed him a plate

with warm oatmeal and treacle cookies piled on it. TR took one and complimented the young cook while Millie poured his tea.

The three of them sat around the table and TR filled Millie in on all his news. 'I heard you'd won a few races and were doing well with the breeding and training. That's good news, TR. You've done well since you left Tingulla.'

Saskia tapped him on the arm. 'Do you have a racehorse?'

'You bet. He's called Bill and he's very big and very smart. Bobby, who looks after him, has taught him a couple of tricks.'

Saskia sighed deeply. 'I would love to ride a racehorse. Do you have any small racehorses?'

TR laughed as she gazed up at him with her serious young face. 'You can come and visit Bill any time you want, Saskia. Maybe in a couple of months you could come to Guneda when all the foals are born.'

'Ooh, Millie, wouldn't that be fun?'

'You'll have to speak to your mother about that, young lady. Guneda is a long way from Tingulla.'

'Mummy and Daddy are over at the Quinns' for two days . . . it's a special party for their anniversary. And Daddy has bought a big surprise present. But I can't tell you what it is, except it's so big we can't wrap it up,' gushed Saskia, her eyes dancing with excitement.

TR watched the impish young girl, so like Queenie with her heart-shaped face and beautiful smile. He could see she had her father's grey eyes and dark curly hair; but her body, bone structure, movements and mannerisms were so similar to Queenie's, TR felt he was seeing Queenie as a child.

He noticed Millie looking at him, enjoying his rapport with Saskia. TR reacted with some embarrassment.

'You're enjoying being back here, aren't you?' said Millie.

'Yes. It's very... ' he paused, searching for the right word, but couldn't quite find it. 'Well, nostalgic. Very nostalgic.'

He pushed his chair away from the table and changed the subject. 'Millie, could I phone Guneda and see if Bobby and Bill got back all right?'

'Help yourself, TR. Use Queenie's study.'

Mum Ryan spoke to TR, assuring him that both trainer and horse were safely back and that there were no problems. Mum continued to shout into the phone and TR grinned. Mum regarded the telephone as a dubious instrument and felt she improved Mr Bell's invention by holding the receiver away from her mouth and shouting at it. 'Anyway, TR... we sent her off in the mail truck. Might take her a couple of days to get to you.'

TR hadn't been paying attention. He snapped back to the phone. 'Repeat that, Mum. Who is coming here?'

'Your lady friend. She was very disappointed you weren't here, and wouldn't wait. Said she wanted to see the fillum-making, so we put her on the mail truck going north.'

'Who?' shouted TR.

'The American lady. Very pretty... I don't remember her name. How many girls you got over there, TR?' boomed Mum Ryan in jolly tones.

TR trudged back into the kitchen. 'When's the mail next due, Millie?'

'Probably Thursday. You expecting something, TR?'

'Yeah. See ya. Hooroo, Saskia.' He walked back into the bright morning light, a slight feeling of dread in the pit of his stomach. Surely Ginny hadn't taken it into her head to rush over and visit her father's property.

Warwick and Saskia, one on either side of Queenie, dragged her eagerly down to the rear of the stables.

'Now, close your eyes, Mummy, and we'll tell you when you can open them.'

Still leading her by the hand, they walked a little further, then Warwick said, 'Open up. Happy Anniversary, Queenie'.

Queenie stared and her hands flew to her mouth in surprise as Saskia jumped up and down. Parked next to one of the sheds was a shiny small aeroplane with a large red bow attached to its nose. 'Warwick... what on earth... this must have cost a fortune...'

He dropped an arm around her shoulders and gave her a squeeze. 'Look at the name...'

Queenie walked to the little red and white Piper and saw painted in red near the cockpit the words, *Red Jack*. 'Warwick, we can't afford this... I mean... it's a lovely idea...'

'Don't worry. Call it an advance on profits

from the film. I can fly, but I'll need to brush up a bit and get a new licence. Just think how useful it will be to zip over to Cricklewood, or up to the auction sales, or Brisbane.'

Queenie smiled at him, seeing a small boy with a new toy. 'Let's hope both Red Jacks fly high then. Thank you, darling.' She kissed him, trying to hide the misgivings she felt about this expensive indulgence.

Queenie took Nareedah for a long ride and came back via the new filmset down by the creek. In a day the crew had completed the home of Red Jack and her father. The cabin looked a solid construction but was only a facade.

'Jonesy' Wilson, the Australian actor playing Red Jack's father, was stretched out in a chair, his hat over his face, a bottle of beer at his feet. Babette Larchmont, the cover-girl American movie star playing Red Jack, was huddled with the director arguing over some fine point of her performance. Tyler (Ty) Barda, the hero — known to the Aussies on the quiet as 'Try Harder' — was nowhere to be seen. Queenie suspected he was probably sleeping off another hangover.

Roger Ambrose took Queenie's arm as they walked to the shade of the trees lining the creek bank, to watch the crew preparing for the shoot. As they sat down in director's chairs, there was suddenly a new sound that made everyone take notice — an aeroplane engine starting.

'Ah-ha,' exclaimed Roger. 'Red Jack is about

to get off the ground,' he smiled at Queenie. 'How do you like your anniversary gift?'

'It was a surprise. I don't know that we need a plane, or can afford it. But it was a sweet gesture... I suppose.'

'If an extravagant one,' added Roger.

Queenie sighed. 'Yes, Warwick is inclined to splurge a bit. He gave me some story about money from the film helping to pay for it. The way the crew eats, I think we'll be out of pocket!'

Roger grinned back at her. 'I think he meant profits from his investment in the picture.'

Queenie stared at him. 'Warwick invested money in the film?'

'Oh dear, have I stepped out of line? Didn't you know?'

'No, I didn't.' Queenie looked puzzled, thinking aloud. 'How could he put money in the film and afford to buy that plane? We've been running pretty close to the wind on our overdraft.'

'It's not my business, I know, Queenie, but I think Alfredo Camboni might have helped out.'

'Helped out!' Queenie's eyes blazed. 'That man doesn't do anything out of the goodness of his heart.' She snatched Nareedah's dangling reins and swung into the saddle. 'This has been a private conversation, Roger. Please don't feel you have broken any confidences.'

She rode off and Roger Ambrose was glad he wasn't in Warwick's shoes, having to face Queenie with an explanation. Warwick had been carried away by the glamour of the film industry and by the idea of quick and easy money. He had conjured up images of Hollywood film moguls and their 'deals'. And as he had put it to Roger, rather naively, he wanted a 'slice of the action'.

Roger sighed, he didn't have the heart to tell Queenie about the dismally low percentage of films that went into profit. Distributors, production companies, the studio, all creamed what they could from the exercise in the guise of fees and expenses for the making of the film, the marketing, the promotion and the selling of it.

Millie quietly put Saskia to bed as the argument between Warwick and Queenie raged behind the closed door of the study. Warwick finally left, slamming the door behind him, and picking up a bottle of rum and a glass, headed for his back bedroom. Yet again, Queenie slept on the sofa in her study.

TR was putting his horse through a stunt jump for the cameras down at the set by the creek when the mail truck, trailing a cloud of dust, trundled to the homestead.

Millie appeared at the front steps wiping her hands on her apron as the driver jumped down and greeted her with a big grin. She peered past his shoulder at the figure in the passenger seat. 'Who's that with you, Tom?'

'A visitor.' His grin widened and he tipped his battered broad-brimmed hat to the back of his head. He called over his shoulder. 'Hey, we're here. You can get out.'

The woman inside had been waiting for her

door to be opened. She impatiently wrenched at the awkward handle and hitched her tight skirt above her knees so she could make the long step down to the ground. Tom continued to grin as he stared at her shapely legs. She slammed the door and strode towards them, an almost comic figure — someone dressed for a *Vogue* fashion spread in New York, but looking hot and bewildered in this outback setting.

'This 'ere is a friend of TR's, Millie. All the way from America,' Tom announced, as if introducing a visitor from outer space.

Millie's eyes widened and she hurried forward. 'Hello, hello. I'm Millie. Come on in out of the sun, you look all hot and bothered.'

'You might say that,' she drawled, and fanned herself as she followed Millie along the verandah. 'I'm Martine Hoxburgh. I was expecting TR to meet me. Is he here? It's been quite an amazing trip. I had no idea the country was so ... primitive.'

She sank into a cane chair. Tom joined them, handing the satchel of mail to Millie. 'Chance of a cuppa, Millie?'

'Of course. What about you, Miss Hoxburgh?'

'A cold drink would be wonderful. I can't tell you what this journey has been like.'

'Aw, go on, tell her,' laughed Tom.

Martine glared at him and said nothing. Millie excused herself and Tom followed her to the kitchen. 'I'll give you a hand, Millie. By crikey, Millie, she doesn't know if she's Arthur or Martha. She comes on like some hoity-toity glamour queen, nice enough, but obviously used to the finer things in life. She was so anxious to see TR she's been on three mail runs. I picked her up only this morning. Everything that could have gone wrong, has. You wouldn't credit it. She's dressed to kill and on one trip they break down, on the other trip they hit a flooded creek and had to be winched out, and then they find a snake in amongst the mail. She's had hysterics so often she can hardly talk. She made me stop in Long-reach at a hotel so she could freshen up. She get's all fancied up in the lav at the George Hotel — '

'The George! Why did you take her there? I wouldn't let a dog in that scummy place.'

'I had mail for them. Anyway, she comes out, picking her way through the drunks, when two Abos start a bloody blue on the verandah and stumble right into her, that sets the dogs off and they start fighting. She took off down the street in them high heels . . . laugh . . . I thought I'd die.'

Tom's laughter dwindled away seeing Millie's set face. 'I don't think it's that funny, Tom Higgins. Here, take this tray outside and keep your mouth shut.'

Queenie had got used to strange people about the place with the film crew and cast drifting around. However, the house with Rose's valuable paintings and pieces of silver was off limits unless it was being used to shoot a scene.

She was therefore somewhat surprised to arrive home and find a beautiful redhead in a cream linen skirt, a silk shirt and sunglasses, flipping through a magazine as she lounged on the verandah.

Queenie greeted her graciously. 'I'm Queenie Redmond. You're new — you must be an actress. I didn't hear the plane come in.'

They shook hands as Martine lowered her dark glasses. 'Plane? I have been to hell and back for three days on trucks. They told me the property was "Just up the track". A quaint interpretation of distance, I must say, but apparently a very Australian understatement. And the men! My God, they're unbelievable. If they are specimens of Australian males, I pity the girls out here.'

Queenie laughed, enjoying her Southern drawl. 'You're American. Yes, the fellows can be a bit rough and ready in their treatment of women, but they're good men underneath. Why on earth did they send you up on the mail run? That's scarcely star treatment. I'm sorry, what was your name? Or should I know you? I've trodden on a few egos, I'm afraid, as I don't keep up with the movie business.'

'I'm Martine Hoxburgh and I'm certainly not an actress. I'm in the fashion business, and I've come out to visit my . . . a friend. I thought I'd surprise him . . . it was a mad idea at the time. Seems even crazier now.'

'I think that's a lovely idea. You're a friend of Roger's , are you?'

'No. TR Hamilton. Do you know him? He doesn't know I'm here, he's still filming in the wilderness somewhere.'

Queenie paused a moment. 'Yes, I know TR.

Martine, would you care for something to drink? If you'll excuse me, I just dropped in to pick up some serum for a sick horse. I'll be back shortly.' Queenie strode into the house. 'Millie...'

Millie hurried downstairs. 'Oh, Queenie. Did you meet TR's girlfriend? She's just arrived. Poor thing. Had a dreadful trip. I put her in one of the spare bedrooms, was that all right?'

'For the moment,' Queenie called as she disappeared into the rear of the house

A short time later Queenie approached Martine. 'Would you like to go down to the filmset and find TR?'

'Oh, that would be great!'

Queenie wanted to be there when TR saw Martine. She reversed the Land Rover with unnecessary force.

Roger Ambrose hurried to the two women and Queenie introduced Martine. Roger's eyes flicked appreciatively over the elegant Southerner. 'TR is just over the rise. They're filming him galloping and jumping the creek. He's doubling for Ty, the main actor,' explained Roger.

From the Land Rover they watched the sequence go smoothly for three takes and when the director called 'Print', TR reined in his horse and dismounted. Roger called to him and TR turned and came towards them. Before he could react to the sight of Martine, she ran forward to embrace him.

'Good lord, Martine! What a shock! How did you get here?'

'Honey, don't ask.' She lifted her face to be kissed. TR kissed her lightly and came towards them with Martine holding his arm. 'You've met Martine?'

'Yes. We've been hearing how she decided to surprise you at Guneda and when she found you were filming out here, she just set off into the wild. A nice surprise, huh, TR?' smiled Roger Ambrose.

'I am surprised.'

Martine smiled and TR looked at Queenie. 'I hope this won't put you out?'

'There's room at the house. You're welcome to stay as long as you wish, Martine. Well, I have work to do.'

Queenie turned away and got back into the Land Rover. She knew it was unfair to feel so jealous. TR was entitled to have a woman in his life — but not under my roof, she thought furiously.

That night at dinner Roger Ambrose raised his glass to make a toast to the three beautiful women gracing the table. 'Our new guest from the States, Martine; Babette, our beautiful star of *Red Jack*; and our hostess, the lovely Queenie.'

TR, Warwick and Roger sipped their Bollinger, but Queenie rose, disguising her discomfort, murmuring, 'I'll see to the dessert.'

'I'm sure Millie has everything under control,' called Warwick, but Queenie had left the room.

As soon as she could excuse herself she fled to her study and the friendly sofa, hoping to avoid Warwick until the morning.

Queenie was asleep when Warwick came in and flung himself into the armchair beside her. 'You awake, Queenie?'

'I am now.'

'That was rude, leaving early like that.'

'Rubbish. They were all having a good time talking about life in America. I was tired. Goodnight, Warwick.'

'TR's got himself a real elegant lady. Can't see her settling into our life style though.'

Queenie didn't answer, and Warwick reluctantly left her alone.

'TR, when are we going to be able to be alone? This is awful, me staying in the house and you in that bunkhouse. I came out to see you.'

'Martine, I'll be finished here in two days. Then we can go back to Guneda. You'll have to face driving, though.'

'It will be different with you. To tell you the truth, darling, I can't take the manners of these Australian men. They don't know how to treat a lady. You certainly are the exception to the rule. But even you seem a bit on edge. The sooner we get away the better.'

'Why did you come, Martine?'

'Why, honey, I hadn't heard from you in so long and I missed you. Besides, you always talked so much about Australia I wanted to see it.'

Martine had her arm around his waist as they walked towards the stables. 'Martine, you really shouldn't be walking about in those high heels, you're going to break an ankle.'

'TR, I was going into town with Roger. I thought I'd have a look around and maybe get my nails and hair done.'

TR stifled a grin. 'Martine, I don't think there's a women's hairdresser in town. There's a barber. And I know there isn't a manicurist for a few hundred miles. Ask Roger if the film crew girls can fix you up.'

'Well, I could do my own hair, but my appliances don't work out here. Wrong power system. No wonder the women are so plain. Not Queenie, of course. Y'know, maybe that's why the men don't have any manners. The women don't bother, so the men think why should they? A beautician would make a fortune out here.'

'I doubt it. Women's priorities in the bush are a bit different. Don't worry about it, you look just fine.'

TR had always admired how well groomed American women were, but here it all seemed rather silly and superficial. He couldn't help comparing the two Americans with Queenie. The movie star was either swathed in a scarf and no make-up, hiding from the world, or else she was in full war paint for the cameras. At home Martine always looked fashionable and immaculate, but here he felt she looked all wrong.

Queenie looked beautiful without any effort. She seldom wore make-up, except for the occasional touch of lipstick, and never painted her nails which were oval and naturally pink. Her face had a soft glow from the sun and her thick hair shone, falling in heavy waves when it wasn't pulled back or braided. Some evenings, when she had pinned it on top of her head and tucked a flower in one side, she looked almost regal.

TR couldn't imagine Queenie fussing with hair curlers and coloured nail polish. He had seen little of her since Martine arrived and felt uncomfortable. He was anxious to get back to Guneda.

Queenie was also restless. The constant problems and confusion with the film were claustrophobic and she wished she could disappear and leave it all to Warwick whose enthusiasm hadn't dimmed. He joined in the crew meals, knew everyone's name, revelled in the 'in' jokes, shared the camaraderie and helped smooth over petty jealousies and tantrums.

Roger, Warwick and Martine had become a friendly little unit while TR and Queenie went about their work.

When one of the stock agents rang Queenie to tell her there was a mob of good cattle for sale, her spirits rose. 'Warwick, we have to get them. They've been fattening out in the Channel Country after the rain. Seven hundred head. A good price, too. We put them with the Brahman bulls at Cricklewood to breed up and we're in business.'

'And where is the money coming from? You're the one always saying we can't afford to spend.'

Queenie's voice was brisk. 'Warwick, this opportunity is too good to miss. We will have to cut corners or sell something to raise the money.'

'Like what, Queenie?'

'Like the plane.'

'No!' Warwick was about to argue but recognised Queenie's stubborn expression. 'All right, I'll talk to the bank about increasing the overdraft.'

'I'm going to walk them down to Tingulla,' continued Queenie. 'I'll take Ernie. You, Jim, Millie and Snowy can run things here.'

'That's a helluva cattle drive. You'll be gone for weeks. You'll miss the wrap party. Contract a droving team to bring the cattle down,' he protested.

'We can't afford it. And I'll miss the what?'

'The end of filming party. It'll all be over by the time you get back.'

'Let's hope things can then get back to normal. I'll say goodbye before I leave.'

Once she had made up her mind and the deal had been sealed, Queenie and Ernie began getting the droving plant together. They'd be on the track, sleeping in swags and on their own, as they slowly walked the cattle out of the remote Channel Country down the stock route to Cricklewood. Queenie estimated they'd be gone six to eight weeks.

They would need a cook who could double as a farrier as the horses would go through many shoes. The cook would take the one supply vehicle and go ahead, setting up each night's camp. The rest of the gear would be carried by three packhorses.

Queenie had her own reasons for doing it herself. She was looking forward to being in the open air and away from the world. Ernie would be company round the campfire at night and invaluable if they struck any problems in the outback. But she knew there would be long quiet days in the saddle plodding along behind the cattle. It all seemed immensely appealing compared to the turmoil created by the film makers.

Before he left, TR found Queenie working in the tackle room at the rear of the stables.

'Sorting out the gear for your drove, huh?'

'Yes. I'm really looking forward to it,' Queenie replied.

'I can understand why. Been a bit of a circus around here, hasn't it?'

'Yes. Thanks for your help. You and Martine are leaving?'

'Yes. I just wanted to say goodbye and...' TR ran his fingers through his thick golden hair, a habit Queenie recognised as an indication that he was feeling uncomfortable.

They gazed at each other. TR wanted to tell her Martine meant little to him, even though in Kentucky she had seemed more important in his life. Perhaps because she was secure and confident running her own business. However, she was a fish out of water in the Australian bush. But there was something more important...

'Queenie, you can tell me this is none of my business, but I feel I have to say something. You're my...' He was going to say friend but it seemed so inadequate. 'I know how much you love Tingulla and I don't want to see you get into trouble...'

'What are you talking about, TR?'

'Please don't get your back up. It's about Warwick. The way he gambles... Queenie, I just wonder if you know how much money he's losing at the racetrack. And other places.'

'Gambles? For godsake's, TR, the man has a few bets now and then. That doesn't make him a gambler. Why are you telling me this? What are you trying to do?' demanded Queenie angrily.

TR spoke softly and calmly. 'Queenie, listen to me. I happen to know Warwick has lost a lot of money at the races this past year. A lot. He's in hock to several SP bookies. I know you've had a hard time at Tingulla with the drought, and it worries me that Warwick has a tendency to spend money he hasn't got. When the day of reckoning comes along I don't want to see you hurt.'

'TR, you're mad. And out of line. How dare you march in here with such wild stories, insult my husband and infer I'm some dumb female who doesn't know what's going on...'

'That's not what I meant, Queenie, and if you don't want to listen to a friend, then more fool you,' retorted TR.

'Keep out of my business, TR. And keep out of my life.' Queenie was shouting, her throat tight, a pain constricting her chest, tears springing to her eyes.

'All right, I will. Don't say I didn't try to help you — or warn you.' TR strode from the stables hurt and angry. He left Tingulla a few hours later without seeing Queenie again.

From a corner of the upper verandah

Queenie stood by a jasmine-covered post watching the Range Rover carrying TR and Martine, and towing the horse float, head for the boundary and the road south. Soon they were just a smudge of dust on the horizon and Queenie turned inside with a heavy heart.

Chapter Twenty-Three

—— ❧ ——

Queenie had her droving team well organised. The plant consisted of six stockhorses, three packhorses and Tubby, the cook and farrier, with his four-wheel drive wagon that carried food, cooking utensils, water and gear to shoe the horses. He would travel ahead of Queenie, the cattle, Ernie and the horses.

Ernie was now in his twenties, still shy, but his infectious humour remained as effervescent as ever. Knowing that he had a multitude of tribal skills — many learned from Snowy — and that he was a good stockman, made Queenie feel secure. Ernie could survive off the land if needed but, above all, he was regarded as part of Tingulla's 'family'. Together they made an easy-going and professional team.

Queenie paused in her packing preparations to smile at the activity around her. Here she was following in the tradition of the overlanders and first settlers who opened up the outback with a horse, a dream and a spirit of adventure; while all around her the twentieth century technicians buzzed frantically in the bizarre, confined world of the movie set, artificially manufacturing dreams and stories.

Snowy, working beside her, read her mind. 'Them fellas take lotsa trouble to tell a story. Much better to just sit round the campfire and sing stories. Or mebbe paint them on bark. This white fella's way — look like too many bosses. Which one's the storyteller?'

'It's true, they seem to have all chiefs and no Indians. It's like a lot of little kingdoms with their own rulers. The cameraman is a boss, the director is a boss, the light man is a boss, the designer's a boss . . . '

'Stan is a boss too,' added Snowy.

Queenie laughed. 'You're not wrong, Snowy . . . a big boss.'

Stan, the shearers' cook, had proved a key element in the smooth running of the filmset. If the food wasn't up to scratch, there was an outbreak of grumbling and tantrums. The film people were unaware or didn't care about the difficult conditions under which Stan and Millie performed miracles at mealtimes.

'If they get the same meal twice in a week, they whinge. How do you reckon they'd get on out in the bush?' Stan asked Millie.

Millie paused in her scone making. 'Stan, can you see any of these people lasting one day out there? They're going to be so happy to get back to fairyland or wherever it is they come from.'

'Disneyland. They told me all about it. Can

you imagine grown-ups spending good money to troop around a huge place that's like a cartoon? Even got flamin' Mickey Mouse and Donald Duck walking about. And as for them orgies in bloody mansions ... America sounds a strange place to me.'

Half the fun of mealtimes for the Los Angeles crew was telling Stan outrageous stories of tinsel town.

Millie's workload would be even heavier with Queenie away, so Sarah and John had offered to take their goddaughter, Saskia, back down to Sydney with them while Queenie was droving. She and Warwick talked it over and agreed it seemed like a good idea.

Saskia was beside herself with excitement at the prospect of going to the city for the first time that she could remember, having Sarah's son Tim as a playmate, and going to *real* school. Sarah had also promised to take her to Taronga Park Zoo and a Saturday matinee picture show in a theatre as big as a palace.

Queenie realised she was going to miss Saskia far more than her daughter would miss her parents and Tingulla.

She and Warwick sat in the study the night before Queenie left. 'The paperwork for the bank loan isn't through yet. I'll have to give you power of attorney so you can sign on my behalf.' Queenie picked up the pen to sign the document which Warwick had asked the solicitor to draw up. For a brief second her hand hesitated over the paper as TR's warning flashed into her mind, but she angrily pushed the recollection aside, signed, and handed the paper to Warwick. 'I guess that's everything. I hope you won't find it too dull when all the film people leave. Though you won't be on your own too long,' said Queenie.

'Well, it will be nice to get our bedroom back.' He grinned at her and reached for her hand. 'Queenie, why don't we have another baby?'

It caught her off guard and she stared at Warwick, then smiled. 'That would be lovely. I'm sort of surprised one hasn't come along before now.'

'Well, let's start tonight.' Warwick clicked off the lamp and stood, gently pulling Queenie to her feet.

Queenie was saying goodbye to each member of the film crew and when she reached Roger Ambrose, he took her aside to talk privately.

'I'm sorry I won't be seeing you any more, Queenie — unless you come to Los Angeles. You have a standing invitation to stay any time. I mean it.' Roger hugged her. 'You are the most fascinating woman I've ever met, Queenie. If you weren't a married lady I would chase you round the world.'

His arms were still around her and he bent his face to kiss her on the lips. Queenie turned her face so the kiss landed softly on her cheek. 'But I *am* married, Roger. Thank you for the compliment, though.' She smiled at him, gently extricating herself from his embrace. It was definitely time to be leaving. 'I hope the film is a big success for you, Roger.'

He sighed. 'To be perfectly frank, Queenie,

we are having a few problems. Nothing to do with our end here, but not all the money for postproduction has appeared yet. I'm sure there's no problem, but wheeler-dealers do like to make you sweat a bit.'

'Oh dear. I'm sorry to hear that.'

'Don't you worry about it, Queenie. That's my job. You have a big task ahead of you. I hadn't realised what you were undertaking until I talked to some of the station hands. There are a few bets riding on you pulling this off. Some of the men say a woman hasn't done anything like this in recent times.'

Queenie laughed. 'There have been a couple — Edna Zigenbine and May Steele in the fifties. It's just a job that has to be done. I have my skills, Roger, and you have yours — they're just different.'

'We come from very different worlds, Queenie. I think you could conquer mine, but I could never survive in yours. Good luck.'

Millie, Jim and Snowy farewelled Ernie with handshakes and few words. Queenie gave them each a swift hug and a kiss before turning to Warwick.

'Go well, Queenie, love. Keep the buggers fat and don't lose any.'

'We'll take it slow and easy, don't worry. I probably won't be able to contact you much. I'll try to get through from the Windorah pub.'

'Righto. Don't worry about anything here.'

Warwick kissed her quickly. They'd said their goodbyes the night before.

Queenie turned to her horse and put one foot in the stirrup. Warwick stepped forward and impulsively put his hands around her waist, murmuring in her ear. 'I'll miss you. Don't forget I love you, Queenie.'

She swung into the saddle, surprised at the whispered endearment. 'I love you too, Warwick.'

She turned the horse and moved to the head of the small contingent. The horses' hooves clicked on the flagged courtyard, taking the first of many steps on the journey which lay before them.

Before they had gone far from the house, she looked back and lifted her arm. Warwick blew her a kiss, Jim raised his hat and Millie fluttered a tea towel.

They detoured past the filmset, where the director called a halt to filming and everyone cheered and whistled. Queenie grinned at them all, tugged her hat firmly in place and, with Ernie and the horses strung behind her, crossed the creek. Soon the little party disappeared into the trees.

Colin and Dina sat with Alfredo Camboni and his lawyer in the Cambonis' darkly panelled library. The lawyer handed a sheaf of documents to Alfredo. 'It is very cut and dried, Alfredo my friend. You have been outstandingly helpful and more than generous for the past two years. However, business is business, it is time to ask for repayment.'

'And if the debt cannot be repaid?'

The lawyer shrugged. 'You have the controlling interest in the collateral. You must call it in.'

Dina turned to Colin with a small smile, but he was staring at the pattern in the Chinese carpet and didn't raise his eyes.

Alfredo folded the papers. 'Very well, then. You do understand, Colin, this is in all our best interests?' Colin looked up and gazed impassively back at the older Italian man. Alfredo had arranged his features into an expression of caring concern. Colin saw only the jowls, the watery eyes, the thick pale lips.

Alfredo continued, 'She may not see it as being in her best interests at first, but things could get far worse if he tries to pay us back and only gets in deeper with the wrong people. This way, we keep the collateral within the family. You agree it is the better way, *si*?'

Colin nodded, rose and left the room. He was clearly distressed.

Alfredo lifted his eyebrows and turned to his daughter.

'He is still adjusting to the idea,' said Dina.

The lawyer spoke quietly behind them. 'He is probably feeling a little manipulated. You must restore his ego, Dina.'

Roger Ambrose rubbed a hand across his tired eyes. The entire film crew and cast were gathered in the dusk on the verandah of the homestead. Warwick stood in the background, his arms folded, his face grim. Roger had been talking to them for twenty minutes. He finished and there was silence.

Then one of the gaffers spoke up. 'So what's the bottom line here — moneywise? We haven't been paid for the last four weeks, a lot of us don't have return tickets or transport. Is it going to be paid, or what?'

'I'm arranging travel to Sydney. Flights back to the US will be organised from there. As for salaries — I can only promise you I will do my best. It's very difficult from this distance to know what the exact situation is. I will have more control and power back in LA.'

'Sure,' came a surly mutter.

'The union isn't going to like this,' came another disgruntled voice.

'I know. And frankly, they have my support in putting pressure on the studio.'

'It's going to kill the prospects of any other film company that wants to come and shoot in Australia,' said the cinematographer.

'Yeah, we get ripped off to prove a point. Is the picture salvageable?'

Roger looked uncomfortable. 'There are only a few scenes not shot. They could be tricked up in LA. The problem is the money needed to complete the picture, the editing, the postproduction and so on.'

'What about the "suits" — and the investors? I bet they're getting paid.'

'No, I'm afraid most investors went in on a deferred basis, to be paid from net profits after the production company had been paid from the gross.' Roger didn't look at Warwick.

'What exactly went wrong?' asked the make-up girl.

'It's not a new scenario. A power shift at the top, pressure from the banks on the studio, the new guys decide to push their own projects. There's a lot of politics and power games being played that have nothing to do with us. I know it seems strange to dump a film that's looking good and is almost finished, but I think we are pawns in a personal vendetta as well.'

'Jesus, what a business. I just want to make movies. Why does all this crap get in the way?'

Roger rose. 'I agree with you. I can only reiterate: I am doing what I can. Although it is out of my hands I feel responsible and will fight for *Red Jack* as hard as I can.'

'Just get us what we're owed,' said the focus puller.

The group broke up and Roger went over to Warwick who grinned ruefully. 'That couldn't have been easy for you.'

'No. And it's not easy telling you I don't know when, or if, you and Queenie will be paid for Tingulla. As for your investment... I would say that's in serious doubt.'

'As one of the crew said... what a business. Does this happen often?'

'I'm afraid so. Swings and roundabouts, as they say. It's addictive, though. Anyone with any business sense would stick to accounting or growing beans, but I find myself diving head first into another project full of hope and optimism right on the heels of a disaster.'

Warwick didn't answer. The two men walked along the verandah in the still night.

'You're lucky to live here away from the rat race with your lovely family. I think you've come out on top no matter what, Warwick.' Roger headed off to the shearing shed where beer was flowing to soften the blow of *Red Jack*'s fate.

Warwick retreated to the study with a bottle of rum and a glass. Thank God Queenie was away. How was he going to tell her this news? Warwick opened a drawer and took out a small cash box, found the key he had secreted on a shelf, and unlocked it. He spread the papers from it on the desk and studied them carefully.

At daybreak he stirred, his head resting on his arms, his neck stiff, the bottle empty. The figures on the paper hadn't changed.

The Channel Country of southwest Queensland is generally dry, barren, and red. Its flat, scorched surface is crisscrossed by a maze of cracks and splits like parched wrinkles in an ageing face. When heavy rains come to the far north and the Gulf Country, the flood waters flow south, dribbling and gushing into the channels and forming creeks and rivers which fill up and overflow, so the land becomes a giant lake or inland sea. When the waters eventually recede, dormant grasses, seeds and flowers spring up to make a verdant carpet on the soaked, ochre earth. It is feed that fattens cattle, and for a brief time the face of the land looks youthful.

Once it belonged to the Aborigines. It was their mother — the source of all life, all meaning. Strewn across it were secret places and features of special spiritual significance, all tangible links with the time of creation — the Dreamtime. It was a relationship with the land, the past, the eternity, that few white people knew about, and even fewer understood.

To most whites the Channel Country was tough country when dry; impossible when wet. Only when it bloomed and fattened cattle and made stock routes passable was it of any real use.

Queenie and her team picked up their seven hundred head of Herefords in the small township of Boulia on the edge of the Channel Country. The cattle were in holding yards, fretful and nervous at their confinement.

Queenie shook hands with the sales agent and climbed the fence to sit beside Ernie. In the yards close by, two drovers were having trouble guiding cattle into the back of a large truck. The animals' hooves clattered and slipped on the wooden ramp as cracking whips startled them into the dark and crowded cavern.

'I reckon we got a good buy here,' said Queenie.

Ernie was watching the men loading the cattle trucks. 'How come we're droving the old way, walking ours and not trucking them down to Cricklewood?'

Queenie smiled. 'I wondered when you'd ask, Ernie. One reason is it costs too much. Second reason — I want to do it this way. I think it's better for the animals and if we take it slow and easy they shouldn't lose condition. Three... ' Here Queenie stared into the distance seemingly talking to herself. 'It's also good for me. I need some time and space and peace. I want to calm my spirit and find my own Dreaming. I love this land but every so often you have to make contact and be with it — breathe the air, sleep on the earth, follow its rhythms, get back in harmony with it.'

Ernie understood. His face broke into a wide grin. 'Like going walkabout ... to sing the Dreaming songs.'

'I'm glad you understand, Ernie. Tubby doesn't see it that way, but he's happy enough for the job. Come on, then. Let's get this show on the road, as the picture people say.' Queenie lifted the scarf knotted around her throat and tied it bandit-style over her nose and mouth, and uncoiling her stock whip, jumped down from the fence.

A cloud of red dust rose above the pens, men shouted, whips cracked and cattle bellowed as the animals were herded from the yards and headed down the dusty road to the outskirts of town.

Two men standing on the pub verandah holding schooners of beer watched their noisy, dusty progress. 'That's the mob with a sheila boss drover.'

'Flaming hell, what next? Does she know what she's doin'?'

'They reckon. Hanlon's daughter, Queenie. You know — the bloke whose wife was murdered and he drowned in the big flood.'

'Oh yeah. She doesn't have a big plant. Good looking mob, though.'

'Kinda miss the droving days. Using motorbikes for mustering, sending the cattle round the place crammed in trucks ... not the same as going down the track.'

'Yeah, you're right. I miss it a bit meself. 'Nother beer?'

The two old drovers turned inside as the last of Queenie's mob plodded past with Ernie on the tail.

Once they were out in open country the days fell into a quiet rhythm as the cattle moved steadily towards Cricklewood. Ernie and Queenie rarely had contact during the day although they were in sight of each other. Evenings were spent around the campfire quietly chatting. Occasionally someone made a joke, but often the time passed in companionable silence.

Tubby went ahead each morning in the truck and made camp for the night. A cooked meal with fresh damper was always waiting. Tubby also checked the horses' shoes, replaced any when needed, and took a turn as ringer riding night watch.

The ringer's job was to circle the resting cattle, all the while singing softly or reciting to the stars, the familiar voice soothing the animals. While most cattle slept, legs awkwardly folded beneath them, some would stay on their feet as sentinels, and others might stand to urinate before settling down once more. A sleepless beast might poke out into the edges for a feed. The ringer would settle it back with the mob and continue his rounds.

It didn't take long for drovers to get to know their herd; like a schoolteacher with a new class, they were quick to spot the troublemakers and the leaders. On this trip there were two cows that had adopted the role of teacher's pet. They were first on their feet to lead the cranky mob away at dawn — if there was good feed about the animals were reluctant to move on — then they'd slowly drift back through the herd to plod along with whoever was riding as tail-ender, seeming to prefer human companionship.

Experienced drovers knew never to relax their vigilance, especially at night when the chance of a rush was greatest. Anything could spook a herd and a rush was a terrifying thing to experience. Stories were told of bad rushes, how mobs had thundered over a camp, killing stockmen and hammering gear into the hard-packed earth.

At daybreak, after dishing up breakfast, Tubby packed the camp while Queenie, the cattle and Ernie headed out for the day's walk. The midday meal was simple fare: corned beef, damper and sweet rock cakes with a billy of black tea, eaten by a small fire in the shade of a tree — if there was one.

Sitting comfortably in the saddle, Queenie thought how few travellers appreciated these paths that traversed the outback. Most people roared past on bitumen roads that speared across the desolate plains, or raced through skies with scarcely a glance at what lay below; others sat in trains bound to one set of tracks, confined in a capsule that didn't allow you to smell the air, feel the sun on your face or hear the call of birds. Unseen were the songlines of Aboriginal belonging that linked one tribe's territory to the next.

Also unrecognised by such travellers were the stock routes, where the travelling sheep and cattle slowly munched their way from one part of the country to another. The land looked almost like desert but to the initiated there was a complexity of highways spreading in every direction, each with its own folklore and mythology.

As suddenly as it had grown, the greenness disappeared. Between sunup and morning smoko, they travelled off the green carpet onto the terracotta dirt where the feed for the cattle was sparse. Most of the channels still held water, but the sun was quickly shrivelling what little growth was left.

Queenie looked across to where Ernie was riding on the left flank. He pointed his whip towards a dead tree, a bleached skeleton in the stark terrain. When she rode closer Queenie grinned at the sight of a rusting iron canoe in this arid scene. Roughly made from galvanised iron, someone had used it during the floods many years before. But on what errand, wondered Queenie. Now it lay incongruously under the blazing sun, a nautical body on a hard red sea.

At sunset they reached the Diamantina River — a broad, bare, gouged ribbon with a trickle of water at its centre. Tubby had made camp and the billy of tea was a welcome sight.

After eating, when the last of the light had faded from the sky, and the lone evening star shone beside the moon, Queenie announced she'd take the late watch. She rolled into her swag, comfortably tired, idly thinking that people in the cities were probably pushing and shoving their various ways home from crowded offices in noisy traffic. Here her day was dictated by the rising and setting of the sun.

She had specifically asked for Sparky to be her night mount, a small roan which had the best night sight of the horses. It was a skill some had and others didn't. The night horse was kept saddled and standing close by the camp, ready to be ridden at a split-second's notice if the cattle rushed in the night. Ernie was on first watch so she closed her eyes and slept.

In the early hours the wind rose and growled around the cattle, causing the campfire to spark and Ernie's chanting song to be blown away.

Then it stopped, as swiftly as if a switch had been pulled. Queenie stirred, maybe it was the uncanny silence and stillness, or some second sense that alerted her. She started out of her swag, still wearing her boots, as the bellowing cattle chorus swelled to a roar and she heard the yell from Ernie — 'Rush!'

A shuddering wall of animals began moving en masse, running recklessly into the blackness, driven by fear and the unknown. Ernie had been able to swing the mob away from the camp but couldn't see where the leaders were as he raced alongside the terrified beasts.

Queenie was in the saddle and lungeing after the mob in seconds. Sparky swung instinctively towards the head of the mob, galloping flat out without putting a foot wrong, and seeing exactly where he was racing. Queenie crouched low and forward giving the horse its head.

They overtook most of the charging cattle, and Queenie unleashed her stock whip, cracking it wildly to turn them. A dust cloud gathered above them, filtering what little moonlight there was. Over the pounding hooves she heard a whip crack and knew Ernie was up with her on the other side, but although her feet brushed the solid mass of charging flesh next to her, they were not yet up with the leaders.

It was then that fear struck Queenie as she heard a distant roar and knew what had set off the rush. The animals had heard, or felt, the subterranean tremble of an approaching flash flood.

Instant flooding was a phenomenon of the outback. When it rained to the north, weeks later the accumulated water would explode into a dry river bed, turning it in minutes from dust bowl to surging torrent carrying away all before it. Sometimes word got through to warn others that it was on the way, and sightseers would head to the banks to watch the dramatic appearance of a flood sweeping through a desert. But with no warning, in the dark, and with the cattle heading for the river bed, Queenie imagined a disaster of mammoth proportions.

She screamed aloud though no one could hear her. 'We'll lose them if they go into the river!'

She kicked Sparky, heading him towards the

previously dry river, and without hesitating the horse responded, squelching through mud and splashing into the first gush of water. Queenie hoped to get into the river first so she could charge the cattle and frighten them into turning away.

To her amazement she found her horse was swimming. It was deeper than expected and the current was strong. The flood was more advanced than she had anticipated. She swung around to face the bank they'd just left, feeling the current pull her along.

In the dim light she saw the leaders reach the bank. With terrified bellowing they faltered as their feet sank in the mud and in that instant Queenie thought she could swing them around. But she had been swept too far downstream by the current, and the pressure from the raging mob behind pushed the leaders into the water.

Helplessly, Queenie watched the cattle surge into the river. Suddenly she glimpsed Ernie riding down the bank, his horse striking out into the deep water.

'Swim with them!' he shouted.

Queenie gathered her strength and realised there was no turning them back now. In the darkness the mob had to be encouraged to swim for the other bank. With luck they could prevent them from panicking and drowning.

She nudged her horse in close to the first animals who were beginning to swim downstream. With Ernie now on the other side, the horses swam beside the frightened and confused animals. The riders pushed their mounts in close, shouting to the cattle in firm, loud voices.

Although the current grew stronger by the minute, they managed to head the animals around so they were facing the opposite bank and swimming purposefully rather than fighting and kicking in the wrong direction. Queenie's horse slipped and staggered as its feet hit the muddy bottom and together Sparky and the leading cattle struggled up the bank. The swim had taken the fear and flight from them and they stood forlorn and disoriented. Queenie snapped her whip and moved them forward as several others were nudged up the bank by Ernie.

Then Queenie wheeled her horse around and plunged back into the river to guide more of the cattle across as they fell lemming-like into the water. But already she knew they were going to have losses. There were too many animals to shepherd across in the appalling conditions, made worse now by concealed logs and debris. Ernie worked them up the bank. Queenie and Sparky swam back over, encouraging them to cross the dark swirling water.

The main stream of the river had swollen to double its width, spilling over its banks and flooding across the plain for half a mile. Queenie could feel her horse tiring as she headed back yet again with the stragglers.

Ernie caught up with her midstream. 'Some are in trouble at the tail!'

Several beasts had been trampled by the mob close to the far bank. Two were stuck and struggling in the mud but looked as if they could be saved. Swiftly Queenie pulled the rope from her saddle, throwing a lasso over an animal's head. She rode up the bank and round a tree which gave the rope enough leverage to pull the animal to its feet, and then she chased it into the water.

She rescued the second the same way, then rounded up two strays and guided them all across to join the herd, now standing quietly on the other side.

'How many have we lost, Ernie?'

'Hard to tell till daybreak. A lot, I think.' Ernie surveyed the mob now standing meekly on the opposite bank. 'Well, that's one way to cross 'em over,' he remarked drily.

Queenie glanced at the pearliness beginning to light the sky. 'In a couple of hours it will be light. We'll bring the gear and packhorses over then. Tubby will have to take the truck upstream and meet us further on.'

'I'll light a fire and we can dry a bit, eh?' said Ernie comfortingly.

Queenie shivered, realising she was soaked to the skin. Ernie found a small bush and gathered some dry leaves and grass and took from his small saddle bag his emergency lighter — two small fire sticks which he rubbed together, grinding and blowing on them until the friction caused a thin sliver of smoke to rise, followed by a spark.

He blew gently on the shredded dead leaves till they caught and blazed. In minutes the heaped wood of the fire was burning cheerfully. And with saddles for pillows and saddle blankets for cover they gradually relaxed and slept.

In the dawn light Ernie and Queenie rode back across the river. It had stopped rising but it would be weeks before it subsided. As Queenie and Tubby packed up camp, Ernie rode along the bank looking for cattle that had been left behind. He found ten still alive but all partially crippled. Without feeling, he shot them.

Both newborn calves which had been born along the way were missing, presumably drowned and swept down river.

It had been a sad blow to Queenie, but she knew this was the nature of the outback. Philosophically she remarked to Ernie, 'Well, it could have been worse.'

The last of the trucks with Mountain Pictures stencilled on their sides rattled down the dirt road, leaving Tingulla silent and abandoned after the weeks of frenzied activity.

Jim went into town for a few days to pick up spare parts that had arrived for two of the vehicles and the bulldozer. Millie set about a massive spring clean. Stan moved on to another cooking job, and down by the creek where the remains of the filmset stood incongruously, a family of Aborigines moved in and set up camp. Warwick stayed closeted in the study doing paperwork.

Millie tapped at the study door. 'Lunch is ready.'

There was no answer so she cautiously opened the door. Warwick was asleep in the chair. He hadn't shaved for several days, his face looked lined and tired. Millie sighed when she saw the open bottle of rum on the desk. Quietly she shut the door.

It was late afternoon when Warwick emerged. Millie saw him walking slowly around the garden deep in thought. She made tea and carried a tray with a sandwich on a plate onto the verandah. 'Tea, Warwick.'

He started and lifted a hand. Millie left him alone but was relieved when she heard his boots thunking on the verandah, the creak of timber as he sat in the squatter's chair, and the rattle of china.

That night Warwick returned to the bedroom he had shared with Queenie for the first time since filming had started. The peacefulness that always settled on the house at night was missing. It seemed sad and quiet and lonely. Warwick longed for Queenie. He needed her strength, her love and her understanding.

He rolled onto the bed, buried his head in a pillow and moaned. 'Queenie, my love, I've let you down.'

Under the same night sky Queenie gazed up at the Southern Cross from the snugness of her swag by the campfire. She was thinking of Warwick; his presence seemed close by. She knew she would never love him as she loved TR, but Warwick was loyal and good and solid. If their life had been sliding into the doldrums it was her fault for being so preoccupied with Tingulla, Cricklewood and Saskia. She was going to make more of an effort to be attentive and caring.

She smiled, remembering how they had

talked of having another child and was suddenly overwhelmed by a feeling of loss and guilt as she thought of the child she had given up. It was a heavy burden in her heart, carrying the secret known only to Millie, Jim and old Snowy. It all seemed like some terrible, distant dream that periodically haunted and tortured her.

She longed to feel Warwick's familiar shape beside her. She shifted in her swag, sighing sadly.

At sunrise Millie stirred and opened her eyes. Jim was still away and his side of their bed was cold. She turned over to doze and then it registered what had awakened her. Above the dawn chorus, she heard the spluttering drone of an aircraft engine.

Draping a faded chenille dressing gown around her shoulders, Millie sleepily plodded outside and stared into the sky. Who would be coming in unannounced at this hour? Then she realised it was a plane taking off, not landing. The red and white Piper rose into the gold and lilac streaked sky and turned east.

It was soon obliterated from her sight by the burning ball of light that rose above the low line of shadowy blue hills.

'Now where would Warwick be headed?' she wondered. Strange, he didn't say anything last night. But then, he'd been quite distracted since the film people had left. Millie was now alone on the property save for the station hands.

She went towards the kitchen to put the kettle on as usual, then paused, and swung around and went back to her bed to enjoy the rare luxury of sleeping in past sunup.

The news came into Longreach first and spread through the town in minutes. Men shook their heads. Everyone had a different theory about what had happened.

Jim had been set to leave town when Kevin Hooper, the flying doctor, found him and had taken him aside to speak quietly to him. Within half an hour they were on the runway.

With a map spread on his knees, Jim sat beside Kevin as they taxied down the tarmac. Kevin spoke to the small control tower beside the strip. 'This is Charlie Alpha November, six zero nine, ready for clearance.'

'You are cleared for take off, climb to flight level five thousand feet heading due west. Report at ten hundred for further clearance. Do you have a specific destination?'

'She left Windorah two days ago, it shouldn't be too hard to locate them. She's travelling with a pretty big mob. There are clay pans in the area I can drop down on.'

'Roger. Keep us notified. Tell Queenie... we're all real sorry. Over and out.'

Kevin returned the microphone to its clip on the control panel and glanced at Jim who was staring into the blue distance as they climbed. Jim's gnarled hand crumpled a corner of the map. He wondered how he was going to find the words to tell Queenie the terrible news that Warwick's plane had crashed.

Chapter Twenty-Four

❧

Queenie wanted everyone to leave. She
wanted to be alone with her grief. She was
tired of being brave and strong. So many
friends had hurried to be with her, they were
kind and supportive and marvelled at how
Queenie was coping.

After the initial shock, her greatest concern
had been for Saskia. Queenie comforted her, but
allowed her time and space to mourn her father
in her own way. She was determined not to
cling, or suffocate her daughter with the overwhelming burden of 'You're all I've got now'.

Warwick had been cremated and his ashes
returned to his family in Western Australia
as they had requested. His mother was too
upset to travel. His sisters had flown over for
the funeral and the memorial service at Tingulla's little church, which overflowed with
mourners; many clustered outside during the
service.

Colin came alone, the Cambonis sent an embarrassing mountain of flowers from Sydney. Colin had arrived the night before the service and spoke quietly to Queenie in a corner of the crowded living room. 'Warwick was a good bloke, Queenie. I hope Saskia will get over it all right.'

Queenie nodded. There was an awkwardness between them. They were uncomfortable together. Colin mumbled and Queenie couldn't think of anything to say to him to break down the barrier that had grown between them over the years.

'How's Dina?'

'She couldn't come and sends her apologies. She's not well.' Then in a confidential rush he decided to tell his sister the truth. 'She had a miscarriage.'

'Oh, Colin, I'm so sorry.' Queenie reached out and touched his arm, genuinely sad. 'Things will go well next time, I'm sure. Please tell her how sad I am for you both.'

'I doubt we'll try again. She thinks she's too old.'

For a moment Colin wanted to unburden himself to Queenie who was still touching his arm, her eyes full of compassion and caring. As always, something prevented him, and he turned away. 'You're not the only one who suffers in this world, Queenie.'

Sadly, Queenie watched him go. 'What happened to you, Colin, to make you so bitter?' she wondered. Sighing, she headed for the kitchen to ask Millie to put out the food for the buffet.

TR mingled unobtrusively with the mourners, waiting for the right moment to speak to Queenie privately. They hadn't spoken since the last day of their filming for *Red Jack*. He knew she was avoiding him, and he suspected she was uncomfortable about the passionate kiss they had exchanged and probably angry about his criticism of Warwick. He patiently watched her and waited. In the simple, slim-fitting black dress, her hair tied back with a black bow and no jewellery, she looked fragile and young. TR's heart ached for her and Saskia.

At that moment he spotted Saskia, red-eyed and sad-faced, carrying a platter of ham slices which Millie directed her to put on the sideboard. TR went over to her. 'Remember me? How are you doing, Saskia?'

'Yes — you're TR. I'm fine, thanks,' she answered quietly.

'Want to get out of here for a bit? Come and take a turn around the garden with me. Do you know, I have seven new foals at Guneda?'

'What are they like?' Her interest was aroused and TR took her hand. Together they headed out to the verandah and into the evening garden.

By the time they turned back towards the house where softly lit rooms shone through the night with a friendly warmth, Saskia was chatting with more animation about riding and horses.

'Did your Dad ever tell you the funny story about the first time the boys put him on a horse at Tingulla?'

Saskia stopped in her tracks, tears suddenly spilling from her eyes as she gave TR a hurt look. For a brief moment she had almost forgotten the loss of her father, now TR had hit her cruelly in the face with a thoughtless remark.

He crouched down before her. 'Saskia, you have to talk about him. He was a special and important part of your life and now he's gone you can't pretend he was never here. You'll never forget him, so treasure all the memories. I know it seems hard, but it will make it easier for you and for other people if you talk about them. Don't feel embarrassed to mention your Dad. The more you talk about him, the closer you'll feel to him.'

TR hugged the young girl as Queenie's voice rang through the dark gardens. 'Saskia, are you out there?'

TR recognised the note of fear in Queenie's voice. 'Yes, we're here, we're coming.'

Saskia ran towards her mother silhouetted in the gold light from the front entrance. 'What are you doing out here in the dark?'

'It's all right Mummy. I was just taking a walk with TR.' She glanced at him shyly. 'We were talking about Dad.' Saskia hugged her mother tightly and ran indoors.

Slowly TR mounted the steps to face Queenie. 'I think she will be all right. She's a great little girl, Queenie. But what about you? Are you okay?'

'TR, I appreciate you taking time to talk to Saskia, but I'd prefer her to come to me. I'm ... managing. I have to go inside.'

She turned away but TR caught her arm, making her face him. 'Queenie, you can't keep on being a rock. You have to let go, too... You need me, Queenie. Let me look after you.'

'I don't need anyone, TR. I can look after myself. I don't want to see you, TR. It's too hard for me.' Her composure crumbled. 'How do you think I feel? Knowing a short time before Warwick died, that I was kissing you and wanting you and then you tried to turn me against him... I've been punished, TR. You only bring me heartbreak and pain.' The words gushed out between sobbing breaths and tears splashed from her hurt and angry eyes.

TR stepped forward, wrapping his arms about her in anguish. 'Queenie, no. Don't say that. You mustn't think that. It's crazy.'

She struggled to free herself, but he gripped her by the shoulders. 'Listen,' he said harshly, 'that day by the creek, you kissed me and I kissed you back simply because we thought of ourselves as two different people. It was a fantasy, like the whole film. Forget it. It meant nothing... it was nice, but that was all. You and Warwick had a lot of good years together. Cherish them. Don't blame yourself. And don't blame me.'

'Please let me be, TR.' She spoke quietly now. TR's fingers loosened their grip and he gave her a gentle squeeze as he looked at her downcast eyes before dropping his arms.

Queenie didn't see the tortured expression in his eyes as he left, walking down the steps and into the darkness.

*

Gradually the house guests at Tingulla drifted home, and only close friends remained.

Sarah gently spoke to Queenie. 'John and I are going back to Sydney in a day or so. I've talked to Saskia and she says she'd like to come and stay for a little while, but she's worried about leaving you alone.'

Queenie touched her friend's arm. 'I won't be alone. I'll suggest it to her myself. I think it would be good. Distract her a little.'

Dingo was the last to leave. The old bushman gave Queenie a hug, smoothing her hair. 'Poor Queenie. You've had more than your fair share, girl.' He stared into her pale face. 'But you're strong, Queenie, and you'll weather this one, too. Your time for peace and happiness will come, even if the track is a bit crooked and rough right here. Walk on, girl, walk on.'

'I will, Dingo.' She sighed and hugged him back.

'Ah, Queenie, a sigh like that could break a man in two.' Dingo squashed his hat on his now thinning white hair. 'I'll come whenever you need me.'

'Thanks, Dingo. I think I have to do this by myself.'

Dingo nodded. He understood Queenie's nature. He knew she had to find reserves of strength within herself, to reflect and reason and slowly come to terms with her pain and loss, and whatever lay ahead. No one could help Queenie as much as herself.

Millie and Jim left Queenie alone a lot of the time. She rode about the property, sat by the creek, walked through the gums. The tranquillity of the land she loved began to heal and restore her wounded spirit.

Millie tried to explain it to Jim. 'The place you belong to, your Dreaming place, is the earth mother who reaches out to love you. You are never truly home, Jim, till you rest on your Dreaming land. Then you get fixed up. Tingulla will make Queenie better — you'll see. Time and Tingulla, that's all she needs.'

But there wasn't time. The serenity was shattered with the unannounced arrival of a black car carrying two men in dark suits.

Millie watched them get out in the driveway. 'Now, who might them fellas be? Either undertakers or vultures by the look of them.' She gave them tea and sent Jim to find Queenie.

The two men rose to their feet. 'Mrs Redmond. We are from Turner and Berkley, solicitors in Sydney...'

Queenie raised her eyebrows. 'Solicitors? I understood all the paperwork concerning my husband was completed.'

'This is a different matter. It does concern your husband's estate, however.'

Queenie's skin began to prickle and her heart beat faster. Outwardly she remained calm. She sat down and crossed her ankles. 'You'd better tell me what you've come about.'

The two men talked in tandem, their story, facts and figures down pat, one often finishing the other's sentence.

Queenie's tea grew cold in her cup. She did

not move. She was frozen in shock as she listened. Beneath her calm exterior, jumbled, confused and fearful emotions churned.

'It is all most unfortunate,' concluded one.

'Most distressing,' added the other.

With an effort Queenie rose to her feet. 'I will have my own solicitor get in touch with you. Good day, gentlemen.' She turned, and with her head held high, walked stiffly indoors.

The men glanced at each other and shrugged. One slipped a business card onto the tea tray and picking up their snap-brimmed hats, returned to the car and disappeared silently back into the landscape.

Millie looked at the closed door to the study. Queenie had locked herself away when the visitors left and had not appeared for dinner. Millie sensed something was very wrong. She tapped on the door. 'Queenie, I have some dinner for you on a tray, shall I bring it in?'

'No,' she snapped. Then softly, 'Yes . . . yes . . . come in, Millie.'

Millie placed the tray to one side, noting the jumble of papers on the desk and Queenie's red eyes. 'I'll bring you some tea. What's up, Queenie? Do you want to talk?'

'Oh, Millie. It's too difficult to explain . . . I'm having trouble taking it all in myself.'

'I know I'm just a simple murri girl, but sometimes talking it through or aloud helps.'

'This can't be talked away, Millie.' Queenie's shoulders sagged. 'Those men were from a Sydney legal firm.'

'I knew they were trouble,' sniffed Millie, sitting on the arm of a chair.

Queenie drew a deep breath. 'It seems Warwick had something of a secret life — he gambled. Far more than I ever suspected or realised. He had a lot of debts and while I was away droving the cattle down from the Channel Country, he had power of attorney — and in effect he signed away my ownership in Tingulla. The place had already been mortgaged. I knew we owed the bank a large sum, but it was a temporary thing. I guess he was trying to raise the money. But he died before he could do anything about it. The finances are an almighty mess.' Queenie took a deep breath, 'Tingulla now belongs lock, stock and barrel to Signor Alfredo Camboni and Associates.'

'What does that mean?'

'It means, Millie, I no longer have any right to be here. Here — on *my land*.' She banged her fist angrily on the desk, tears of frustration burning in her eyes.

'How come Mr Camboni is the boss? He is in-law, family, he'll let you stay here. You talk to your solicitor, I bet he can sort it out.'

'I phoned him. My solicitor says there's little we can do, though we'll try to fight it. Warwick owed Camboni money from loans going back years; from the racetrack and from that wretched film. Camboni is calling in the loan. If I can't pay it — which I can't — he takes over. I bet the rat planned this all along. Took advantage of Warwick. I wouldn't be surprised if Colin had a hand in this, too.'

'Surely not,' gasped Millie in disbelief. 'Queenie, you can't leave Tingulla.'

'I know. But I might have to go.' The tears ran down her face and Millie hurried to comfort her, wrapping her sturdy arms around Queenie's trembling shoulders.

Queenie was totally bereft. This blow had shattered the last of her strength. Tingulla was more than a home. It was her link with the past, the generations of her family that had lived — and loved this land. It was her physical and spiritual home. It was her future, for her daughter and grandchildren. It was not a piece of property to be bought or sold. Or gambled away.

After Millie left the room, Queenie hid her face in her hands and sobbed. 'Oh, Warwick, how could you do this to me?' A chilling thought suddenly struck her. Did Warwick know about this before he took off on the flight that killed him? Had he chosen death rather than face her? He would have known losing Tingulla would devastate her.

The shock of the idea cleared her head and she began pacing distractedly about the room, running her hands wildly through her hair. Poor Warwick. How he must have suffered knowing how deeply he had trapped himself. 'If only I had guessed. If only he had come to me earlier... perhaps I could have helped him.'

Queenie stopped, her arms about her shoulders. If only she had listened to TR. For a moment she wanted to run to him and ask for help. But she stilled the thought. No one could help her now.

Like fragments from a film — certain incidents, comments, Warwick's unexplained trips away, his evasive behaviour, his impetuous generosity — everything began to fit into place. He would go for months without gambling. Then he'd break out in a spree where sometimes he won and other times he lost. That he had managed to keep it all from her was the surprising thing.

Though, Queenie supposed, it wasn't so surprising, really. It was the last thing she ever would have imagined. She had never questioned or queried his motives or his time away from Tingulla. She was so wrapped up in her life at Tingulla she wasn't interested in anything else. She had been a trusting fool.

Two days later, sitting in her solicitor's office with her bank manager and a financial consultant, the full extent of the nightmare was exposed and set before her.

Queenie was brisk. 'What can be done? I will do anything to hold onto the station. Those men don't want it — they want their money. There must be some way to raise the money, even if I just have to be a tenant at Tingulla for a while.'

The solicitor kept his voice steady. 'I'm afraid they do want the property. Even selling off as many assets as we can, with the outstanding debts, there is no way you can hold onto the property. I understand Camboni intends that Colin and his wife should move in and run it.'

Queenie stared at him, a pink flush spreading across her cheeks. 'And where do my daughter and I fit in?'

'They have made a provision in this contract that you and your child are welcome to remain in the guest quarters. If you choose to help Colin work the property a small remuneration would be paid.'

'That does it! *Help* Colin! While Dina swans around playing mistress of the manor! Certainly not.'

'Queenie, don't be too hasty. Where will you go?'

'I'll live in a tent if I have to. What is happening to Cricklewood?' she asked suddenly.

'It's an asset and will have to be sold. Of course, if you declare bankruptcy, you can write off some of your debts.'

'You mean people like the grain merchants, the vet, the fellow who runs the equipment agency for the tractor, bulldozer and other gear, they're the people who won't get paid. Write them off — I won't do it.'

'Then you will have to sell what you can. The new owners will not want to inherit your debts.'

'I pay my own bills.'

The men shifted uncomfortably in their seats. 'If there is anything we can do...'

'Just do whatever is necessary. I will give you a list of what I intend to sell. The personal items left to me in my parents' wills, are I hope, still my property?'

The solicitor nodded.

Queenie stood and the men scrambled to their feet. At the door she turned, 'Tell my brother and that family he married, I do not want to see any of them. I'd appreciate it if you'd handle all communication.' The door snapped behind her and the men glanced at each other.

'What a terrible thing to happen.'

'God, she's got guts. Anyone else would eat humble pie or cave in. This is not some little property we are talking about here.'

'No,' agreed the bank manager. 'Tingulla is part of the country's history.'

'It's the Hanlons' heritage, so at least it's staying in the family's hands.'

'I give Colin six months at the outside,' said the solicitor.

Methodically, Queenie set about selling what she could. Jim walked about the property with her. 'Too bad we can't sell the heavy equipment. The 'dozer and so on.'

'They're not paid for. They're being repossessed. I tell you, Jim, I feel like stripping the place. Let them start from scratch and struggle.' Her voice was bitter.

'You don't want to see Tingulla go under, Queenie.'

'You're right, Jim. But it just seems so unfair ... after all our hard work. Dad's too. After getting through the drought, things were just starting to pick up again.'

Inside the house, Queenie went from room to room. Every piece of furniture held memories — Rose telling her about the old wood turner who had made so many of the pieces, the antiques she had brought out from England. There were few things she and Warwick had put in the house other than personal pictures, ornaments, and slightly more updated office equipment. Even Saskia had inherited Queenie's childhood bedroom and favourite toys.

Queenie packed her jewellery in a small box. She knew she would never get back its full value when sold but she needed every penny she could get at this crisis point in her life.

Saskia came and sat on the bed beside her. 'You're not selling all your jewellery?'

'I'm afraid I will have to, Sas . . . '

Saskia silently reached out and picked up the long strand of heavy pearls which had belonged to Rose's grandmother. She draped them about her neck, fingering the luminous globules.

'Saskia . . . I'm not selling those. They belonged to my great-grandmother and they're meant for you. I always thought you'd wear them on your wedding day,' smiled Queenie. 'And these. I won't part with my opals either.' With a determined air, Queenie pulled out the fiery opals Patrick and Rose had given her for her twenty-first birthday and clasped them around her neck.

Mother and daughter sat there with the necklaces shining on their old clothes. Queenie suddenly burst out laughing and hugged Saskia. 'Oh, Sas, don't we look a pair of grand ladies? Things will never get so bad that I have to sell these. Somehow I'll manage to work things out, you'll see. Let's go get a pot of tea.'

'Let's wear our necklaces down to show Millie.'

'And let's use the silver teapot and the good china for our tea.'

'It'll be like playing kings and queens!'

Holding hands the 'royalty' swept downstairs, wearing jeans and old riding pants with their simple cotton shirts, one with a glorious strand of pearls swinging to her waist, the other with opal lights of green, gold and rose sparkling at her throat.

Saskia had taken the news of their move from Tingulla well. Since returning from her two weeks in Sydney with Sarah and John and young Tim she seemed calmer, adjusting to the gaping hole in their lives.

Queenie had told her there were money problems, that Uncle Colin would be taking over running Tingulla for a while. 'There are too many memories here for us at the moment, Saskia. I think we need to make a change in our lives.'

'But we will come back to Tingulla, Mummy?'

'Of course, we'll be back, my sweet. And,' Queenie added firmly under her breath, 'I promise you that, my darling. If it's the last thing I do.'

She resolved with steely determination that every moment of every day would be put towards regaining her property, her heritage, her Dreaming land — her rightful home in this world.

Queenie had no clear plans. She knew she could never tolerate a moment at Tingulla under the same roof as Colin and Dina.

The stock at Cricklewood had been sold.

The Brahmans and the Herefords had fetched high prices. The auctioneer made a big point of the value of the beasts, calling it a pioneering herd that would be worth double the investment of ordinary stock, and had pointedly added it was a forced sale from Tingulla. Everyone knew who was selling and why, and when it was knocked down to Reg Coombes from Kilarney, he admitted he'd paid 'a bit over the odds'. But, he added 'if it's helping Queenie Hanlon, it's worth it. Besides, she knows what she's doing, so I'll go along with these Brahmans if she reckons they're good.'

Queenie was able to pay off what was owing to the local merchants. That left the personal loan at the bank still outstanding. She told the bank manager she intended moving to Sydney, to stay with Sarah and John, and she'd try and get on her feet in the city.

'Is that wise, Queenie? You're a country girl. Your skills are on the land. I can't see you in the city. What will you do?'

'I don't know. But I have faith in myself. And I just sense it's the right thing. I need a total change. Somehow I'll make money.'

She and Saskia took their clothes, but little else. Saskia had her favourite books and the blue wool wombat she'd loved since a baby, but she had to leave Devil, her young dingo behind. Jim promised he'd take care of the yellow-eyed dog who never left Saskia's side.

Jim and Millie would stay on, there was nowhere for them to go, and they would be needed. Queenie felt a little better knowing they would both be there looking after Tingulla and watching over its spirit.

Millie was especially upset. She kept rushing up to Saskia to give her a hug, pleading with Queenie to let her come to Sydney and help them get settled.

'Millie, I don't know what I'll be doing. I'll stay with Sarah and John till I decide what I'm going to do.'

'Then you'll send for me, Queenie? You and Saskia need me.'

'Jim needs you too, Millie.'

'Not as much as you two do. And he understands.'

Queenie hugged her. 'We'll see, Millie, we'll see.'

The only other personal items Queenie took were the collection of fine works of art her mother had left to her. The twelve paintings included work by some early Australian artists who had painted poignant scenes of outback life — Frederick McCubbin, Tom Roberts and Julian Ashton. Also inherited from her mother were several valuable English paintings including a Turner landscape. Patrick and Rose had some Aboriginal bark paintings which Queenie packed, but did not intend to sell. Snowy had explained the Dreaming story depicted in each one and Queenie felt they were tangible and important links with the soul of Tingulla. Besides, she knew Aboriginal art work was not yet considered 'collectable'. Her plan was to sell the rest of the collection to pay off the bank and give her a toehold in Sydney.

*

Inevitably the day came when Queenie had to leave Tingulla. She had mulled over in her mind how she would cope with it. Days before, she found herself walking about the property, touching the trunk of a tree, picking a flower and putting it between the pages of a book, running her hands over the sun-warmed sandstone blocks of the homestead.

She took Nareedah for long rides, not wanting to think each time might be the last. Nareedah stared at her with mournful eyes, sensing the sadness in Queenie's heart. She wrapped her arms about the Arabian's strong neck and laid her cheek against the velvety skin.

'Jim will look after you, old girl,' she whispered. 'Till I come back.'

On the last morning Jim and Millie put the bags in the car ready to drive Queenie and Saskia into town to catch the train. They had decided the long train ride south would be nicer than rushing in a plane. There was no hurry. Queenie had no commitments, no plans, no one waiting.

Millie bustled, hurrying them about, trying to avoid any prolonged and agonising goodbyes. She was brisk and bossy. Snowy stood quietly by, watching the proceedings. Taking off their hats, the remaining men on the station drifted up to stand awkwardly in the background. They each shook Queenie's hand and wished her luck.

Queenie stood before Snowy, Saskia at her side. 'Well, Snowy... keep an eye on things for me. I'll miss you.'

'Don't you worry. I'll be here when you

come back. When you come back as boss,' he added.

Queenie hugged the old man as he pushed a small package into her hand. He swung Saskia into the air. 'My spirit watch you every day so you be one good girl, orright? And if the spirit come back and tell me Saskia not happy, Saskia afraid, or Saskia lonely, then I send good spirits back to cheer you up. Old Snowy be looking out for you, okay?'

'Thanks, Snowy.' She kissed his kindly smiling face.

'Now you and your mumma go. And don't look back. Bad luck to look behind. You keep walking forward.'

'We will, Snowy,' Queenie's voice was husky. Taking Saskia's hand she climbed into the back seat behind Millie and Jim.

Jim revved the engine, and the wheels crunched on the loose stones and the car moved away from Tingulla homestead. Queenie took Saskia's hand and squeezed it.

Saskia squeezed it back whispering, 'Remember what Snowy said, Mummy, don't look back.'

Holding hands tightly, Queenie and Saskia sat silently in the back of the car watching the familiar trees slide by as they headed for the unknown challenges of the city. It seemed impossible that they were leaving behind everything they loved so deeply.

Queenie clenched her free hand and realised she was still holding the tiny package Snowy had given her. She unrolled the soft wrapping of paper bark and found a small carved song stick, painted with the symbolic markings of the tribes who had first known and named Tingulla.

Quickly she wrapped it back up so no other eyes would see its sacred markings. Queenie felt this precious totem would keep her safe but like herself, one day it must be returned to its rightful Dreaming place — Tingulla.

III

---

*1980s
Return to the Dreaming*

Chapter Twenty-Five

The first few weeks in Sydney passed in a blur of faces, noise, movement and a claustrophobic mass of buildings towering above and pressing in on all sides.

Queenie felt constricted, as if she couldn't take a deep breath. She longed for the peace of the bush.

Sarah knew what she was experiencing. 'Queenie, I went through the same thing when John and I were first married and I realised I was staying in the city and not going back to the country to live.'

'I feel I'm on a strange kind of holiday and then it hits me, I can't go back ... home. I don't have a home.'

'You know you and Saskia can stay with us as long as you like — there's plenty of room.'

'You've been wonderful. Saskia has settled into school and it's good for her to come home to a busy and happy household. But I have to start sorting out my life, Sarah.'

'I understand. How is your money situation? John and I will give you a loan... until you get on your feet,' Sarah quickly added, seeing Queenie's mouth set in a stubborn line.

'Thanks, but no, Sarah. We'll manage. I never want to borrow another cent ever again.'

'I won't try and talk you out of it, Queenie. I know you. As much as we love having you stay here, perhaps you'd feel better in your own place — more settled. We'll talk to John about finding a place tonight.'

John returned from taking Saskia and young Tim to feed the ducks in Centennial Park; and while Sarah took the children upstairs to bathe and get ready for dinner, John showed Queenie a list of houses and apartments to rent.

'I wish you could afford to buy something rather than rent. What about the flats Colin owned in Double Bay — are they all rented?'

'I don't know. I assume they are, knowing how money-conscious Dina can be. But I'm not about to ask any favours from them. What have you got?'

They studied the list of rental places John had on his books. 'I'm more into the selling and developing side so I haven't seen any of them. My secretary suggested these as possibilities.'

'None of these mean a thing to me. Where's Balmain?'

'It's not the most desirable area, but it's close to the city, right on the edge of the harbour.'

'It has water views?'

'Not of the most salubrious part of the harbour... it's close to where freighters and the less glamorous shipping comes in.'

'I like the idea of looking at the water because it would be different. I certainly can't afford the harbour views in posh suburbs. Let's look at this one.'

The next morning John drove slowly along narrow winding Wharf Street, pulling up before a rusty gate, an overgrown garden and a flight of steps disappearing through a grove of creaking bamboo. Echoing from below came the blast of a ship's whistle and the answering bleat of a tug's horn.

'I don't know about this, Queenie.'

'It's different,' she grinned at him.

The house was a tiny Federation cottage, dust-covered and musty from eighteen months of being closed up.

'It's small — three bedrooms — but it has a nice little patio out the front... somewhere under the leaves,' said John cheerfully.

Queenie wasn't looking at the antiquated kitchen with its old Kookaburra gas stove, or the terrace littered with debris from the overhanging orange and mandarine trees. She was watching the activity on the water directly below their miniature front garden.

Cranes swung from freighter to dock and, on Russian and Japanese cargo vessels, crew in dark uniforms scurried about their decks. A dark sinister submarine lay in the shadows of an inland dockyard and moored midstream was a small grey naval battleship.

'I like this. It's interesting. I like the activity. We don't have to look any further, John.'

He gave her a quizzical look. 'Sure you're not being impulsive? The house and garden need work — though the rent is cheap enough. It's not a fashionable area.'

'I have made up my mind and I'll stick to it. Saskia will like it too,' she said decisively, and John shrugged his shoulders amicably.

Sarah and John sent a team of professional cleaners and a gardener over to work on the house and garden as a house-warming present.

Saskia was entranced with the quaint location and scrambled through the front garden fence down to the dockyard and in two hours she had made friends with an old man who ran a boat shed. He told her she could use one of the dinghies to paddle around that part of the harbour any time she wished.

Queenie went to Lawson's auctions on a rainy day when few buyers were about and picked up antique furniture from a deceased estate for a fraction of its value. In three weeks the house was charming.

John shook his head. 'Queenie, you're amazing. I wish you'd transform some of the houses I have to sell. This is a picture.'

'Oh, it's not finished yet, wait until I've done the garden. I found a potter who makes great urns which I'm planting with geraniums and flowers for the terrace.'

John sat in the swinging love seat, watching Queenie pour tea. 'And where did you find all this wrought iron furniture?'

'It's Victorian. Now I've got wheels I'm finding my way all over the city.'

'Queenie, you must be the only woman in Sydney driving about in a Range Rover. You don't need a four-wheel drive in the city.'

'It's practical. It's been great for throwing furniture in the back and it's what I'm used to driving. Can't get about on horseback down here.'

John was pleased to see how well she was adjusting to the city and that her sense of humour was surfacing again. 'So what now? How's your money holding out?'

'I'll have to look for some kind of work. But first I need to sell my mother's art collection. I'm paying back that bank debt and I need money to live on.'

'I know a reputable dealer I could put you in touch with.'

'Thanks, John. I thought I might do a bit of homework and investigate the art scene myself. If I do sell through your dealer I still want to have some sort of knowledge.'

'Sarah said you'd want to do it all yourself. You certainly are thorough.'

'I appreciate your help and kindness. You and Sarah have been wonderful.'

John stood and lightly rested his hand on her shoulder. 'You're like family, Queenie. We're here for you, day or night.'

Queenie waved to John as he drove away. He was such a good kind man, and he and Sarah seemed so happy. She sighed. People had probably thought the same about her and Warwick. Well, they had been happy. And there had been lots of good times. If their relationship had been a bit stolid maybe it was because you weren't supposed to experience or expect the wild and delirious passion of youth in a marriage. But why not? She paused, hidden in the archway of massive bamboo that creaked and sighed above her. The filtered light was green and dreamy and for a moment Queenie closed her eyes remembering...

She shook her head and marched down the steps to the house. Tingulla, TR, her past life had to be put behind her. Whenever she caught herself wallowing in memories she forced herself back into the present. 'Live for the moment. Day by day.' That was what she kept telling herself. 'Let go of the past. It's over. Don't look back.'

After she had dropped Saskia at school each day, Queenie began visiting art galleries, art schools, dealers and artist's studios. She talked to everyone and slowly began to piece together a picture of Sydney's art world.

Painters were moving away from the small élitist groups of the sixties into a broader sphere now that the government was funding young artists. Art schools were booming and established painters were winning wider acceptance. There was a lot more recognition and understanding of abstract art although the purchase by the Whitlam Government of Jackson Pollock's *Blue Poles* for more than one million dollars still caused heated arguments.

Queenie discovered class and snob systems still operated and there were buyers who paid high prices for the signature rather than the painting. She thought the gallery commissions were far too high but it was the only way to reach the high-paying clients. She was reluctant to let a gallery buy her collection and charge her a high commission; and she would have no control over the purchase price. So she decided to put it up for auction with a high reserve price.

As the day of the auction drew near she sat nervously in Sarah's sunroom. 'I just hope enough people with money come along to the auction. They've done a lovely discreet catalogue, but I wish they'd bang the drum a bit more loudly,' said Queenie.

'Let's do it ourselves then! Make another pot of coffee.'

Sarah sat on the telephone for the next half hour and, adopting a snooty accent, rang all the newspapers, radio and television stations inquiring about the fabulous mystery art collection she'd heard was being auctioned. Could they tell her something about it?

'Naturally none of the news editors knew a thing about it,' giggled Sarah. 'But they sounded a bit interested. Now you mail them all a catalogue and I'll follow up with another round of calls.'

'I've told the auctioneers I don't want my name revealed,' said Queenie.

'All the better. I'll plant a few hints about the mystery seller and is it true that a Malaysian tunku, a Japanese industrialist and Australia's two richest men, as well as overseas galleries, will be bidding against our own galleries?'

'Sarah! You're outrageous! What are you doing?'

'Just asking questions. I'm saying no more than that. You know how one hears things, dahling,' she joked.

The auctioneer nervously adjusted his polka dot bow tie. The press had been trumpeting about the auction for days, creating more interest in this art sale than any for several years. It had turned into a media event with the social press covering the well-heeled buyers and the evening TV news services setting up cameras in the hope of covering a big sale or a bidding duel between the financial heavies.

The seller was a mystery and several wealthy prospective bidders sat on the end of international phone lines, while the art press raged at the idea of early Australian art possibly being sent out of the country.

The mystery seller kept away. Her adrenalin pumping, she spent the morning slashing at the weeds at the bottom of the garden.

At the end of the day, Sarah arrived with John triumphantly waving bottles of Bollinger. 'Queenie, you've done brilliantly. Made masses of money. You should have been there. It was so exciting, everyone kept applauding. You'll see it on the news tonight.'

Queenie sipped her champagne. 'Have I made enough to pay back the bank?'

'The auction rooms will call you soon, but yes. The Turner went for a huge price — two galleries wanted it, one here and one in

England, then some Hong Kong buyer stepped in and the bidding went through the roof.'

'What a relief. But I'm sad, too. They were my mother's. I kept her portrait, the one of Tingulla, and the Aboriginal works.'

'Your mother was not materialistic, Queenie. Rose loved beautiful things, but family and people and Tingulla came first. She would have told you to sell them straight away,' said Sarah gently.

'I hope so.' Queenie raised her glass. 'To step one. And to you Sarah, for banging the drum so well.'

'What's step one?' asked John.

'I plan to get back Tingulla if it's the last thing I do. Clearing my debts is step one.'

'What's step two?'

'I don't know.'

Sarah and John exchanged a swift look. Queenie had to let go of Tingulla or she'd never settle and be completely happy.

Queenie paid off Tingulla's massive loan to the bank, kept a small nest egg for herself and Saskia, and invested what was left. Somehow she had to use that to make more money to buy out Colin and Dina — to own Tingulla once more.

She was driving through a back street of elegant Bellevue Hill when she came upon a small art gallery she hadn't seen before. As soon as she stepped inside she realised it was a quality gallery, small but select. The owner, an American with a silver goatee and red bow tie, left her to browse in peace.

She studied the delicate pencil sketches of Cedric Flower; the lewdly humorous water colours of Norman Lindsay; and the outback oils of Russell Drysdale. Several oil paintings by Sali Herman caught her eye.

'You have been staring at these for longer than normal. Can I answer any questions?' came the quiet voice of the gallery owner beside her.

'I like these. I like his work and I was wondering where he painted them.'

'Sali is Swiss, but has lived in Sydney for years. He's in his seventies now, still painting like a fiend. But these are particularly fine examples of his work from the fifties and sixties. They're titled *Terrace Houses*.'

'Where are they? Are these places still standing?'

'I have no idea. I don't know Sydney that well myself. If you're interested I could find out. I'll call him.'

Queenie could hear the gruff, heavily accented voice booming down the phone.

'A lady wants to know? Is she pretty?' asked the incorrigible old painter.

'Oh, very,' replied the gallery owner, giving Queenie a smile.

There was a brief exchange and he hung up. He wrote on a piece of paper and handed it to Queenie. 'You're invited round for tea at his studio. Watch out though, he's a terrible flirt.'

Queenie laughed and did indeed ring and make an appointment with the old artist.

Sali Herman was a charmer. Short, balding and overflowing with European manners, he looked twenty years younger than he was. He pushed his hugely fat black and white cat off a chair and waved Queenie to be seated.

He started by asking her about herself — she was brief, but when she mentioned she was from the bush, Sali clapped his hands and told her of his experiences in the outback, which he adored. He told her of growing up in a family of nineteen children in Switzerland, of coming to Australia as a young man, his many love affairs, his wartime experiences in New Guinea. Several hours were swallowed in a flash.

Sali took Queenie's arm and led her into the dining room. Fresh tropical fruit, cheeses, French bread and good wine and rich cakes were spread on the table under a gauze cloth. 'Our lunch,' he announced.

'It looks too good to eat. Like a still life, perhaps you should paint it,' laughed Queenie.

'I prefer to feed my stomach, then I can satisfy my artistic spirit,' said Sali.

'Sali, I nearly forgot to ask, where are the terrace houses you painted? Are they in Australia?'

'They're here in Sydney. In my secret place. I will take you there. To Glebe.'

Glebe turned out to be an inner suburb, close to the city. Parts of it were neglected and overlooked, only the larger, wealthier homes on its fringes looked impressive. Tucked away in its leafy back streets were Sali's row of two-storey terrace houses. They were run down, and badly in need of paint; and although some had the remains of attractive wrought iron balconies, other balconies had been enclosed with ugly fibro sheeting and glass.

Queenie stared thoughtfully at the last house in the row. A peeling yellow and black 'For Sale' sign was stuck in the downstairs front window. She went through the wrought iron gate and rapped at the door.

John stood on the footpath staring at the row of terrace houses. 'You want to buy this house? For God's sake — why, Queenie? It's cheap, but you can do a lot, lot better.'

'Don't sound so exasperated, John,' said Queenie calmly. 'You don't know what I want to do with it. Remember you said I was good at transforming places when I moved into the Balmain house.'

'Decorating a rental place is one thing. Buying a derelict joint in a rundown area is quite a different matter.'

'Before I buy it, I want to make a few enquiries and I need your help. I want to contact the owners of all the other places in the row.'

'What on earth for?'

'Because I want to buy those as well.'

'Are you out of your mind? That will take, at the very least, every cent you've got!'

John paced up and down the kitchen as Sarah made dinner. 'I can't just stand by and watch her sink every cent — plus take out a loan — for a bunch of old houses. She'll never get her money back on rental and they're certainly not an investment. Who'd want to live there?'

'Queenie says she's going to live in one of them. Maybe she has a clever idea. At least hear her out, John.'

'It'd better be good,' he muttered.

Queenie spread her sketches of the proposed renovations of the terrace houses before John. Beside it she placed several sheets of paper outlining the potential of Glebe.

'It's minutes from the city. It's quiet. It has lots of trees, small shops run by Europeans, buildings that could be turned into restaurants yet remain in character with the area, galleries, trendy boutiques, arty shops.'

John studied her plans thoughtfully. 'I see what you're aiming at... and it's certainly ambitious. Very Parisienne. But how are you going to persuade other people not only to restore these houses to Victorian and Federation elegance, but to also move here?'

'Once they see what I do... others will follow. I'll get Sarah to do some more publicity and promotion work for me.'

John laughed in open admiration. 'It's a hell of a bloody gamble, Queenie.'

'If I fail, I might get my money back. If I succeed I will have accomplished step two.'

'As a real estate agent, I can see the potential and the sense of what you're saying. As a friend, I'm a bit worried. I don't suppose I can talk you out of it,' sighed John.

'No,' smiled Queenie.

The locals around Scone, used to wealthy and attractive women, still gave Martine a second look. TR's glamorous American girlfriend was used to turning heads and this was her third visit to the area. She'd been staying at Guneda for a month now, and in her heart she knew this would be her last visit.

She waited for the right moment, when TR was relaxed and receptive. Handing him a cold beer at the end of the day, she watched him lean back in his chair and stretch his long legs.

'Thanks, Martine ... nothing like a cold beer to finish off a hot and productive day.' He eyed her reflectively. 'Do you miss your sunset mint juleps?'

'Sometimes ... TR, I've been thinking. I feel it's time that you and I came to some sort of understanding.'

TR lowered his glass and sat upright. 'I've been waiting for this. I guess it is time we talked.'

'Just where are we going, TR? You and I? I love being with you, I think we have a lovely relationship. I know you don't want me to say it, but I do love you. I can see that you will never love me ... at least, not any more than you are prepared to now. But time is passing and I've come to realise I could never settle here in the bush and that you are devoted to the land. But more than that, I can't compete with whatever memory you hold in your heart. You're not prepared to give yourself, TR, and I'm no longer prepared to wait.' She took a deep breath, tears shining in her eyes.

TR looked at her tenderly, with deep affection and sadness. 'You are right, Martine. I've tended to just drift along, enjoying the moments with you — with no thought of any future, any commitment.' He turned away and his voice was husky. 'I can't do that.'

Martine stood. 'I know, TR. Whatever or whoever has hold of you . . . until you lay that ghost to rest you will never truly start living.'

She left him and he wanted to wrap his arms about her and comfort her, but now he didn't want to offer false hope. She was right and he knew it was best for both of them if they went their separate ways. He hoped they would remain friends and that she would make a new life for herself back in America, with someone more suited to her.

His heart ached and he felt very alone.

Chapter Twenty-Six

Dressed in paint-stained Yakka overalls, old riding boots, her hair tied back in a pony tail and without makeup, Queenie scrambled through the junk yard with a measuring tape and a notepad covered with scribbled figures.

'I'll take the lot,' said Queenie to the old man in charge.

'Ninety-eight dollars.'

'Get away! *Ninety-eight* dollars? Make it fifty.'

'Eighty even.'

'Sixty, and that's your lot.'

'I can get more for scrap. Seventy-five is the lowest I can go, lady.'

'Sixty-five, cash, and I'll take it off your hands now. Take it or leave it.'

He shrugged. What the hell did she want broken bits of rusty wrought iron and lead-light window panes for anyway?

Feeling pleased with herself, Queenie counted out the notes; she had been prepared to go to seventy-five dollars. The old man watched her load up the back of her four-wheel drive, not offering to help.

She had searched everywhere for matching pieces of iron lace to restore the upstairs balcony of her new Glebe house. In her expeditions around the industrial scrap merchants and small junk dealers, she had discovered a treasure trove of pieces salvaged from demolished homes. It saddened her to see the way the old houses were being bulldozed for the modern angular boxes of rendered cement, brick, and tinted glass.

She bought light fittings, plaster mouldings, and a stack of Victorian tiles hand painted with dainty flowers, to lay around the fireplace. She had been thrilled when she ripped away the old electric heater and plywood covering to discover a beautiful marble fireplace.

Queenie backed into her small rear courtyard and began dragging her latest haul from the rear of the Range Rover.

'That's too heavy for you. Let me give you a hand.'

Queenie spun around to find Millie standing by the back door, dressed in a good dress and straw hat, grinning at her. Queenie dropped a piece of iron with a clatter and rushed to hug her. 'Millie ... what a wonderful surprise. What are you doing here? How did you get here? Where's Jim?'

'Slow down, girl. Invite me in and give me a cuppa and I'll tell you all. Where's Sas?'

'She's at school. Oh, Millie, she loves it. Look, I'm sorry the place is such a mess,' said

Queenie, stepping over piles of building materials as she led Millie indoors.

Queenie put the kettle on and pushed the Weet Bix packet and remains of breakfast to one side of the scrubbed pine kitchen table. 'Had to leave early to take Saskia to school then get to the junk dealers to see what I could scrounge.'

'You fixing this place up, then?'

'More than that — restoring it, Millie. I want to get it back to its original condition then decorate it and do the courtyard. It's going to look lovely.'

'Lot of work.'

'I know. I feel a bit like a labourer's apprentice, but I can't afford to pay people — besides no one quite understands what I'm doing,' smiled Queenie ruefully.

'Good thing I turned up then,' said Millie standing up and lifting the steaming kettle off the stove.

'What do you mean, Millie?'

Millie poured the boiling water into the teapot. 'I've left Tingulla. Couldn't take that foreign biddy bossing me around any more.'

'Oh, Millie, I am sorry. That's terrible. How can you leave Tingulla? And where's Jim?'

'Don't you fret about it. Things have worked out real good. I'm going to stay here and look after you and Saskia, same as before, and . . . '

'Millie! I can't pay you, this place is tiny, you won't like the city, and what about Jim?'

'Let me finish,' said Millie calmly, bringing the pot to the table and settling herself opposite Queenie. 'I belong with you and Sas. I can see you need me. I don't care where I live for the moment. It'll just be till you get on your feet. I know you want to get back to Tingulla one day, and you'll do it, Queenie luv, I know you will. Besides, it may be sooner than you think. Colin is making a right mess of the place.'

'Oh, no!'

'He wouldn't listen to Jim or Mr Quinn. That wife of his has him buying this and doing that. The place is like a flipping hotel — party after party, all these people up from Sydney. I didn't mind the work... it was her being such a bossy boots, never a thank you, just complain all the time. You know what the problems can be like when the generator breaks down and there's no water being pumped to the house, no power... my goodness, did she throw a turn,' Millie commented with grim satisfaction.

'I can imagine.'

'Jim didn't have it any better with young Colin. Even Snowy was gettin' fed up. Took off and went walkabout for a couple of weeks, and he hasn't done that in a long time. So we had a bit of a mag about it all and decided we'd leave. Jim has gone to work for TR at Guneda, I'm staying with you — forget about the money, I got a bit put away — and I'll go up to Guneda when I can... holidays and like... to stay with Jim.'

'And Snowy and the boys?'

'Don't worry. Snowy says he'll stay and watch over the place. He just keeps to himself.'

Queenie sighed and sipped the tea Millie had poured during this speech. 'It breaks my heart to think of everyone and everything being so... uprooted.'

'Don't you worry. Just put it out of your mind. You got to get yourself back on top. Now — what are you doing and what do you want me to do?' She smiled at the dishevelled Queenie, who was staring at her with tears glistening in her eyes.

'Millie, I don't know what to say.'

'I'm here and there's nothing you can do about it. You got a spare bed, or you going to put me out in the street?'

'Well, you can start by taking off your hat.' Queenie reached out and patted her hand. 'Thanks, Millie, you're wonderful.'

Queenie collected Saskia from school and told her there was a surprise waiting for her at home. Saskia bolted through the narrow house and squealed with joy to find Millie making biscuits in the tiny kitchen. She dropped her school bag and flung her arms around Millie's waist.

Watching in delight Queenie explained that Millie had come to stay and would sleep in the small downstairs bedroom, and that Jim would be working at Guneda.

'Can I go with you when you visit?' asked Saskia promptly.

'If it's school holiday time and your mumma agrees. Now pick up your bag, young lady, there's enough mess about here as it is.'

'Yes, Millie.' Saskia grinned at her mother giving her a conspiratorial wink. The boss was back.

*

The weeks flew by, and with Millie running the household and helping to look after Saskia Queenie accomplished a lot more than she had anticipated. Millie also helped with stripping paint, wallpapering and assisting Queenie as she balanced atop ladders, knocking out partitions and cupboards to open up rooms which had been divided into cubicle-like bedrooms.

Light, air and space gave the formerly pokey cottage a spacious look and a happy atmosphere.

'I'll have to get an electrician in to rewire the kitchen. That is totally beyond me,' said Queenie.

'There's a fella down at the boat shed does that sort of work, he's one of Saskia's mates. He'd probably moonlight and do it on the cheap for you,' suggested Millie.

'Provided he knows what he's doing. I'll talk to him, anyway.'

Saskia took her mother to meet her boat-building friends and told Queenie how she was still trying to persuade Millie to go for a row with her. 'She won't set foot off land — she's funny. But she likes fishing off the wharf with me,' laughed Saskia.

The electrician turned out to be willing and helpful, telling Queenie about one of the old men who worked at the shipwright's and did beautiful wood finishing. 'He'd do those stairs and get that panelling back into shape in no time. He loves good wood... damned shame it's been let go.'

Queenie's refurbishing generated a lot of interest among the boat builders and they took to dropping in for cups of tea — a pretence for helping out. They lent her tools, and gave her a hand with heavy work. The old craftsman who did the decking and cabinet making on luxury boats, offered to do work for Queenie, saying, 'Pay me when you can, luv. It's a pleasure to see you save all this lovely old stuff.'

She flagged the courtyard and used wooden lattice and a series of old iron lampposts to make an outdoor eating area. Millie worked in the garden, transforming the tiny area into a small rainforest.

'Those tree ferns and palms must have been there fifty years,' said Queenie, helping Millie drag terracotta urns into the garden ready to be planted with flowers.

'And there's a couple of fruit trees hanging along the fence and behind the old dunny,' said Millie.

'The outdoor loo will have to go. Now that we have internal plumbing we don't need that dunny... I know — I'll put a gazebo there,' laughed Queenie.

'You could always grow chokos and passion-fruit over it and hide it. That's what all the neighbours seem to do,' said Millie.

John and Sarah came by each weekend and enjoyed poring over paint colours, fabric, and books on historical houses of the period. John kept tabs on any structural changes Queenie planned, worried she was going to knock down a supporting beam.

'I have to admit, Queenie, you're doing a helluva a job. It's really looking good. Puts the rest of the places to shame.'

'I've been thinking about that, John. Now that I can see that this restoration is possible — and I learn something new almost everyday, so it's getting easier and I don't make quite so many mistakes — could you find out if any other places in the block are for sale?'

'Queenie! How could you bear to go through all this again? And how will you pay for it?' asked Sarah.

'It seems to me I'd stand a better chance of making a bigger profit if we sold several places already fixed up in one street, rather than just one. A lot of people wouldn't want to do this,' replied Queenie.

'Most people wouldn't know where to start — or have your creative ideas,' said Sarah.

John looked thoughtful. 'I wonder... the area is taking off. An art gallery has opened around the corner, and there are a couple of places being turned into arty boutiques. I think the timing could be spot-on. I'll make a few inquiries.'

'And the money? How does Queenie pay for it?' asked Sarah raising a quizzical eyebrow.

'Let me worry about that. First things first,' grinned John.

In the shearers' quarters at Tingulla, Snowy and Ernie sat with a tearful Ruthie. 'Now she's got this lady housekeeper from Brisbane who don't know nothing about a station and she expects me to do all the dirty work,' sniffed Ruthie.

'Bloody wog bitch. Don't worry, Ruthie. Maybe we can all go over to TR's place at Guneda.'

'Watch what you're sayin', Ernie,' admonished Snowy.

'What for? She calls me a thick-in-the-head-blackfella. I heard her,' retorted Ernie. 'I reckon we should all just pack up and go. Leave them up a creek without a paddle.'

Snowy patted Ruthie's hand. 'Just go 'bout your work, and keep out of Mrs Colin's way. Things can't stay like this much longer, I reckon. Besides, we gotta keep an eye on things here for Queenie.'

In the big house, Colin and Dina were having a similar discussion. 'Colin, Mrs Thompson has a list of problems as long as my arm. She says she can't possibly cook this menu for next Saturday, the food supplies haven't come in and if the generator isn't fixed she can't cook at all. She doesn't know how to use the wood burning stove. Colin, you'll just have to fly in the food and get someone out to fix the generator. What's taking so long?'

'Dina, it's not that simple. Cancel the bloody dinner, we've had too many parties. I have problems of my own with the vehicles and sick sheep.' He stomped from the room.

Dina slumped in a chair and, picking up a magazine, fanned herself. The novelty of Tingulla was wearing thin.

At dinner that night, as Ruthie sullenly put their meal before them, Dina smiled brightly at Colin. 'I've solved our party problem. I cancelled it.'

'Good.'

'I mean I've cancelled it here. It's now going to be held at Jingles.'

Colin lowered his fork. 'Where and what is Jingles?'

'It's a divine new restaurant that's opened up in Surfers Paradise, we can all meet there and stay for ... '

'Surfers Paradise? We're going all the way to the Gold Coast for another of your flaming parties?'

'*Caro*, we'll make a weekend of it. Daddy and some of his friends are coming up from Sydney, there's a race meeting on the Saturday and we can have our party at Jingles Saturday night, stay in the new hotel, relax on Sunday and drive back Monday. It will be fun, Colin ... ' She leaned across the table touching his arm, one foot rubbing his leg.

'And what do I do about my problems here? Since Jim left, it's been chaos. I can't get a shearing contract arranged — I sometimes think the station blokes are deliberately going out of their way not to be helpful.'

'Get a manager to run everything. You're the boss, why should you do all this work?'

'Because that's a boss's job, Dina,' said Colin in exasperation. 'Besides, it will cost too much. This place is a huge drain on our resources. And weekends at the bloody Gold Coast don't help.'

'You're tired. Come to bed, we'll talk about it later.'

But Dina's usual solution for getting her way didn't work this time. Colin sat on the verandah outside their bedroom in his jeans and boots while Dina tossed alone in their bed.

Dina pulled her peignoir about her and moved outside, looking at Colin's bare chest in the moonlight. 'All this work here has built up your muscles. You look very sexy, darling,' she purred, sitting on his lap.

'Jesus, Dina. Give it a rest. I'm thinking.'

'And you can't do two things at once? Think *and* cuddle your wife?' She got up in a huff and flounced back into the bedroom.

Colin drained the glass beside his chair. 'Now listen, Dina . . . ' he flung himself on the bed beside her. 'I think we should get out of here. You only spend half your time here as it is — you're always going down to Sydney, over to Brisbane and the coast, or else you're shipping half your mates up here to party. I'm going to talk to the accountant and see what he suggests. I reckon we should sell up and move.'

'We'd get good money for Tingulla? And where would we go?'

'I'm sure you'll have a few ideas.'

'Mmmm . . . Will Queenie come back here?'

'No. She can't afford it. And you're not to breathe a word about this. It's just an idea at the moment.'

Dina rolled across him, kissing the hairs on his chest and murmuring, 'How does the Italian Riviera sound? A nice little villa . . . long sunny days . . . *la dolce vita* . . . mmmm.'

'Sounds pretty good at the moment. I knew it wouldn't take you long to come up with an idea.'

'I have another good idea . . . take your boots off . . .'

*

478

Queenie flung herself onto a seat in John and Sarah's garden. 'Well, I've done it now.'

'What have you done?' asked Sarah curiously, as she handed her a cold fruit juice.

'Bought a houseful of furniture... even down to jugs.'

John sat forward in his chair, 'What sort of furniture?'

'We could have loaned you any extra you needed, Queenie.'

'Sarah, this is not "extra" furniture. This is extraordinary furniture.' She grinned at her friends. 'My old boat builder mate doing the floor for me just happened to mention his aunty's deceased estate was going to be auctioned, and would I like to have first pick of it? So, I bought the lot. The whole house — a small house, mind you — but the most exquisite Victoriana. Good antiques, all in mint condition. The aunt was in her eighties and she'd inherited stuff from her mother. I even bought the china and old paintings, and washstands with bone china jug and bowl sets... It cost a lot, but one twentieth of what we'd pay at auction. I can furnish the whole house now in period, plus sell a few bits and pieces. Sarah, you'll adore it.'

'How much?' asked John, loosening his tie and attempting to look stern.

Sarah laughed at him. 'John, stop trying to look fatherly. You are as excited as Queenie. What a pair! But seriously, Queenie... it must have taken everything you've got.'

'It has. But it will be worth it.'

John threw his suit jacket on a chair. 'Well,

I've had a fruitful day at the office too... I found out about the rest of the terraces in your block. Would you believe they're all owned by one man? He lives in Melbourne and hasn't seen them in years. He could be talked into selling. Thinks they're only worth pulling down and is prepared to sell at the land site value. He doesn't need the money — he runs some big company.'

'What an opportunity. How could we raise the money?'

'We?' asked Sarah, looking from Queenie to John.

'By going into partnership, mortgaging everything to the hilt, and taking a bit of a punt,' grinned John. 'I think Queenie has stumbled onto a gold mine, and once people see what she's done with her place, we offer to develop the others. We'll make more than selling outright and hoping buyers fix them up properly. This way we become the developers. It's a whole concept that will catch on given the right exposure and publicity. There are inner city terrace blocks all over the place which are suitable. Traffic is so bad people are sick of spreading north and south and driving for an hour or more to get into the city. I've done some research and I'm convinced it will be a new trend. And we'll be in on the ground floor.'

Queenie looked worried. 'John, having just gone through losing Tingulla I don't want you to stick your neck out for me. I couldn't bear being responsible for you and Sarah losing your home.'

'Queenie, you're not responsible. I'm doing it for my family. I see the chance to make money here and make my mark as a developer, and you will be in there to oversee the design and restoration.' He reached out and touched her arm. 'Rest assured I'm not taking any risks.' He stood and dropped his arms about Sarah. 'At least not any that I can't deal with. What do you think, Sarah?'

She linked her fingers through his. 'I trust John's judgment. He's a cautious man, Queenie. Whatever he says, I'll go along with.'

Queenie was speechless for a moment. She couldn't help comparing John to Warwick, who'd been so reckless.

Sarah went and sat beside her, giving Queenie a hug. 'I think it's exciting and I'm sure it will work out, even though it's going to be a lot of work. Actually, I'm quite envious — this project will keep you both so busy and stimulated.'

'You'll be roped in, too, Sarah, there'll be plenty for you to do, don't worry. Now, do you want to see my bargains? I have the key to the old aunt's house ... you're not going to believe the treasures ... '

Sarah looked at her watch. 'It's nearly time to collect Tim and Saskia from their piano lessons, let's take them along, too.'

John and Queenie formalised their partnership, calling themselves Heirloom Cottages, and Queenie was amazed at how smoothly John arranged the finance once the owner had agreed to sell.

'He thinks he's unloading a real lemon on us,' laughed John. 'He kept asking had we *seen* the row of terraces, hinting they were in pretty crummy condition.'

'They are. But they've been surveyed and are structurally sound. They knew how to build solid homes in those days. And you know the stone walls that divide all those overgrown gardens? It turns out they're sandstone!' exclaimed Queenie.

Three of the houses were empty, and two were occupied — one by a scruffy group of unemployed young people who slept on dirty mattresses and seemed to drift through days and nights in a stupor of marijuana and alcohol. 'The lost tribe,' Millie called them. Queenie wasn't sure who was living in the last house on the corner of the block. She'd seen lights burning behind the tightly drawn curtains but had been too busy with the purchasing and building plans to pay much attention.

John had delivered notification of the sale of the buildings and informed the unofficial residents they would have to vacate the premises.

'They're not paying rent, according to the records. Or if they are it's a cash in the pocket deal. The bloke selling them told me all the places were empty. In fact, not habitable,' John told Queenie.

'Those kids are just squatting. I'd better check out the last house then,' said Queenie.

It took a long time for the door of number thirty-seven to be opened, and then a double bolt was slid back and the door only opened a slit. Blinking from the bright sunlight Queenie couldn't see into the darkness of the doorway. She introduced herself and said she was the new owner of the building.

The bolt was lifted and the door opened, and a middle-aged lady dressed in a smart skirt and embroidered jacket stepped outside, closing the door behind her. She shook Queenie's hand. 'Gail Sweet. How do you do?'

Queenie was taken aback; she had expected some little old lady, not this brisk businesslike woman. 'I hope you got the notification that you have a month to move. It was my understanding none of these houses were occupied,' said Queenie.

'I was given permission to stay here by the local council, dear. You see, I'm a social worker and I work in this area... counselling and so forth.'

'Oh. That must be interesting work, but I'm afraid you will still have to move in the next few weeks. Perhaps you could give me the name of the man at the council...'

'Don't you worry. Matters will be taken care of. Er, may I ask what you plan to do with these places?'

'Renovate, restore and sell them. Possibly they will be up for rent again — we think business people and young couples are interested in moving back into the inner city.'

The woman looked unconvinced and Queenie didn't like the way her smile became more of a smirk. 'Well, good luck then. I suppose we'll be talking again. Good morning.' She turned inside and the bolt clicked into place.

Queenie could hear a telephone ringing inside the house as she went thoughtfully through the front gate.

John mulled over this information. 'Something doesn't seem quite right about all that. There's been no council permission given, and no services are supposed to be connected... It's very strange.'

'If she's a social worker, she could start with the mob in number thirty-three,' added Queenie. 'I've tried talking to them all but it's useless. Those kids are zonked out of their heads most of the time.'

'We might have to get the strong arm of the law to move them on,' said John.

The eviction deadline came and went and nobody even looked like moving. John called in the local police and a male and female sergeant arrived, backed up by a paddy wagon, to move out the young squatters.

Queenie and John followed the officers inside as they began firmly and politely asking the groggy young people to leave the premises. There was a feeble, 'Who's gonna make me?' but most mumbled sullenly as they scooped up their few possessions.

Queenie and John looked at each other, wrinkling their noses at the stench and filth in the rooms.

It was a forlorn group which stood in a bewildered huddle on the footpath. The two police officers were telling them to move along when a station wagon marked with a TV station's logo swept into the street. A news film crew began setting up their gear as an aggressive reporter began demanding to know why these people were being thrown into the street.

John's jaw dropped and Queenie's mouth set in a grim line. She stepped forward. 'Just a minute. What do you think you're doing? These are not innocent victims, as you put it. They're trespassers.'

The cameraman and reporter switched their attention to Queenie. 'Who are you?'

'I own these houses. They've had more than a month's notice. They have been squatting here illegally.'

'Are you a mother by any chance, ma'am?'

Queenie was thrown for a moment. 'Yes... but what has that...'

'And so you feel no compunction over throwing a pregnant woman and homeless teenagers into the street?'

'What are you talking about?' Queenie's eyes narrowed dangerously, but the reporter pressed on.

'That young woman is expecting a child,' he pointed to a lank-haired girl whose baggy sweater almost concealed her pregnancy, 'and these two twelve-year-olds have run away from homes where they've been beaten and abused. Here they had shelter and protection.'

Queenie looked at the two young boys staring defiantly at her. She turned her back to the reporter and strode towards John. 'I've never seen that girl or those kids before. I think we've been set up. Who told these TV people about this, anyway?'

The reporter, trailing his microphone,

hurried after Queenie. 'I understand you want to throw these poor people onto the street and fix these places up to rent to rich people?'

Queenie spun around and spoke in a low, icy voice. 'Your information is incorrect and unsubstantiated. Please give me your name, your network and the name of your chief of staff.'

The reporter hesitated, then began hastily writing on a page of his notepad which he tore out and handed to Queenie. The cameraman lowered his camera.

Queenie took the paper and glanced at it. 'Thank you, Mr Cameron. I'll be in touch with your station. Next time, check your sources.'

Queenie strode away, followed by John who whispered, 'Do you think they'll run it?'

'I doubt it. But they might follow it up. Let's hope everything just dies down.'

Within two nights the original group were back in the house again, living by candlelight, eating junk food and sleeping on the floor.

'We should have boarded the place up. I think calling the police again would be a useless exercise. They just get back in. We could hire a security guard for a week or so,' said John.

Millie placed a plate of biscuits in front of Queenie and John and remarked, 'If you don't mind me saying so, I reckon a blast of birdshot up their backsides would shift them lazy galoots.'

Queenie and John laughed. Queenie grinned. 'That's a damned good idea, Millie.' She left the room and came back carrying an old shotgun.

John put his plate down with a clatter. 'Queenie! You're not serious? You're not supposed to have that thing in the city, are you?'

She gave an innocent shrug. 'You don't have to be a party to this.' Queenie slung the gun over her shoulder and picked up her coiled stock whip which had been hanging over the edge of a bookcase.

'Oh, my Lord... Queenie, what are you up to...?' John hurried behind her, turning to shake a fist at Millie who stood holding a teapot and smiling broadly.

'You fix 'em, Queenie luv.'

Queenie arrived at the house, flung open the front door and strode into the downstairs living room where three people lounged on a filthy sofa. She pointed the shotgun at them. 'You've got five minutes to get your stuff and get out.'

They gave her a dazed look and as she clicked the safety catch back, two of them began scrambling for their things.

With John trailing behind her, Queenie stomped upstairs and pushed open a door where others lay sleeping on old mattresses spread around the empty room. Candle wax lay in congealed puddles and food wrappings were scattered in corners.

Queenie leaned the gun by the door, unhooked the stock whip from her shoulder, and flicked it delicately onto each sleeping form. With a bullet-like crack, the thin blankets were whipped off them.

The figures sat up in shock to see Queenie standing over them, her legs astride and a shotgun pointed at them. 'Out. Now. For good.'

'You bloody shot at us. We can dob you in for that.'

'I used a stock whip. Next time it's the gun. You're trespassing.'

They began to mutter, wrapping their belongings in blankets and filing outside.

'Some more in here,' called John from another room. 'They seem unconscious. They're really out of it.'

Four people lay sprawled on the floor, spilled bottles of beer and hash pipes beside them.

Queenie took careful aim at the plaster wall between them. The blast reverberated round the room and, en masse, the sleeping bodies rose, shaking their ringing heads.

Queenie didn't have to speak. One look was enough. They followed her down the stairs.

John slammed the front door behind the last of them and watched Queenie walk swiftly away. He waited till the last of the stragglers had drifted down the block, noting the two young boys and pregnant girl were not in the group.

They had barely settled back in the house when there was a loud banging at the front door. Queenie waved a hand at John. 'I'll go.'

John heard her calm and friendly voice drift back. 'Gunshots? No, can't say I did, officer. There's always a a lot of cars backfiring in the area ... trouble? No, we had some squatters, but the police evicted them. Thanks for your concern. Good day to you, too.'

Queenie shut the door and walked back into

the room and winked at John. As she sipped her fresh cup of tea she said, 'Y'know, the neighbours were pretty quick off the mark calling the police. I wonder if our friend from the TV station might be around. John, I think it's time I had another talk with Mrs Sweet, the social worker at the end of the block.'

The visit was unproductive.

'No luck?' asked John.

'She didn't answer the door. But I felt sure she was there. I thought I heard a giggle when I left.'

'I'll get my mate down at the council to do a bit of detective work,' said John.

It was Saskia who provided the first clue. Sarah had brought her over to Glebe after school and put her bicycle in the back of the station wagon. While Queenie and Sarah worked in the house, Saskia toured the quaint little neighbourhood.

'Our houses are the nicest of them all, though there are lots of old ones like ours,' she said on her return. 'Who lives in the last house down there, Mummy?'

'A Mrs Gail Sweet — and she's not. I think she should be called Mrs Strange. She is supposed to have moved out by now,' answered Queenie.

'Maybe she's having a goodbye party. She has lots of visitors.'

'What do you mean, Sas?'

'I went down the back lane and there were cars and a taxi and these men went inside.'

Queenie glanced at Sarah. 'That's very interesting. When John comes over, maybe we'll have him go knock at the back door.'

John arrived with his own news. 'It seems Mrs Sweet must have friends in high places.'

'We think we know why,' said Queenie. 'We'd like you to make a few discreet inquiries at the rear of number thirty seven.'

'But that's all, John,' admonished Sarah.

That evening at Sarah and John's house, while Tim and Saskia watched 'Dr Who' on the ABC, Queenie sighed. 'A brothel. I can't believe my luck. How are we going to get her out?'

'It's illegal. Just report her,' said Sarah.

John shrugged. 'It's not that simple. Half her clients are members of the council, or in big business, and there's a rumour she has a few friendly detectives looking after her as well.'

'You can't go in with a rifle this time, Queenie.'

'No. But this time I have a story for Mr Kim Cameron of the "Six PM Newsline".'

'Queenie, if you go to the media, remember you are the owner of the building housing a brothel. This could backfire,' cautioned John.

'We'll see.'

Queenie called the young TV reporter and they sat in an Italian coffee shop around the corner from Mrs Sweet's establishment. She told him of her plans for the restoration of the houses and her belief that the neglected area would be developed as a unique part of the city.

'I'm impressed. I admit that before, we did get a tip-off that some tough woman was throwing women and kids into the street.'

'Who had never set foot in the place before you arrived.'

He had the grace to look embarrassed. 'Yeah... well, when I got back to the office I did do a bit of checking. We have a file on you. You're something of a heroine... droving all those cattle on your own, the er... loss... of your mother and father. And husband... plane crash, wasn't it?'

He sipped his short black. 'You've had it tough, all right. But what is the mistress of Tingulla doing in Glebe?'

Queenie bit her lip. 'That's another story. My brother is running the station. I wanted a fresh start. Too many memories there.' She hoped he wouldn't probe further, and he seemed satisfied.

'Well, I'd have a hard job making you out to be the bad guy. Let's go after Mrs Sweet, eh?'

At the end of the week Queenie visited number thirty-seven. 'Mrs Sweet... it's about your moving out...'

'Well, dear, I'm afraid it would be very inconvenient for me to leave.'

'I understand. However, I think it might be even more inconvenient for your, er... social cases, if you don't leave my house,' said Queenie.

The smirk changed to a hard expression as Mrs Sweet demanded, 'And what exactly does that mean?'

'Let's not play games any longer. It means that a TV cameraman and reporter have photographed the comings and goings to your establishment and the story will go to air, with a nice preview in the *Sunday Telegraph*.

'You wouldn't dare.'

'I'm afraid I would. In fact our conversation is being recorded and filmed.'

Mrs Sweet glanced behind Queenie, suddenly noticing the camera poking around the edge of a parked van. She turned inside and slammed the door.

Queenie lifted the metal flap of the letter slot in the front door and called through it, 'Out. By tomorrow, Mrs Sweet. And the girls.'

A furniture van arrived early in the morning and Mrs Sweet and entourage disappeared with no more fuss.

Queenie called Kim Cameron. 'She's gone. What are you going to do with your story?'

'There isn't one, I'm afraid. It got killed. I suspect there might have been a newspaper editor or TV proprietor among her customers.'

'Oh, Kim, that's too bad. After all your work.' Privately Queenie was elated. 'I'll send you an invitation to the launch party for Heirloom Cottages. Maybe you could do a story on that.'

Kim Cameron thanked her but doubted he'd do a story on trendy homes. However, he wouldn't turn down an invitation to free food and booze. 'Thanks, Queenie, I'll look forward to it.'

With the row of terrace houses now safely in their possession and ready to be renovated Queenie concentrated on putting the finishing touches to her house, which would be used as the model. She moved in the antique furniture and added the final touches of Brussels lace curtains and old embroidered bedspreads she'd found in spotless condition at a church bazaar.

Sarah took on promotions and publicity and soon had the interior design magazines, the newspapers, the trade press, the historical societies and preservation trust out in force.

Millie and Saskia kept out of the house as much as possible as there was a never-ending stream of photographers and visitors wandering about, marvelling at what Queenie had done.

Sarah put together a brochure featuring photographs of Queenie's model house and the proposed plans for others in the row. John sold the remaining houses in a matter of weeks.

'This is easier than selling iced water in the Sahara. It's bloody amazing,' said John.

'Nonsense. It's a great idea, and what with Queenie's decorating and my publicity push, you had half your work done for you,' retorted Sarah.

'You're absolutely right. What say we ask Millie to baby-sit and I take you two hard-working girls out to a slap up dinner?'

'John, that's a lovely idea. I don't think I've been out of these overalls in weeks.'

Sarah studied Queenie. 'Y'know Queenie, you do look like you've been building a house. Your nails are broken, your hair has been hidden under a scarf for weeks and you haven't seen a lipstick in months. I'm taking you to the beauty parlour in David Jones. Besides,

I've lined up a photo session and interview with you for the *Women's Weekly* next week.'

'It's nice to have frank friends isn't it, John?' mocked Queenie. 'No beauty parlours... I'll get myself together. Really, Sarah, I promise.'

Millie mailed a copy of the magazine and newspaper articles about Queenie, Heirloom Cottages and Glebe, Sydney's 'in' place to live, to Jim.

Jim handed them to TR. 'Look what Queenie's up to now... never thought she'd take to the city so well.'

'She's a very determined woman. I don't think she'll stay there though, Jim. I suspect it's all part of a grand plan to get back to Tingulla one day.'

Jim looked thoughtful. 'I talked to Millie on the phone a coupla days ago. Funny thing, she mentioned Tingulla. Said she was getting bad feelings 'bout things there.'

'The old bush instinct at work, eh? Had she heard from Snowy?'

'Nope. She didn't say nothing, but I think she's feeling worried in her bones. Said she kept having warning dreams about Tingulla.'

'In that case maybe I'd better drop by and check things out,' said TR. 'I have to go up north and pick up a horse. It wouldn't be far out of my way. But don't say anything to Millie. Let me find out how things are going.'

Chapter Twenty-Seven

The summer holidays arrived and Sydney sweltered under a heat wave. The newspapers had photographs of people frying eggs on the pavement and elderly citizens being treated for heat exhaustion in the crush of Christmas shoppers. The beaches were crowded, the golden sand blanketed with beach towels and colourful cotton umbrellas. Sunbathers burned under the sun's fierce rays before plunging reddened bodies into the cold blue surf for momentary relief.

At sunset the southerly buster with black clouds, high winds and coin-sized rain drops, swept in from the ocean to bang doors, whip washing from clotheslines and send umbrellas cartwheeling along the beach. Families hurriedly packed and headed for their oven-hot cars standing on roads where steam rose as the rain hit the melting tar.

The storms passed quickly, and in the

evening coolness barbecues were lit and a haze of smoke and the aroma of grilling meat hung over the suburbs.

Millie prepared to go to Guneda to spend several weeks with Jim. She broached the idea of Saskia going with her for some of the time. Queenie was reluctant. She tried most of the time to push TR to the back of her mind but the contact between him and Saskia brought back painful memories. She couldn't explain to Millie that TR had been the love of her life and that the loss of their child was a wound in her soul that had never healed.

'It will be so hot out there. What will she do? I don't want to put TR to any trouble looking after a young girl,' muttered Queenie.

'Jim says TR has more rooms than he knows what to do with, there's a housekeeper and, besides, I'll be there to look after her. What's she going to do here? She's not much of a beach girl, she'd much rather spend her days with horses. TR said she can work in the mornings mucking out the stables and he'll pay her pocket money for doing it.'

'You seem to have had a lot of discussions with TR.'

'Aw, come on, Queenie. If you weren't so stubborn you could come with us. A break would do you good. Spend some time with your kid. You're her mother — not me.'

Queenie knew she'd been neglecting Saskia since she'd got involved with Heirloom Cottages. She'd been tired every evening and barely listened to Saskia's chatter about her day. She couldn't remember when they'd last spent time alone together enjoying themselves.

'I'll think about it,' she said, and walked away. But Millie knew she would not go to Guneda. She just hoped she'd allow Saskia the holiday trip.

Queenie packed a picnic the following Saturday and she and Saskia caught the ferry across the sparkling harbour to Manly and walked around the rocky headland to Shelley Beach. They found a shady corner against the craggy headland and swam and explored the rock pools as the tide went out.

They ate their lunch and spread their towels out to lie in the sun. Saskia picked up her book.

'Sas... before you get your nose buried in that book... I know it's holiday time for you, but I still have a lot of work to do getting the houses finished and looking for some more work. I want to build on what we've done so far, it's the only way to make money.'

'You don't have to entertain me,' came the gruff response.

'I know. But Millie mentioned to me about you spending time with her at Guneda...'

Saskia didn't raise her head and continued to stare at the page of her book, but Queenie knew she wasn't reading.

'I just don't know about it. I know you love the bush and horses... I did too at your age — and I still do. I just don't want to put TR to any trouble.'

'Why don't you like TR?' asked Saskia in a low voice, still not looking at her mother.

Queenie bit her lip. 'It's not that I don't like him...'

Saskia flared angrily. 'Well, what then? You won't talk about him. You never see him when he comes to Sydney. Dad said you used to be friends. You grew up together.'

'That's not quite true... about us growing up together. I met him at my twenty-first birthday party.' Queenie's voice trailed away. 'People change as they grow older. Lives go in different directions, I suppose. But you're right, I shouldn't deprive you of the pleasure and fun I'm sure you'll have at Guneda. We'll try it for two weeks and see how it works out. If everyone is happy with the arrangement you can stay on a few more weeks. I'll miss you, though.'

Saskia rolled over and gave her mother a hug. 'Thanks... I'll write, and you can phone me up.' Contentedly she turned on her back pulling her straw hat over her face.

They lay in silence for a moment.

'Mum...'

'Yes...?'

'Tell me about your twenty-first party. What was it like, what did you wear? Who was there...?'

'Oh, it was a wonderful party... how I wish you'd known your grandparents. I ended up wearing your grandmother's satin gown. I still have it put away... I tore my dress.'

Saskia giggled. 'Tell me the whole story...'

Smiling softly, Queenie told her daughter of the party, climbing on the roof after jasmine, TR breaking up the fight with Colin, how Patrick had danced with all the young girls and of the beautiful opal necklace they'd given her.

'I love that necklace,' interjected Saskia. 'You've promised never to sell it no matter how hard things might get.'

'I remember, Sas.'

'And at the end of the party... that was when Grandma was killed?'

Queenie had never spoken of Rose's death in detail to Saskia. She had been told the facts since a young girl but had never expressed any curiosity before. Queenie now found herself telling her daughter in a small voice how hard it had been, how Colin had always blamed her for the death of their mother, maintaining that if Rose hadn't worked so hard at Queenie's party she wouldn't have gone back early and alone to the empty homestead and disturbed the intruders.

Queenie lay with her eyes closed, her lips trembling as she spoke. From under the hat covering Saskia's face, a tear trickled.

She reached out and found her mother's hand. 'Uncle Colin is mean. He's different to the rest of us. I never think of him as family.'

'Sas... that's not fair, he can't help how he is...'

'Well, I don't like him, and I don't like the way he treats you. You're too much of a Pollyanna, Mum.'

Queenie laughed. 'I've been called lots of things before but never that!

'Some of my friends think you are so strong and independent, but I know you're a real softie.'

'Don't tell anyone, Sas.'

'I won't.'

The two lay in the sun in silence as the tears dried on Saskia's cheeks and Queenie fell into a peaceful sleep, knowing the love of her daughter would always be with her.

With Saskia away at Guneda, Queenie knew Sarah was plotting for her to meet eligible men, and she dreaded the prospect. She wasn't interested in the delicate probing and fencing, the small overtures, insistent questioning and eventual courting by men fascinated by this elusive, mysterious and beautiful woman.

Sarah persisted, telling Queenie she had to come out of her shell. 'Just for fun, Queenie, and to have some social life. I'm not suggesting that you have an affair — though that might be a good idea — or marry them. You're becoming a recluse.'

Queenie laughed it off, saying she was too busy being a career girl. But in the loneliness of her bed, she lay between the cold linen sheets and longed for the comfort of Warwick's arms, while in her dreams TR's laughing blue eyes and burning mouth haunted her.

She hated waking to the thought of TR. She still felt guilty about him, as though she had betrayed Warwick. The hurt and grief TR had caused her was lodged like a knot in her body, strangling all feeling, energy, and passion.

TR left his car towing the horse float in the shade of some trees alongside the road leading to Tingulla's homestead, took the foal out and hobbled it in the grass, and set out to walk the half mile to the house.

Snowy appeared before he reached the main driveway and TR shook his gnarled hand. Snowy didn't seem surprised to see him.

'Glad to see you, Snowy. I was hoping I'd find you before I got to the house. So . . . how are things at Tingulla?'

The two men ambled to the fence and leaned on the splintery wooden rails. 'Not too good, TR. One dam bin poisoned with something, made plenty sheep sick — some died. There's bin a bad outbreak of flies and Colin got in some cowboy shearing outfit, made a big mess of the wool clip — did a terrible job.'

'Colin couldn't get Samuelson's team in to shear this year?'

'Dunno what the problem was . . . mebbe he wouldn't pay their rates, but none of the regulars came. Just this new mob, no bloody good mob.'

'Colin hasn't been managing too well?'

'Wants to change everything, do things his way. No good, no one could tell him nothing. And that missus of his . . . ' words failed Snowy. 'She thinks she still in the big smoke. Nope, things pretty crook here. I promised Queenie I'd keep an eye out, so I'll stick it. Most of the boys have gone. New blokes come . . . and go . . . '

'You're a good man, Snowy. Jim sends his regards. Well, I'll head down to the house.'

The garden looked neglected but everything else seemed normal. However, without Queenie in residence the house seemed forlorn. The housekeeper, a starched and snooty woman who reminded TR of a hospital matron, bustled away to fetch 'the mistress'. TR was not invited indoors. In his dusty and casual clothes the housekeeper obviously did not consider him respectable or important enough to cross the threshold. TR didn't sit in a chair on the verandah, he knew he wouldn't be staying long.

Dina swept out to greet him, not looking too pleased at being caught without make-up and in a plain skirt and blouse. 'Why, TR, this is a surprise. I wish you'd let me know you were coming by, I would have been prepared for you. At least let me offer you a cold drink... wine? Gin or whiskey? No? A beer, I suppose.'

'Nothing thanks, Dina. I'm sorry, I'm not accustomed to making appointments to visit friends. I picked up a horse from a property near here and thought I'd drop in to see how Colin is doing.'

'He is doing just fine thanks, TR.'

'Is that so? And what about you, Dina — how are you liking country life? Bit of a change from the social scene in Sydney — don't you miss it?'

'Not at all. We entertain a lot, and go to the coast regularly, things are working out very well,' said Dina brightly.

'I'm glad to hear it. Is Colin around?'

'I'm afraid not. He's in Longreach on business of some sort. I really couldn't say when he'll be back.'

'I'm sorry I missed him. Tell him hello.' TR

was about to add if he needed any help to call, but figured Colin wouldn't do that, so he kept quiet.

TR put his hat back on. 'Nice to see you again, Dina.'

'How are your horses doing, TR? I've been telling Colin he should get into racehorses, Daddy would love that.'

'You couldn't breed racehorses in this country, Dina. Guneda is doing very well. Seems we're all doing well, doesn't it? G'day then.'

'See you at the races some time, TR,' called Dina and disappeared into the house.

TR walked down to the stables and found Snowy waiting for him. 'I got the billy on in the quarters — want a mug of tea before you go?'

'Bloody oath I do, my tongue's hanging out. She's not up on country hospitality is she?' remarked TR as he followed Snowy. 'If I believed what she had to tell me, Tingulla is doing fabulously well. But things don't look too good. How long do you reckon they'll stick it out here?'

Snowy shrugged. 'Hard to say. Bin a bad season and he's done stupid things. His father must be turning in his grave,' said Snowy. 'What they teach them boys at that fancy school he went to anyway?'

'I think Colin's problem is he won't listen to advice, he's out of touch and he has a definite problem with a wife who doesn't understand country life.'

'Well, I hope Colin gets fed up and gets out before he ruin the whole place. Tingulla needs Queenie bad.'

*

Queenie slung the antique silk shawl around her bare shoulders, covering the strapless black dress, and headed out into the still night. Gingerly she hitched up the short tight skirt and in her black stiletto shoes climbed into the Range Rover and eased it into gear.

With a damaged muffler amplifying the exhaust, she roared into the gracious driveway of Sarah and John's home as a smartly dressed, attractive man stepped from a sleek Jaguar. He watched in amusement as Queenie parked and slid down from the driver's seat.

'Someone who looks as elegant as you shouldn't look so at home behind the wheel of a four-wheel drive,' he remarked.

'You obviously haven't spent much time in the bush. We country girls consider these quite chic.'

'So I see. I must go bush if this is what I'm missing. You don't see too many of these trundling around the city. Or have you just arrived from the wilds?'

They turned and headed for the brightly lit entrance of the house. 'No, I'm a city girl . . . for the time being.'

'I'm Anthony Tureau. I assume you are a friend of John and Sarah's?'

'Queenie Hanlon. How do you do.' Queenie had gone back to using her maiden name on John's advice in order to promote Heirloom Cottages. The Hanlon name was well known and Tingulla's fame widespread.

They shook hands as Sarah came to the door beaming. 'Well, how convenient — my last two guests arrive together.' She kissed Anthony lightly and gave Queenie a meaningful look. Queenie realised this was her blind date for the evening. She pursed her lips at Sarah behind Anthony's back.

It was a large group and dinner was a buffet so Queenie was relieved she wasn't trapped at a sit-down dinner. Anthony was attentive and rather charming but Queenie found herself enjoying the company of a jolly woman called Judith Thomas. Judy was close to fifty, buxom with greying hair. She was lively, warm and intelligent, and the two women took an instant liking to each other. They quickly settled themselves in a corner where they talked so animatedly and were so engrossed no one wanted to interrupt them.

Judy admired Queenie's opal necklace. 'Those are superb opals. I know quite a bit about them even though Australian women don't seem to favour them much... yet. All the good ones are sold overseas.'

'Some people think they're unlucky. I love these — they were a twenty-first birthday gift from my parents.'

'Don't you believe that nonsense about opals being unlucky, it was all a rumour started by the goldminers and the jewellers when opals were first found.'

Judy's husband Eric was a stockbroker in Sydney and the Thomases were obviously well-to-do, with old money and good connections. But in the manner of those with good breeding, she made no reference to her status, didn't name drop or give any clues.

Her interest in Queenie was so genuine and

caring, Queenie was amazed to find herself telling Judy about the loss of Tingulla and the struggle she'd had to get established in Sydney.

Judy clapped her hands together when Queenie began to explain about the terrace houses. 'Heirloom Cottages! I know them. We read about them... of course — now I realise who you are. Congratulations, you deserve everything you've worked for... in fact, I believe a friend of ours has bought one as a town house. I admire you tremendously, not many women would have achieved so much with such odds against them. Good on you, my dear. So, what's next?'

'I'm not sure. I guess developing and designing more Heirloom Cottages. I have to push myself a bit to drum up some business now the initial flush is over with the places in Glebe. I'm in partnership with John.'

Judy put down her coffee cup. 'Why don't we meet for lunch next week? Perhaps I can help. Besides, I'd enjoy seeing you again.'

'I would too,' smiled Queenie. She hadn't been so stimulated by anyone's company in months.

To Sarah's dismay Queenie hadn't given Anthony any time at all, but when she bid her good night after all the guests had left, Queenie hugged her. 'Thanks for introducing me to a new friend. I really like Judy Thomas.'

'She and Eric are a wonderful couple. Really special people. Well, if I couldn't line up a lover at least you have an entrée into the best circles in town.'

'That's not the reason at all. I like her as

a friend. I found I could share things with her
that, apart from you, I haven't told anyone.
I like a woman's company. There's always sex-
ual games and a competitiveness with men.'

'Shall I leave you two?' asked John.

Queenie and Sarah laughed. 'Good night . . .
and thanks for inviting Anthony, Sarah. I'm
sure he's a lovely man, but I'm not interested.'

'Anthony's loss I'm afraid,' murmured John
as Queenie headed down their drive. 'He was
most smitten.'

'It seems such a waste. I just hope she
doesn't fall for some loser,' sighed Sarah. 'I'm
glad she and Judy got on so well, though, even
if there is such an age gap. But come to think
of it, she has some of those gracious qualities
of Queenie's mother, Rose.'

The next week Queenie met Judy in a small
coffee shop and later took her back to show
her the house in Glebe.

'Queenie, it's exquisite. You have superb
taste, a real talent for this. You must do more.'

'I only want to do things that appeal to me.
Now I have a bit of money I can afford to
be choosy. Frankly, as I told you, I want to
make a lot of money.'

'So you can buy back your Tingulla?'

Queenie nodded.

'Right then. First I'm going to hold a series
of small soirées . . . my "famous little dinners"
as Eric calls them. I get roped in for all kinds
of charity work which is boring because the
women are generally such pains. But I have
a certain clout on committees and such, so

everyone who is anyone turns up when I ask them to dinner. I can introduce you into a circle of wealthy clientele who will outdo each other in demanding your services. But you have to play the game too, my dear.'

'Judy . . . you are wonderful . . . what do I do?'

'You are a rare flower who is naturally beautiful, but we have to gild the lily a bit. These women only respect what they recognise — the labels and the trappings. So we're going shopping. And to the hair stylist, and to Arabella.'

'Oh no, must I? Who's Arabella?'

'She runs a very exclusive boutique. She will happily outfit you in her designs. It will be good publicity for her, trust me.'

Sarah was thrilled when Queenie told her Judy's plans. 'Queenie, I think that's wonderful. You have to play them at their own game. It's infuriating how you look glamorous in old moleskins, but here you have to outclass the social set. The more expensive you look, the more snooty you are, the more exclusive you seem, the more they'll want you.'

'My lord, between you and Judy doing an Eliza Doolittle on me, poor Saskia won't know her own mother when she gets back from holidays.'

While Queenie reluctantly submitted herself to the hands of hair stylists, beauticians and fashion consultants, Saskia was knee-deep in horse dung and loving it.

Old Bobby had taken her under his wing and talked about horses for hours on end as they tended the foals and pregnant mares. Saskia was allowed to ride several of the quiet horses and Bobby and TR taught her some finer points of horse riding. In the evenings with Millie and Jim, she recounted her day with great enthusiasm before her eyes drooped and she fell into bed. She was up at sunrise and out watching TR and Tango, the new jackaroo, train the horses.

Mick, the young Aboriginal jockey came several mornings a week to ride Bill, but for the rest of the time Tango helped with the training.

'Why is he called Tango?' Saskia asked Bobby.

'There was a bush dance the first week he was here and although he's a shy young kid he's a good dancer, so they nicknamed him Tango.'

'What's a tango?'

'A sexy dance, luv. One of them foreign Latin numbers.'

'I don't like dancing. Riding is better.'

Bobby grinned at the lanky young girl. 'You'll change your mind in a couple of years.'

Saskia didn't answer but continued to watch Tango put a skittish young thoroughbred through its paces.

Tango was nearly seventeen, shy and good-looking. He was tall, of slim wiry build, with still a lot of growing to do despite being almost six feet in height. He had bright blue eyes and sun-bronzed hair. His voice was soft, not the harsh nasal twang of most country boys. He tolerated Saskia dogging his footsteps with good humour, recognising her love of horses. 'You like horses better than people, I think,' he once teased her.

She had considered this remark with deep concentration before smiling back at him. 'Just some people.'

Along with their mutual love of horses, Saskia and Tango shared a deep respect and affection for TR. As did Bobby. The old man considered him the son he never had, and each day thanked whatever lucky star had sent TR to his daughter's house in Brisbane to rescue him from turning into a cabbage. He complained to TR that his daughter and her family either ignored him or treated him like a 'wobbly old man'.

'You've given me a new lease of life, TR,' he would add.

'And I couldn't do this without you,' rejoined TR. 'We're partners, you silly old coot.'

Queenie felt strangely nervous as she presented herself early at Judy's for the first dinner party for Heirloom Cottages. She kept glancing at herself in mirrors, marvelling at the ultra chic woman who looked back in surprise.

Judy circled Queenie, studying her, and stepped back. 'You're perfect,' she announced.

Queenie's hair gleamed in a series of coils and braids glittering with jewelled combs. Her emerald eyes were heavily made up to look more dramatic than ever, and her high cheek bones and sensuous mouth were a fashion photographer's delight. Her slender figure was swathed in deep turquoise bands of chiffon with a length floating like a sari from one shoulder. It was strapless and long and she wore very high heeled sandals that were mere wisps of leather created by an Italian crafts-man. Queenie had been appalled at paying so much for so little.

Her nails were painted a clear coral. A mag-nificent and unusual silver and turquoise neck-lace with matching long earrings gave a stunning finish to the outfit.

'I feel so... conspicuous... and I'm certain I'm going to fall on my face in these heels,' muttered Queenie.

'Take tiny steps. And yes, you do stand out... gorgeously, so — that's the whole idea. The other women are going to be beside them-selves,' grinned Judy with satisfaction.

Queenie found the evening long and tiring, as if she were on stage performing the whole time, aware she was being scrutinised by the ladies, and covertly leered at by the men.

At first the women wanted to know about Heirloom Cottage's decor and furnishings and chatted about buying antiques.

'They sound quite divine, what a clever idea,' said one of the lady guests.

One of the husbands chimed in, 'Yes, indeed. Just whose concept was it? Exactly?'

Queenie lowered her wine glass before an-swering in a firm but gentle voice, smiling steadily across the table. 'It was my concept, my development, my hard work and my gamble that paid off. Exactly.'

There was a brief silence, then one of the other men leaned back in his chair. 'So, who's the big money behind that pretty face? Surely you are just a figurehead, my dear. Prospective investors might want a little reassurance they are dealing with someone more... ah, experienced in business.'

'My track record speaks for itself. I planned and fought for a project and brought it to fruition under budget — and it has exceeded expectations in record time. I have more ideas which I know will also be successful. Frankly, city business is a piece of cake compared to not only surviving, but making a success of a large outback station. I think that sort of experience makes me a pretty strong investment.'

The men around the table broke into a spontaneous round of applause. 'I'll drink to that! Here's to Queenie's Heirloom Cottages,' grinned the man who had baited her initially.

'Touché. Well done, Queenie,' thought Judy as she rang the bell for the maid to bring the next course.

By the time they had finished the liqueurs and coffee, most of the guests had picked up one of Queenie's small engraved business cards from the sideboard.

When everyone had left, Queenie and Judy sank onto a sofa kicking off their shoes. 'You were magnificent, Queenie. A few more of these and you'll feel more comfortable, *and* you'll have more business than you need. Most of them will call, you'll see.'

'Judy... I'm exhausted, but it was great. How can I ever thank you?'

'Don't ever get too busy to see a friend.'

'Never.'

*

They called indeed. Suddenly every socialite in the eastern suburbs, followed by those from the North Shore, was on a nostalgia kick, wanting a heritage inspired theme, or room, or house, or country cottage done by Queenie. People started to simply call them Queenie's houses and she was booked solid for months.

John found a street of grand old Victorian homes in Randwick which had been turned into flats and bedsitters. These were added to the agenda to be restored and sold as 'Gentleman's Residences; close to the city and the racecourse' said John, trying out his advertising skills.

'John, I can't do all these myself!'

'Hire people, start training them. But you oversee what goes into every house, every room.'

Queenie dropped her head into her hands, groaning aloud. 'It all seems too much. It's getting out of control.'

'You were the one who wanted to make money,' teased Sarah.

Queenie lifted her head. 'You're right. I'm not quite there but it's looking good.'

'Having the money is one thing. How are you going to get Colin to sell to you when you have enough?' asked Sarah.

'I don't know. Except he mustn't know I want to buy Tingulla or he definitely won't let it go. I might have to be a bit devious and get John to work something out for me.'

'Queenie, how you've changed,' laughed Sarah. 'Normally you would have charged up to Tingulla with a fistful of money, kicked the door open with your boot and demanded Colin sell.'

'I'm learning to play their game,' said Queenie. 'And I intend to win...'

Chapter Twenty-Eight

The tepid air blew in from the night sea, lifting the gold-flecked drapes in the penthouse of Paradise Gardens. Colin walked onto the broad balcony on the twentieth floor and gazed into the warm Queensland night. Below, floodlights shone onto the sand, illuminating the white foamy crests of the surf as it rolled sleepily to shore. Colin wondered what lurked in the dark water beyond the beam of the spotlights.

Dina's laughter floated ahead of her as she joined him. 'Colin, come on, a pile of us are getting into the jacuzzi with a couple of bottles of Bollinger.'

'Not me. I don't like communal bathing.'

'Don't be such a drag, it's just for fun.' She leaned her head against his shoulder. 'I just adore it here. I love the sea breeze and there's always something going on. Why don't we buy one of these units?'

'Because I'm not made of money, Dina. If you want a place in Surfers Paradise, we'd have to sell Tingulla.'

'Maybe that wouldn't be such a bad idea. It's not making us any money and it has turned you into a real misery, *caro mio*. Perhaps we should go back to my idea about Italy... a nice villa on the Riviera, you can zip to Roma or Milano in your convertible and look after business for Daddy.'

Colin drained his champagne glass. He said nothing but at this moment the idea had great appeal. He was tired. Running Tingulla was a strain and he knew he wasn't managing well, though he kept telling himself he'd had a run of bad luck. But in his heart he knew that surmounting such obstacles was all part of running a big station. Maybe he should get out rather than slowly go under or wait for a really good season to pull up the finances. The run of bad seasons could last for years. It annoyed him that Queenie had run the place so successfully for so long before Warwick dragged her down.

He turned back to the party. 'Let's get another drink and think about it.'

Dina did more than think. Rather than return to Tingulla after the weekend festivities at the coast, she flew to Sydney to do some shopping and spend time with her father.

'Colin isn't happy. And why should he work so hard? For what? I'm bored, he's tired and neglects me. He loves Europe. I have family and friends there. Surely you could find something for him to do, Pappa?'

Dina hadn't called her father that in years and Alfredo Camboni knew he was being manipulated. Nevertheless, he was pleased at the loving attentions of his daughter. 'If Tingulla is sold, a goodly portion of the proceeds are due to me, but there would be enough for you two to set yourselves up in Italy... if your plans are not too grand... a villa, not a *palazzo*, Dina. And *si*, there are small business matters Colin could look after for me, but he will not make his fortune.'

'If we need money, Colin can sell one of his flats in Double Bay. That's a good investment he has sitting there. Going back to Europe will be wonderful. Tingulla is beautiful, but so far away from everything.' Dina leaned forward taking her father's hand. 'Colin would not want Queenie to know about this, of course.'

Camboni nodded. 'Tell him I will arrange matters discreetly. There is much jealousy between that boy and his sister. Does he know how successful Queenie has become in Sydney?'

Dina flicked her hair in annoyance. She was none too pleased at Queenie — 'the hick horsewoman', as she called her — now being one of the most sought after women in Sydney, socially and professionally.

'He knows she is doing interior design work, that's all. He's not really interested. So... how long before we can move to Europe, Pappa?'

Camboni smiled paternally at his glamorous womanly daughter who could still behave like a spoiled and wilful ten-year-old. 'Don't be impatient. I cannot wave a magic wand. I'll see what I can do. Incidentally, you'd better tell Colin what you have decided for you both!' he laughed.

John and Queenie studied the plans and building applications for the old Victorian homes in Randwick's George Street. John was frowning and Queenie chewed her bottom lip as Sarah came in carrying a tray of coffee and cake.

'Problems?'

'Yes, some other company has also made an offer. Substantially higher, we understand. We have to decide by the end of the week if we are going through with renovating these places or not,' said John.

'I don't like the way we're being pushed. It makes me suspicious,' said Queenie.

'I agree. I don't want to get caught in a bidding battle. I think we have to decide on our limit and if we lose, *c'est la vie*, eh, Queenie?'

John reached for the cup Sarah held out to him. 'There's something going on we don't know about. I just feel it in my bones.'

Queenie continued to stare at the papers.

Saskia watched Bobby massage a special liniment he had made into Bill's long powerful legs. 'You really love Bill, don't you?'

Bobby straightened up, gave a little groan and began rubbing his back. 'I guess I do, Saskia. I've looked after a lot of horses in my time but this bloke is special.' He winked confidentially. 'But for goodness sake, don't tell him.'

Saskia laughed. 'Tango says he's doing great times in training.'

'Yeah. Quite amazing really.'

'So, do you reckon he'll qualify for the Melbourne Cup?'

'We'll see, we'll see. Time for our walk. See ya, Sas.'

Bobby headed away from the stables with the big horse quietly following like a dog. Once they'd crossed the paddock, Bill would start running in circles around Bobby, following the rules of some game between the two of them.

Saskia saw Tango strolling towards her. 'Can I help you wash down those two thoroughbreds?' she asked.

'It's okay, Mick has done it. He's a good bloke as well as an excellent jockey. I was just going for a walk along the creek before lunch. Want to come?'

'You bet.'

The creek was four feet across and mainly shallow, though after heavy rains it sometimes churned along like a small, angry river. Today, under the clear blue sky, dotted with puffs of cloud, it flowed quietly, making soft music at mini-waterfalls as it dropped into small pools. Grasses, shrubs and reeds fringed the stream and Tango led the way as the two of them picked their way along its edge, following the creek's meandering path through the paddock.

Saskia had come to regard Tango as a man because of his adult physique and his acceptance as a peer by other adults. But now, as they paddled, peered under rocks and just wandered in silence, Tango seemed like any teenage boy enjoying the pleasures of a favourite haunt.

They both stopped as they rounded a bend to find an ibis standing mid-stream on spindly legs, his white head and long black beak prodding under the water. The bird lifted its head, swallowed and stepped forward, gracefully probing under the water and eating as it made its way upstream with Saskia and Tango following slowly and softly a short distance behind.

Dragonflies dipped and hovered above the water like shimmering, twitching jewels of turquoise, gold, and red. Small fish darted in pools and a kookaburra chortled in a tree whose roots dipped into the water. The two stopped pointing out things and talking and became silent as if caught in a spell. Stealthily they crept around a large boulder shadowing a deep pool. On the flat edge of the rock, wet and glistening, lay a small brown creature, its dark fur shining in the sun.

Saskia caught her breath in delight as the platypus slid with a plop into the water, its stumpy tail waggling, its broad flat bill poking into the roots of the rushes. 'I've never seen one before,' she whispered.

Tango grinned back. 'Nor have I.'

They watched its darting progress through the water, marvelling at its grace before it disappeared under a log embedded in the bank.

The sun was directly above them now and they were feeling the heat. The water was clear, cool and inviting. 'Do you want to go in?' asked Tango.

'It's hot. Let's.' Unselfconsciously they pulled off boots, pants and shirts, Saskia wading into the cool water in her panties and camisole top — she didn't need to wear a bra. Tango splashed in beside her in his underwear.

'Not deep enough to swim, but deeper than a bath,' he said.

'You could drink this water.'

'I wouldn't though, probably full of sheep's piddle.'

'Oh yuck, and I was enjoying this,' giggled Saskia.

Saskia lay in the water hugging a small protruding rock. Tango lay across the upstream opening to the pool and let the water flow across his chest.

'I wish I didn't have to go back to Sydney,' sighed Saskia.

'What's your life like down there?'

'It's nice. I'm glad my mother is doing well now. But I miss the bush.'

'Do you miss your father?'

'Yes. Sometimes. That's why I like it here so much... I have Jim and Bobby and TR. I miss old Snowy, too.'

'Who's he?'

'The head stockman at Tingulla. He's sort of like a grandfather. He's Aboriginal.'

'What's your mother like?'

Saskia laughed. 'I couldn't describe her. You'll have to meet her for yourself.'

'I once asked TR what your mother was like and he said the same thing — I'd just have to meet her.'

'I like TR.'

'Me too.'

'Where are your parents?'

'Dead. They were killed in a car accident a couple of years ago. That's when I came away to the bush. I never liked the city, I always wanted to get to the country. But they were my adoptive parents — dunno where my real parents are.'

'Did you finish school?'

'High school. But TR is trying to talk me into going to uni. I'm doing a correspondence course,' said Tango shyly.

'That's terrific. My mother wants me to go to uni, too but I can't imagine what I'll do with my life.'

'I feel a bit the same way. I do know I want to stay on the land, though.'

Saskia nodded. She didn't confide in Tango and tell him her dream was the same as her mother's . . . to return to Tingulla.

They left the pool and picked up their clothes, walking along the bank letting the sun dry them before getting dressed again. Tango followed the track that led away from the creek. 'We'll go back this way.'

The path led through a paddock smothered in golden dandelions and Paterson's curse — the prickly, purple-flowered weed. The track dipped down a small hill and as Saskia wandered ahead of Tango she disturbed a blanket of thousands of white butterflies which had been resting on the ground with their wings upright and together. They rose in a great cloud, the tips of their wings edged in black lace, a gold dot in the centre of each wing.

They rose endlessly from around their feet, fluttering about their heads, and several alighted in Saskia's dark curls like pretty clips.

'It's a plague,' laughed Tango, waving his arms at the army of silent wings.

'They don't do any damage, and they're so pretty,' said Saskia. Spontaneously she stretched out her arms and began dancing, spinning and laughing in the cloud of swirling butterflies.

Joining in her laughter, Tango took her hand and they finally emerged from the moving cloud. As the young couple moved away, the butterflies floated back to nestle on the ground in their hollow.

Queenie was poring over plans at her kitchen table when the phone rang.

'It's me — John.'

'I was just thinking of you! I've been looking at our development ideas . . . '

'We lost,' interjected John bluntly.

'Oh. By how much?'

'Quite a lot. Whoever wanted those Randwick places paid through the nose for them. They must figure they're going to make a killing.'

'We'll have to find something else to throw our money at then.'

John drew a deep breath. 'Queenie, I've been thinking, and it seems to me I have to put my capital to work. Now this deal has fallen through I've been considering investing in a big waterfront property that's come on the market. It's costly but I figure in a few years

Sydney waterfront mansions will be up there with Californian prices.'

'I understand, John. You go ahead. I'll look around some more. I still need to raise a lot more money before I can make an offer for Tingulla. Something will come along.'

'You need something that will turn over and make money, rather than a long-term investment. I'll keep my eyes open too.'

Queenie talked to Judy about looking for a new investment opportunity. 'But while I'm looking, I guess I'll go ahead and do the Woollahra house for the Ashleys, then,' sighed Queenie.

'Frankly, I think you need a bit of a holiday, Queenie.'

'I can't afford the time. But I might take this weekend off and go somewhere. Saskia is staying over with a girlfriend, so I'll have some time to spare.'

'Go to the mountains, you haven't been there yet, it'll be a change.'

'That sounds like a lovely idea.'

Once Saskia had been waved off on Saturday morning, the house seemed very quiet, so Queenie threw some clothes in a small bag, told Millie she was taking off for the weekend, backed the Range Rover out of the drive and was soon travelling along Parramatta Road on her way to the Blue Mountains.

She left the old town of Penrith, crossed the Nepean River and began the steep climb up the escarpment. Queenie's heart lifted at the sight of miles of empty rugged bushland.

Sheer jagged cliffs with smooth orange and cream sandstone faces stood across valleys which dipped and dived, then soared steeply in impenetrable dark green waves forming the Great Dividing Range.

After driving through a string of small towns in the mountains, Queenie stopped in Katoomba — once a fashionable and popular holiday resort, now just a stopover point for travellers. Queenie wandered down the main street with its slightly rundown, old-fashioned shops with striped awnings over the footpath. She continued past the once grand cinema, and turned into the only cheerful spot, the Paragon Cafe. The smell of homemade chocolates, pastries and rich coffee was appetising. She ordered Earl Grey tea and scones and chatted to the dignified elderly woman who had owned the Paragon for over thirty years.

'Times have changed in the mountains. It used to be the favourite place for honeymooners and holiday makers. Most of the old guesthouses are a bit rundown, not too many visitors come up here now. Though a lot of people are moving here to live. I sense our time might be coming again.'

The woman suggested Queenie stay out of town in a small boarding house, the Echoes.

Finishing her tea, Queenie set out to explore the small town, its antique shops and tearooms, finding it all charming, if rather economically depressed. By late afternoon she had put on her riding boots, thrown a sweater over her shoulders and set off on a bush walk.

Within a mile she came across a small farm where a wooden sign advertised, *Horses for Hire*. She decided to explore further on horseback.

The poor old mare she rode was tired, but pricked her ears and stepped out under Queenie's gentle hand, seemingly glad to be away from the confines of the farm. They meandered through thickly timbered bush, where ferns and lush damp growth obscured the sunlight, and the earth smelt rich and dank. A rivulet trickled through the shadows on its way to join a larger flow of water tumbling into huge falls several miles further along. The horse drank the icy water and then splashed through it and on up the bank on the other side.

They reached open ground some time later and followed the path along the edge of a ravine. The track detoured round a grove of tall pine trees and Queenie's horse plodded slowly. She didn't mind the slow pace. It was peaceful, with only the call of the bellbirds and the noisy darting of scarlet and blue rosella parrots, to interrupt the silence.

A broken wooden sign with peeling white paint lying on the ground caught her eye. *Hotel* was all it said. Queenie stopped and dismounted. An overgrown track led into the grove of pines.

It was only one hundred yards through the pines when she came across two stone posts and rusty grand gates hanging crookedly at the end of a driveway. She looped the reins over the gate and walked up the driveway, past the old fountain and overgrown gardens, and caught her breath as she saw for the first time... the hotel.

It looked like it had fallen off a Bavarian mountain — a pastiche of a romantic, fantasy castle, its turrets, balconies and domed roofs faded and peeling.

The building was immense, perched on the edge of the cliff facing the breadth of the valley. All the rooms looked across to the Kurrajong Mountains — sandstone cliffs capped by dense bush. Once-formal gardens ran in tiers on either side of the building.

Queenie spent an hour wandering about entranced, attempting to peer through dusty windows and stained glass doors. It was impossible to tell how many rooms and chimneys there were, but it had all been built on a grand and lavish scale.

A growing feeling of excitement crept over her as she stood on the deserted terrace. Then she swivelled on her heel and marched purposefully back down the drive, mounted the browsing horse and kicked her into a reluctant trot back to the farm.

The next day Queenie visited a local real estate agent who scratched his head and confessed he didn't know a thing about the old hotel. 'Been closed up for years. Used to be a real posh place in the twenties, from pictures I've seen. Then it got a bit seedy... was the place blokes brought their girlfriends for a dirty weekend. Then it finally folded. No, I don't know who owns it. It's not listed for sale, that I can tell you! No one in their right mind would buy it. Motels get all the trade now.'

Queenie returned to the Paragon for a coffee and unearthed some more local knowledge. The hotel had been built by a British shipping magnate just before the First World War, and she was told that there was a lot of information about it in the local historical society.

In the small museum Queenie found a helpful old man who agreed to do a little detective work for her. 'I want to find out who owns it and if they'll sell it.'

'My goodness, whatever for?'

'It's a hotel, isn't it?'

The old man simply shook his head and took Queenie's phone number in Sydney.

John and Sarah were aghast when she told them her plan.

'A hotel in the mountains? Nobody goes there.'

'They will when I open the Kurrajong.'

'How much work is there to do? It may be beyond restoring.'

'I have the keys and I'm taking a builder up to check it out on Wednesday. I'd like you both to come.'

John muttered all the way to the mountains, listing the negative aspects and the craziness of the whole idea.

Until he saw it. Then he, too, fell under the spell of the building and its setting.

'It's like a dream,' breathed Sarah. 'A fairy-tale place.'

'But it certainly needs work,' said John.

'Do you still think I'm crazy?'

'Yes!' They both laughed.

*

In the cold, rational light of the next day, Queenie explained to John that her plan to restore the old hotel was based on more than a romantic whim. There was a huge swing towards interest in nostalgia and 'the good old days'. Life styles were changing, the affluent middle class and young couples were looking for weekend pastures. There was a creeping awareness of environmental and conservation movements and with the peaceful and beautiful Blue Mountains only one and a half hours from Sydney, it's time for resuscitation was near.

The negotiations went smoothly. A tired old man, the last of the family who originally built the hotel, was only too happy to have this white elephant off his hands. He readily agreed to Queenie's absurdly low offer.

Triumphantly she told Millie and Saskia. 'We're in the hotel business. I've called it the Kurrajong and it's going to put the Blue Mountains back on the map as a tourist resort. You wait and see.'

Saskia hugged her mother in delight, thinking it a great adventure. Millie raised a sceptical eyebrow. 'Is it going to make money?'

'That's the idea, Millie. I'm moving closer to my dream — I know it.'

Later, Queenie sat in John's office with the final papers and picked up the pen. John stilled her hand with his. 'Are you absolutely sure you want to sink all your savings into this crazy venture?'

'Yes, I am. Would you?'

'I'm not sure. I bought that waterfront place

so thankfully I'm not forced to decide. It's a big gamble ... but if you pull it off ... '

Queenie patted his hand and signed the documents. 'There, it's done now, for better or worse.'

Queenie spent the next few weeks travelling to and from the mountains, drawing up plans, seeking advice and quotations, and getting a pile of paperwork from the council. It was while waiting for some documents to be certified at the council that she idly mentioned to the fellow behind the counter that she had decided on renovating a hotel rather than a whole street of houses in Randwick.

'What street in Randwick?' asked the councillor with sudden interest.

'George Street, beautiful old homes that ...'

'Lady, were you ever smart.'

'What do you mean?'

'They're putting a freeway through there, the whole lot are coming down. I gather the guy that bought it lost a packet. Someone pulled a bit of a swifty on him.'

'Who was it, do you know?'

'Yeah, some Italian millionaire — or now ex millionaire — Camboni. That was the name. Apparently he paid way over the odds in the first place.'

'Too bad,' said Queenie, picking up her papers, and smiling, left the council chambers.

Chapter Twenty-Nine

———— ❧ ————

The months sped by at Guneda with the routine broken by the sudden arrival of Clayton Hindmarsh. The American was astounded and pleased at what TR had achieved. After inspecting every horse, building and paddock, TR introduced him to his and Bobby's personal investment — Sweet William.

The horse and its trainer intrigued Clayton. He spent a lot of time watching Bobby put Bill through his paces, and over dinner one night said to TR, 'That's a damned fast horse, TR, with a goodly string of wins on the city circuit. You should enter him in your Melbourne Cup.'

'Bobby beat you to it, Clayton. It's been his dream for two years now. The race is only a couple of weeks away and he has Bill on this amazing training programme. That horse has a heart and stamina you wouldn't believe.'

The next morning they joined Tango at the

little racetrack and watched Mick take Bill for his early morning sprint.

'I'd sure like to be there when he crosses the finish line,' sighed Tango. 'I think Bill stands a good chance.'

TR slapped the boy on the back. 'You'll be there. You have to help Bobby, me and Bill get to Melbourne. It's a long drive and there'll be a lot of stopovers. We'll need an extra hand to keep an eye on Bill round the clock.'

Tango grinned at TR, his eyes shining. 'Wow, thanks, TR. I never thought I'd be helping get a horse in the Cup.'

'Heck, I'm gonna stay for the Cup, too,' declared Clayton. 'I'll be there with bells on, and the celebration after Bill wins is on me! Say, who you gonna get to ride him?'

Tango stared in amazement at Clayton. 'Why, Mick's our jockey.'

Clayton turned to TR. 'He's just a hick jockey, TR. Sure, this black kid can ride okay... but in the Melbourne Cup?'

'This isn't like in the South, Clayton. That Mick is an Aborigine doesn't come into it. And some of our bush jockeys are pretty damned smart riders. It's the relationship between horse and rider that counts.'

Clayton smiled. 'I consider I'm put in my place, TR. You're right, it'll be an advantage for you. Some jockeys have never ridden their mount before the race. Good luck to y'all.'

They allowed themselves at least two weeks for the trip, making it a bit of a holiday, and taking the drive at a leisurely pace. They often camped at a local showground or racecourse, keeping up Bill's training sessions on whatever track they could find.

Country newspapers soon picked up their story. It made good copy — the bushies with their well-known horse rambling through the countryside in an almost absurd approach to the biggest horse race in Australia. People came to watch Bill run at their local track and he left behind a trail of fans who all promised to 'put a bob or two on him in the Cup'.

At Wagga Wagga Bill ran a sluggish time and Bobby checked him with a worried frown. 'He's off his feed a bit. I reckon we should rest up a day or two.'

They rented a box at stables near the racetrack and Bobby concocted medicine for Bill, who looked lethargic but was still happy to play and go for walks with his mate, Bobby.

Bobby slept on a shelf in the box, a sleeping bag thrown on the hay, to be on hand in case Bill developed any complications. However, Bill soon returned to strength and seemed as robust as ever — but Bobby looked grey and haggard.

'Taken a lot out of him,' muttered TR. 'He frets over that horse worse than any mother with a sick baby.'

'Just like you do over Bobby,' said Tango who was very aware of the bond between TR and the old man.

When Bobby decided Bill was fit again, they set off, Tango and TR sharing the driving while Bobby kept an anxious eye on the float carrying Bill, towed behind their Holden station wagon.

'There's the New South Wales–Victoria border. Not far now, Bobby,' said TR buoyantly. The old man didn't reply.

'Just as well, we're cutting it a bit fine for time,' said Tango, filling the vacuum in the conversation.

TR glanced at Bobby, 'I think we'll stop at the next town and check into a pub for the night. Get a decent night's sleep.'

They checked in to the Commercial Hotel but Bobby excused himself halfway through dinner. 'I feel a bit crook. Tired as hell. I'm going upstairs to bed.'

'I'll sleep with Bill, don't worry about him, Bobby,' said Tango.

TR headed into the bar for a nightcap. The man beside him gave him a nod. 'Just got in?'

'Yeah, on the way to Melbourne.'

'For the Cup?'

'Yeah, bringing my horse down, slow and easy. Taking a couple of weeks to do it.'

'Cripes. Are you walking him like Zulu?' laughed the man.

At TR's blank expression the old man explained. 'Zulu. Won the Cup in 1868. They reckon he walked down from Sydney and went on to win. Hey, what's your horse called, I'd better put some money on him.'

Later TR walked down the hall to the shared bathroom and hesitated outside Bobby's door. He tapped quietly and pushed the door open. Bobby was asleep, his bedside light still burning. TR tiptoed over to the bed to turn it off.

One look at Bobby's ashen face and laboured

breathing had him running down to the manager's office. 'My mate's ill. Get an ambulance. Fast.'

Queenie planned to have the gala opening of the Kurrajong Hotel in the New Year. She was now spending several days a week in the hotel supervising the details of decoration and finish. The other days she was in Sydney haunting the antique shops and auction rooms for furniture, fittings, and accessories.

She was thrilled at how the forlorn old building had blossomed. Local craftsmen had been recruited for most of the internal renovations and they took pride and pleasure in bringing 'the old lady' — as the hotel was fondly known — back to life.

The carved woodwork gleamed under new French polish, the stained lead-light windows had been replaced and repaired where necessary, the fireplaces were opened up and chimneys cleaned, walls marble-washed in soft pastels, the bedrooms wallpapered in Victorian flower patterns. Old-fashioned washstands topped with hand-painted Victorian tiles stood in each bedroom with fine china jug and washbowl sets filled with flowers from the garden. Big beds, some cedar four-posters, others brass with ceramic inlays, were covered in quilted feather eiderdowns.

Despite the period appearance of the furnishings, ultra modern conveniences like concealed heating and air conditioning, added to the comfort. Drawing and sitting rooms, sun rooms, and reading rooms with big log fires made the Kurrajong seem like a stately home.

Queenie fitted out a billiards and games room and installed a library. On the western side she added a conservatory. Its partially glassed roof and walls were screened with plants to filter the sun. Exotic tropical plants flourished and flowered in pretty hand-painted ceramics and old Chinese pots. The white cane furniture was upholstered in pastel pink and green chintz and, from the garden-like protected indoor environment, guests could watch the activity on the miniature lake, or the gentle swaying of the big old trees.

Members of the local horticultural society had offered their help on a voluntary basis to restore the gardens. They researched the original design and replanted and pruned, bringing the rose arbour and banks of pink and mauve hydrangeas back to life. They trimmed the old magnolia trees and gardenia bushes and planted beds with English flowers which did well in the mountains. Victorian era garden-edges of lacy ironwork were found in an old shed and painted and put back in place around the formal garden.

What had first appeared to be an overgrown swamp turned out to be a miniature lake. It was drained and cleaned and planted with water lilies and irises. A photo from the historical society showed a small gazebo in the lake's centre, so Queenie had a new one built and had Saskia's friend, the boat builder from Balmain, build punts for the guests to paddle on this tranquil waterway or to row to the gazebo. Wild ducks quickly made the lake their new home.

The kitchens were modernised to meet health department and fire safety regulations. Huge old wooden refectory tables were found in storage and were dragged into the kitchen, and freezers and a cool room were installed in the spacious pantry.

Through the Paragon staff Queenie unearthed a one-time *haute cuisine* chef who had retired to the mountains from Sydney. Monsieur Ambert was getting bored and embraced Queenie with gusto when she offered him the job of head chef.

Queenie had heard how temperamental and unpredictable chefs could be. She took him on a tour of inspection of the hotel and his domain. 'So, Monsieur Ambert, does the kitchen meet with your approval?'

'*Oui*. Inside is very good. But Madame Queenie . . . the garden . . . ' He raised his eyes to the heavens and flung up his arms in despair.

'What do you mean? I've spent a fortune on the gardens, they are looking superb!'

'*Non, non*. My garden. Where is the '*erb* garden?'

Queenie breathed a sigh of relief. A kitchen and herb garden was not an impossible demand. 'If that's all you require, I will send the head gardener to speak to you. Tell him what you want planted.'

Several *sous chefs*, kitchen staff, parlour maids and administrative staff were found among local residents and an immediate loyal fraternity was established.

Queenie spent hours in her little office

overlooking the main terrace and out to the valley and mountains, working on her launch party. There was a constant flow of interruptions and requests for her to come and look at something or give an opinion.

The opening of the Kurrajong was already generating a lot of interest, as well as bringing new life to the business community in the mountains. The curious local real estate agent kept popping in to check on the progress, hopeful that guests to the hotel might like to purchase a little property in the area. There was speculation in the travel and burgeoning tourist industry as to whether the magnificent hotel in the mountains would succeed.

In her mail one morning Queenie opened an invitation to a prestigious cocktail party in Sydney being given by the newly restructured State Tourist Board. She decided it was essential to attend, even though she didn't feel like travelling to Sydney to stand around making small talk. However, she knew promotion of her hotel was essential and she needed to develop contacts in the tourist industry.

It had been a long time since she had gone out socially and Judy and Sarah persuaded her to buy a madly expensive but exquisite Dior gown... stunning in its simple but superbly cut lines. It was deep purple, almost black, and set off Queenie's opal necklace perfectly.

There were a few professional women at the function, mainly from travel agencies, and several wives also attended; but it was primarily a sea of suits, with drifting waiters bearing silver hors d'oeuvre trays and cocktails.

Holding a now-warm Campari and soda Queenie extricated herself from a circle of travel agents and headed across the room to introduce herself to the director of the Tourist Board who had made a pompous and boring speech. He was delighted to meet the new owner of the Kurrajong and held her hand longer than was necessary. Queenie was introduced to the rest of the circle standing around the director. The names went in a blur as she shook hands. The last man gave her a warm smile and repeated his name in a soft, slight French accent.

'Henri Barnard. Montpelier Incorporated.'

'*The* Montpelier hotels?' asked Queenie. As he nodded modestly, she asked, 'Are you planning on one opening in Australia?'

He gave a Gallic shrug. 'Perhaps.'

'Not in the Blue Mountains, I hope,' said Queenie with a smile.

He laughed. '*Mais non.* But I have heard of your Kurrajong. It sounds most intriguing. Would you tell me about it?'

They drifted away from the others and he led her to a quiet lounge in a corner of the room.

As they chatted, Queenie observed Henri, wondering where he was from. She guessed he was in his late thirties. He was tanned, with dark brown eyes behind large square glasses, straight brown hair and perfect teeth. He was impeccably dressed and emanated power, prestige and wealth; but his manner was relaxed and unpretentious.

He, in turn, was fascinated by Queenie's beauty, style and business acumen.

A passing waiter held out a tray of drinks and as they took a glass of Great Western champagne, Henri lifted his in a toast. 'Here is to the success of your Kurrajong and good luck to a beautiful lady in a Dior gown.'

Queenie sipped her drink and asked, 'Are you French?'

'A little. I'm French Canadian. I combine the romanticism of Europe with the pragmatism of North America. My headquarters are in New York.'

Queenie now recalled reading about the handsome, rich and eligible head of Montpelier and how he had taken an old family hotel chain and turned it into a string of luxurious hotels around the world. 'What are your plans in Australia?'

'I have been looking around at possible hotels to buy and locations suitable for one of our hotels. Australia is an expanding market. I would very much like to see the Kurrajong.'

'It's not for sale, I'm afraid — nor is it finished... but if you don't mind seeing it as it is...' relented Queenie.

'I would enjoy that very much. I'd like to visit some places outside Sydney, seeing that this is my first trip here.'

'Allow me to be your tour guide for a day.'

'I'd be enchanted. *Merci.*'

Queenie hesitated about driving the famous head of one of the world's great hotel chains to the mountains in her Range Rover four-wheel drive, but decided he'd have to take her as she was.

Henri enjoyed the drive. They took the scenic Bells Line of Road into the mountains and stopped for coffee at a roadside orchard stall in Bilpin and bought apples, then drove through Mount Victoria to Katoomba and Queenie's hotel.

Henri was amazed as they drove to the entrance. '*Mon Dieu*. I wasn't expecting anything as fabulous as this.'

He wandered with Queenie all over the building, making small suggestions and asking questions before they lunched on the terrace.

Monsieur Ambert had prepared a simple meal, not flamboyant, but exquisitely cooked and presented. Henri eyed the cracked blue swimmer crabs on their bed of ice, the Sydney rock oysters and the smoked salmon, fresh fruit, green salad and cheese.

'I hope you like seafood. Sydney is famous for it. I had it brought up fresh from the fish markets this morning.'

Henri sighed over the fresh fruit flan and coffee. 'My compliments to your chef. I think you are going to do well here, Queenie. A satisfying meal means a satisfied customer; an exceptional meal like this turns a satisfied customer into a passionate one. It's hard to believe you are a novice in this industry. You have a natural instinct for style, comfort and presentation. I hope you have a practical streak as well.'

Queenie flushed with pleasure at his compliment. There was a sincerity about his words. 'I avoid unnecessary extravagance, but spend money where and when I think it's effective.'

'Admirable. You have also trained your staff well. Now all you need are the guests.'

'I know. This is all a bit of a gamble for me. Most people told me I was crazy to do it. I'm hoping my launch extravaganza will spread the word.'

It was early evening when Queenie dropped Henri outside the Wentworth Hotel.

'It has been a delightful day. Allow me to reciprocate. May we dine together tomorrow evening?'

Queenie shook his hand. 'I'd love to, Henri. I've had a nice day too.'

Queenie found herself changing her mind several times over what to wear to dinner with Henri Barnard and taking special care with her hair. He called for her in a limousine and smiled mysteriously when she asked where they were going.

Queenie shrugged, smiled and relaxed, happy to go along with whatever plans he had concocted.

The chauffeur sped across the Harbour Bridge and headed through the scalloped string of northern beaches until they arrived at the narrow Palm Beach peninsula, the northern tip of Sydney. It had taken almost an hour, though time had passed swiftly as they chatted amiably. They wound around the Palm Beach headland, glimpsing the old sandstone lighthouse atop the nearby Barrenjoey headland, the beam flashing across Pittwater, the mouth of the Hawkesbury River and the Pacific Ocean.

'We're running out of land — where are we going?' joked Queenie.

The car glided along the narrow cliff road past luxurious homes nestling amongst the trees.

'The opera star, Joan Sutherland, has a home here, I believe,' said Henri, peering into the gathering darkness where the houses climbed down the cliff from the road to face the wide open sea.

The car swung into the circular driveway of what appeared to be a large home but from its discreet sign, Queenie realised it was a small hotel.

'I never knew about this place, or this part of Sydney,' said Queenie.

'A friend of mine owns it, so I had to visit. It's primarily an exclusive restaurant but it has several small suites on the level below,' said Henri as the maitre d' ushered them into the plush and elegant drawing room which served as the restaurant's bar.

Henri spoke softly in French and they were led through the bar, past the candlelit restaurant and through the French doors onto a stone terrace. 'It's not as grand as the terrace at the Kurrajong, but rather special, don't you agree?'

'It certainly is,' said Queenie with enthusiasm.

The terrace was narrow, studded with potted palms and small tables and chairs. It faced the expanse of the Pacific Ocean stretching to the distant dark horizon. A full moon painted a path of shimmering light across the swell of the water. Below the terrace, the surf crashed rhythmically and pleasantly on the rocky shoreline.

'I thought we'd eat out here, if that is acceptable to you.'

'Henri, it's magic!'

He smiled at Queenie, seeing the wind lift her hair away from the nape of her neck. 'The moonlight suits you, Queenie. You are a very beautiful woman.'

Queenie looked down at her hands on the table.

Henri reached across and rested a hand on hers. 'It was merely an observation, a statement. My French nature appreciates a beautiful woman like a work of art. It was not, as my Canadian side might put it — a pass.'

Henri passed lightly on to talk of other things, charming and amusing her. Queenie felt drawn to this attractive man, and it disturbed her. It was late when he dropped her at her door, kissing her lightly on the cheek.

Queenie soon fell asleep, but her dreams were troubled and her body ached with loneliness.

TR sat by Bobby's bedside in the small intensive care ward of the country hospital. He looked so pale and insubstantial, as if he could float to the ceiling, save for the restricting lengths of tubes and wires attached to his body and the clicking machine beside the bed monitoring his frail heart.

A nurse in a starched uniform appeared silently, giving TR a brief sympathetic smile as she changed the drip bag hanging above Bobby, made notes on the chart at the foot of his bed and swished out of the room, black shoes creaking on the polished floor.

Bobby moved his head. TR bent closer and was startled when Bobby opened his eyes. 'Bobby ... mate, can you hear? It's me — TR.'

Bobby struggled to focus and his mouth dropped, sounding a gasping rasp.

'Don't try to talk. It's all right, mate.'

Bobby's fingers twitched and TR took his hand as the old man struggled to speak. TR bent down, his ear close to his mouth.

'Race ... gotta go.'

'Don't worry about the race, Bobby. You're more important.'

'No.' The twiggy fingers attempted to grip TR's hand.

'You go ... Bill race ... please.'

The old man shut his eyes, his breath coming in short rapid gasps. TR reached for the button and rang for the nurse. 'Calm down, Bobby ...'

The ward sister hurried to the bedside. 'You'd better leave us, Mr Hamilton. It's too much for him. He's too weak to talk.'

TR walked slowly down the corridor lined with windows that looked onto the bush-like gardens of the small hospital. He found Tango sitting on a bench at the end of the corridor.

'How is he?'

'He spoke for a minute. Wants us to go on and race Bill.'

'Jeez, the stubborn old bugger. He really wants Bill to run in the Cup.'

'Yeah, a shame. After all his work. Bill stands a good chance, but we'd never make it in time anyway.'

Tango looked at his watch and thought for a moment. 'It'd be close. But we could try.'

'No way. I'm not leaving Bobby!' snapped TR, exhausted from tiredness and emotionally drained.

Tango said nothing, giving TR a sympathetic look. They sat in silence for a moment, TR staring at his clasped hands hanging between his knees.

Then Tango said softly, 'I could give it a go.'

TR looked up and Tango gave him a small smile. A sudden rush of hope and affection for this lanky lad surged through TR. 'If you drove straight through, you might make it in time for the check-in deadline — all the paperwork is lodged. Hell, what have we got to lose? Let's try.'

Tango slid behind the wheel and TR slammed the driver's door. 'Good luck, kid. Just do your best and take it easy.'

'I won't let you down, TR.'

'We're all in this together, kid. Just take good care of Bill . . . for Bobby's sake.'

TR watched Tango drive away, towing the horse float, and said a silent prayer.

Chapter Thirty

Since early morning, the crowds had poured through the turnstiles into the racecourse, filling the car park and grounds. Tables and chairs, rugs, mats and beach umbrellas, were spread out; and picnics ranged from catered hampers to casual plastic food coolers filled with ice, cold drinks and sandwiches.

The men came in tails and top hats, the women in designer gowns and hats — more elaborate than any Easter parade. Girls came in fancy dress, from flappers to crinolines, while their male dates appeared in anything from formal wear to wet suits.

The bookmakers had set up their stands and touts did the rounds of their 'connections' to get the inside tips. Much of the activity centred around the stables where the expensive stars of the day waited, watched over by trusted minders and candidly discussed by the public as they read of their life history. At around three that afternoon, over a two mile course, one of them would go down in racing history as a champion.

The stall labelled Sweet William was still empty.

Mick had slept in the empty stall reserved for Bill, wondering what had happened to Bobby and Tango. The pink and navy silks that had belonged to TR's father and which Mick would wear, hung on a peg on the wall. Once again Mick trudged around to the office to see if there were any messages.

The steward looked up at the shy young Aboriginal boy looking hopefully at him. 'You're in luck, Mick. Let's see here... TR rang, Bobby's had a heart attack but Tango is on his way with Bill.'

'Did he say how Bobby was doin'?'

'Nope. But your horse will be here if they don't hang about. Good luck, sport.'

Mick found Clayton Hindmarsh, decked out in a grey top hat and tails, pacing about the stalls. 'Where the hell are they?'

Mick told him.

'Let's hope that kid gets here okay. Well, there's nothing else can be done in the meantime.'

The big Southerner slapped the small jockey on the shoulder. 'I figure you need some chow, Mick. C'mon, I'll treat you — then you'd better hang by the gates.'

Tango, used to driving in the bush, found the highway traffic hard going. He stopped at a truck café for coffee to keep himself awake. He bought a Violet Crumble bar, ripped it open and ate it as he checked on Bill in the float, who gave a soft, unhappy whinny.

The constant flip-flip of the broken white lines dividing the road began to mesmerise him, but his concentration soon returned when he found himself in a stream of traffic and began looking for directions.

The car began to jerk and make a slight grinding sound. Tango swore under his breath and eased down a gear. It slipped and the gears screamed. He knew there was something dramatically wrong with the gearbox, and in a few moments his fears were confirmed. He pulled over to the side of the road.

Tango peered into the engine and saw that it was a major problem. Desperately he looked at the unheeding flow of traffic, then at his watch. There wasn't time to thumb a ride to a garage, get the car fixed, and go on.

Gingerly he opened the float and backed out a nervous Bill. He stroked the big horse, calming him. Bill didn't like the noise and rush of passing cars, but as Tango talked softly to him and smoothed his head, he settled down.

Suddenly decisive, Tango locked the car, took the saddle from the float, threw the horse rug on Bill, buckled the saddle in place and swung into it.

'Only one thing for it. Let's go, mate.'

All over Australia lunch parties in hotels, restaurants, homes and offices were getting underway. Sarah had arranged a big party and Queenie and Judy were explaining the significance of the Melbourne Cup to Henri. 'It's bigger than our

National Day, the whole country stops. Now, you have to buy your sweep ticket.'

'My what?'

'Everyone runs a sweep. You put your money in and the names of all the runners are put in a hat and everyone draws one. Whoever gets the winner, gets the money.'

A similar party was being given by Sarah's parents. However, the Quinns had arranged a barbecue for all hands on the property, and their sweep was being drawn around the beer keg.

At Guneda and in Scone excitement was running high and the pubs overflowed as TV sets tuned in to the live coverage and everyone was set to cheer home their local heroes, Bill and Bobby.

In the Champagne Bar at Flemington Racecourse, Alfredo Camboni, Colin, Dina and a group of friends were laughing loudly and raising their glasses to toast their own horse running in the Melbourne Cup — Silver Lining.

Nearby, one man watching the raucous group commented to his friend, 'I thought Camboni did his dough in some real estate deal?'

'Yeah, he did. He's got everything riding on this horse. It's his last chance to win back some of the money he lost.'

Tango and Bill were cantering steadily down the side of the highway. Tango was trying to judge the timing without tiring Bill who was a bit edgy at the stream of passing cars.

Some drivers added to the problem by blaring their horns.

A police car passed and pulled in, and a well-built officer stepped from the car and motioned Tango to stop. 'Against the law to ride a horse on a main thoroughfare, sonny. You trying to run the Melbourne Cup by yourself?'

'We're in the Cup. My horse float broke down. I figured I could still make it in time.'

'Pull the other one, kid.' The officer looked at Bill. 'Strong looking horse. Where did you come from? Where did you say you broke down?'

'Couple of miles back. We're from Guneda, near Scone. We were taking it easy, then our trainer had a heart turn and we stopped to put him in the hospital. He insisted we try to get his horse here.'

'Scone, eh? Got a cousin up that way. Rich part of New South Wales. Who owns your place?'

'An American — Hindmarsh. But it's run by TR Hamilton.'

'Hamilton ... TR ... say, isn't he the rodeo champ who made it big in America some years back?'

'Yeah. Sarge, I hate to be rude, but I've got to get moving. How far is it to the racecourse?'

'Now just a minute, son.' The policeman went back to his car and spoke on his radio.

He strolled back to where Tango was waiting impatiently. 'What's your name, kid?'

'Tango.'

'Your real name.'

'Tobias White.'

'I see why you prefer Tango. What's the horse called?'

'Sweet William — Bill,' answered Tango between gritted teeth.

'You two are a bit of a traffic hazard. I'd better escort you.'

He got back in his car, turned on the flashing blue light and drove ahead, followed by Tango and Bill.

The police radio was monitored in the newsrooms of radio and TV stations and created background noise in the news chief's office in newspaper buildings around the city. They all pounced on the brief conversation between the traffic cop and his base about escorting a kid from the bush riding his racehorse to the Cup. Racing to the highway, they began photographing and filming Tango and Bill, talking to him from their cars as they cruised beside the cantering horse.

It didn't take long for the full story to emerge — of the once-famous trainer, Bobby Fenton, lying in the country hospital willing his horse to go on without him; and the young strapper's desperate bid to get to the course on time, where the Aboriginal bush jockey waited for his ride of a lifetime. Embellished with racing rhetoric, the story was beaten up to whirlwind proportions in the news slump prior to the afternoon race.

In the last two miles leading to the racecourse, people who'd heard the story on radio and TV began lining the streets. Cars stopped and people shouted and waved encouragement to Tango and Bill. The grinning cop leading them in his police car waved back to the crowd.

A small boy tugged at his father's arm as they passed. 'Is that horse going to win, Dad?'

'I don't reckon he stands a chance after the effort to get here. But, by God, I'm going to put a couple of dollars on him. They call him Bill, son, give him a wave.'

There were cameramen and press photographers waiting as the police car nosed through the crowd to lead Bill to the horse gate. The white-coated steward glanced at his watch and quickly directed the policeman, while Tango and Bill followed.

'You're just going to make the two-hour deadline.'

Tango was close to tears as the crowd of well-wishers pressed forward. Mick pushed through them and grasped Bill's reins as Tango pulled him to a halt and slid stiffly from the saddle.

'How's Bobby?'

'Dunno, Mick. All he wants is for Bill to run in this race. Am I in time?'

'Yeah. You done good, Tango.'

'Well, it's up to you now, Mick.'

Leading Bill, Tango followed the hurrying young jockey.

Over the public address system the announcer confirmed the arrival of the missing starter. 'Sweet William, number seventeen in the Melbourne Cup, is here. He's arrived, ladies and gentlemen, with barely minutes to spare.'

A cheer rose from the hundred thousand people gathered around the course.

Relentlessly the cameras followed their last-minute preparations. Mick weighed in and Bill was vetted and declared fit. Several of the mounts were paraded around the saddling enclosure as the crowd, many still undecided which horse to back, eyed the gleaming horses.

Tango hurried to the betting ring and looked at the bookmakers' scrawled figures on the blackboards under their umbrellas. A red-faced bookie, his leather money bag clutched at his bulging belly, eyed Tango. 'What's it to be, kid?'

'What are the odds on Sweet William?'

'A hundred to one long shot this morning, now he's down to ten to one. Been a sentimental surge on him since he turned up.'

Tango emptied his wallet. 'A hundred and fifteen dollars on Bill.'

'I hope that's not every last penny you own, kid,' commented the bookie scribbling on a ticket stub.

'If it is, I'll be ahead then, won't I?' quickly replied Tango.

There was a laugh beside them. 'You want a tip, young fella? Back Silver Lining.'

Tango turned to find a smartly dressed man beside him. 'Why?'

'He belongs to my father-in-law.'

'Well, Bill belongs to my boss.'

The man's expression hardened. 'TR Hamilton?'

'Yeah. I just brought Bill down for TR and Bobby.'

'G'arn, you're having me on,' interjected the bookie with a big grin.

The man beside Tango turned away saying bitterly, 'After this race is over, tell TR that Colin Hanlon told you he'd never win.'

Tango looked at the stranger disappearing into the crowd, shrugged at the bookie and went to find Mick.

Clayton Hindmarsh had adopted a protective role towards Mick and Bill. Tango told him that the odds on Bill had slipped. 'Don't worry, I put a couple grand on him this morning.'

'At a hundred to one?'

'Yep,' grinned Clayton.

Mick's eyes bulged. 'That's *a lot* of money.'

'Don't worry about it, Mick. You'll clean up with the jockey's cut.'

Mick looked nervous. Changing the subject, Tango told Clayton of the exchange with Colin Hanlon at the bookies.

Clayton looked thoughtful. 'Silver Lining, eh? Mick, check that horse's number and watch out for him during the race.'

The crowd began to line the rails and the grandstands filled as the procession of twenty-four horses began to file down towards the start. With his binoculars dangling round his neck, his top hat still in place, Clayton gave Mick a boost into the saddle. 'You got your race worked out in your head; you know Bill; relax, enjoy it, and just be in goddamned front at the finish!'

Mick flashed Tango a white toothy grin and tipped his crop to his skull cap.

Tango smiled at him. 'Don't get lost, Mick.'

'I'll try not to, mate.'

Tango touched Bill lightly. 'Do your best

for Bobby.' The horse rubbed his nose against his hand. Tango followed Clayton.

'Pin this pass on you, Tango — we're in the Members' Stand,' said Clayton.

Bill eyed the small wire cage and, gently urged by Mick, nosed into it. Both looked apprehensively down the long empty expanse of green track with its white rails curving away before them.

The gates were banging behind other horses. Mick closed his eyes briefly and softly began chanting in a sing-song dialect.

'You pointing the bone or casting a spell, mate?' the jockey beside him said scathingly.

Mick took no notice, but slowly turned and looked at the other jockey and saw the number — six — Silver Lining. Mick turned away.

With a clang the gates sprang open and Bill leapt forward, responding instantly to Mick's guiding hand. The horses bunched together and for Mick the race became a blur of coloured silks, flying clods of dirt and pounding hooves. His entire concentration was on his horse, timing himself to Bill's rhythm and judging how much energy Bill was expending. He soon realised Bill had a lot in reserve and Mick began looking for the chance to move in to the rails or get to the outside and make a break. He eyed the horses in front of him, looking for the slightest gap.

Tango was numb as he watched. It was as if he was in a vacuum, the cheering roar sounded distant, coming from some other place. He stood motionless, riding with Mick and Bill as they began inching forward, horse by horse, to fifth position. It seemed an eternity and they were only at the halfway point in the race.

Mick was suddenly aware of the horse beside him pressing in close. He glanced across to see the jockey on Silver Lining angling his horse into Bill's path. His stirrup and heel of his boot caught against Mick's foot trying to dislodge him.

It took a split second for Mick to realise this other rider was maliciously trying to do him harm. He tensed, and it was Bill who took the initiative — with a slight shake of his mane, he stretched forward yanking on Mick's arms, sidestepped around the horses to the far outside and simply started to run.

If Mick thought Bill had been galloping at full throttle he realised now this horse had amazing reserves of energy and strength, but most importantly, a desire to lead.

Bill powered past the other horses, taking the lead as the watching crowd went berserk. Above the pounding hooves behind him, Mick heard the cheers and knew they were for them.

TR had tears running down his face as he held the transistor radio close to Bobby's head.

In the quiet hospital room, the race commentator's voice echoed incongruously, but Bobby gave no indication of hearing anything as he lay unmoving, his breathing shallow and irregular.

The commentator's voice was strident with delight and disbelief. 'He's won it! Sweet

William, number seventeen, has romped home in an unbelievable victory against incredible odds . . . this is one for the history books, ladies and gentlemen. The horse is fantastic. He's won by lengths. A bolter from the bush, that's for sure.'

The voice raged on, but TR wasn't listening. He smoothed Bobby's forehead and lifted his thin hand. 'Did you hear that, Bobby? Bill has won. Your Bill has won the Cup, mate . . . Bobby?'

There was the slightest pressure against TR's fingers and Bobby's eyelashes fluttered, the corners of his lips lifted and he whispered, 'You bloody beauty'.

'And it's all because of you, mate . . . '

But Bobby had heard all he needed to hear and TR felt the old man's hand relax and his fingers fall away from his as the last breath whistled from his body.

TR sat holding his hand and wept. The radio continued to fill the room with cheering and Mick's emotion-filled voice . . . 'at the end I was just hanging on. Bobby Fenton, his trainer, said give him his head, Bill would know when to go. And he did . . . Bill won the cup for Bobby . . . his mate.'

Colin and Dina closed down Tingulla. They had their possessions packed and sent to Sydney. Ruthie stayed on in Millie and Jim's old quarters as caretaker.

The station hands had all been let go, save for Snowy who remained on the property sharing the caretaking duties with Ruthie.

Ernie took a droving job, promising Ruthie he'd be back and would 'look her up'.

The sheep were auctioned. Colin said nothing to anyone local, but rumours spread quickly and it was soon known Tingulla was being wound up. No one knew what its future was or if it would be sold.

Alfredo Camboni had arranged for the sale of Tingulla to be conducted discreetly by private tender. Colin insisted that there be no publicity. At the same time he easily sold one of the flats in his block at Double Bay and he and Dina made arrangements to move to Europe.

'Dina, it's just for a six months trial,' Colin had insisted.

'Of course, *caro*,' she replied reassuringly, but had every intention of settling in Europe and had already planned to buy a villa in Porto Ercole. 'Daddy has arranged for you to look after his business dealings in Europe. You'll find this suits you much better than being a farmer,' she murmured, winding her arms about him.

Colin let the remark pass. He felt he had failed with Tingulla and blamed Queenie for his own inadequacies. But he was damned if he was going to let her get back there and prove he hadn't been able to manage. As he signed the transfer papers he realised this would be the end of the Hanlon line owning Tingulla. If he heard any misgivings from the graves of his great-grandfather, grandfather and father, he ignored them and held the pen firmly.

Two weeks later Colin flew to Rome with Dina without any family farewells.

The Kurrajong was almost finished and Queenie moved back to Sydney to work on publicity for her launch and party.

She planned to open the hotel after Christmas with a gala weekend extravaganza for a hundred and twenty influential guests from the media, the travel and tourism industry, the social scene and heads of large corporations. She also wanted her friends to share the occasion and she invited Dingo, Millie and Jim, Snowy, Sarah's parents, old Alf from Neptune Island and Judy and Eric Thomas. John and Sarah would be on hand to help out if she needed any assistance.

She hesitated about asking TR. She was saddened at the death of his trainer, Bobby, and impressed about what she had heard of Guneda from Millie and Saskia. Sarah had shown her several articles about TR and the stud in magazines, and she agreed it looked a spectacular set up. But Queenie still found being near him unsettling. Also, unaware Martine had returned to America, the thought of him bringing his girlfriend along disturbed her. She decided to spare herself the anguish and his name never appeared on the guest list.

Henri Barnard had decided to stay on a few months in Australia and was included among the guests. He was in Adelaide for two weeks and Queenie was surprised and flattered when he sent her a bouquet of native flowers and a note saying he was thinking of her. He hoped all was progressing smoothly and asked if she would dine with him again.

Because of the hotel launch, Queenie made no grand plans for Christmas. As Sarah, John and young Tim were taking a break on Neptune Island, she accepted an invitation from Judy and Eric Thomas to have Christmas lunch with them.

'We're going out... I'm not cooking this year,' said Judy. 'It's going to be seafood, outdoors in a dear little restaurant on the water.'

Millie would be with Jim and TR at Guneda, and Saskia said she too would rather be there, than sitting in a restaurant. Queenie was reluctant, and finally promised her she could spend the last two weeks of her school holidays there after the launch of the Kurrajong.

'You don't want to miss my opening do you, Sas? Besides, I need you to act as co-hostess.'

'You think I can do that all right? It all makes me feel nervous.'

Queenie regarded her daughter fondly. 'Have you looked in the mirror lately, my sweet girl?' Queenie turned Saskia around to face the oval mirror on the wall. With arms about each other, mother and daughter stared at their reflection. 'See, you're nearly as tall as me... and how pretty you are, Sas. You're going to look wonderful in your new evening dress.'

'If I don't trip over.'

Queenie laughed, then paused, her eyes misty.

'What are you thinking, Mum?' asked Saskia gently.

'I was thinking of my twenty-first birthday . . . when I ruined my dress and my mother took me to a mirror to show me how pretty I looked . . . and you know, she also told me not to fall over in my silver sandals.'

'I bet you were more at home in riding boots!'

Queenie hugged her daughter. 'You're right. I was, Sas. Come on, we still have Christmas shopping to do.'

This Christmas seemed a bit of an anticlimax — the year had gone so swiftly. Queenie shopped for gifts in a rush and really didn't feel at all festive while she had so much on her mind.

Henri returned to town and they had lunch or dinner together at least twice a week. Queenie was grateful for his knowledge, advice and calm manner. It was reassuring to be with him and to listen to his comments about the details of the hotel. He had warned her with a twinkle in his eye, that inevitably something disastrous happened. Whenever you opened a hotel, he said, there was a drama — ranging from the chef running away or getting drunk, food or last minute equipment not arriving, or a major piece of equipment breaking down.

Queenie was determined to cover any and every eventuality to prevent such a nightmare happening at the opening of the Kurrajong. Her planned safeguards and carefully prepared check lists amused and impressed him.

She enjoyed Henri's company too. He was charming and witty and they shared a professional interest. She knew he was interested in her romantically, but he never pushed himself forward. He kissed her on the cheek in greeting and when saying goodbye. He was well aware of her vulnerability and while he had never questioned her directly about her past loves or her marriage, he realised he should deal gently with her emotionally. Queenie began to relax in his company, feeling safe without the need to be on the defensive all the time.

He courted her nonetheless. Small, thoughtful, silly or sweet gifts turned up at Queenie's door with little notes that simply said, 'I thought this might make you smile', or, 'I saw this and thought of you'.

Several times they included Saskia in their outings. On one occasion Henri hired a cruiser and took Saskia and Queenie for a day trip on the Hawkesbury River. They spent one Sunday at Taronga Park Zoo finishing up at Luna Park funfair where Saskia squealed her way through every wild ride. Another day he took them both ice skating for the first time. While towing Saskia around the ice he asked her, 'Would you like to visit America? I could take you snow skiing over there.'

'Not on your life,' retorted Saskia. 'I like the bush, even if it does get hot.'

'Like mother, like daughter,' smiled Henri easily.

But Saskia was generally busy with her own activities and school work and only occasionally did she long for life at Tingulla. Mostly Henri and Queenie spent time alone together. Queenie found she was enjoying the company of this urbane and sophisticated man more and more; and his talk of Europe and America made her think for the first time in years of travelling abroad.

Henri, however, planned to be around Sydney for some time. He had found a location for his hotel, in the historic Rocks area which was being redeveloped in line with the preservation of the remaining buildings of Sydney's first settlement.

Queenie heard from TR for the first time since their last unhappy meeting, when he sent her a formal note asking if it would be all right if he gave Saskia a horse for Christmas.

> She seems to enjoy her times here and we certainly like having her cheerful company about the place. The horse is a steady animal — though I have discovered Saskia can handle almost any horse, like her mother — and it is not an expensive thoroughbred, so she would be doing us a favour to take it on. I hasten to add this is Tango's idea and I think it a good one. So, if it's all right with you, we'll let her know what we have in store.

This gesture surprised, touched and troubled Queenie. TR had hurt her terribly, yet she couldn't deny the deep feelings she still held for him. For her own tranquillity these had to be pushed aside as she got on with her life. But she realised she was dealing with her own problems and depriving Saskia of the joy of owning a horse. Queenie knew her daughter missed the bush and the country life style, so she sent TR a brief card thanking him and Tango, and agreeing to the gift.

Saskia solved her problem of what to give Tango for Christmas when she found a beautiful old wooden box in a junk store. She decorated it with a hot poker, burning a design of horses, birds and his initials into the lid. Inside she put, 'December 1984, your friend, Saskia'. Beneath her name, she burned a design of a small butterfly.

The Christmas meal at the Cottage Point Restaurant proved a huge success. A converted boat shed, with its own wharf and small deck over the water, the owners specialised in local seafood.

Saskia and Queenie ordered the seafood platter between them and were overcome by the huge plate of fish, crabs, crayfish, mussels, calamari, octopus and oysters. 'And what's this?' asked Saskia, lifting a brown shellfish from the bottom of the dish.

'A Balmain bug... surely you've tried one before! You lived at Balmain.'

'If you like lobster and crab you'll like that... it's very tender and sweet,' said Eric.

Traditional pudding was served despite the brilliant sunshine glittering on the water.

Judy handed each person a small package which turned out to be a threepence or sixpence minted in the year of their birth. 'I haven't put coins in the pudding since Eric broke a tooth on one years ago, but I thought it might be a nice memento of this Christmas. I bought them from a coin dealer. The equivalent in decimal currency just doesn't seem the same...'

Queenie looked at the small shiny coin. 'My

mother and Millie always put threepences and sixpences in the Christmas pudding. What a lovely idea, Judy.'

Queenie gave hers to Saskia who was born after the change to decimal currency. Saskia put it carefully in her pocket. 'I'm going to give it to Tango. I'll put it in the box I made him.'

Queenie looked at Saskia. There was obviously a very close bond between the two of them and it hit her for the first time that perhaps Saskia had a crush on Tango. Her heart lurched, partly from the knowledge of how swiftly time was passing, of the loneliness in her own heart, and the memory of her own first — and only love. She prayed Saskia would never suffer the same agony she had over her love for TR.

Queenie and Saskia drove home in comfortable and happy silence after the long Christmas meal.

Saskia leaned her head against the back of the seat and Queenie thought she was asleep. Then she sighed. 'You know what I want for next Christmas? I want to have Christmas at home... at Tingulla.'

Chapter Thirty-One

━━━━ ❧ ━━━━

Snowy was sitting under the shade of a tree, making a stock whip from long strips of leather, when he heard a car approaching Tingulla homestead. By the time he got to the house, three men were at the front door jangling a bunch of keys as they tried to fit the right key in the lock.

'Can I help you fellas?' asked Snowy.

'It's all right, mate ... you work here?'

'I'm lookin' after Tingulla. I'm Snowy.'

'I'm Dick Brighton. We're from Sydney, and these gentlemen are just going to have a look through the house,' said the man doing all the talking. 'Just seeing what they're getting for their money.'

'Tingulla's being sold?'

'Maybe,' said the man evasively.

'Who's gonna buy Tingulla?'

'No one you know, mate. It's a syndicate. They'll put in a manager, he'll see you right, I'm sure.'

The men disappeared inside. With a worried expression Snowy drifted back to the shade.

Millie and Jim were working in the vegetable garden that Millie had created at Guneda. Saskia and Tango were out riding and TR walked from his office studying a sheaf of papers.

With Millie staying for the holidays, the housekeeper, Mum Ryan, had taken off for a break with her sister down the south coast.

'Hey, Millie, we're not going into the market garden business,' exclaimed TR, looking at the rows of freshly planted vegetables.

'What you don't eat fresh, you can freeze or give to the horses.'

'Good for man or beast, hey, Millie? Well, at the moment I'll settle for a cup of tea,' said TR.

'Yeah, I reckon it's smoko time,' said Jim, straightening up.

Millie put her hoe to one side. 'I'll go put the kettle on.'

Ten minutes later the men washed their hands and headed to the verandah where Millie had the tea things laid out with large slabs of fruit cake.

Jim and TR chatted quietly about moving some horses and making repairs to one of the stables. Millie was silent as she poured the tea then sat back and stared into the distance. She didn't have more than two or three sips of her tea before she became perfectly still. She no longer heard the drone of conversation and her tea grew cold. It was as if she had become hypnotised.

Jim noticed her distracted expression. 'What's up, Millie?'

She didn't reply for a moment and slowly her eyes refocused on Jim. 'I think Snowy wants to reach us. There might be something happening at Tingulla. Maybe something wrong.'

TR was about to ask how she figured that, but held his tongue. He had experienced Aboriginal telepathy — or intuition — several times before, and while he couldn't explain how messages seemed to be transmitted between Aboriginal people over vast empty distances, he accepted that it happened. 'What do you want to do, Millie?' he asked gently.

'No good phoning, the house is locked up,' said Jim.

'Someone should go see if everything is all right,' said Millie.

'Millie! That's a big trip,' said Jim, a little surprised at the suggestion, but not in a challenging way. He knew his wife.

TR thought a moment. It might seem like a crazy idea to travel such a long way because of Millie's sixth sense, but he didn't like the idea that there might be trouble at Tingulla. Things hadn't looked good on his last visit. 'I know — Tango can drive up. I'll give him a week off,' said TR.

Millie nodded and, satisfied, picked up her cup of cold tea.

Now that Henri had found a location for his Sydney Montpelier Hotel, he began the convoluted procedure of setting up an administrative infrastructure to get the project underway.

'I'm bringing out some of my people from New York and an architect from Paris. I'm in the middle of the financial negotiations at the moment. The trouble with being a known international quantity, you have to negotiate downwards,' he told Queenie.

'I'm lucky, nobody has heard of the Kur-rajong... yet... so I can haggle better,' laughed Queenie.

They were walking along the long sweep of Palm Beach after a lazy and casual lunch of fish and chips eaten out of paper on the grass by the beach. The local fish shop was famed for its fresh and tasty fish.

'Let's walk up the cliff to the lighthouse and work off those chips,' suggested Queenie.

Henri sighed. 'Don't you ever run out of energy?'

But he strode easily behind her as Queenie picked her way along the rocky path that wound its way up to the top of Barrenjoey Headland.

Henri stumbled and realised he had been admiring Queenie's neat round bottom in her crisp white shorts rather than watching where he was stepping. She looked like a schoolgirl, he thought. Suntanned, streaks of sun lightening the bronze glints in her windswept hair, a cotton striped top, long shapely legs emerging from the shorts, simple, sturdy sandals and no make-up.

Three-quarters of the way up they paused to look out over the sail-studded Broken Bay and Pittwater to the hilly green bushland of Ku-rin-gai Chase National Park. To the east they looked out over the Pacific, clear and blue, dotted with surfboard riders and swimmers, and the long stretch of sand sprinkled with multicoloured umbrellas and sunbathers.

They walked on, admiring the scarlet bottle-brush flowers, tiny honeyeaters darting amongst them, before stepping onto the smooth path that led to the lighthouse keeper's sandstone house.

'What a romantic place to live. Look at the view. It's like an eyrie,' said Henri.

'Think of dragging the groceries up here,' said Queenie. 'They used a donkey in the old days, I guess. Like in Greece. The place is empty now that the lighthouse is electronic.'

They explored the overgrown headstones of a woman and a child who died at the top of the cliff in 1924. They crouched and pushed their way beneath the canopy of matted wattle trees to emerge on the tip of the headland, knee deep in prickly, sticky lantana bushes. Queenie leaned against a boulder, peering nervously at the cliff edge and the surf pounding two hundred feet below.

She shivered and grinned at Henri who moved closer to her and wrapped his arm about her shoulders. 'Scared of heights?'

'No . . . but there's always the fear that this wind could whip you over the edge, or the ground give way.' She grinned up at him and impulsively he kissed her.

To his surprise — and even more so Queenie's — she didn't pull away, but let him gently kiss her, tightening his arm about her.

Henri pulled slightly away and gazed into

her eyes. 'I've been wanting to do that for a very long time.'

Queenie's mouth curved in a teasing smile. 'What took you so long?'

Henri smiled and wrapped both arms about her, giving her a lingering kiss. They returned to the car holding hands.

Henri kissed Queenie again at her door but made no move to be asked inside or to appear too passionate. He judged that one step at a time with Queenie would be the wisest move, although not the easiest for him.

Tango stopped the car and stared in amazement at Tingulla. Despite everything he'd heard about it, nothing had prepared him for this. He could imagine how it must have looked when Saskia was growing up. At the moment, closed and empty, it looked neglected and sad.

At the sight of an elderly Aborigine with a shock of white hair coming towards him, Tango got out of the car, extending his hand. 'You must be Snowy, Saskia has told me a lot about you. I'm Tango, I work with TR at Guneda.'

Snowy beamed and shook his hand warmly. 'Millie sent you, eh?'

'She was worried something might be wrong.'

'Come and have some tea. Nothin' wrong ... yet.'

'But?'

'Some men bin here.'

'What sort of men?'

'Fellas in city suits. Said they were selling Tingulla.'

'Ah, I see. That explains why Millie had some sense something might be up.'

'I dunno anything. Wouldn't tell me nothing.'

'I'll see what I can find out. Saskia says it's all her mother thinks about... getting back here. Funny they didn't hear it was up for sale.'

Snowy shrugged. 'Bin some funny business goin' on, I reckon.'

Tango slept in the shearers' quarters, but it was a restless night and he woke early, the shadows of a dream drifting at the fringes of his unconscious. He got up, pulled on his boots and walked outside.

He strolled about the property in the soft dream-like dawn. He wandered down to the creek and sat by a willow that Queenie had always favoured. Of all the properties he had been to, none held the magic of Tingulla.

He found Snowy at the stables, fondling the mane of the large white Arabian. 'What a magnificent horse,' exclaimed Tango.

'This is Nareedah.'

'Could I ride her?'

'If you like.' Snowy stood back and watched Tango make friends with the horse and ease into the saddle.

'See you later, Snowy.'

'I'll get breakfast started.' Snowy didn't make a move, however. With a thoughtful expression in his black eyes he studied Tango on Nareedah until they were out of sight.

Tango threw his small swag into the back of his car and leaned on the door, delaying saying goodbye to Snowy. He was reluctant to leave Tingulla. He had explored as much as he could, knowing Saskia would want to know every detail. 'I'll see what information I can dig up around the traps in town. I'm glad you're here, Snowy.'

'I wouldn't leave this place to the dingoes, don't you worry.'

'It certainly is a special place. It's got a certain feel... a presence about it. I can't explain it.'

Snowy nodded, and clasped Tango's hand in both of his as they shook hands.

'Some spirits are happy and bilong here. Everyone got to find their Dreaming place.'

Tango slid into the car and started the engine. 'I'll give Saskia your best, eh?'

'Tell her old Snowy is looking out for Tingulla.'

Tango could dig up no information but passed on Snowy's news to Millie who phoned Queenie from Guneda.

Queenie also hit a blank wall when she tried to find out where Colin had gone and why Tingulla was abandoned. Finally she phoned her old friend Dingo to ask if he had heard anything about Tingulla being sold, and he was as surprised as she had been. 'Where's Colin?'

'I don't know. I haven't been able to raise any of the Cambonis either.'

With John and Sarah's help Queenie began some detective work around the big real estate offices, investment companies and large accountancy firms.

It was Judy Thomas who led them to the

first clue, giving them the name of a friend's husband who was a merchant banker.

'Yes.' he said. 'I was offered Tingulla a couple of weeks back. Not really the sort of thing that interests our clients. Hang on and I'll see if I made a note of the offer.'

That led Queenie and John to another discreet market speculator who had handled the sale for the anonymous vendor.

'The vendor must have been Colin Hanlon,' said John.

The financier shook his head. 'No. I don't believe it was. It was a big fish.'

'What's the state of play at present.'

'Gone, I'm afraid. I know it's been taken off the market. I think it went to a syndicate.' He could tell them no more.

Queenie slammed a fist into the palm of her hand. 'Dear God, why doesn't anyone use their names?'

John shrugged. 'I'll keep trying. But frankly, Queenie, I think we're too late.'

'Find out who bought it and we can make them a better offer.'

'Queenie, where are you going to get the money? You've sunk everything into the Kurrajong.'

'I don't know. But if there's a chance I can buy Tingulla, I will. It hurts me that Colin did this without telling me.'

'It sounds like it was very deliberately done,' said John gently.

'Let's keep digging,' said Queenie.

A week later John took Henri to lunch at the

Tattersalls Club. The two men had become friends, though John was aware Henri wanted to talk about Queenie more than any other subject.

The club secretary came into the dining room and quietly told John he had a phone call. He excused himself, wondering who would interrupt his lunch at the club.

Henri sipped his Rosemount Chardonnay as John returned to the table. 'Bad news?'

'That was Sarah. They found out that Queenie's brother Colin and his wife have moved away to Italy. To live.'

'How did Queenie take that news?'

'She told Sarah she hopes he chokes on garlic.'

The two men grinned at each other, knowing Queenie. 'There was more news which Queenie doesn't know yet. Judy's husband Eric is a stockbroker and he's found out that Tingulla was bought as a long-term investment by some private company no one has ever heard of and no further negotiations will be considered. Queenie is going to be very disappointed.'

'I shall go and see her,' said Henri.

The next evening, armed with roses, Bollinger champagne and Je Reviens perfume, Henri headed for the mountains, on his way to the now completed Kurrajong Hotel, and the woman he loved and wanted to marry.

Chapter Thirty-Two

Queenie signed each embossed invitation to the opening of the Kurrajong Hotel with her favourite fountain pen, making her distinctive little circle above the 'i' of Queenie.

John and Henri had persuaded her to use her maiden name because the Hanlons of Tingulla were well known. People would expect that a hotel owned and run by the daughter of one of the country's most beautiful properties must have a certain style.

Initial invitations had gone out weeks before, she was now sending confirmed invitations and passes. Queenie sipped iced water from a crystal glass with a slice of lime in it. She wished it was a winter opening and not at the height of a scalding Australian summer. A winter launch party with log fires, frosty grass, mist in the valleys and hearty meals would be more suited to the ambience of the Kurrajong.

Yet again she ran through the sequence of events for the opening weekend. Family and friends would make their own way to the Blue Mountains. Dingo was flying from Western Australia. Dear Alf, who still ran Neptune Island, was coming south for the first time in years and even promised to wear shoes. Saskia had insisted Tango be invited and Snowy was taking his first train trip to get there. Millie said he told her he shook like a leaf every time he thought about it. 'From excitement as much as nerves! I think he'd rather walk,' laughed Millie.

The official guests were mainly from Sydney — travel and tourism luminaries, journalists and photographers, TV news crews, including her friend Kim Cameron who promised to do a splashy piece on the hotel, and politicians and radio personalities. Everyone was coming by train, but not the normal electric train which ran from Central Railway Station.

Queenie had met Damien McPhee, a former football star now head of the State Rail Authority, and he offered her the use of two antique commissioner's carriages which would be hooked up to two more restored 1950s carriages, to be hauled by the famous 3801 steam locomotive.

All the carriages, once used for the commissioner's tours of inspection, were immaculately restored and preserved. The polished cedar interiors had marquetry inlays of Australian wildflowers and animals worked in lighter coloured woods. There were shining brass fittings, lots of leather and it even boasted a four-poster bed. The main section of the carriages resembled a Victorian sitting room with comfortable chintz and leather lounges, a bar and a small piano.

On boarding, waiters would serve champagne cocktails and give each guest an impressive press kit with details of the Kurrajong's facilities and history including the programme of the weekend activities.

Guests would be collected at the tiny railway station in horse-drawn sulkies and wagons from the district's carriage club. In the warm night air the horses would clip-clop through the bush to the dramatically floodlit building for cocktails and a light supper. The spectacular view from each room would have its full impact on the guests when they woke in the morning.

On Saturday morning a lavish breakfast would be served on the terrace with its heart-stopping view. Then there was time to dawdle through the delights of the gardens; paddle around the lake, go for bush walks or horse riding. Lunch was planned as a picnic at the base of the nearby waterfall, although only a narrow veil of sparkling water was flowing at this dry time of year. It would be an upmarket barbecue under a marquee on a private property which the hotel would lease for such occasions.

In the afternoon the guests could rest, or stroll down to the village and browse through the antique and craft shops. It wouldn't take long for guests to later discover the shady swing seats and hammocks scattered invitingly in peaceful corners of the grounds.

Saturday evening was to be the main event; apéritifs and a few brief speeches followed by a grand dinner and formal ball. On Sunday afternoon the guests would return to Sydney, suitably impressed — so Queenie hoped — by the stupendous Kurrajong Hotel in the mountains.

Midweek Millie arrived with Saskia. The next day Queenie waited at the station to meet Snowy. They embraced warmly and she saw that although Snowy had aged a bit, he was still strong and his wise eyes still twinkled. He walked to the front of the train and studied the hissing engine. Shaking his head he reached out and patted the black metal. 'He's one mighty fella orright.'

'Was it a good trip, Snowy? Comfortable?'

Snowy was still a bit overwhelmed. 'Not like riding a horse. Them clickety-clacks started talking to me.'

Queenie laughed and picked up his small suitcase, linking her arm through his. 'I know what you mean. Something comes into your head and it starts repeating itself with the rhythm of the wheels.' She didn't add that every time she had taken a train journey the wheels always sang to her, 'Tin... gulla... Tin... gulla... Tin... gulla.'

'Just you wait till you see the Kurrajong, Snowy... it's a pretty swish place now I've fixed it up.'

'You never do anything by halves, Queenie. What mob's coming to this party then? What they gonna say when they see an old black fella here?'

'They're going to see a dear old friend, who's looked after me all my life. And besides, I think you'll be more than a match for them. I reckon the press are going to love you, Snowy.' She squeezed his arm as she opened the car door. 'Making this a success means a lot to me, Snowy. It's a way of getting back Tingulla. But that's just between us.'

Snowy settled into the car. 'Ah, that's okay then. I reckoned you weren't turning into some city slicker.'

Millie and Saskia showed Snowy over the hotel and he began to take everything in his stride, adjusting with great aplomb to this different world.

The staff were nervous and excited and small dramas kept flaring up to be quietly doused by Queenie. 'It's as if opening night nerves are hitting everyone. I'm jittery too,' Queenie confessed to Millie.

'Everything will be alright. So just relax,' she said calmly. Behind Queenie's back Millie was double checking things as well, determined that nothing would go wrong or fluster Queenie.

'I can't control everything or everyone... but, like the Boy Scouts, I'm prepared,' said Queenie, giving a Scout's three finger salute.

She did tell Henri on the phone that she didn't feel quite as prepared as she had told Millie. 'You know that awful feeling at the back of your mind, that you've forgotten something terribly important and obvious? I just hope it's only in my mind.'

Henri laughed. 'I know the feeling well, *chérie*. Would you like me to come and run my eye over things in a professional capacity as well as a friend?'

'Yes, I'd love that. I would really appreciate it, Henri, if it's not's putting you out. I know how busy you are with your own hotel plans.'

'Queenie, when are you going to understand I enjoy it. You are so capable, it's nice to feel you might have a vulnerable spot. Accept a helping hand without feeling you've stumbled in any way. Besides, I want to see you.'

He spoke gently and Queenie was touched. 'Your French charm and Canadian practicality have won me over. Please come with a notebook and white gloves and see if we pass the test.'

Queenie left Henri alone as she was busy during the day with last minute details such as the supply of fresh food coming from Sydney and the flower arrangements which she had designed. She drew sketches for the decorator, inspired by her mother's imaginative flower displays which had always graced the house at Tingulla.

Henri drifted about the Kurrajong chatting casually with the staff, but behind his glasses, his sharp brown eyes missed nothing. 'Let me take you to dinner at the local Chinese ... for a change,' suggested Henri.

'Yes I think I need to get out of here. I don't think I've seen daylight for days!'

They decided to walk through the dusk to

Katoomba, and Queenie ate heartily, her nerves calmed by Henri's amusing chatter about his youthful days in Lake Toba in Sumatra.

'There was nothing there, then... an old Dutch Hotel where Sukarno stayed, and a huge volcanic lake filled with goldfish. No people from the outside ever went there. I saw some strange and exotic things while I was there.'

'You're not going to put me off my dinner with stories of eating live monkey's brains are you?'

'Never. I'll tell you instead about the secret rites of the Island of Niias.'

The town was quiet and dark as they walked back to the hotel, following the path through the trees in the moonlight.

'I hope you don't walk alone in the bush at night,' said Henri.

'I'm never afraid in the bush,' said Queenie with quiet confidence.

Henri put his arm about her waist and gave her a squeeze. 'You miss your home in the bush?'

'I do, Henri. It has just been sold, which came as a bit of a shock, but I'll own it again one day.'

'Maybe you need a change for a while... why not come to New York and visit me?'

'A lovely idea... if not very practical,' smiled Queenie.

Henri didn't press her. 'Think about it,' he said.

All was quiet in the hotel. They walked

along the dark terrace, looking over the moon-lit valley and sharing the companionable silence with foraging possums and a distant night owl.

Queenie spoke first. 'I'm not sleepy, I guess I'm keyed up. They all arrive tomorrow night... after so many months of planning, it's hard to believe.'

'I have a Moet Petite Liqueur in my suite... which is charming, thank you very much. Would you care for a nightcap?'

Queenie nodded. His room was off the terrace and she settled into an easy chair, kicking off her shoes while Henri took two glasses from the small bar.

An hour passed before Queenie realised the time. 'Henri, I had no idea it was getting so late... time passes very pleasantly with you.'

She picked up her shoes as he drew her from the chair to her feet. 'Good night and sweet dreams... have no fears, all will be well this weekend.'

He kissed her lightly but his mouth lingered and Queenie found she was kissing him back with a surge of emotion. His arms went around her and her shoes dropped to the floor as she reached her arms about him.

Henri lifted her slim body in his arms and carried her unprotestingly to the bed. Between kisses he tenderly slipped the clothes from her body, catching his breath at the sight of her firm flat belly, slim hips, the length of her legs and the soft fullness of her breasts. 'Oh, Queenie, you are so beautiful... so sweet...'

She reached up and drew him close, and

with eyes closed, her fingers tangled in his hair and she lost herself in their loving embrace.

Henri was a considerate and skilled lover, and Queenie quivered with pleasure at his touch. But later, as he held her in his arms, he didn't see the tears that rolled down her cheeks.

She realised it was only with TR that she had experienced overwhelming passion and unbounded love and that she would never find it again. It had not just been the magic of a first love, she knew now how special their love had been, and it made her heart ache. She knew she had always felt Warwick was second best, but he had been so good and affectionate in other ways she had accepted the loss of passion. And now with Henri. Was this to be her fate — never to give her heart? She had given it once and could never do so again.

As she lay in the darkness in Henri's arms she slowly realised how she would have to compromise and adjust. It was time she grew up, faced reality, dismissed a once-cherished dream and got on with her life as it was to be. There were good things and good people in her life. She could be happy and at peace.

Yet the memories came flooding back ... of TR telling her not to be content with being merely happy when he could make her joyously and deliriously happy. And then how they had hurt each other. It was time to realise that all that belonged to yesterday and was finished. The future was what mattered. She trembled and Henri whispered. 'Are you cold? Come under the covers.'

'No... I must go back to my room.' She pulled her dress over her head as he pulled on his trousers to walk her down the corridor.

'It is I who should be tiptoeing down the darkened hall,' he smiled, kissing her at her door.

'Goodnight, Henri. See you in the morning.' The door clicked softly behind her.

Henri padded back down the carpeted corridor thinking, 'Ah, Queenie, you are like a bird who must fly free. No one will ever cage your heart and soul. But I will be content with whatever you decide to share with me.'

It was Saturday afternoon. So far everything had gone smoothly and as planned, even though it had been a stiflingly hot day. The compliments from the guests came freely and effusively and, apart from some minor hitches behind the scenes, the launch of the Kurrajong was going well. Tonight was the grand dinner and ball.

Queenie had planned to make a short speech and as yet she hadn't given it much thought. She walked onto the deserted terrace with a cup of tea. The guests were either in the village, bushwalking, horse riding, or in the gardens. Some were resting, or preparing for the ball.

She sipped her tea and stared across the valley where the sun was beginning to slide behind the sandstone cliffs. Queenie narrowed her eyes and stared at the sky, lowering her cup into the saucer. A dusty gold light hung in the sky. It was too early for the often spectacular displays of colour that came with summer sunsets. It looked as though a yellow scrim, or sheet of plastic film like the movie people had used to diffuse the light, had been slipped across the sun. Slowly the realisation inched into her mind, much as she didn't want to believe what she instinctively knew. She lifted her head and drew a deep breath. Unmistakably there came the faint smell of distant smoke. Bushfire.

Snowy found her on the staircase and, seeing his face, Queenie spoke first. 'I know, Snowy. Let's hope it's not as bad as it could be.

'Lot of big scrub out there.'

Where it was, how far away, in what direction the wind was driving it, all were unknown. What Queenie did know was that the Kurrajong was vulnerable.

She went to the phone and the local Volunteer Bushfire Brigade confirmed her fears. 'It's still over the western ridge, but it could sweep through the valley and up to you in no time. You'd best start preparations just in case. We'll do our best, but if the fire is on a wide front we won't be able to cover all of it.'

Quietly Queenie asked the staff to assemble in the privacy of the large kitchen where she briefly told them the news. 'Those who wish to leave and see to the safety of their homes please do so. Those who can stay to help with preparations here in case the fire does threaten us, their assistance would be appreciated. I will notify the guests and arrange for them to leave if there is any chance of danger.'

Henri had just come through the swinging

doors and he spoke up in the silence. 'Queenie, what if the fire doesn't come over this side?'

'Then we have a party as planned,' said Chef Ambert.

'That's right, Mrs Hanlon. We're not going to let all this work go for nothing. We'll see to our homes and be back.'

There was a chorus of agreement and Queenie had tears in her eyes as she thanked them.

Henri came and gave her a hug. 'I told you there would be a little drama . . . have no fears. It will be all right.'

'Henri, you have never seen a bushfire. It's a terrifying, savage beast.'

'Then let us prepare to slay this dragon in case he comes to our door. Maybe he will get lost on the way.' Taking her hand he led her back to her office. 'Tell me what to do.'

With guidance from two men from the bushfire brigade the staff began clearing combustible material from near the buildings, hoses were readied, more sent for, and a water tanker was driven up and parked discreetly out of sight.

The staff who had gone home began returning and were given tasks in addition to seeing to the last minute details for the dinner and the ball. The sun had set and the sky still glowed ominously. Henri kept monitoring the progress of the fire through the headquarters of the fire brigade.

Jim and Millie burst into Queenie's office where she was packing documents and personal effects into her fireproof safe. 'Queenie, there's a bushfire over the ridge. We were down in the valley and came up on the little train and couldn't believe it when we got to the top and saw the sky,' exclaimed Millie. 'What are you going to do?'

'All we can — and hope it doesn't turn this way. Where are Sarah and John?'

'Horse riding on one of the trails,' said Jim.

'My God, the horses! Jim, will you see to them. Put halters on them in case we have to grab them in a hurry.'

'Righto, Queenie. I'll go see what else needs doing.'

Jim had been through a few bushfires and knew the dangers well, the destruction and the unpredictability of a fire out of control. He also knew how fast it could travel.

Queenie went upstairs and changed into her evening clothes, flinging old clothes and boots on a chair ready in case she needed them.

Sarah knocked on her door as she was pinning up her hair. 'Queenie, John and I just got back. What news?'

'Not much. It's at a critical point, apparently. It can go one way or the other... towards us or away. The timing is crucial here, I'll have to tell the guests now, so they can get ready in case we have to evacuate.'

When everyone was assembled in the sitting room, Queenie with Saskia at her side, made a brief announcement that there was a bushfire on the ridge and it could threaten them or head the other way. There was a slight communal gasp, but Queenie's calmness, her air of authority and sensible comments, stilled their fears. They listened attentively as she offered them two options — to leave as soon as they were ready, or to stay on until the situation was known and then be evacuated if necessary.

Tremulously, one lady asked. 'If we wait, how safe will we be getting out?' Queenie explained that there were several safe roads out and they would have plenty of warning.

'Then we stay!' called out a man from the back of the room. There was a chorus of 'Hear! Hear!' and Queenie quickly sent the waiters around with trays of Bollinger.

Several guests moved out onto the terrace to watch the glow in the sky, treating it as a 'light show' — an unplanned feature of the hotel opening.

Dingo and Alf joined Queenie. 'Well handled, girl,' smiled Dingo.

Alf sipped his champagne. 'Never seen a bushfire. I always figured if I had a fire I'd dive in the surf and to hell with the joint. But then, my place is made of banana leaves, more or less. Not quite like what you've got here.'

'Neptune Island has it's own charm and beauty, Alf.'

'We're right here with you, anyway,' said Dingo.

Queenie touched the two older men on the hands. 'I couldn't ask for more. You're good friends.'

Laughter began to drift through the hotel as the guests relaxed. Queenie noticed, however, that the film, TV and radio people, along with the press photographers, kept their gear within easy reach and kept making phone calls to their offices.

At a querying look from Chef Ambert, Queenie nodded and the chimes rang, and everyone was ushered into dinner. Guests were seated at circular tables in the ballroom. The small orchestra — many of them locals — filed in and began playing in the background.

The meal was splendid and as Queenie circulated she heard nothing but praise. Henri sat beside her and squeezed her hand as the dessert appeared. Jim, looking uncomfortable in a hired tuxedo, slid to Queenie's side and whispered in her ear. She excused herself and followed him into her office and picked up the telephone from her desk. 'Hello, Queenie Hanlon here.'

'It's turned, Mrs Hanlon, it's over the ridge and heading your way. You'd better get people out of there. I'm real sorry to tell you this,' said the fire chief.

'Not your fault. Thanks for your help.'

'We'll send as many men as we can spare. Goodbye.'

Queenie returned to the ballroom and went to the microphone. The orchestra stumbled to a halt. 'The fire is heading this way, ladies and gentlemen. We don't know if it will reach us, but I've asked the buses to be out the front in twenty minutes to take you into Katoomba.'

No one in the room moved. 'What are you going to do?' called out one of the journalists.

'Stay and fight. This place means a lot to me,' smiled Queenie ruefully.

'Then we'll stay,' came another shout which was followed by a cheer.

'We're with you. Hell, this place is too precious to lose,' came another voice.

One of the radio journalists turned to a newspaper colleague and shrugged. 'Bit like being on the Titanic, isn't it?'

'Bloody good story, though,' came back the other. They both reached for the Bollinger bottle and poured another drink. 'Could be a long, thirsty night, mate,' said the radio man, raising his glass.

Everyone hurried to their rooms to pack for a last minute dash if they had to run for it, and to put on practical clothes. Then they assembled on the floodlit terrace where the volunteer bushfire fighters issued instructions for fighting the blaze and for their personal safety.

The fire could now be seen coming over the ridge like an army marching in close formation wearing uniforms of burning yellow beneath a huge black flag of death, smoke and ash. Occasionally there were explosions like fireworks going off as giant gum trees ignited, their eucalyptus oil burning like fuel. The wind had picked up and the fire was gathering pace, jumping streams and roads and racing towards the hotel.

The smoke reached them, bringing an acrid smell of burning wood and eucalyptus oil.

The hoses were turned on to damp down as much of the building as possible. Downpipes were blocked and gutters filled with water. Piles of hessian wheat bags were handed out and large tubs of water placed in as many places as possible to wet the bags, a simple but effective weapon in combating small fires.

Soon a powdery ash began to drop on them like warm black snow. The heat could be felt in the air and, most frightening, was the crashing roar as the beast lunged forward, devouring everything in its fiery path.

The wine cellars were stocked with food, water, bedding and first aid supplies, ready to be used as a shelter if needed.

Teams of guests were organised to tend hoses, or as bucket brigades, to stand at the ready around the grounds, armed with the wet bags waiting like a rag-tag army for the enemy.

'It's like Custer's Last Stand,' quipped the TV cameraman to Kim Cameron who was holding a microphone in one hand and a champagne glass in the other.

'From such stuff are awards made. Stand by for a piece to camera,' replied the intrepid reporter.

The advance line of the fire sneaked into the grounds in small embers, flaring and catching isolated dry grass. As soon as a fire was spotted the shout went up and the wet bag brigade attacked, smacking down the bags until all that was left was a singed and steaming patch of black. But behind these first windborne sparks came the ominous roar of the main fire, and all of a sudden all the lights went out... the power lines had been destroyed.

Fire fighters all around the grounds were

forced towards the buildings as the roaring fire raced into the grounds on all fronts, pushed along by a heat-powered wind. Trees in the garden exploded into flames. The guests could feel the heated air scorching their skin and the smell of the burning bushland was overpowering. They began to choke on the smoke and exchanged fearful looks.

Almost immediately the fire brigade captain came along the line telling everyone to retreat to the main building.

The grounds were left to burn as water from the lake and the tanker was poured onto the hotel. Hoses played on the roof and on the walls of the building. The boat house and the furniture in the gardens were blazing, and even the gazebo in the middle of the lake was alight.

Henri left the grounds where he had been beating sporadic mini-fires with the back of a shovel — the only thing close by when he had seen a flying spark land, multiply, and start a chain reaction of small fires. His shirt was burned, he had singed hair and sore hands. Hurriedly he asked where Queenie was — he knew it must be breaking her heart to see so much being destroyed.

Henri stopped John as he rushed past with two sloshing buckets of water. 'Where's Queenie?'

'We tried to get the horses out but they were panicking. She's gone to do it.'

'Will she be all right, is someone helping her? I'd better go.'

'Leave her. She knows what she's doing.

If you go she'll have to watch out for you. Queenie will manage.'

Henri nodded. He wouldn't be much help coping with frightened horses.

Smoke was filtering into the stables and the horses were terrified. There were four of them and each time Queenie grasped one by the halter, another reared and raised its hooves, trying to knock down the stable door with its front legs.

Holding one horse, she managed to free the second from its adjoining box and grasping each by the halter she ran with them on either side of her, leading them down the path towards the driveway. She dropped their halters, slapped them hard on the rump and for a split second watched them gallop down the drive and away from the fire, before turning around to let the other ones out.

As she reached the stables she realised the roof was alight. Wooden shingles had dropped into the pile of hay which had burst into flames. The horse in this box was almost demented with fear. Queenie lifted her shirt, and holding it over her nose and mouth and shielding her face with an arm, fumbled to unbolt the stable door.

Queenie knew what would happen but was not quick enough to grab the terrified horse as it crashed through the doorway, slamming her head against the door. She groaned and slid to the ground. As a black blanket of unconsciousness enveloped her, she prayed the horses would follow the others and not turn towards the oncoming fire.

The stables were now burning fiercely.

Everyone who wasn't immediately involved in fighting the fire gathered indoors. Millie and Judy Thomas led a small group of women down to the wine cellar shelter.

'There's a chartered bus on the way to take you out, but it might be wise to wait in here,' Judy spoke to the group.

'Just in case the fire does come through... just in case...' added Millie reassuringly. 'Lie on the floor and throw the blankets over you. Breathe low down. Don't stand up. Smoke rises.'

Saskia hurried along the terrace and seeing Tango wrenching the full length drapes from the huge French doors, called out, 'Where's my mother?'

'I don't know, Sas.'

'She's seeing to the horses,' came a response in the dark.

Tango left the damask drapes in a heap on the floor. 'She'll need help. Stay here, Saskia.'

'No, I'm coming too.'

The two of them ran through the dark gardens which smelt of dampened fire. The hotel was dark, save for emergency lanterns and candles, while outside, the red glow of the fire was reflected in the windows.

Seeing the stables Saskia cried out, 'Oh, no, they're on fire... Mum, *Mum*?'

One end of the stables was completely demolished and the last section was about to collapse on the flames burning inside.

Tango spotted the figure in the white shirt on the ground and dashed forward, dragging

Queenie away. 'She's all right, Sas... just knocked out, I think. I guess she breathed in smoke.'

'There's no doctor here, Tango...' sobbed Saskia.

Tango didn't reply. He gently tilted back Queenie's head and dropped his mouth onto hers, steadily breathing into her, and pushing grimly on her chest.

Tears running down her face, Saskia crouched, holding her mother's hand while Tango worked. In minutes Queenie began coughing and opened her eyes, turning her head away.

'It's all right. Don't talk, just breathe slowly and deeply,' said Tango.

Queenie nodded and did as he said, finding her head clearing and her eyes focusing properly again, despite the sudden glare of a hand-held light from a TV news crew, swift on the scene.

She smiled at Saskia and Tango. 'Thanks, my darlings. God, I hope the horses went the right way.'

Tango and Saskia exchanged a relieved grin as they helped Queenie to her feet.

'I'll be fine.'

'Bloody great stuff,' exalted the Channel Nine reporter to his cameraman.

Back inside the hotel, the fire chief called everyone into the ballroom. 'The bus is here, there isn't room for everyone. Those who are willing to stay in the cellars, could you please make your way there now. The evacuation is precautionary now. We think the hotel is safe.'

Queenie sipped a glass of water Dingo handed to her, marvelling at the calm manner of everyone about her.

Quietly they split into two groups in an organised fashion, the larger group heading for the cellars. Only forty could fit on the bus.

A TV cameraman switched on the portable light on top of his camera and began filming the sad exodus.

Two firefighters came into the room and went to their chief, speaking animatedly to him. The chief headed back outdoors.

As the last of the guests climbed onto the bus, welcomed cheerfully by the driver, the fire chief stepped onto the bus and made an announcement. 'Driver, wait just one minute. The wind has changed. Turned right around, it's burning back on itself. If it doesn't swing round again, we're safe.'

A cheer rang through the bus. The driver licked his finger and stuck it out his window. 'Yep, nor'easter. She'll be right now.'

'Give it a few more minutes. I'll go tell those down below they might not have to spend the night in the cellar after all.'

There were a few more moments of indecision and chatter, then the group left the bus and filed back into the hotel.

The bus driver shrugged. 'I guess I'll join the party.' He eased out of his seat and followed.

Those who had been sheltering in the cellar came back into the ballroom and joined the others as groups gathered at windows watching the retreating fire begin to burn itself out.

Henri and two young waiters began opening more Bollinger and Chef Ambert set out platters of his famous chocolate torte, hastily flung back in the fridge several hours before. The band members, in dinner suits dishevelled and dirty with ash, but cheerful nevertheless, began playing a lively tune and a festive air of celebration, relief and the exhilaration of having survived danger, swept through the room.

Saskia squeezed her mother's arm. 'Everyone's having a better time than before.'

'Whatever the damage, it can be repaired. I think this hotel has now become part of local folklore. In a strange way fate has actually done you a favour', added Henri.

As the party got into full swing, Queenie, Jim, Tango, Snowy, and Dingo prowled outside the hotel, shining torches into the smouldering darkness.

Returning to the candelit ballroom, Queenie walked to the front of the band and waited for them to finish the number, then stepped up to the microphone. It took a drum roll to still the dancers and groups at the tables who eventually quietened and turned their attention to Queenie. The cameramen picked up their cameras.

'Ladies and gentlemen, dear friends, each of you. How can I begin to thank you all for what you have done tonight? You have shown great courage and friendship which I will never forget. Thanks to you, the Kurrajong is saved and although we have water damage within the hotel and the grounds are destroyed, there is nothing which cannot be put right in time.'

At this point a cheer rang through the room.

Queenie smiled. 'I'm sorry for the interruption to the festivities. I did have a speech prepared in which I planned to extol the virtues of my hotel, but I now realise a building is only a shell, and while one can offer hospitality and comfort to the best of one's ability, the true spirit of a place comes from the people who care for it. I can say I don't think you'll find more loyal or caring people than the staff of the Kurrajong and the first guests we have embraced. You will always be welcome here and I hope you share the feelings we have of being present at a special if traumatic birth.'

Applause rang out. 'Long life to the Kurrajong,' called out a man raising his glass.

'To the Kurrajong!' Glasses were raised as the toast rang through the room.

'And to you, Queenie.'

'Three cheers to our hostess! Hip-hip hooray!'

Tears sprang to Queenie's eyes as the crowd rose to their feet and three loud cheers rang through the room. Unable to speak, she blew them a kiss and hurried through the well-wishers.

Millie followed Queenie into the kitchen and hugged her. 'You've come through this one, girl. It'll be all right.'

'I don't know how I'm going to raise the money to rebuild and repair. The insurance won't cover all of it. But I'll face that tomorrow. I'm going to enjoy my party.'

Queenie joined the overflowing table of her family and friends, squeezing between Alf and Sarah.

The bus driver took another slice of torte and headed for his bus as the media people clamoured to get back to the city with their stories for the morning news. 'She's going to get more coverage out of this for her hotel than if everything had rolled along without a hitch,' said a cameraman, slinging his tripod into the luggage compartment.

'There wasn't a hitch,' replied the reporter from the *Australian*. 'It was just different to the planned itinerary.'

They were right. The fire at the Kurrajong with its dramatic film, TV, radio and pictures on the front page of the newspapers, dominated the news the next morning. The hotel had become famous overnight; and so had Queenie.

Plans to close the hotel until repairs had been completed were shelved as the phones ran hot with people wanting to come and stay despite the damage; and offers of help poured in.

TR followed the news and when Jim returned to Guneda he listened to his first-hand account of the events.

'Jim, it sounds strange, but that night I had a premonition Queenie was in danger. Personal danger, I mean.'

Jim gazed steadily at him. 'Yeah, she nearly got burned up in the stables. Tango saved her.'

TR's eyes closed briefly as a stab of fear hit him at the thought of anything happening to Queenie. It was swiftly followed by a rush of affection for Tango. 'I'm glad he was there.'

'Saskia was with him, too. She wouldn't stay and wait while they looked for Queenie.'

TR grinned. 'His shadow. Though I can see Saskia is like her mother and has a mind of her own.'

'Yeah, that's for sure. Well, hopefully this hotel thing will work out and Queenie will be able to get the money together to buy back Tingulla one day. That is, if she doesn't get dragged off to America by the French bloke who's always hanging around.'

Jim turned away and didn't see the effect these last words had on TR.

Chapter Thirty-Three

❧

Jim shook his head in disbelief as he watched Tango, TR and two of the workers pound around the freshly cleared and fenced playing field at Guneda. They were riding hard and fast on sprightly new polo ponies, cutting and swerving with agility as they swung their mallets, missing more often than connecting with the ball.

'You blokes are still a bunch of amateurs,' muttered Jim, trudging away. He didn't see the point of polo, TR's new passion. TR and several other property owners in the district had formed polo teams and they played with enthusiasm, if not skill.

TR and Tango spelled their ponies and TR grinned at Jim's retreating back. 'Jim thinks this charging around chasing a ball on horseback is a bit of a waste of time.'

'Well, this is only practice. Wait till he sees the Guneda team thrash the opposition next weekend.'

But Jim decided not to stay for Guneda's first tournament. Instead he told TR he'd like to take off for a few days to visit Snowy at Tingulla. Jim had a feeling Snowy had news of the new owners. Queenie had asked him to find out what he could, but he'd been unable to discover any details in the district or through the country grapevine. He now had a feeling there was news.

'Been living with an Aborigine too long,' he muttered to himself. Millie often told him his 'sixth sense', or intuition, was the same as her ability to receive messages by some unfathomable ancient telepathic sense.

Whatever news there was, Jim hoped Snowy would be kept on at Tingulla no matter who was running the property. They all regarded Snowy as Tingulla's spiritual guardian.

Snowy recognised Jim's car as it swung around the stables at Tingulla several days later, and came to greet him, grinning broadly. 'G'day.'

'G'day, Snowy. How you goin', all right?'

'Orright,' replied Snowy, completing the laconic outback greeting ritual.

'Place looks a bit quiet — what's the score, Snowy?'

'No one seems to know who's the new big boss. Some mystery man in Sydney paid the money. New manager came out to inspect the place. Moving in next week.'

'I thought there might be news. Good fella?'

'Seems to know what's what. Old bloke, no missus, bin on the land all his life. Just goin' to run the place, he said. Putting sheep back on it.'

'That's good. You stayin'?'

'Yeah, he wants to get back as many of them old boys as we can. Word has gone around the district. All them fellas that left Colin'll come back, I reckon. Good for the place.'

'What about the house?'

Snowy shrugged, 'Dunno. Manager bloke didn't seem too interested. Mebbe it'll stay locked up.'

'Queenie won't like that.'

'Well, at least they ain't gonna turn it into a fancy hotel like her other place,' said Snowy with a wry grin. He was still talking about his visit to the opening of the Kurrajong to anyone who'd listen.

'I'll pass the news on to Millie for Queenie. Do you know what price they paid?'

'No one knows anything 'bout the sale. All done real quiet. Don't reckon the manager bloke knows either.'

Jim stayed the night, yarning with Snowy and the young jackeroo helping with the fences, before heading back to Guneda.

Under Queenie's gentle but firm persistence the Kurrajong began to return to a state of grace and beauty. The horticultural society flung themselves into the resuscitation of the grounds, though it would take a season or more for their efforts to blossom. The water damage was repaired and broken fixtures and furnishings replaced. The gazebo, the lake boats and the garden furniture were replaced by a young artist who created rustic furniture from the blackened, twisted bodies of the burnt trees, polishing and lacquering them into small, beautiful monuments.

Henri came to visit, bringing Judy and Eric with him.

Judy scrutinised Queenie sternly. 'My dear, you need a rest. The launch itself was demanding, let alone having to fight a bushfire. And restore the place. You need a holiday. You should go away.'

'I can't leave,' protested Queenie.

'What you need is a good manager, like you put on a valuable property,' suggested Eric. 'Surely there's someone you could hire to run this place. You didn't plan to spend the rest of your days managing a hotel in the mountains?'

Queenie knew they were right, but finding a suitable person to run the Kurrajong and maintain her standards would not be easy.

Once more Henri came to her rescue. 'I have the perfect couple. But I cannot take the credit. Monsieur Ambert, your devoted chef, suggested them and I took them out to lunch one day.'

'Who are they, Henri?'

'A retired couple who have done everything from running a hamburger joint near the Newport Arms in Sydney, and a bush pub in Wee Waa, to owning a caravan park at Seal Rocks, and a children's holiday hostel at Manly.'

'God, the last thing I'd want after that would be to take on a grand hotel in the mountains. Running the Kurrajong is a bit different.'

'They have retired up here, but they are

still only in their late fifties — they are practical, sensible and enthusiastic. Meet them at least, Queenie, and see what you think.'

Carol and John Macquarie were ideal. Queenie liked them immediately and saw they had a lot to offer. What they lacked in sophistication, Chef Ambert was swift to make up for with his European flair.

Queenie felt as though she was growing small wings and could rise above, and float away from, the day-to-day hassles. It was a nice feeling. 'How can I thank you, Henri?'

'By coming to New York with me. You will find it stimulating and exciting, I promise.'

'I am tempted. I do need a holiday.'

'I was not thinking of a holiday.'

Queenie stared at him. His craggy, tanned face with gentle brown eyes magnified behind his flattering square glasses, was filled with love. Henri was not tall but years of kayaking down white water rapids and winter skiing had given him a strong physique. He radiated strength and security.

'Just what were you thinking of, then?'

'Queenie, you must know I love you dearly. I want to marry you. If you are not prepared for that commitment yet, at least come with me and see for yourself what America has to offer. Think what an opportunity it would be for Saskia.'

Queenie lowered her eyes. 'Henri... I... need time. Time to think about it.' Her voice was husky with emotion.

'I didn't expect an answer right away.' He smoothed her hair and kissed her lightly.

Henri was not the type to sweep her up in his arms, smother her with fervent kisses and insist she come with him *now*. Although a small voice in Queenie wanted him to do just that. Involuntarily it jumped into her mind that it was just the impulsive passionate thing TR would do.

At the thought of TR, the familiar pain stabbed her. She had to rid herself of the anguish that burned inside her like a constant small flame. Somehow she had to extinguish it forever.

'Henri, I will think about it. Seriously. But I need to go away to think. Give me a few days.'

'Of course, *chérie*. But Queenie, don't go to the Kurrajong and get caught up in work. Go somewhere peaceful where you can think clearly. I want you to be very sure in your heart.'

'I know, Henri. I have a special place to go.' She kissed him gently on the cheek. He squeezed her arm, his touch filled with longing.

'I'm sorry to put you through this,' she whispered, and turned and left him.

While Jim was strolling about Tingulla visiting his favourite spots in peace and quiet, at Guneda it was all action and high spirits.

The First Scone Polo Tournament was underway at Guneda. Knockout competitions were being held between the various teams which ranged from raw beginners to more practised players. Somehow the teams balanced out with experienced players and rank amateurs on each side. It was the horses that proved the most knowledgeable.

At the end of a chukka, TR, his tight riding pants stained, his face streaked with dirt and perspiration, his gold hair flattened beneath his helmet, changed horses, commenting to Tango, 'Y'know, one day we'll get the Argentinians over here and play them into the dust. Then we'll prove how good we are.'

'Cripes, give us a chance, TR! I don't think I know all the rules yet.'

'Don't hang back, kid, get in there and ride 'em into the ground.'

Saskia and Millie were about to leave for Guneda and the polo match when Queenie spoke to them. 'I'm going to Cricklewood for a few days, I have something important to think about.'

'Oh?'

'Is something wrong, Mum?'

'Henri has asked me to marry him. I need to think about it.'

'What's there to think about! He's lovely. Do you love him?' bubbled Saskia.

'No, she doesn't, and I think it would be a big mistake,' snapped Millie, shocking Queenie and Saskia.

'Please, Millie, this is very personal and very important. I'll talk it through with you later, but first I have to think about it. For several reasons. One big one being he wants us to live with him in New York.'

'Oh no! What about *my* life?' Saskia's attitude changed immediately. 'I don't want to go

to America and leave my horse and Tango at
Guneda. And what about Millie? Leave us
here, put me in boarding school. Please...'
Saskia pleaded. Queenie put an arm about her.

'It would be a wonderful opportunity for
you, Sas. And Millie, I was hoping you'd come
with us. At least till we were settled.'

'No. If you take one step on this walkabout
you'll find it's in the wrong direction, Queenie.'

'I'm not asking you to come just because
I need your help, but because you're all the
family I've got, Millie.'

'Millie, don't leave me,' wailed Saskia.

'Look, I haven't decided yet. But let's leave
it this way for the moment. Perhaps you might
try it for six months, Saskia; and if you don't
like it, then you can come back here to boarding school.'

They both stared at her in angry silence.

'You aren't helping me come to any decision,
you know.'

No more was said. Millie and Saskia left
for Guneda and Queenie threw a few things
in the back of her faithful Range Rover and
headed north, to Cricklewood.

The property had never sold and she'd taken
it off the market. Now that she was in a position where she didn't need to sell it, she had
decided to keep it for Saskia. She knew her
daughter loved the land and the bush and
might one day want to settle there. It would
never replace Tingulla, but it was still part
of their heritage. Saskia knew of her grandfather's dreams for Cricklewood and that it
held a special place in Queenie's heart, too.

Queenie had faced crises and turning points in her life at Cricklewood and thought that perhaps there she would find answers, something that would point to the direction she should take. The land was as familiar as always and when she lifted the rusty piece of wire to unlatch the first of the four gates on the track to the homestead, she immediately felt a peace settling on her.

The small house was filled with dust. She opened the windows, lit the stove, brushed off a chair and sat on the little verandah, sticking her feet up on the railing while she waited for the kettle to boil. The quiet midday sounds of the bush were comforting and there was a warm and welcoming feeling about the humble cottage, despite years of neglect.

Later, carrying her chipped enamel mug of tea, she walked about the overgrown garden, remembering how she and Millie had struggled to clear the ground around the house during the months of her pregnancy.

She drove the Range Rover down to the creek, pulled a string hammock from behind the back seat and fastened it between two strong young gums. There, in the dappled light, Queenie swung gently, while two willy wagtails quietly preened their feathers in the branches above her and an occasional dragonfly buzzed lazily past. She let her mind become blank and slowly slipped into a light sleep.

Refreshed and relaxed she headed back to the house at sunset, made a simple meal and flung her swag on the bare wire-sprung bed and settled down for the night.

She woke as she always did in the bush, at piccaninny light. She stretched and lay there watching the pearly dawn seep into the room, listening to the chorus of the morning birds. How she missed the sounds of the bush and station life.

Whenever she thought of Tingulla the images came to her with sound... the wild bush animals and birds; the bleating of sheep; the whinny of a horse; rain spattering on a tin roof; the soft swish of wind through the branches of the she-oaks at the creek; the shouts and whistles and cracks of stock whips from the stockmen; the barking of the working dogs as they rounded up the sheep.

These were sounds she had known since birth, and in her heart this was the music of her Dreaming songs; unlearned internal, rhythms and harmonies — threads which linked her to her spiritual home. The first time she had ever been away from Tingulla as a little girl, she had run to Snowy on her return, overwhelmed at the relief she felt to be back at Tingulla. Later, he had gently explained to her the Aboriginal belief in one's Dreaming place and how she would always be tied to that special place.

The more she reflected, the more Queenie realised she was experiencing a joy and a tranquillity she hadn't experienced for many years. She was back in the bush, in the land she loved, close to her Dreaming land. And although Tingulla was lost to her, she was close enough to feel and hear its songs.

For two days Queenie drifted, her mind shut

down in meditative stillness as she walked and slept and watched the patterns of clouds, the crimson and golden sunsets, the graceful sway of tree tops, or paused to watch the busy progress of an ant or insect. Gradually through the layers of her mind, from the quiet, still depths, like a tiny bubble making its way from the ocean floor to the surface of the sea, her future direction became clear.

Her marriage to Warwick had been scarred by her love for TR and the loss of their child, and she had never given herself completely to him. She realised she would be cheating Henri if she married him, once again settling for second best. Queenie didn't know what the future held for her, but she knew she had to let go of the past, forget TR, and lead her own life. If that meant being alone, so be it. She was strong and learning to find peace and happiness within herself. Being alone no longer frightened her.

Once she had come to this decision, she knew she had made a positive step and felt flooded with renewed energy. She breezed into the house, washing, scrubbing and cleaning. It was an unnecessary exercise, because as soon as she was finished she promptly locked the door, threw her swag into the Range Rover and drove purposefully away.

The small crowd ringing the playing field at Guneda were cheering their teams in the final moments of a closely fought match. The horsemen were riding with reckless abandon, the Guneda polo team determined to hold the one point lead that meant victory, the other team as determined to level the score in the last few minutes of play. There was a madness about their riding, as if reason had been totally abandoned.

Saskia jumped up and down by the fence, alternatively clutching Millie's arm or chewing her nails.

Millie stood impassively, holding a large black umbrella to shade her head, but she, too, was concerned at the reckless way Tango was riding. 'He's gonna hurt himself, or the horse, or both. He wants to win too much,' she muttered.

'It's so close, Millie, and he scored the last point . . .'

Saskia's sentence caught in her throat. A gasp rose from the crowd as Tango, stretching out to swing his mallet, lost his balance and fell from the saddle under the feet of two horses.

In the melee of horses and dust, it was difficult to see what was happening. TR ran across the field followed by Saskia and Millie.

One player caught the riderless horse, while the others left the field. A doctor, a reserve player from the visiting team, dashed forward.

'TR, is he all right?' asked Saskia in a small voice.

Tango was lying in a twisted position on the ground, moaning softly, his eyes closed, his face ashen.

The doctor finished his examination and stood up. 'Broken femur — the thigh bone. He'll have to be moved carefully.'

The ambulance was on its way to take Tango into the Scone hospital. He was resting on a temporary stretcher in the shade of the beer tent. The doctor returned and handed Millie a pair of scissors.

'Would you mind helping? I've given him a shot, he's quite heavily sedated. If you could cut away those pants I'll see what I can do about dressing the wounds that are bleeding.'

Millie nodded and began snipping away at the heavy cotton. Saskia smoothed a hank of hair from Tango's closed eyes. In a few strokes Millie had cut away the torn riding pants revealing Tango's pale skin. Saskia turned her head away at the sight of the protruding thigh bone. The doctor swabbed down the bleeding around the fracture and carefully peeled back more of the trouser leg to check for excessive bruising.

At a choking sound from Millie, he smiled reassuringly. 'It looks worse than it is. It's a clean break, once it's set in plaster it should knit well.'

But Millie seemed not to hear him. She was staring at the bare skin on Tango's upper thigh. There was a small birthmark, a series of dots and lines in the rough shape of a small butterfly. It was faint, but very distinctive.

The doctor looked at Millie as she gazed fixedly at the small mark. 'You've never seen a birthmark before? That's a rather definitive one, but they are quite common.'

Saskia glanced at Millie curiously, wondering why her face looked pale and sickly beneath her dark skin. Then the ambulance men and

TR arrived, there was a bustle of activity, and Tango was carried away.

'Millie, what's wrong? The doctor says he'll be all right.' Saskia reached out and touched Millie who hadn't moved.

'Help me up, girl, I feel a bit weak.'

Saskia linked her arm through Millie's and carrying her black umbrella walked with her to find a ride back to the homestead.

Tango was resting in the hospital, Millie hadn't left her room and Saskia hung about the kitchen talking to Mum Ryan, who kept saying she knew this polo business was going to lead to trouble.

TR stayed at the hospital with Tango whose first words after he came around were, 'Did we win the match?'

'Yeah, your final point did the trick. And the horse is fine.'

Tango smiled and relaxed.

'I'll be back to see you later.' TR stood, then leaned down and awkwardly patted the boy's arm. 'Don't do this again — it hurts me, too.'

'Millie? Millie, would you like a cup of tea?' Saskia tiptoed into the darkened room. 'How are you feeling?'

'Thanks for the tea. I'll be all right.'

'You didn't look too well at the match.'

'I wasn't . . . too much excitement, too much heat. I must be getting old.'

'Rubbish. You're ageless, Millie.'

Saskia soon returned to Sydney to go back to school and as Millie wanted to stay on and see Jim when he got back from Tingulla, Sarah agreed to look after Saskia until Queenie arrived back from Cricklewood.

'You know, Aunt Sarah, I feel everyone has secrets and problems they're not sharing with me,' said Saskia. 'What's going on?'

'I don't know either, Sas. All we can do is wait until they decide to tell us.'

'What do you think Mum is going to do? I wish she'd talk to me about it.'

'Sas, you and your mother are wonderfully close. You've already told her your feelings about her marrying Henri. Your mum hasn't had an easy life. It was hard losing her parents the way she did, and then losing your dad. We grew up together, but to be honest I don't know that I could have coped with what she has had to face.'

'Plus not having any money and starting over again in the city,' added Saskia thoughtfully.

'And just look how brilliantly she's done. You should be very proud of her.'

'I am. But I want her to be happy.'

Sarah hugged the tall young girl. 'We both do, Sas. But it has to be her decision. Now, do you want to come with me while I take young Tim for his swimming lesson and then go down to Manly pier for an ice cream?'

Queenie and Jim were travelling south at the same time without knowing it. When he reached Guneda, Jim went directly into the kitchen where Mum Ryan told him about Tango and explained that Millie seemed to be in some sort of 'state', and was waiting to see him.

'I thought she and Saskia would be back in Sydney.'

Mum Ryan sniffed. 'The girl is all right. She's back down south but something is bothering your old lady.'

It was dusk and Millie was sitting in a fraying wicker rocking chair when Jim came quietly into the room. 'I'm back. Didn't expect you to still be here.'

'I needed to talk to you.'

'What's up?'

'Tango hurt himself.'

'So I heard, but Mum Ryan says he's coming along real good.'

'I saw it, Jim.'

'Eh? Saw what?'

'He had a birthmark, on his thigh. The same one I saw so long ago. On Queenie's baby.'

There was a brief, stunned silence. 'What are you saying, Millie?'

'Facts is facts. Tango is Queenie's son.'

'You sure?'

'I'm sure, all right. The mark on that baby boy was a little butterfly on his left thigh.'

They stared at each other in the fast falling twilight as the truth dawned on them.

Millie reached out and took Jim's hand. 'What are we going to do?'

Chapter Thirty-Four

&

Henri perched at his makeshift desk in the dusty construction office of the proposed site of the Montpelier Hotel. The multi-million dollar complex was merely a hole in the ground, littered with rubble and rain puddles. It was sandwiched between old city buildings and surrounded by a wooden fence already plastered in peeling posters for pop bands.

He blew a layer of dust from the architect's plans spread on his desk and chewed the end of a pencil.

'Perhaps you should call your hotel The Phoenix,' came a soft voice. 'It appears something beautiful is going to rise from the ashes of the old.' Queenie grinned at him and his heart lurched as he leapt to his feet, coming around the desk to reach her. He was about to take her in his arms, but hesitated, afraid to speak.

She stood still, her face solemn, and slowly she shook her head.

'Oh, Queenie, are you sure?' breathed Henri.

'It would not be fair to you. You are a wonderful man, but I cannot love you completely and I don't want to hurt you.'

'I would accept whatever love you were prepared to give.'

'No, Henri, it wouldn't work. I'm sorry. Truly sad and sorry, but I know it is the right thing — for both of us. Our lives are too different. I realise I have to go back to the bush — I couldn't settle in New York.'

'But I can give you the world, Queenie. You can live wherever you want, for any length of time... travel...'

'No, Henri. That's not for me. I'm very fond of you, but I can't love you.'

He shut his eyes in pain and gripped the desk. Queenie touched his arm hesitantly, then turned and left him, tears stinging her own eyes.

Sarah visited Queenie the next day and was astounded that she was sorting and packing up the elegant terrace house. 'What's going on? You going somewhere?'

'Sarah, I've made up my mind. I can't leave the land. I belong in the bush and so does Saskia. I'm moving to Cricklewood and will start developing that property... as Dad always dreamed. I can't marry Henri.'

'You're obviously very sure,' said Sarah, looking at Queenie's peaceful expression. 'Millie will be pleased to hear the news.'

Before Queenie could relay the news to

Millie, who was still visiting Jim at Guneda, Millie and Jim had come to a decision of their own. Together they went to TR who was by one of the shady paddocks watching a foal follow its mother on wobbly legs.

'TR, come and sit under a tree with us. There's something we have to tell you,' said Millie gently.

When Millie had finished her story, TR ran a hand across his face. It was a dream, his heart ached for what Queenie had been through, the lost and wasted years. No wonder she had been so hurt and defensive. Tango... in his heart he knew what Millie was saying was true.

'Millie, we have to be terribly sure. Don't you have any facts?'

'We can check with the authorities, I suppose,' said Jim.

'He was born in Charters Towers on 9 June, 1966. I held him and saw that birthmark. Queenie never knew whether the baby was a boy or girl. And she doesn't know I've known all these years that you were the father. Those eyes... he looked just like you.'

'He looks like both of them... I guess we weren't looking, eh?' added Jim.

'It hardly seems worth checking the records — I just know it's true. Tango told me he was adopted by a wonderful couple when he was a baby. He was shattered when they were killed. Said he felt he'd lost two sets of parents.'

Millie touched TR's twisted hands. 'Now it's up to his real parents to make it up to him.'

'My poor Queenie. All these years... I've never stopped loving her, you know.'

Millie nodded. 'That was obvious to me. And even though she's been fighting it all along, she's never stopped loving you, TR. Isn't it time you fixed all this up?'

'What happened... back then?' asked Jim shyly.

TR looked thoughtful. 'I wrote to her, she says she never got the letters...'

He and Millie looked at each other and spoke simultaneously. 'Colin...'

'It had to be. The bastard was always jealous of her... and me. God, if I ever get my hands on him.' TR slammed a fist into the palm of his hand. Then he stopped. 'Millie, does Queenie know? About all this?'

'No. I figured you'd be best telling her. It's between you both now. But I'd get a move on. You know Queenie — when she makes up her mind to do something, she does it. She could be on her way to America with Henri.'

Having made the decision not to marry Henri or go to America, but head back to the bush and start over again, Queenie moved like a whirlwind, flinging herself into packing up their Sydney home. Saskia complained it was disrupting her school studies, so she moved in temporarily with John and Sarah.

Pictures came off walls, books rose in a pile on the floor and clothes were flung in heaps.

Queenie took a break, made a cup of tea and sat on the floor to drink it, studying the beautiful portrait of her mother propped before her. She was deep in thought, lost in the memories of the warm and gracious woman she had loved so dearly. Sighing, she pushed a strand of her hair behind her ear.

'That portrait of Rose always hung in the landing above the staircase at Tingulla, didn't it?'

Queenie gasped, and lowered her cup with a shaking hand as she saw TR standing in the room. 'How did you get in?'

'The door was open. I'm sorry, I didn't mean to startle you.'

'What are you doing here . . . why?'

In three strides he was before her and reached out and took her hand, pulling her to her feet. 'Queenie. Please don't say a word, just listen to me. This is our last chance.'

He lifted his hand as Queenie opened her mouth to protest. He spoke calmly but firmly. 'I love you, and I know you've never stopped loving me. I think I know where the whole bloody misunderstanding between us began. I want you to come with me, now, as there is someone I want you to meet. There is a lot you have to know.'

'What are you talking about? I can't just leave.'

'Queenie, for once in your life listen to me. Do this one thing — it's all I ask. For everybody's sake. Millie is waiting for us at Guneda, throw some things in a bag and come now. Hear me out, please. Then I'll leave you alone, you can go to America, get married, do what you want. But this is important.'

The intensity of his speech knocked the wind from Queenie and she stood stunned. 'I'll call Saskia.' In a trance-like state she left the room.

*

They drove in near silence for five hours. Their only conversation was inconsequential and stilted. Each was wrapped in their own thoughts. Once he asked her if she'd like to stop for a cup of tea and a sandwich, but she shook her head. A dull ache throbbed at the back of her head and she sat with her eyes closed, sitting far across the seat from TR. Once or twice her eyes fluttered open and from the corner of her eye she glimpsed his strong tanned hands flecked with golden hairs, gripping the wheel. It made her heart ache and she closed her eyes again.

They arrived at Guneda at sunset, the lights were on and a curl of smoke rose from several of the chimneys. Taking her arm, he led her into the living room.

Awkwardly Tango rose to his feet.

TR was matter of fact. 'Queenie, I have something to tell you. Tango is our son.'

So much explaining, confusion, misunderstanding.

'I was desperate for news of you when you went away, TR. I couldn't believe you didn't write at least *one* letter...' Queenie shook her head in disbelief.

'What about me? How do you think I felt when I received this?' TR took from his wallet a worn letter, the creases of the folds beginning to tear. He handed it to Queenie.

When she got to the part, *So I think it best we forget each other*, tears blurred her eyes. 'TR, I didn't write this... it's Colin's handwriting... I just can't believe his treachery... he's sick. It's so sad... why... why?'

TR embraced her and crumpled the letter. 'It's over, Queenie. There's no going back. But we've won, we beat him. That's all that matters.'

With Millie and Jim they talked long into the night. Overwhelmed, tearful, but above all, overjoyed, Queenie went to bed after kissing Tango on the cheek and hugging him briefly. There was a shyness between them. They needed time, and time alone.

Once the shock and surprise had passed, TR had accepted the situation more easily. He'd shared a lot with Tango, knew him well and had grown to love him as a son.

Queenie woke to sounds of kookaburras singing and the smell of toast drifting through the house with the rattle of cups. Slowly she focused on the strange room. It hadn't been a dream. She clasped her hands together in a childlike gesture and, with tears spilling from her eyes, said a prayer of thanks and gratitude to whatever power it was which had returned her lost child.

There was a tap at the door and she hastily wiped her eyes with the sheet before calling out, 'Come in'.

Tango inched into the room, carefully balancing a cup of tea and plate with a slice of toast. He sat them by the bed. 'Good morning . . .'

Queenie smiled at him and moved over, patting the side of the bed. 'Sit down.'

'Millie told me how you like your tea. I . . . I . . . don't know what to call you,' he blurted.

'Let's get to know each other better and see what happens.'

'I'm still getting used to all this.'

'Me too.'

'Does Saskia know yet?'

'No. It's all been so... sudden. I'll call her and get her up here today. I'll ask Sarah to put her on a plane.'

Tango stood. 'Is your tea all right?'

Queenie gazed up at the tall, handsome young man and couldn't speak. She nodded.

'Maybe we could go for a ride later? I can manage now I only have bandages and not plaster on my leg,' he suggested.

'Yes. Let's.'

Queenie debated telling Saskia the news after she arrived, but Saskia knew something was up immediately, and demanded to know what was going on.

Slowly Queenie began, then with a rush the story poured out.

Saskia was initially hurt and stunned that her mother had never shared this secret with her.

'What was the point, Sas... I didn't think I would ever see that child again and I have never forgiven myself. It has been a secret that has tortured me every day of my life.'

'Oh, Mum, don't feel like that. I understand, I really do... ' Now they were both in tears. 'Well... I guess that explains why I feel such an attachment to Tango.'

'He said the same about you. He's anxious to see you.'

'You'll want time alone with him, won't you? I won't be jealous, I promise. Gee... overnight, I've got a family!'

Saskia's high good spirits returned and excitement replaced the shock. Relieved, Queenie hung up the phone.

Later that morning she and Tango saddled two of the horses and headed out towards the low hills. Curiously they watched each other ride, each suddenly noticing their similar style and ease on horseback.

'Race you to the far fence,' called Tango and, laughing, they galloped side by side.

Later they sat in the grass and Queenie spoke frankly of the events leading up to his birth.

'I always thought if I found my real mother I'd want to have a go at her for giving me up. But my adopted parents always said she must have had a very good reason, and they were glad they were able to adopt me, instead. They were wonderful people . . . ' said Tango sadly.

'I'm glad. I always worried about what sort of a life you'd have. I prayed you'd gone to loving parents.'

'I was fourteen when they died. It was tough, but they gave me a good start in life, I reckon.'

'We have a lot of catching up and making up to do.'

'I'd like to think of this as a new beginning. And not dwell on the past too much . . . you know — blaming anyone or anything,' said Tango awkwardly.

'That's very wise, Tango. I have carried so much guilt and regret for so long, it eats away at you. Let's call it a new day, shall we?'

She held out her hand, and Tango took it, and they sat, mother and son, hand in hand, as the horses contentedly nibbled the grass by their feet.

There were no reservations between Saskia and Tango, she ran to him and they hugged in delight and he swung her around and around.

For the next few days, everyone allowed Tango and Queenie time to themselves. They walked and talked and they rode and spent time with the horses. He confided his dreams, told her of a small boy's hurts and failures, of silly incidents and birthday parties and his first crush on a schoolteacher. Queenie told him of her life, and especially of Tingulla.

'I went there once and I felt so strange,' he said.

'You did? When?'

'A few months back. TR sent me because Millie thought something might be wrong. I met Snowy and I felt like . . . like I'd been there before. I can't explain it.'

'Snowy could explain it to you better. Tingulla is your Dreaming place, too. It's where we all belong. Ah, one day, Tango . . . who knows . . . ' She sighed.

He dropped a comforting arm over her shoulders. 'One day at a time . . . eh, Mum?'

From an upstairs window TR saw the gesture and smiled to himself. He had kept in the background knowing Queenie needed space to come to terms with this and build the link with her son. But TR, too, had a longing. He ached to take Queenie in his arms, but he knew he couldn't rush her. 'Give it time,' he kept telling himself impatiently.

At the end of the week Saskia had to return to school for exams, and would stay on with Sarah and John.

'That's all right with you is it, Sarah?' asked Queenie on the phone from Guneda.

'Of course. Queenie, I'm so thrilled for you. But I just can't believe you went through all that and never told me. We were best friends...'

'Sarah, you were overseas, and we were both wrapped up in our own lives at the time. I'm just thankful I had Millie to turn to...'

'Dear old Millie. She must be as smug as a mother hen,' laughed Sarah.

'She is going round preening and fluffing up her feathers,' admitted Queenie.

'So, what are your plans?'

'Plans? For once in my life I haven't thought past the next moment.'

'Just enjoy Tango, Queenie.'

'I am. Thanks, Sarah.'

It was TR who made plans.

He took Millie to one side and spoke to her at length. He sought out Saskia and spoke privately to her. She flung her arms about his neck and kissed his cheek. Together they went to Tango who grinned and nodded.

Queenie was oblivious to the plotting. Each day brought her closer to Tango, closing the gap of years, as they discovered things in common and came to know each other.

Millie came to Queenie and announced she

was going back down to Sydney to finish packing up the house. 'You stay here with Tango. There's no need for you to go. I'm sure you've done most of the work anyway.'

'You are a dear, Millie. I could get the packing company in to do it, but I'd nearly finished when TR turned up. Just throw it in cartons and I'll sort it out when I get to Cricklewood.'

Millie nodded. 'Oh, by the way, John called earlier. Said to call him at the office. Said he might have a buyer lined up for your place in Sydney.'

'Is that why you've offered to go back, Millie... Oh dear, maybe I should go.'

'No way. Me and Sarah and John will fix it all up. Take a holiday.'

With Millie away, Jim drifted back into his routine, leaving Tango, TR and Queenie in the house. Mum Ryan was nursing her sick sister and was still away. Queenie suddenly felt uncomfortable. And TR knew it.

While Tango was working he caught her alone on the verandah and pulled up a chair. He took off his hat and spun it slowly in his hands, not looking at her as he spoke. 'Queenie... don't you think it's time we talked? I've tried to leave you and Tango alone together... but now I think it's time we spoke. We had a deal, remember?'

'We did?'

'I wanted you to come with me to Guneda for a special reason, after which I said I'd leave you alone. It's up to you.'

'What is?'

He lifted his eyes, a bemused look on his

face. 'I know you're being deliberately obtuse. I want you to come away with me for a few days... just as a friend, no pressure. I mean it...' he grinned, seeing her quizzical glance.

'We have to get to know each other again too... I want us to be friends. I was going to go to all sorts of lengths and subterfuge to get you to go away, but then I thought, no, I'll just ask you straight out. Just a short trip... there's some land I'd like you to see, just out of interest. We'd only be gone a day or so. What do you say?'

She was silent. She could find no good reason to refuse. She was having a difficult time coming to terms with her past. Maybe she needed to settle all the ghosts.

'No pressure?'

TR lifted his hands. 'Mates, okay?'

'Okay.' Queenie stood and walked away.

TR took a deep breath, he'd given his word. Damn it.

The next day he had his Range Rover packed, had found Tango and told him they were going bush for a few days.

Tango grinned. 'You look after my mother, TR.'

'I will. And son, take that knowing look off your face.'

They embraced unselfconsciously.

The first night they stopped at a country motel and stayed in separate rooms, meeting for breakfast.

'After today we'll be bush, so it'll be swag time. Weather's good, so we'll be all right,' said TR solicitously as he smothered his toast in Vegemite.

'I have been into the bush once or twice before, TR,' joked Queenie.

By the second day Queenie was relaxing and enjoying TR's easy friendliness and his swift wit. He made her laugh often and at night he played his harmonica to her. She fell asleep rolled snugly in her sleeping bag, her cheek pillowed on her arms, the sweet sounds of the harmonica filling her dreams.

They inspected the property TR had been told about, but didn't think it looked much of an investment. He told her about Clayton Hindmarsh, who still had plans for more development in Australia. And he told her of being pursued by Ginny, imitating her coy Southern drawl.

They were still heading northwest. As the day began to draw in Queenie peered into the setting sun. 'Are we heading for anywhere in particular?'

The Range Rover bounced through some spindly scrub till they came to a stand of tall trees by a billabong. 'This is where I was heading.'

'It's pretty.'

'Let's make camp before dark.'

They worked together swiftly and efficiently. TR cooked their meal, and Queenie took their plates down to wash in the billabong. 'The cook never washes up,' she reminded him.

It was still early and they lay on their swags on either side of the fire, gazing at the diamond-bright stars.

TR was first to break the silence. 'So, Queenie... tell me about Tango. I need to know, too.'

They hadn't talked about Tango or the past till now.

'What do you want to know?' she asked in a low voice.

'Everything. I know it couldn't have been easy and I would give anything to be able to go back and spare you all that pain.'

'We can't go back, TR.'

'If it hadn't been for bloody Colin... taking my letters... goddamn him.' TR leapt to his feet and kicked a rock, his voice choked and full of anger. 'I feel like going to Italy and... I don't know what. One day I'll have it out with him.'

'TR! No. Sit down. Please don't be angry. There has been enough pain and bitterness. Let it be. You have to let it go... it's the only way. I've come to understand that. I've forgiven him. Poor Colin, I feel so sad and sorry for him,' said Queenie gently.

'You've got a bigger heart than I have, Queenie,' said TR, sitting beside her. 'I don't think I will ever forgive him for what he did to us.'

Queenie looked thoughtful. 'Looking back now I can see he had such anger about him ever since he was a little kid. Even before Mum and Dad died... he was so jealous of me, we were so competitive. I never realised how it affected him.'

'You mean because you were always better at everything... more of a success than he was?'

'I suppose so. But I never thought for one moment I was replacing him in Dad's affections. Jealousy is such a sickness, it twists how you look at the world.'

'And how you interpret actions. Ah, Queenie...'

He looked at her, his eyes filled with love and longing. He reached out and gently took her hand, tenderly touching each finger. 'Tell me about Tango. God, how you must have hated me...'

'I was confused... and hurt, yes. It wasn't easy giving him up, you know.' Her voice was barely a whisper, her eyes closed. 'If only, if only...'

TR blindly reached for her, wrapping his arms about her, his voice tearful. 'I understand, I know... I know...' He rocked her gently.

Slowly the pain she had carried in her heart for so many years slipped away. She took a deep shuddering breath.

'There, oh, my darling Queenie...' TR kissed the top of her head. 'Oh God, I love you. How I love you.'

Queenie drew away and stared solemnly at him. 'I've always loved you too, TR. But then, you knew that.'

They stared at each other. TR wanted to grab her with all the fierce passion that was welling inside him. But he kept still.

'So, here we are then,' Queenie smiled softly at him. 'What next, TR?'

He continued to stare at her lovely face illuminated in the firelight, but didn't move.

'Oh, TR.' Queenie reached out to him and softly kissed his mouth. She drew back and smiled at him then kissed him tenderly once more.

TR wrapped his arms about her and embraced her with all the urgency and passion he had kept buried for so long. She kissed him back wildly, and without taking his mouth from hers, he lifted her in his arms and carried her to his swag.

There, wrapped in each other's arms, the years fell away and they were once again two ardent lovers whose passion and deep love had never died, and who had waited so long for this reunion of bodies, souls and hearts.

They stayed at the camp site for two more days, then TR packed up and announced they had one more stop to make.

Queenie was sitting on a log brushing her hair. Without make-up, and wearing TR's loose blue shirt, she looked like a teenager. TR sat beside her, took the brush from her and continued stroking it through her hair. Queenie closed her eyes contentedly as the morning sun sent bright lights shining through her burnished golden brown hair.

'Queenie... there's just one thing...' he began softly.

'Ummm...' she didn't open her eyes but moved her head slightly as he lifted the thick river of soft hair in his hands.

'You will marry me, now... won't you?'

Her eyes flew open in surprise and joy, love dancing from their emerald depths. 'TR... I love you.' Her lips parted in a smile to reveal her perfect teeth. 'You never give up do you?'

'I said I'd wait for you ... for as long as it took.'

She tilted her face to his to be kissed. 'The waiting's over, my darling ... '

Queenie didn't ask where they were headed. She floated in a blissful state, carried along by TR who whistled as he drove; and when Queenie took over the driving, he sang and played his harmonica to her.

Queenie stared at the sweeping landscape unfolding before them. The dusty red earth faded to pink in the distance where it met a mauve sky which spread upwards to azure blue. Hazy grey-green trees seemed to dance above the surface of the ground, and an eagle drifted lazily across the empty sky. Queenie felt a lump come to her throat. This was her country.

In another hour they were on the familiar road. TR reached over and held her hand, steering with the other.

Queenie gripped his hand, tears rolling down her cheeks as they passed under the great archway carved by grandfather Hanlon who'd burned the word *Tingulla* into the top log.

'Why are we here, TR?'

'You'll see.' He released her hand and hit the car horn as they wound up the driveway. The lawns were green, the fountain splashed, and the windows of the grand house were open, with lace curtains fluttering in the breeze. The front door stood open, wide and welcoming.

TR turned off the motor.

'Who lives here, TR? I can't go in. I can't.'

'Queenie, darling, look . . . '

She looked up and spilling from the house came . . . everyone. Millie and Jim, Snowy, Sarah and John, Dingo, Alf, Sarah's parents, friends and neighbours she'd known all her life, and leading them all were Saskia and Tango.

'Why are they here?'

'There's only one place we could get married. Here . . . '

He kissed her and everyone surrounding the car began cheering and clapping and banging on the dusty metal.

'There's just one more thing.' TR opened the glove box and took out a thick envelope and handed it to her. 'This belongs to you.'

Puzzled, she opened it, pulling out the heavy papers. They crackled as she unfolded them, to find the deeds to Tingulla made out in her name.

'I was the last mystery buyer. I was just waiting for the right time to give it to you. Welcome home, Queenie.'

Epilogue

—— 🐦 ——

Millie was dusting the small walnut table in the upper hall when she picked up the silver framed photograph.

Queenie and TR smiled at her, their faces aglow, arms linked, joy radiating from the coloured photograph. Queenie held a bouquet of freesias, wattle and jasmine and she was wearing the silvery gown and opal necklace she'd worn at her twenty-first birthday party. This time her hair was coiled elegantly atop her head, crowned by a wreath of dainty flowers and ferns.

'Ah, Queenie, you looked no different on your wedding day than the day you two met . . . seventeen years ago.' Millie sighed nostalgically.

'Milleeeee . . . ' Ruthie's call echoed up the sweeping Tingulla staircase.

Millie headed downstairs, the dust rag wiping the banister as she went. 'What's up, Ruthie?'

'A letter for you from Saskia at her school.'

'Oh, she's a good girl,' smiled Millie, sitting down in the middle of the stairs to open the letter.

'What does she say?' Ruthie sat beside her.

'She says she's writing this in boring old science class ... ' began Millie with a laugh.

The two dark heads, one now specked with grey, bent over the page covered by the sprawling writing. Above their heads hung the portrait of Rose — back in its place once more. To one side now hung another painting — of Patrick on horseback. The two pictures seemed to beam down upon the peaceful scene below.

In the far saddling yards TR and Tango were breaking a colt, TR showing his son the gentle skill which had made him such a master.

Further away, Queenie rode beside Snowy.

They reined in their horses at the crest of the small rise overlooking Tingulla homestead and the creek with the blue hills shimmering in the distance.

Queenie patted Nareedah. 'Well done, not bad for an old lady.' She gazed over her land spread before her. 'It's so beautiful. It's good to be home.'

'I always knew you'd come back, Queenie. This is where you belong.'

'Your home too, Snowy.'

The old Aborigine looked into the distance, his eyes seeing through time. 'More than home. This our Dreaming place.'

Queenie leaned down and undid the small

buckle on her saddle bag. 'You've been Tingulla's spiritual guardian, Snowy.'

She took the small song stick from the bag, turning it over in her hands, looking at the abstract pattern of lines burned into the wood. She handed it to Snowy, remembering the day he had given it to her when she and Saskia had driven away from Tingulla. 'This brought me back to my Dreaming. Now it should come back to you.' She handed the sacred totem to him.

Nodding to himself, Snowy put it in his shirt pocket and patted it. 'We safe now.'

Together the horses trotted back down the hill as a magpie sang in the distance, rippling scales of contentment that drifted towards the bright blue sky.

Dear Friend

I hope you have enjoyed *Heart of the Dreaming*. I have now written its sequel called *Follow the Morning Star*.

For Queenie and TR, now happily living at Tingulla, with Saskia and Tango pursuing their own lives, life seems perfect.

But then one day Queenie's life comes crashing down around her...

Her beloved TR is seriously injured in a riding accident and can no longer recall the life they shared...

Colin, her bitter and still vengeful brother, returns from Italy with a new scheme to lay claim to his inheritance...

Her precious daughter is seduced by her uncle into giving up all she's strived for...

Once before Queenie was robbed of everything she loved...surely it can't happen to her all over again?

But it is old Snowy who tells Queenie if she 'follows the morning star, dat fella see her right'.

Follow the Morning Star is a story of one woman's unshakeable love and faith despite terrible odds.

I hope you enjoy it!

With kind thoughts and warm wishes,

Di Morrissey

Di Morrissey
The Last Rose of Summer

Following the success of Di Morrissey's first novel,
Heart of the Dreaming, comes another stunning saga –
the compelling story of two beautiful and remarkable
women...

Kate, a strong-willed heiress determined to defy
Edwardian convention...

Odette, a fiercely independent and idealistic young
journalist...

Years apart yet inextricably linked by Zanana, the
magnificent mansion they both love...

From turn of the century India to contemporary
Sydney, *The Last Rose of Summer* is a spellbinding
saga of love, possession and intrigue, a story of bitter
struggle and jealousy...of two women connected
across the decades by the men who love them...and
the magic of Zanana.

Evan Green
Dust and Glory

The world's toughest car race. Twenty-one days
and ten thousand miles of searing heat and rock-
hard desert tracks; of driving rain, flooded rivers and
icy mountain trails. Twenty-one days of blowouts
and breakdowns; of subterfuge and sabotage. Ten
thousand miles of dust and glory.

Driving at breakneck speed over Australia's
roughest roads and through the most appalling
conditions imaginable, six competitors break free
from the pack and fight for the lead, gradually
finding themselves entangled in a web of deceit,
betrayal and danger:

Jack Davey, the radio star, whose tragic secret
threatens the lives of those closest to him;
Kit Armstrong, Davey's co-driver, determined to
beat the ex-lover she believes has betrayed her;
Harley Alexander, the idealistic young reporter who
uncovers underworld sabotage attempts ... and
becomes their next target;
Gelignite Jack Murray, the legendary Redex winner,
larrikin and cult hero, who must fight to clear the
name of a mate;
JJ Chesterfield, the ace American driver who is
forced to cheat in the race by a Mafia boss who is
holding his daughter hostage;
Carey Roberts, a Mafia strongman sent to Australia
to make sure Chesterfield wins, who realises, too
late, that his own life depends on the outcome of
the race.

Dust and Glory is best-selling author Evan Green's
stirring account of the most gruelling race of them
all, a hair-raising, careering ride that accelerates to
a gripping and unforgettable finish.